Trail of Death

Chronicles of the Dawnblade Book 5

Andrew Claydon

Trail of Death

By Andrew Claydon

Published by Andrew Claydon

Edited by Danielle Fine

Cover Design by MiblArt

Just because you're chosen, doesn't mean you want to be.
Reluctance is a thing of the past for Nicolas Percival Carnegie as his party embarks on a quest to rescue the people of Hablock. To do that, they must track down Alric Tavish, their one link to the mysterious group causing chaos in Etherius.

Their pursuit takes a surprising turn when the group save Billy Bobknobs from Alric's clutches, and the hunters quickly become the hunted. Soon enough Nicolas will discover that his promise to keep his new companion safe is a monumental task better suited to an entire army. For it isn't just Tavish who's after Billy. Everyone is!

Finding themselves under constant attack by new and surprising enemies, Nicolas and his companions will have to come together as never before, at a time when the gap between them seems to be widening. Only then can they survive long enough to learn why Billy is so important to the Maestro.

But they are also about to learn something even more surprising: that taverns can be the least hospitable places of all.

Dedicated to my daughter, and favourite roller disco diva, Emie (aka Emelina).
And to everyone who loves a good adventure.

'The much vaunted Ale Trail *boasts a truly impressive amount of taverns along it's route. These range from the high quality – which is priced accordingly – to the 'rough and ready', and everything in between. Whilst I shall lay out fuller reviews for each later in the chapter, please note (in case you follow the trail before you have a chance to read this chapter fully): avoid the* Rat's Tail *like the plague associated with the creature it is named for. Whilst I am not normally so biased when it comes to businesses, from the experience I had in that* 'establishment', *I heartily believe the place would be better served burnt to the ground.'*

Etherius, A Travellers Guide – Dieter Von Ostric

rringsburg
The Cyclop's Second Eye
The Rat's Tail
The Golden Wand
The Buried Nugget
The Dragon's Tooth
The Merry Ogre

Chapter 1

'**G**ood morning, sir.' The boy gave him a hearty wave and a bright smile as he walked toward the tavern. The sandy-haired young man was over by the stable door, sweeping up some hay that had escaped its confines. 'Going to be a lovely day, isn't it?'

Briefly, he glanced at the early morning sky, where bright blue was breaking through the last few clouds that dared stain it. 'I reckon so.' He waved back.

As the sweeper went back to his chores, whistling merrily, he stepped onto the wooden porch, the planks creaking slightly underfoot. On the door was a sign with the name of the tavern and a crudely drawn picture of a grinning ogre holding a tankard aloft.

Can't imagine they look that genial in real life.

He pursed his lips before entering, taking a moment to gather himself. Uncertainty nipped at his heels, but then it always did when he visited somewhere new, never mind the urgent business that had brought him here.

I don't have the luxury of uncertainty anymore.

Gripping the handle tightly, he turned it and stepped inside.

The Merry Ogre was bustling. Strangely, though, it appeared to be mostly staff—the only exceptions being himself, an old, cloaked man thoughtfully nursing a tankard at a table close to the bar, and, for some bizarre reason, a man in a tub. The moustached gentleman was lying back with his eyes closed, some bubbles visible around his chin as steam rose from the water. He quickly turned his gaze to other things. At some point, the man would be getting out of that tub, and he didn't want to be looking even vaguely in that direction when it happened.

If only that was the oddest thing I've seen.

The best way to describe the place was quaint. And big. Certainly bigger than any tavern he'd visited in the past. Bigger than some barns, even. The main floor was a large open area of dark wooden beams offset by light-coloured walls decorated with the occasional picture. Everything was laid out in an almost homely fashion. Old tables of knotted wood sat waiting for patrons. At the back of the room, behind the bar, a rotund fellow with a walrus moustache hummed cheerfully as he cleaned glasses with a rag that didn't look fit for purpose. At the far end of the room, a chef and his two apprentices toiled over a pot of amazing-smelling stew, whilst near the door, a bard played a gentle tune on his harp, accompanied by the brush strokes of a boy sweeping the floor with the smile of someone who enjoyed their work.

What a nice place.

Another one of the staff—a fellow about his age, with long hair tied back—passed by with an armful of firewood. 'Good morning, sir,' he greeted with a happy nod 'Hope you're having a nice day so far?'

Sir again? Everyone's so polite here. Though I'm not sure Sir *suits me.*

'It's off to a decent start,' he replied with a smile

It'll get even better if I find what I'm looking for here.

Picking a table near the centre of the room, he sat down. Deities, that stew smelled delicious, its pleasant aroma tantalising his stomach. Part of him hoped he could sneak in a quick bowl before he got down to business...except his business was too important to be kept waiting. Still, the aroma was undeniably pleasant.

Less pleasant was the Helstrum pamphlet on the table beside him. It looked worn from over reading. Not good. No one should've been ingesting that garbage. After checking to ensure he wasn't being watched, he flicked the document onto the floor. Having that sort of literature nearby was likely to sour any food placed near it.

'Good morning, my luvver,' the matronly woman greeted him loudly, with a smile as beaming as the firewood-carrier's, as she ambled over to him. 'And welcome to The Merry Ogre. Looks like it's going to be a lovely day out there.'

They take a keen interest in the weather here.

It made sense, though, since it might be a predictor of the day's trade. And like the stable sweeper, she was right. He would like to make the most of the nice days while he could. It'd be winter before he could blink—time passing quickly now he was out adventuring—and then *nice* would be in short supply.

And it will make it harder to complete our quest.

'It's got all the signs of being one,' he replied.

'Ah,' the woman said, wagging a finger at him. 'You're a local—of Yarringsburg, anyway. And you've not been here before. Well, old Wilf and I will have to make sure to treat you well so you come back regularly. Nice, polite human boy like you.' She reached out and ruffled his hair, which was a very strange thing to do to someone you'd just met. 'That's the kind of customer we like here, my luvver.' Turning, she bellowed to the man behind the bar, 'Isn't that right, Wilf?'

The barman clearly hadn't a clue what she was on about. 'Yes, dear.' He nodded anyway, before turning his attention back to his rag and the glasses.

'Quiet day?' he enquired politely.

The plump faced woman nodded, smiling pleasantly. 'Calm before the storm, methinks, my luvver. It'll get busy later. Old chef Jona's stew's so good the smell brings 'em in from miles around.' He could believe it. 'Then once Savan gets playing his tunes proper and the drinks start flowing, they'll be 'ere for the afternoon. You picked a good time to come, my luvver.'

He really had. Though he wasn't sure he fancied being called *my luvver* any more than *sir*.

The woman leant against the table, moving in a laborious fashion. 'So, what can I get you then, my luvver? Gots about a twenty-minute wait on the food.'

The lure of the stew was nearly irresistible, but so was the urgency of his mission. 'Actually, I was hoping for some information, if you wouldn't mind?'

The woman chuckled heartily. 'Oh Deities, I'm sure we can 'elp a strapping young lad like yourself. What I don't know about the area, Wilf, my dear old hubby, will. So, what is it, my luvver?' She looked at him expectantly, her cheeks red, giving her a jolly look that matched her smile.

Here we go then. 'I'm looking for Alric Tavish. I was told I could find him here.'

The woman rose and let out a cheerful whistle. 'Well, I definitely knows him, young sir. Buts I need to know who's asking after him first. Mr Tavish is a fella that likes his privacy, my luvver. Very careful sort, if you gets my drift.' She punctuated that with a theatrical wink.

He did. Meeting the woman's eyes directly, he gave her an equally pleasant smile. 'The name's Nick Carnage.'

'Well, bless me soul,' the woman said, folding her arms. 'Turns out I knows you too, my luvver. And I knows exactly what you need.'

Nicolas kept his face neutral. 'Oh? And what would that be?'

'To *die*!'

He pushed himself away from the table, and the tip of the knife the woman produced from her sleeve missed his nose by an inch, if that. Going with the momentum of the chair, which was already tipping, he used his arm to cushion the fall and scrambled to his feet. The woman came at him again, her face contorted with rage, as if she'd just turned into some kind of demonic creature.

He blocked the blow with his forearm, thankfully not catching the knife on it. Turning his hand, he gripped the knife arm at the wrist and punched the woman in the face as hard as he could. Once. Twice. Three times. She blinked rapidly as the strikes dazed her, blood pouring from her nose and over her off-white apron—which, by the third punch, had become quite the mess.

Taking advantage of the moment, Nicolas turned in towards her, lowering his hips and using the hostage arm as leverage to propel her over his body just as Silva had taught him. There was a second when he took the sizeable woman's weight and thought his knees might buckle, but then the momentum took over and that weight hit the floor with a loud thud. He gave her one more punch, for luck, before removing the knife from her hand and throwing it across the room.

Resting his hands on his knees, he took a second to catch his breath. Then he pressed his fingers to his nose, just to check that his reflexes had, in fact, been faster than a large woman with a knife. There was no blood.

Phew. I'm getting better at this.

He suddenly became very aware of the loaded silence around him. Rising slowly, he flicked his cloak to the side, revealing the hilt of his sword, and took in the room. Everyone was staring at him with stupefied expressions, save the cloaked man at the table, who was smirking inanely. Then, several things happened at once.

The boy brushing the floor put a single foot on the broom's head, yanking the handle free of it to reveal a deadly spear tip, which he brandished at Nicolas. The chef and his apprentices drew pairs of cleavers from behind the pot, sliding the blades across each other and looking at him like a butcher looked at the cow he was about to bone and joint. The wood carrier dropped his load, the logs clattering to the floor as he reached back into his belt. When his hands reappeared, each had a set of spiked metal knuckles adorning it, and he set himself into a practised fighter's stance. The bard pulled a spare string from his bag and held it tightly between his hands, ready to use as a garrotte. The stable boy who'd greeted him outside kicked his way into the tavern brandishing a double-bladed axe. The barman, Wilf, panted like a minotaur about to charge—something Nicolas had experienced firsthand—as he eyed a crossbow hanging above the bar.

This is going to be tricky.

Good job he wasn't alone.

A powerful kick burst open the door at the rear of the tavern, shards of wood from around the handle and hinges exploding in all directions, and Silva strode into the room, sword drawn. The chef, the closest to the warrior, cursed loudly and gestured to the intruder with one of his cleavers. His apprentices surged forward at his command, waving their own weapons and making yipping noises, as if they were two small, but very angry, dogs.

Auron appeared through the wall in the corner of the tavern, his ethereal essence shimmering as he walked through the solid wood. The deceased hero took a moment to study his surroundings, before grabbing plates from a pile neatly—and handily—stacked where he'd entered. One by one, he launched them like discuses at the boy with the metal knuckles, who was understandably surprised to have plates flinging themselves at him. Cursing in confusion, he brought his forearms up to defend his face from the onslaught.

On the other side of the room, the old man leapt up, crossing the gap between table and bar in a sprightlier fashion than seemed plausible. Jumping over the counter in a single fluid motion, Shift changed back to their preferred form mid-air, landing behind the bar and grabbing the crossbow from the barman's hands just as he levelled it at Nicolas. A furious wrestling match over the weapon ensued, with inventive curses exchanged along with blows.

A heavy thud caused Nicolas to whirl around, just in time to see the stable boy's limp body drop to the floor. Garaz had, Nicolas assumed, slammed the boy's head into the top of the door frame. The orc filled the doorway, pursing his lips as the bard charged him, shouting something that sounded like, *'Have at you, monster.'*

That's pretty optimistic, considering all he has on him is a piece of wire and Garaz can fling fireballs.

Garaz moved to meet the challenge, swinging his staff like a club. The bard rolled under it with ease.

'Kid, concentrate!' Auron yelled as he ran out of plates and found more things to throw at Knuckles Guy, who was crying, *'Ghost, ghost.'* Judging by his dark grin, the spirit was starting to enjoy his work now that the boy had used the dreaded *G word*.

Nicolas, pay attention to the fight dammit.

He turned again and quickly stepped to the side, the spear tip missing him by almost as narrow a margin as the knife. The kid, who was shorter than him but a lot angrier, snarled as he pulled back his weapon and spun it around his body at speed. It was quite impressive, and very hard to follow. Around and around it went, his eyes trying to keep track of it whilst attempting to discern the angle the next attack would come from.

But the weapon was a blur. Acting purely on instinct, Nicolas ducked low, the spear ruffling his hair as it sailed past. The attacker did a full three hundred and sixty degree turn before bringing the spear in for a low sweep. This time, he was ready for it.

Timing his jump perfectly, Nicolas landed with one foot on the spear, pinning it to the ground, much to the surprise of its bearer. Nicolas grabbed the shaft, released it from under his boot, and yanked, pulling his much smaller attacker toward him and right into the swinging right hook he threw out. The sweeper spun a full circle before hitting the floor.

I'm not chopping anything off him. But a punch in the mouth is the least he deserves.

After grabbing the tray the matronly woman had left on the table, Nicolas smashed it over Knuckles Guy's head as he continued to try to work out who was throwing stuff at him. He fell to his knees, dazed. Surprised the young man was still conscious, Nicolas followed up by hitting him in the jaw with one of the pieces of wood he'd recently been carrying. That did the trick.

When he looked around, he'd actually done a better job than some of his companions. Silva was sparring with the chef and his deadly cleavers, their blades moving like a blur. Both apprentices were sprawled on the floor. As Silva was much less forgiving than Nicolas, and more prone to violence, it wasn't a massive leap of logic to assume they were dead. The amount of blood around them backed up his hypothesis.

Somehow, the bard had managed to climb onto Garaz's back and was now trying to bring his deadly garrotet into play. The orc had the bard's hands at the wrists, doing his best to hold him back. When the piece of wire was around his throat, there would be no chance. Just as Nicolas was about to intercede, Garaz threw himself backwards with an angry grunt, slamming the bard into the wall. Yet the tenacious musician hung on. Twice more, the orc charged backwards, until finally the musician-slash-assassin slid to the floor, where Garaz set about him with his large green fists.

Shift had won the wrestling match and had old Wilf's head pressed to the bar by threat of his own crossbow.

'This is going well,' he whispered.

Thunk.

Wide-eyed, he looked at the knife embedded in the post right beside his head. The blade vibrated fiercely from the force of the impact that had stuck it into the thick wood.

I had to say it.

Following the line of the blade, Nicolas gawped at the man in the bathtub, who was already brandishing another throwing knife. Nicolas ducked aside just as he launched the blade, the wall taking the hit for him again. Quickly, he upturned the nearest table and used it as a shield. Two *thunks* followed, suggesting that a pair of knives were now embedded in the piece of furniture.

'Care to help?' he asked Auron, as the spirit watched the scene with folded arms.

'No,' Auron answered simply. 'You'll never learn if I hold your hand...metaphorically speaking. Besides, his aim is shit. I would've got you with the first one.'

Wet hands will do that.

'Thanks for the feedback, honoured master,' he snapped back sarcastically.

Thunk, thunk, thunk. The knives kept coming.

Where in the Underworld is a naked guy in a bathtub getting so many knives?

'So, what're you going to do, kid?' Auron asked, his casual look turning irritated as a knife ricocheted off the edge of the table and passed right through him.

'Can't stay like this forever,' he muttered to himself. Rising, Nicolas grabbed a nearby stool and advanced on the man, holding the stool in front of him like a shield. Several knives stuck into the seat, and several bounced away as they hit its edge, but he kept edging closer to the soggy knife flinger.

When he was close enough, Nicolas turned full circle, swinging the stool in an arc before bringing it down across the back of the knife thrower's head. The stool shattered into pieces, and his attacker flopped forwards. He sank into the tub, and for a second, Nicolas thought about letting him drown. Instead, as the air bubbles dwindled, he reached into the murky water—very carefully in case he pulled the wrong thing—and yanked the man's head up by his hair, leaving it to rest on the side of the tub. Out of curiosity, he walked around to look at the other side of the metal bath. Attached to it were rows of throwing knives. He wouldn't have run out for a while. Which, come to think of it, might've been a good thing.

What would he have done if he had *run out? Got out and charged me?*

Nicolas was getting used to fighting, but duking it out with a wet, naked man was something he'd like to avoid as much as a mermaid would avoid a desert.

An elongated scream of pain drew his attention to the other corner of the room. Nicolas gagged slightly at the sight of the chef's soaked head, the skin red and blistering as pieces of onion and mushroom ran down his cheeks. Apparently, Silva had dunked him headfirst into his own boiling stew. The warrior watched with a raised eyebrow as the blinded chef scrabbled for a towel. Silva's eye caught his as she readied her blade.

'I think you've done enough to him,' Nicolas remarked as the chef dabbed his ruined face tenderly, whimpering all the while.

The warrior shrugged and brought the hilt of her weapon down on the back of the chef's head. He crumpled to the floor.

So much for trying the stew.

And that was it. They'd taken the room *and* managed to keep someone conscious to question. Judging by the curses he was throwing at Shift, old Wilf felt quite chatty.

Good.

CHAPTER 2

The Merry Ogre looked...a little less quaint now. Bodies were strewn everywhere, with several pieces of furniture either upturned or broken – or both. The wall now had the added decoration of a fair few knives sticking out of it too. But at least Nicolas and his companions were all unharmed.

I think.

'Garaz, are you okay?' He approached the orc, who was staring furiously down at the bard, as if willing him to get up and try something else. The orc's hands were still clenched in shaking fists that gave Nicolas a moment's pause.

'I am well.' His tone said otherwise, but the orc let out a large breath and Nicolas could practically see the tension disappear. Garaz offered him a laboured smile. As genial as the orc had been lately, he clearly wasn't himself. According to Shift, he'd been slightly off since the fight on the freighter with the faun and his toad-like bodyguard.

But Nicolas understood the mental toll this adventuring lark took better than anyone. Having his entire village taken, being half-killed, and having his soul sent to the Underworld had left him more than a little out of sorts himself.

There's an understatement.

At least he had finally found his focus. His desire to find his parents and the people of his village was being poured into his training. To find them, rescue them and bring them home, he was going to need it. Because he doubted those who took them intended to part with them without a fight. It'd been nearly a week since his return from the land of the dead, and he'd made the most of it whilst they'd regrouped and prepared for whatever would come next. Silva and Auron were proving to be great instructors now that they had a willing pupil.

Looking around the room, he noted how many times he'd come close to being one of the bodies on the floor.

Still a lot to learn.

Which would have to happen on the road now. Every day the people of Hablock could be getting further away from him...

At least they had somewhere to begin their search, thanks to an insane necromancer. Hoping they would come here to meet their deaths, the spiritual remnant of Avus Arex had given Nicolas the name of this place and the man they needed to find: Alric Tavish, who'd acted as an intermediary between the necromancer and this Maestro he'd been hearing so much about.

And will find.

His people had been taken by the Maestro's demonic fixer, whose name he couldn't even bring himself to think, as retribution for Nicolas and his companions ruining his schemes. He should've seen it coming. Should've known there'd be consequences for his actions. Now he would be the consequence for the Maestro's actions.

He won't be getting the same leeway as the boy with the spear.

When they'd come upon the tavern, he'd been all for kicking the door down and storming in, sword swinging. Normally, he would've been the voice of reason, but Silva's suggestion had stoked a fire in him, one that could've easily raged out of control. It had been Auron who'd pressed for the subtler approach, for the spirit to go in and scout the place. When he'd seen nothing untoward, Nicolas had been sent in to ask some questions and see what happened. At the time, it'd rankled him, but now he saw the sense in it. Though Silva had still managed to kick at least one door in.

Cussing made him turn towards the bar. Wilf was being surprisingly rude for someone with a crossbow pressed to his temple.

'Oh, yer gonna get yers,' he huffed from beneath his large moustache. 'Ye and all yer friends are gonna pay for this. Oh boy, are ye all gonna pay.'

Shift looked half-tempted to squeeze the trigger.

As he approached the bar, he passed Silva, standing over the unconscious old woman. It took him a second to figure out exactly what the look on the warrior's face was—she was appraising his work.

'You were very thorough in putting her down,' Silva said when she realised he was looking at her. 'Good to see an improvement.'

What do you say to that?

How did one respond to being praised for turning an old lady's face into a bloody mess? Eventually, he settled for a polite smile and continued to the bar. Where Shift and Auron were grinning at him inanely.

'What?' His tone was defensive. He was most likely about to be ridiculed.

The pair looked at each other before Shift said, 'You used the name.'

'What?' he asked again, frowning. 'What name? What are you...' Suddenly, his stomach dropped.

Oh. That.

'You finally called yourself *Nick Carnage*,' Auron said with dramatic flair. For a second, Nicolas was sure his aura had glowed slightly brighter. 'It's about time you took ownership of it. Though I think some apt middle name would finish it off perfectly.' The spirit ran his tongue across his teeth as he thought. 'Nick *Evil's Bane* Carnage. Nick *Vanquisher* Carnage. Nick—'

'Nick *Granny Puncher* Carnage,' Shift suggested with a smirk.

'Will you two cut it out?' Nicolas snapped. That bloody name had dogged him since the wagon ride to the Oracle's cottage and the beginning of his first *adventure*. Apparently, everyone thought he should have a name more suited to his new life. He disagreed, quite passionately. 'I only used it because it's how they know me.'

Except they don't. K...the demon knew my real name well enough.

'It's how everyone knows you.' Shift grinned.

'Sorry, kid.' Auron shrugged in a mocking fashion. 'It's who you are now.'

No, it bloody isn't.

He wouldn't allow the things he would have to do, or the things he had done already, to change him. He was Nicolas Percival Carnegie, and he always would be.

I have enough identity issues without that stupid name hounding me.

'You shouldn't be so invested in changing me.' He smiled at Shift. 'Especially when you like me just as I am.'

Shift's face dropped, and an awkward chill ran up his spine.

I thought we were making progress.

'It won't matter what yer name is once we gets through with ye.' Wilf huffed, rather stupidly bringing attention back to himself.

'I suppose we'd best get back to the matter at hand?' Nicolas indicated the red and sweaty barman.

'Yup,' Shift said quietly before looking down at Wilf. 'Where's Alric Tavish?'

'Ye broke me wife's face!' the barman whimpered indignantly.

Nicolas looked back at the floor where the woman lay unconscious and bleeding. Her stubby nose *was* a bit of a pulp now. Because of him. 'Oh...I...I'm sorry about that.'

'Kiiiiiiid,' Auron moaned in exasperation. 'You don't apologise to the bad guys. Instead, you say something like *I'd call that an improvement. Or I hope I beat the evil right out of her.*'

Maybe the spirit wasn't wrong, but it seemed really rude. Also, the moment was gone.

'Tavish?' Nicolas asked instead, allowing the edge of irritability nagging at him into his tone.

'Up yers,' the barman spat, though he looked hesitantly at the crossbow first. 'I ain't telling ye race traitors nothing.'

Race traitors?

Fists clenched, he turned to Garaz. The orc stood quietly in the corner of the room shaking his head sadly.

What's so bad about giving others a chance?

Garaz was wise, and kind, and caring, yet people still treated him like he was...well, what most believed an orc to be. It boiled his blood. It wasn't necessarily the narrow mindedness - annoying as that was - but it was using it to fuel some *us* and *them* nonsense in a world that everyone shares.

This is what happens when you read too much of that Helstrum nonsense. Though I doubt Garaz beating the crap out of the local bard and stable boy will do much to change opinions around here.

But they were here for answers, not to discuss the finer points of xenophobia in local drinking establishments. Returning his attention to Wilf, he was about to repeat the question when Silva grabbed the barman's podgy hand and, with a crack that made both him and Shift wince, snapped all his fingers. Wilf cried out in pain.

'You only had to snap *one*!' Nicolas admonished as the barman went redder, panting heavily. If he had a heart attack, they'd find out nothing.

Or, you know, maybe it's just wrong to casually break an old man's fingers.

'It is prudent to show him we are not messing around.' The muscular warrior shrugged.

That...made sense. 'Want me to let her loose on the other hand?' Nicolas asked the barman. 'Or...anything else?'

'He's not here,' Wilf shouted between gasping breaths that made his moustache quiver. 'Ye missed him by half an hour.'

'Where did he go?' Shift asked, pressing the crossbow into the barman's furrowed brow.

'South,' the squirming man spat petulantly after a moment. Silva took his other hand and held his fingers. '*Northwest.* He went Northwest. Followed the Ale Trail. He and his men took some guy out of here.'

'What guy?' Auron asked, then rolled his pupilless white eyes when he remembered that no one but his companions could hear him.

Nicolas repeated the question.

'I don't know.' Shift prodded Wilf with the crossbow. '*I don't.* I don't. I swear. They didn't tell me that. All I know is, four of Tavish's men brought this guy here then Mr Tavish took his leave. Though if ye ask me, it looked like he was a prisoner. He didn't seem too keen to be around them or go off with them, but Mr Tavish isn't one to take no for an answer.'

'That everything?' Shift asked.

Wilf nodded, clutching his ruined hand.

Swinging the crossbow, Shift connected the butt of the weapon with all three of the barman's chins. He flopped to the floor unconscious. 'Northwest it is then,' they said with a smile.

'Time to continue on our quest,' Nicolas smiled back.

Shift frowned. '*Quest?*' the shapeshifter shook their head. 'You know who you're beginning to sound like?' They nodded toward Auron. 'I think you're starting to get into this a little too much Mr Carnegie.'

'Well,' he replied with a theatrical shrug. 'This adventuring does have its upsides. I get to travel with some...great people.'

For a moment, he found himself staring into Shift's green eyes. There was a twinkle in them that caused an odd flutter in his stomach. Then the shapeshifter blinked, coughed awkwardly and walked away.

Inwardly, Nicolas sighed.

He was about to turn to leave, when Silva got in his way. 'What are we doing with this lot?' She indicated the bodies.

'Silva has a point, kid,' Auron said. 'Lovely as it is, this place is a den of villainy. I think it's safe to say that once they all regain consciousness, it'll be business as usual.' The spirit glanced in disgust at the chef on the floor. 'Though maybe less so for the man whose face Silva burnt off.'

Nicolas took in the room. It was a truly nice tavern, but Auron was right. In these walls, plans had been laid to unleash a horde of vampires on a city...and who knew what else?

'We drag them outside then burn it down,' he said finally.

'I like half of what you said,' Auron replied dryly. 'Why are we going to the trouble of dragging villains outside?'

'Because they're people,' he said, looking over the bodies that littered the floor. 'And hopefully they'll learn something from this.'

'Kid...' Auron began reprovingly.

'No,' he said firmly. 'I've learnt my lesson about killing bad guys. But burning a group of unconscious, misguided village folk to death is a step too far. Hopefully, when they see the tavern burnt down, they'll reassess their life choices.'

'Or come after us for vengeance,' Silva remarked.

'Do you really see Wilf and his wife riding across the country in pursuit?'

'Look, kid,' Auron began slowly, 'I get that—'

'I said *no*.' Nicolas understood the spirit's point, and respected his wisdom. But these weren't evil marauders or monsters, just morons.

The spirit, shook his head, then gave him a half smile. 'You know kid, that good heart of yours is made of strong stuff. They can live this time. Though if we ever see any of this lot again and they appear even annoyed to see us, I expect you to kill them on sight. Yes?'

'Deal.'

Auron seemed placated by this. Silva, on the other hand, looked as if Nicolas had just dropped his breeches and defecated on her boots. 'Very well,' she said finally. 'But you are dragging out the overweight ones. It will be good exercise for you.' The warrior was about to walk away when her gaze flicked to the bath in the corner of the room. 'You can also drag out the wet, naked man.'

My cup runneth over.

CHAPTER 3

I t was a strange thing, being on the back of a horse. Who'd first looked at such a large beast and thought, *I wonder if I can ride that?* He supposed it made a little more sense than the first person to look at a cow's udder and wonder, *if I tug on that, can I drink what comes out?*

Getting used to riding was an ongoing process. Up until recently, he'd only travelled via wagon and, it turned out, those were two very different things. The first few hours had been punctuated by the constant worry that the beast would randomly throw him off, but his preoccupation soon changed to how painful the experience was. When he'd said as much aloud, Auron's immediate response had been, 'Do you mean your balls hurt?' Now the spirit enquired at regular intervals as to the state of his nether regions. The answer was always the same: sore.

Still, he was gradually warming to his horse, named Vigour. The animal seemed nice and compliant. And he'd stood patiently when Nicolas needed multiple tries to get on his back. And now Nicolas was getting the rhythm of bouncing in time with the horse's movement instead of completely at random, riding was getting more comfortable.

Really, he ought to be grateful they even had horses. Hunting down these elusive villains required a bit more than a pair of decent walking boots, but their money situation had been quite poor of late. A stroke of luck had come in the village they'd visited the day before reaching The Merry Ogre. The area had been plagued by a succubus, and the local magistrate had put a hefty bounty on the creature's head. Auron thought it'd be a great opportunity for some *'on the job'* training—though Garaz had been the one to subdue their prey in the end. The reward money had been enough to buy them a horse each, and the grateful townsfolk had thrown in some supplies for their journey as a token of gratitude. It had been quite the blessing.

Though it didn't feel like one now, as the group galloped down the road in pursuit of Tavish and his cohorts, the column of smoke from The Merry Ogre staining the sky behind them. The speed was causing the saddle to renew its assault on his groin with, funnily enough, vigour. Foliage whizzed by in a single green blur as the five horses bolted down the track, throwing up loose dirt in their wake. If he'd been cautious at a trot, now that the beast ran full pelt, he was positively panicking, holding onto the reins for dear life as the wind whipped his face—along with the odd branch when he failed to duck in good time.

Is Vigour going to veer off the track? Will I get knocked off by a low-hanging branch?

The questions soon became a panicked mantra.

Please don't fall. Please don't fall. Please don't fall.

Please don't fail.

The last thought surprised him. He wasn't going to fail. Too much depended on catching Tavish and making him talk. He was their one link to whatever group was stirring up trouble in the Nine Kingdoms of Man, the one link to the demonic creature that had burnt his home to ash, taken his parents and his people, and half killed him.

Memories threatened to cloud his mind, but he dismissed them quickly. He needed to focus. Their objective was so close now, and he wasn't about to let him get away. Auron had gone to great lengths to bring Nicolas back to life, to give him a second chance, and he intended to use it.

Get Tavish. Save the people of Hablock. Track down the demon, then find the Maestro and make him account for every death he's caused.

It sounded so easy, but he knew it'd end up being a bloody affair, one that he was preparing for diligently. He was even learning to glean a little satisfaction from the aches and pains after his sessions with Auron and Silva; it meant he was growing. Though he had no idea how they would subdue the demon when they crossed its path again. The creature was ridiculously formidable, even if it did cheat in a fight and use arrows. Still, Nicolas had spent enough time listening to Auron's stories to get the impression that for almost half his adventuring career the hero had winged it as often as he'd actually planned anything. He just hoped they had as much luck with that strategy.

One thing at a time. First, find Tavish and make him talk.

'How will we know it's him when we catch up?' he shouted over the thundering of hooves. What if they accidentally set upon some poor innocent merchants or a family out for a morning ride? Such a mistake would lose them valuable time and allow Tavish to get even further away.

Also, not hugely heroic to assault innocents.

'Trust me, kid, I know a bad guy when I see him.'

Great, so they were relying completely on Auron's instincts. He trusted the hero, of course, but this was too important to leave it to any kind of chance...even though, right now, it was all they had.

'What do we do when we catch up to them?' Shift shouted. 'I doubt they'll come quietly.'

'We take them,' Silva replied. 'Those with him can go free, or they can fight and die. We only need Tavish.'

'We need him alive,' Nicolas reiterated. 'We need to get him to talk.'

Shift's face suggested he was repeating himself unnecessarily, but he didn't care. Tavish had the answers, and he needed to be completely sure everyone knew the plan. Capturing him was the only way to know for sure whether his parents were alive or...

They're alive. They must be. I'll find them.

And that would happen a lot faster if he focused on the task at hand instead of considering the *what ifs* of it all. As much as he was improving every day, they did still slip in from time to time. And who can guard their mind properly in a galloping pursuit?

Anyone who isn't me, most likely.

'There,' Silva shouted, pointing off road.

Between a gap in the trees, he saw sprawling fields, one of which contained six distant figures—but not so distant they couldn't catch up. In time with his companions, he veered Vigour from the main road, jumping over the small bush bordering it. As the horse landed, he was winded for a moment, and in danger of slipping off, but he held firm.

I'm never going to be able to have children.

It was like coming out of a tunnel. On the road, all they'd been able to see was the border of trees, leaves, and bushes on either side of them, but they were now in the open with rolling green hills ahead and a bright morning sky. It *was* turning out to be a lovely day.

Even lovelier when we get Tavish.

As they closed on the group, a sudden thought occurred to him. Considering the welcome they'd received at The Merry Ogre, it was highly unlikely Tavish would surrender without a fight, which most likely meant fighting on horseback. He couldn't imagine everyone politely dismounting first.

I've barely mastered fighting on my own two feet. Which meant he needed to ask an embarrassing question.

'How do you fight on a horse?' he yelled quickly, despite knowing he had no time right now to be properly schooled in mounted combat.

'Just swing your sword.' Shift smiled back at him. 'You usually manage to hit something. Lately.'

Very encouraging.

After a moment of looking at Shift, he realised his gaze became oddly dreamy, and shook himself out of it.

There's another distraction I don't need.

When he'd returned from the Underworld, Shift had kissed him. Then slapped him. It was confusing, to say the least. But what was worse was that, since the kiss, Shift had put a strange wall between them. They still teased him at every opportunity, so that was business as usual. Yet at times in the past, he'd had half an idea they were flirting with him, but having no experience to go on, he could never really be sure. That had definitely gone now. He'd tried to replicate it a few times since his return, but to no avail. He found himself missing it.

For Deities' sake Nicolas. Focus on the damned chase.

'If you're worried about fighting on horseback,' Auron said with a wink as he pulled alongside on Mare, the ethereal steed gifted to him by Sha'then, Lord of the Underworld, for his part in saving his realm, 'I could possess you and do the fighting for you.'

When the demon had attacked him, Auron had followed Nicolas to the Underworld to save his soul and put it back in his body. In that terrible realm, Auron had a solid form again, able to touch things and, more importantly, fight. Since returning, Auron had suggested possessing him a few times, which the spirit had played off as jests. Nicolas wasn't so sure they were, but he felt for his companion. Coming back to such an insubstantial form must've been like dying all over again. But Auron had possessed him once, and it had been an unpleasant experience—mostly, to be fair, for the mercenaries he'd killed using Nicolas's hands—and one he never wished to repeat.

'I'll figure it out, thanks.'

Auron shrugged nonchalantly, but Nicolas could tell he was disappointed. He didn't blame him, and he felt guilty for letting him down—especially when the hero had nearly sacrificed his eternal soul for him—but at the same time, he didn't want Auron inside him again. He was still getting used to being back in his own body without hosting guests.

Ahead of them the six were riding in formation: four armoured men around an unarmoured man in the centre and one in pitch-black armour leading. The man in the centre did a double take as he glanced back and caught sight of Nicolas and the others. Within an instant he brought his horse around and began to ride straight toward them, spurring the beast to go as fast as it could. There was a shout of surprise, and the other five soon followed, all circling around to close in on the rider who had broken ranks. Their horses were faster. As two of the riders used their mounts to cut him off, blocking his route and forcing him to stop, the other two pulled alongside the unarmoured man, grabbing his reins and pulling him back in the direction they had been riding. The unarmoured man struggled to break free of them, to no avail.

They've stopped. Now's our chance.

He urged Vigour on.

The lead rider brought his horse to a halt just beside the scrum, staring toward the riders bearing down on his group from behind the visor of a helmet flanked by the wings of the carved dragon that sat atop it. His pitch black armour had a red cape hanging from its back. He was obviously in charge. It had to be Tavish.

And we're closing on you.

Nicolas tried his best not to be thrilled by the hunt, but despite his best efforts, adrenaline thundered in his blood and the thought of finally catching his prey exhilarated him. This was the first step to getting his parents and his people back. He would not fail.

Raising his gauntleted hand, the knight extended a single finger toward them. The other four riders spurred their horses into action as Tavish took the unarmoured man's reins and continued to force him in the opposite direction.

As a single line, the men charged. Each rider drew a curved blade.

Even over the sound of hooves, Nicolas heard their battle cry.

CHAPTER 4

As the line of enemies thundered toward him, Nicolas repeated another mantra in his head.

I can fight on horseback.

He'd learned a lot of new mantras since clambering onto a horse for the first time, but even with repetition, he remained unconvinced. Not that he had a choice in the matter. Taking a deep breath, he drew his sword. He'd been tentative on his galloping mount before, but it was even worse with just one hand on the reins. Holding the *Dawn Blade* as he was bounced all over the place wasn't an easy task either, yet the sword in his hand was comforting, especially with the battle looming. He hoped it would at least be quick, as every second they dallied with minions was another second Tavish, with his captive, could use to increase the gap between them. Though said captive was still putting up a fierce struggle against the knight to ensure that didn't happen.

Nicolas and his companions spread out parallel to those they'd pursued, who were now their attackers. Beyond the oncoming riders, the unarmoured figure threw himself from his horse, evidently giving up any chance of winning the tug of war against Tavish. The man landed on the ground awkwardly as the black knight dismounted and closed in on him quickly.

Yes.

The scene was intriguing—and he was more than a little thankful that Tavish was getting delayed—but Nicolas had a fight to focus on.

His eyes widened as the sword came swinging toward him. Quickly, he leant to the side, ducking the blade. His relief at saving his neck was momentary, as he overbalanced in the saddle and began to slip right out of it. Letting go of the reins so that Vigour didn't end up dragging him across the field, he fell from his mount. Hands flailing in the air, he managed to grab something, hoping desperately it would arrest his fall. Instead it gave way beneath the sudden weight put on it. The ground came up to greet him at speed.

There was the agonising moment of impact then he found himself bouncing painfully several times, before finally rolling to a stop, staring up at the sky, which was spinning in slow circles. Blinking, he tried to focus. Fortunately, or not, he was becoming so adept at being knocked about that he knew nothing was broken—thank the Deities—but he would have a few fresh bruises screaming at him for attention.

You're still in a fight. Get up.

He tried to jump up, but though nothing was broken, he was in no fit state for jumping. Instead, supporting himself with his hands, he got to his knees. Sounds were still muted by the impact, but he could see his companions around him, locked in battle. Garaz, Shift, and Silva were each sparring with one of the enemy riders. Only Auron was not—the spirit was staring at him wide-eyed, his ethereal mouth moving up and down. It took Nicolas a minute to realise Auron was yelling at him urgently. Narrowing his eyes, he focused on the spirit, which was no easy task at the moment.

'Kid, get up. Now.'

What's he pointing...oh no.

Beside him was a horse, not Vigour, and on the grass nearby an armoured man was shakily trying to stand, stumbling several times in the process. He must've grabbed his attacker's leg during his fall and taken the warrior to the ground with him.

And he's already on his feet. Shit.

He frowned as his attacker bent over. His eyebrows then went high with panic as the warrior rose, sword in hand.

Shit.

Nicolas looked at his own empty hand.

Shit.

You dropped your sword again. Idiot.

But I did just fall off a horse.

In the middle of a battle...where you need a sword...idiot.

He frantically searched for the *Dawn Blade* as the warrior to look at Nicolas. But the only thing around him was grass, the occasional daisy, two riderless horses...and, of course, the man about to try to kill him.

'You,' the warrior shouted, gesturing towards him with the tip of his blade.

Fear took a firm hold of Nicolas, with a grip that only increased when he saw the man's face. Beneath his helmet, he wore a metal mask fashioned into a grotesque, demonic parody of a man, with a hooked nose and fanged mouth. From the eyeholes in the mask, rage-filled eyes glared at him.

Angry professional fighter with sword in hand versus inept swordless boy who's still on the floor. How do I fight? I can't win this.

The warrior stomped towards him.

'Kid, do something.'

Couldn't the spirit, *for once*, just tell him *what* to do?

Okay. Okay. I need to buy some time.

Hopefully, time he could use to find his sword. He grabbed a nearby stone off the ground and flung it at the warrior. With a metallic ping, the projectile bounced harmlessly off of his mask. The man chuckled derisively, shaking his head. A less spectacular diversion than he'd hoped.

With a cry, the warrior charged him. And Nicolas was still knelt on the floor. He scrabbled backwards, but running at someone was, shockingly, much faster than shuffling away from them. With a yelp, he rolled to the side just in time, the sword taking a chunk out of the grass instead of him. The attacker tugged at his blade, but the sword had cut deep into the mud, which was now unwilling to let it go.

Using the opening, Nicolas pulled the knife his father had given him from his boot, just as the warrior finally freed his sword and readied himself to finish Nicolas off.

'In combat, always strike the most convenient target.'

Silva's voice echoing in his mind gave him a flash of inspiration, and he stabbed down with the knife, driving it into his attacker's foot. The warrior reeled back with a roar of pain—a dark red stain slowly covering the tip of his brown leather boots—but did not drop his sword.

Damn.

Oh well, you can't have everything.

Nicolas got to his feet as the warrior stepped back, taking Nicolas's knife with him, still embedded in his foot.

Not even a weapon, apparently.

On the bright side, at least he was upright. He kept himself loose and ready to move as the warrior came at him again. Nicolas ducked the swing at his head and managed to jump back from the follow-up slash aimed at his stomach. His opponent was slowed by his injured foot, but Nicolas couldn't dance around like this forever. Sidestepping a thrust, Nicolas had to stop himself from throwing a punch at the masked face, knowing that if he did his hand would come off worse in that encounter.

Needing to get some distance between himself and his attacker, Nicolas flung himself to the side, rolling between the legs of the warrior's horse, which was minding its own business, grazing contentedly. Quickly, he searched the saddle for any kind of weapon as his opponent hobbled around his mount.

'Death to Nick Carnage,' the warrior hissed from behind his mask.

Why is that damned name catching on?

Though at least he'd been right about one thing: it *was* how the enemy knew him now. And apparently, they knew him by sight, as well, which was pretty disconcerting.

A glint caught his eye. The *Dawn Blade*, lying in the grass beside his own horse. Nicolas must've smiled, because his opponent suddenly came to a halt and followed his line of sight before lunging at him. Nicolas slipped around the sword thrust aimed at gutting him, kicking the warrior in the side of the knee as he did, before sprinting towards his blade. The warrior pursued, limping surprisingly quickly.

Throwing himself into a roll, he grabbed the blade in one fluid motion and brought himself to his feet, already in his guard position, a movement he'd drilled countless times with Silva, due to his *'penchant for dropping your sword.'*

Thank the Deities for Silva.

The warrior was undeterred by the change in circumstance, coming at him with a sideward cut. Nicolas intercepted the blow with his sword, metal clashing. Pushing back his enemy's blade, Nicolas counterattacked. His opponent sidestepped just in time. Aware that the warrior's curved weapon was already swinging, he ducked, coming back up as the sword passed him by and driving the tip of his blade into his attacker's stomach. There was a choked cry of pain from beneath the mask. Unfortunately, Nicolas's low stance was making him privy to the stench as the dying man soiled himself, so he withdrew his sword and put some distance between them. He'd embarrassed himself enough in this fight without throwing up as well.

His attacker fell to the grass, and after a couple of twitches, finally died. And he'd survived unscathed, save the odd bruise from the fall. He could've done it with a little less flailing around, and sword dropping, but at least he was alive.

Nicolas squinted at the corpse. For a second, he was sure he'd seen the ghostly outline of the warrior he'd just killed. More likely it was a trick of the light or—

'So kid, you dropped your sword again,' Auron chided from the saddle of his ghostly steed.

'Well, I fell from my horse.'

'Yes,' the spirit nodded. 'That's something we also need to address.'

'No, what I meant is that I dropped my sword because I fell from my horse.'

Auron gave him a patient smile. 'Those are the mistakes you made during the fight, yes.'

Nicolas rubbed the bridge of his nose. 'What I mean is, that I only dropped my sword *because* I fell from my horse.'

The spirit pursed his lips thoughtfully. 'So, by your logic, because you made one mistake, it therefore somehow negates the second mistake? Or justifies it?' Auron frowned at him. 'Do you need a story? Because I have a relevant one.'

'I...well...' he sighed heavily. 'Have you never...you know what, never mind.'

Anything else I say will only make me look like a bigger fool anyway. Besides, we still have to get...

His train of thought stopped abruptly as he realised that Tavish was staring right at him, having remounted his rabid looking horse. Threateningly, he pointed the tip of his sword at Nicolas, before riding off as fast as his steed could manage.

'No,' Nicolas cried out as the knight fled.

CHAPTER 5

Despair gripped him. Tavish was getting away, and Nicolas wasn't even on his horse.

'And don't come back,' Shift shouted mockingly in Tavish's wake.

'No,' he cried again, unable to help himself. 'He can't get away.'

We need to know what he knows...

His head from side to side, trying to find some solution, but coming up with nothing.

He's our only link to the Maestro.

His hand went toward his boot, but even if the knife had been in there his skill throwing knives was dubious, at best, against even a stationary target.

He's the key to finding my parents, to finding my people.

The distance between him and Tavish was getting greater. He took a couple of steps in Tavish's direction.

I can't run after him. Think Nicolas. Think. Think!

Finally realising his horse was beside him, he readied himself to leap into the saddle, a leap he knew would not be d in a single go. By the time he managed to remount Vigour, Tavish could be on the next continent.

He can't get away. If only there was someone who could...

'Silva, bring him back. Please.'

Instantly the warrior kicked her horse to a gallop in pursuit of the fleeing knight.

I couldn't have thought of that a few moments ago?

'Bring him back,' he whispered hoarsely in Silva's wake, as if pleading may somehow affect the outcome of the chase.

'It's okay, kid,' Auron said with a firm nod. 'Silva's after him. If anyone can get him, it's her.'

Of course she can. It's Silva. Tavish is already caught.

Movement in the foreground brought his eyes back to the man recently in Tavish's custody, who had risen and was approaching them, his walk a strange, loping stride, most likely due to the leap from his horse.

When he got closer, the man raised his bound hands. 'Don't suppose any of you'd cut these off? Please? They're awfully tight.'

He was an odd kind of fellow, but Nicolas was well-schooled in odd fellows by now. The man's tallness and thinness were accentuated by his huge hair. It puffed out in a large curly sphere from the crown of his head. Beneath his long, squat nose was a neat little goatee. He had a laidback quality about him, as well as an amiable one. He even managed to look endearing with his hands bound. This was someone Nicolas could get along with.

Taking his knife from the foot of his fallen opponent—getting much closer to the soiled undergarments than he cared to—he quickly cleaned the blood from the blade and approached the man, who stepped back, nervously eyeing the knife.

'No, no,' Nicolas reassured him. 'It's for your bonds.'

'Thank the Deities for that.' The man smiled. 'I've had just about enough of being threatened for one day.'

Someone actually found me intimidating.

That shouldn't really have made him proud, but he couldn't help himself.

The rope binding the stranger's wrists fell to the grass, and Nicolas returned his knife to his boot. The stranger rubbed his wrists, which, luckily, showed no sign of injury due to being tied together.

'Glad to be out of those.' The man sighed happily. 'Thank you.'

'Nicolas Percival Carnegie,' he introduced himself, offering his hand and a friendly smile. 'And you're welcome.'

The man looked at his hand for a moment then took it. His handshake was...weird. Like holding an empty glove. Nicolas puffed up slightly at having a better handshake. Another strange thing to be proud of, but he was less physically dominant than ninety-nine percent of the people he met. If not more.

'Nice to meet you, Nicolas Carnegie.' *Finally, someone gets my name right first time.* 'The name's Billy. Billy Bobknobs.'

'Your name is Billy Bobknobs?' Shift asked with a poorly suppressed snigger.

'Yeah,' Billy shrugged. 'I know it sounds daft, but it's the one I was born with, so I'm stuck with it.'

At least people aren't trying to force your daft name onto you. Although, if his parents named him then that actually did *happen, after a fashion.*

'Don't worry about it.' They looked slightly abashed. 'My name's Shift.'

'Garaz, shaman and spell weaver.' The orc introduced himself with a slight bow.

'Nice to meet you all.' Billy smiled. 'And thanks for saving me from those guys. If you hadn't come along...well, don't really want to think about it, to be honest.'

Nicolas could most certainly understand that.

'Not going to introduce me, kid?' Auron feigned offence as he stood next to Billy. Nicolas opened his mouth to speak, but Auron interrupted, 'Don't worry about it. He can't see or hear me anyway.'

They'd inevitably get to the point when Billy would ask, *'Uh, guys, is it just me or are you talking to someone I can't see?'* They'd do the introductions then. Besides, they had more pressing matters.

'So who were they and what did they want with you?' The words rushed out of him. If they came away with even a titbit of information, this whole fight wouldn't have been for naught.

It won't be, though. Silva will get Tavish.

Billy considered the question for a moment, scrutinising his rescuers carefully. 'Can I trust you?'

'We did save you,' Shift replied.

'I know that, and don't think I don't appreciate it,' Billy chuckled. 'But I don't get the impression you were chasing them down to save me. And you chasing them does not automatically make you good folks. I mean...' The man shook his hands in the air. 'You know what, ignore me. I'm just being paranoid. Being kidnapped will do that to a guy.'

'I have some experience with paranoia,' Nicolas offered helpfully. 'I...'

'But yours is usually unjustified.'

He made sure to shoot Shift an unimpressed glare for the remark. They seemed to take it as an achievement.

'I was on my way to the city, to meet Cryus Geld, head of the Guild of Magical Antiquities and advisor to King Eldric on all things...magical and antique.' Billy shrugged. 'I was making a delivery.'

'Of?' Nicolas was unsurprised by the childlike curiosity in Garaz's voice. Talking about things magical and old when Garaz was in earshot was the equivalent of mentioning mining around a dwarf.

Billy chewed his lip thoughtfully for a moment before reaching down to his feet. Taking hold of his boot, he pushed the heel aside with a click, and removed the yellow crystal that had been hidden in the secret compartment therein. He held it up for them all to see.

'Ooh, shiny.' And there was Shift's interest. Billy better keep that safe, lest it end up in the shapeshifter's pocket.

The yellow gem was bright and mesmerising. It looked precious, but Nicolas was no scholar of gemology.

'What is it?' Garaz asked, moving his head so he could look at it from different angles whilst rubbing his small beard thoughtfully.

'Well, that's a bit of a tale,' Billy admitted.

'Ooh, a tale.' And now he had Auron's complete attention too.

Yet he didn't quite have Nicolas's, whose eyes kept flicking in the direction Tavish had fled.

Why isn't Silva back yet?

Billy's mouth became a thin line as he gazed at the stone in his hand. 'I was, funnily enough, already on my way to meet Cyrus. The guild is having its annual get together in Yarringsburg. All the scholars sharing the latest amazing find they happened upon in the grave of some poor sod who died in times long forgotten.' Billy lowered his voice to a conspiratorial whisper. 'I always find it more entertaining hearing about the ones who accidentally tripped the traps and ended up in a pit of snakes or something.'

'You are a member of the guild?' Garaz asked.

'After a fashion. I met some of them on the road once, helped them out and they asked me to join.' Billy answered. 'Unfortunately, I have a real weakness when it comes to people asking me to join things. But I digress.' Judging by the sudden sad look, the next part of Billy's tale was not one he would enjoy retelling. 'I stop at this village and there's this faun…'

'A faun?' Now Billy had Nicolas's full attention too. The group had previous experience with a faun, and it had not been a pleasant one.

'Yup,' Billy nodded. 'He marches into the village, says some words, and starts waving this around. Next thing I know, a bloody giant appears and starts turning the village into a plain, if you get my drift. *Stomp. Stomp. Stomp.* It was dancing around like there was a mouse it was trying to squash. It destroyed everything.' Letting out a deep breath, Billy rubbed his temple before continuing. 'Where the faun waved, the giant stepped. But then he got cocky, starts laughing like a maniac and flinging the jewel this way and that, which is when he got stomped on himself.'

Auron let out a single laugh. 'The irony.'

'After that, the giant shook itself as if it'd been asleep and just wandered off. I ran over to the big foot print that had a squashed faun in it and…' Billy gestured to the gem.

'So, it can control giants?' Garaz asked.

'Not a clue, but seems like it,' came the quick reply. 'Once I had it, I got out of there at speed. Who knew if that thing was coming back? I made it to the next village, and that's when things got really strange.' Billy looked around, as if someone may jump him at any moment. 'I report it to the local magistrate and he tells me to stay put, which I do. Next day he comes to the tavern I'm staying in, covered in blood, and tells me I need to get to the castle. Tells me an escort of knights will meet me at a tavern on the Ale Trail, but he dies before telling me which one.'

'Who killed him?' Nicolas asked.

'No idea.' Billy shivered visibly, most likely due to the terrible memory of having someone die in front of him. 'Again, I got out of there at speed. I make it to the nearest tavern on the trail, The Merry Ogre, hoping it's the right one, and next thing I know I'm tied up on a horse being kidnapped.'

'So, Tavish wants the stone?' Nicolas asked, looking at the jewel in a new light.

'No idea,' Billy shrugged. 'He never asked me about it.'

'Did they indicate why they kidnapped you?' Garaz asked, to be answered by another shrug.

'Perhaps they wanted some way into the guild?' Shift ventured. 'These people like infiltrating places. I'm sure getting access to rare magical artefacts would be of great interest to the Maestro.'

That was true enough. In the past, this mysterious organisation had used puppets belonging to the Criminal Guild—Big Boss and his gang – to achieve their nefarious goals, as well as any magical weapon they could get their evil little hands on. Well, whatever they wanted with Billy, Nicolas was going to enjoy disappointing them.

'So you guys are, like, great warriors then?' Billy looked at the bodies around him.

'We try,' Nicolas found himself saying with a touch of out-of-character pride. Wasn't like him to lack modesty. But then winning his first fight on horseback was a bit of an ego inflator, even if he wasn't actually on the horse when he did it.

Warily, Billy glanced back in the direction Tavish had fled. 'Look, I know you've already done me a big favour, but I'm a little worried about those guys coming back and trying to grab me again. I don't suppose you'd help me find my escort? Please?'

'Of course we will,' he answered eagerly.

It was the right thing to do. And if it buggered up the Maestro's plans, all the better. Besides, there was a chance the Maestro would send more of his minions after Billy, so Nicolas was going to stick to him like hair on a troll until he was safe in the company of heavily armed knights.

Hopefully these knights are easier to catch up to than the black knight.

Frowning, he glanced again in the direction Tavish had gone. Silva should have been back by now.

'Perhaps we should take the jewel?' Shift suggested.

'No,' Nicolas said. 'Billy will still be a target even if we have it. Besides, he has that handy hiding spot.'

'And...well, I feel like this is my burden to carry now,' Billy said nervously. 'I took it, and I want to see it gets put in a safe place. That village...I don't think I can rest until I know that can never happen again.'

Sticking with the quest you've been given, I can respect that. Though sometimes I can't help but wonder how different things would have been had I let Potter deliver that message instead...

Nicolas quickly decided that was a train of thought he did not want to follow. This was his reality now.

Billy has a quest and he needs our help.

Nicolas put his hand on their new companion's shoulder. 'Don't worry,' he smiled. 'We will make sure you...' Nicolas looked past the man they'd rescued. He struggled to take in what he was seeing. '...what in the Underworld?'

CHAPTER 6

If she's gone and bloody killed him...

Silva eased her horse to a halt just in front of the group. Her jaw was clenched in annoyance, but Nicolas barely noticed. He was too busy examining her horse, for some clue as to why she had returned alone. Or to see if Tavish's head was hanging from her saddle.

'Where is he?' he asked, trying to keep his voice level. Judging by the odd look the warrior gave him, he hadn't succeeded.

'I lost him,' Silva replied finally.

It took a second for that to sink it. 'You did *what*? For Deities' sake, Silva. How in the *Underworld* did you lose him? He's wearing black armour. He's hardly inconspicuous.'

Silva pursed her lips in annoyance. Nicolas guessed losing him had stung her pride more than a little. 'I do not know,' she admitted. 'He simply...got away.'

Her words roused an uncharacteristic burst of annoyance in him which he quickly quashed. Coming so close and losing the black knight was frustrating. It meant it would take longer to find his parents and people. But he could hardly chide his companion for something he knew he couldn't have done better himself.

We will get there though.

Right now, the priority was to get Billy to safety.

Who knows, maybe Tavish will try to grab Billy again? We can grab him then.

Either way, Nicolas had a feeling – maybe false hope – that Tavish wouldn't go far. Once they delivered Billy to his escort, they could return to hunting him down. Surely a black knight couldn't remain hidden for long in this type of area?

'We came close on our first try kid, we will get a chance again.' Nicolas couldn't help but smile at how well Auron could read him.

Though it's hardly a special skill. Everyone seems able to do it.

'I'm...sorry.'

Nicolas looked up at his companion. Though Silva was not one for letting her emotions show – she was practically the opposite of him...save for when she was annoyed – he was starting to learn to notice small tells. From the very slight pause between the two words he guessed the warrior believed she'd let him down.

'It's no problem.' He tried to give her a reassuring smile, despite the nagging worry about those he loved getting further away with each passing minute. 'We will get him.'

'We will,' the warrior replied firmly.

'Perhaps you'll do a better job of catching him the second time around?' Shift cut in with a smirk. 'It's okay. We all have our off days.'

'Is that helpful?' Garaz chided softly.

Shift shrugged. 'If I only start saying things that are helpful, I'd never speak.'

'That would be a shame,' Silva remarked coolly.

'It's fine guys,' Auron said, staring in the direction Tavish had fled with a nod. 'The bad guys always come back around. Villains have this unfortunate tendency toward single-mindedness.' The spirit hunched himself forward with narrowed eyes, putting on a nasally voice. *'My evil plan is foiled and I barely escaped with my life. Is this a sign that I should renounce my wicked ways? Nah. I'm just going to do the exact same thing as last time...because this time the outcome is* bound *to be different.'* Morons.'

And accurate, given Nicolas's limited experience of adventuring. Even after being killed, Avus Arex had still been planning to use an army of the dead to make people respect him.

The black knight will return. And we will be ready and waiting.

Even Silva seemed placated by the spirit's words. The warrior gave no visible sign, but Nicolas could just sense it.

She's also a good example of Auron's point. After failing to kill me twice, she kept at it. And it didn't end well for her.

'Um, excuse me,' Billy said with a cough. 'But are you all talking to someone I can't see?'

There we go.

'We have a spirit with us,' Shift answered. 'Auron of Tellmark.'

'Oh wow.' Their new companion appeared genuinely impressed. 'Not just a ghost, but a famous ghost.'

Nicolas and Shift both winced.

'*Ghost?*' Auron huffed. 'And he said it twice. I'm not sure I like him. He's probably a bad guy.'

'Do not be so easily offended my friend,' Garaz suggested to the spirit. 'It is a common mistake.'

'Nothing about me is common,' Auron muttered as he stared indignantly into the distance.

Billy frowned. 'Mistake?'

'Auron prefers to be called a spirit,' Shift answered. 'And not a g...'

'As we don't know which tavern the escort is waiting at, I assume we just try all of them until we find these knights?' Nicolas cut in quickly, before the word was said again and Auron became insufferable for the next hour.

'There's plenty to choose from around here,' Shift replied, shaking their head at him slightly for interrupting them. 'But I can't think of a better plan.'

Nicolas noticed Silva's furrowed brow and realised she had missed the whole story about the giant. He quickly filled her in.

'We had best get moving then,' Silva said. 'The sooner he is safe, the sooner we can resume our hunt for Tavish.'

'Mount up,' Auron declared, rubbing his hands together gleefully. 'There's good to be done, and villains to be vanquished.'

Whilst the others remounted their steeds—there being five conveniently riderless ones for Billy to choose from—Nicolas idled behind, hoping to remount Vigour without anyone watching. It was a hit and miss exercise, at best.

Walking around his mount, he smoothed Vigour's long nose.

'Look at me,' he said quietly. 'Horse riding. Fighting. A lot has changed since the bridge.'

I had a home.

Sadness tugged at the edge of his mind, wanting him to focus on everything he had lost. His home. His parents. His ability to go one day without nearly getting killed. His mind kept trying to pose questions which he didn't want to answer. *What if you'd died on that bridge? Did you really come back whole from the Underworld? Are your parents still alive?* He ignored them, just as he had been doing. That path led to a pit of despair, and he had people to save. He'd be no use to anyone if he stood here dwelling.

This is what I do know. This is my purpose. My quest. And I will do what I need to do to...

'Kid? Wake up.'

With a blink, he was back in the moment.

Auron was on his steed, looking at him strangely. 'You okay?'

How long have I been standing here? 'Yeah.'

'Well, we're all waiting for you.' Shift gestured to his horse.

Oh no. However long it had been, it was too long. Now everyone was mounted and waiting for him. With their eyes on him, the hop to the saddle appeared more like a mountain climb. Carefully, he put one foot in the stirrup.

Deities, please let me do this the first time, just this once.

He'd already fallen from his horse *and* dropped his sword. That had to be enough humiliation for one day, right? Trying not to let the deep breath he was taking show, he kicked off the ground, swinging his leg over and landing perfectly in the saddle. The sigh of relief came on so suddenly that he almost let it out, and had to clamp his lips shut to hold it in. He checked around to make sure the others hadn't noticed.

'About time you managed it first time.' Auron smirked as he trotted past.

Ha bloody ha.

'So,' the spirit continued, 'escorting an innocent to safety who possesses a magical weapon capable of untold destruction with the forces of evil potentially on our heels. Sounds like adventure time to me.'

Nicolas looked at the dead bodies around them. He was pretty sure *adventure time* had started when they'd approached the tavern this morning.

I think he just likes saying it.

CHAPTER 7

With every step that Tavish didn't rear his black-helmed head, Nicolas's disappointment increased. But really, it was a good thing. They had to get Billy and the jewel to safety, so not getting attacked went a big way to helping them achieve that goal. Still, he couldn't help those quick glances back, hoping to catch a glimpse of the black knight in pursuit.

Though if he managed to elude Silva, he must be good at hiding. We may not even see him until he strikes.

The itch in the back of his head, telling him that he should be outraged that the warrior failed, tried to get his attention. Mentally, he swatted it away. That kind of thinking wouldn't help anyone.

At least there's promise of a tavern soon. Food and rest will do me the world of good.

There were taverns aplenty on this road, popularly known throughout the Nine Kingdoms of Man as the Ale Trail—purely because of the number of taverns and inns of various shapes, sizes, and qualities peppered along it—which was good business sense. The long trade route, which ran from the far tip of Nalbina all the way through Yarringsburg to the Merida coast, was always bustling with travellers, laden with goods to sell or ship overseas. It was said you could tell how long someone had been travelling the Ale Trail by how hungover they looked.

One of the most popular local legends regarding the Ale Trail surrounded a trader called Auterius the Vast. Each telling of the story disagreed with the last, except on two points: that Old Auterius had challenged himself to visit every single tavern along the route and that on day four, he was so drunk that he stormed a public execution in a nearby town, climbed to the top of the hangman's rigging, stripped completely naked, and threw himself into the very aghast crowd. His nickname was The Vast for a reason, and with him wearing nothing but a smile, no one had been inclined to catch him. After the three weeks it took him to recover from his injuries—it was a miracle he'd lived at all—Auterius was arrested for being a public menace and sentenced to a full week in the stocks, clothed. That more than likely sobered him up.

The road was becoming busy with passing wagons and trains of donkeys laden with goods. Because of this, the group mostly had to ride single file, though Nicolas managed to squeeze in beside Billy without too much issue.

'So, Billy,' he began casually, 'tell me about yourself.'

'If you want my whole life story, we'll be here a while,' Billy said with a charming chuckle, his large hair bobbing in time with the motion of his mount. 'The abridged version: I'm from back East. Had the itch to travel and see the world since I was little, so as soon as I was of age, off I set.'

Nicolas pressed his mouth into a thin line. The tale reminded him of Potter, who had such grand schemes but might now never get to see them through.

Although he is seeing more of the world now, after a fashion...

'I've been all over,' Billy continued. 'Seen some amazing things in my time. People, places, magic. Etherius is an impressive place.' He gave a half-smile. 'Made a lot of friends along the way, like those folks in the Guild of Magical Antiquities.'

'How did you survive, though?' His experience of the world was less amiable than Billy's, so maybe he could learn a thing or two from someone more well-travelled than him. Of course, there were rocks more well-travelled than him. 'Did you work?'

'Like I said, I'm good at making friends,' he said. 'I find if you're approachable enough, there are always some welcoming folk willing to take you in. And there's always work to be done in exchange for a hot meal and a bed.' Billy took a long look at the scenery around them. 'Perhaps I should write a travel guide like that Dieter fellow. *Etherius on a Budget.*' What do you think?'

'I think you need to let me know when it's published. I'm going to need a copy,' Nicolas replied, before adding. 'Actually, you can start dictating it now. I'll take notes.'

As much as it's nice to stay local for this adventure, I have no doubt we'll be flung off to some exotic location soon enough. The more I learn now, the better.

'I'll tell you one thing for sure,' Billy chuckled, 'I feel a lot safer with you guys already. I may be well-travelled, but I'm no fighter. Don't think I'd be capable if I was even inclined.' Nicolas was suddenly aware of his new companion studying him intently. 'So, I take it you're a group of travelling heroes or something?'

Now it was Nicolas's turn to chuckle, though it was more of a surprised snort. 'No, I'm no hero. A group of bandits raided my village and kidnapped my people. My companions and I are trying to find them.'

'Sounds pretty heroic to me.' Billy shrugged.

'It's not.' His firm tone surprised him. 'We're just trying to get my friends and family back.' *And make sure those responsible can't hurt anyone else.* 'We heard that Alric Tavish, the black knight you were with, might know something about their whereabouts.'

'I wouldn't be surprised if he's mixed up with some shady folk.' Billy scoffed, before looking at him askew. 'Sorry, I didn't think. It must be tough to bear, him getting away.' That was certainly true. 'But I'm glad you caught up to him enough to help me, at least. Mind you, I'd feel safer if that black knight wasn't still running around.' Billy shrugged and shook his head. 'It happens, though. I'm sure your friend tried her best. Tavish must be skilled. I can't imagine many can escape her when she sets her mind to catching them.'

There's a first time for everything.

'You might want to relax.' It was only when he saw Billy searching his face that he realised the tension he was feeling. 'I'm sure you'll get another shot at him. And it isn't like she let him get away.'

Of course not. It's Silva.

The woman had taken a crossbow bolt for him. He trusted her implicitly.

Even if she has tried to kill me before.

His eyes flicked to Auron, one person Silva *had* managed to kill. But that was a different Silva altogether. That wasn't the warrior he travelled with now.

The friend.

'Yes, we'll find him.' Nicolas's voice didn't sound as hopeful as he intended it too.

Though it'd be much easier if he came and found us.

At least the scenery around them was beautiful. It was easy to lose himself in the picturesque countryside he caught glimpses of in every break in the treeline. But not for long. Instead, he found himself staring at the horizon, willing Tavish to appear, to return so he could grab him. Beside him, a squirrel ran halfway down the tree and stared at him with bright eyes, nose twitching playfully.

You're not Tavish.

'Coin for your thoughts, kid.'

'Hmmm,' he said absentmindedly as he turned to the spirit.

Auron gave him a sympathetic smile. 'So, this one time, I came across a cult who worshipped some sort of demonic god. Kolotharak, I think was the name. They'd sit by a shrine they made, praying all day, muttering to each other like mad bastards about how he was going to rise any day now and consume the world. Didn't eat, didn't sleep...' Auron curled his ethereal lips in disgust. '...went to the loo where they sat.'

'And obsessively waiting for something to happen consumed them?' he asked with a raised eyebrow.

The spirit smiled. 'Not so much consumed them as they kidnapped some locals to sacrifice to hurry things along, and I slaughtered them all.' Auron shrugged. 'Still, the outcome's the same. Obsession leads to misery.'

'Understood, o' wise one.' Nicolas sighed. 'But I can't get him out of my head.'

'I know,' Auron said quietly. 'He'll be back.'

'Hero instincts?'

The spirit winked at him. 'Hero instincts, kid.'

Nicolas let out his second laugh in one day. 'I trust in those more than some cultists trust that their crazy demon-god is going to rise.'

'Good man.' Auron smiled. 'One day you'll have some hero instincts of your own, and I'll be very proud.'

I'll accept your pride when I get my people back. When I've earnt it.

Nicolas perked up in his saddle expectantly as a group of riders rounded the corner. Craning his neck, he searched the group, who were clearly merchants, for signs of Tavish. All he saw were the wary looks the passing traders cast at Garaz. As Billy waved to the merchants, the orc ignored the looks, sitting upright in his saddle with dignity. Though Nicolas was sure it hurt his companion. What else hurt was that there was no black knight amongst the merchants.

He must be coming.

There was no sign of ambush, no sign of pursuit, no sign of Tavish. With every bush and tree that didn't conceal the black knight, his grip on the reins tightened a little.

You don't just grab someone important, let someone steal them from you, and not do anything about it.

So why wasn't he here yet? He regulated his breathing and tried to recite calming mantras to beat back the frustration rising in him, but every time he did, the image of his burnt-out home appeared in his mind. The outrage and frustration was building from an itch to a full on battering ram, banging on the gate of his mind, refusing to be denied.

I won't give in to it. And I won't fail those who are depending on me.

'Are you okay?'

Am I playing musical companions today?

His head snapped around so fast that Shift started in their saddle. The battering ram in his mind vanished, replaced by a quick, and welcome, memory of a kiss. After a second he realised said daydream was causing him to stare longingly at Shift, so he quickly became very interested in where Billy was.

Doesn't do to lose sight of the person you're supposed to be protecting.

Billy was deep in conversation with Garaz. The orc turned in his saddle, his eyes narrowed toward the merchants who they had just passed.

'Don't do it,' Shift chided beside him.

Do they know what I was just thinking?

'Don't do what?' he said for a poorly faked casualness.

'We missed a chance to get Tavish,' his companion said firmly. 'I know you Nick. You let that sort of thing get into your head, dwell on it, then end up acting a fool. So don't do it.'

They didn't. Thank the Deities.

'I won't.' Maybe the defensiveness in his tone didn't inspire confidence?

'Nick...'

'I won't. I swear.'

Shift didn't appear the slightest bit convinced. 'You're getting better at talking about the craziness that goes on in your head. But there's still room for improvement. You can't even say the name of the demon K...'

'Don't say that name,' he snapped.

'Nick, it's only a name.' There was sympathy in Shift's eyes. 'Saying it can't miraculously summon it.'

'You don't know that for sure,' he scoffed. 'Magic and demons...it's all strange stuff. And I'd rather not take the risk. Not until I'm ready to face...it.'

The image of the demon in his mind caused an involuntary shudder. Vigour seemed to sense it, his mount turning his head and casting him a sideways glance.

'Besides,' he began with a smile. 'I've changed a lot since I came back from the Underworld. I'm practically a zombie now. I no longer have a home and...ow.'

Shift had leant across and punched him in the arm, hard. 'I told you yesterday, no talk about you being a zombie, or some soulless undead creature. Auron's undead, and he is perfectly normal.' *Are they insinuating that I am actually undead?* 'Which does *not* mean I think you're undead, Nick.'

'I hope you're right,' he said with a strained half smile. 'But if you're wrong and I try and eat your brains, then don't complain that I didn't try to warn you.'

'I don't think it's my brains you're interested in.'

He was sure Vigour shook his head as he stiffened awkwardly in the saddle. At least Shift was doing the same thing.

I'm staring.

It took him serious effort to break away from Shift's green eyes. For a moment he could have sworn his companion's face was reddening. His certainly was.

Deities damned lingering gazes.

'And as for your home.' Shift's tone softened as they spoke again, but they refused to look directly at him. 'I don't know where I came from. I just appeared on a roadway one day. No memory, no family. I know what it's like to feel lost and alone.'

That's not the same as having your home taken from you whilst you stood by and watched, helpless to stop it.

He bit his lip slightly to prevent him from saying it aloud, because he knew it was a petulant response. So why did he want to say it?

'I understand,' they continued. 'We all do. And we just want to help you. So make sure you talk to us. Okay?' Briefly, they caught his eye before their gaze flicked away again.

At least whatever happens, I have my companions.

The group had been thrown together by some very crazy circumstances, but it was comforting to know that he wasn't alone. Even if he didn't really know them that well. *What's Shift's favourite food? Does Garaz have siblings? What's Auron's actual last name? What's the history between him and Silva?*

Really, those were mostly just facts. He didn't need to know every detail of their lives to trust his companions. They were a random assortment, thrown together by danger and bound by a common purpose.

But there's no one else I'd rather face this with.

Though maybe a dragon would be a welcome addition to our group? Having something swoop down and burn our enemies to a crisp at a distance would be very welcome.

CHAPTER 8

B etween two fights in one morning, and the energy he was burning on his constant vigil for the black knight, Nicolas was hardly surprised when his stomach started grumbling. The piece of bread he'd snacked on had only angered his hunger for doing a half-assed job of trying to appease it. Rounding the next corner led to the ongoing disappointment that Tavish wasn't there waiting for them, but it was quickly followed by hunger fuelled elation at what was ahead.

A tavern.

His stomach growled in agreement, as if to say, *'Finally.'*

'Looks like we might get to silence Nicolas's stomach soon.' The fact that Silva could hear his complaining gut from that far away was just embarrassing.

'Let's hope the staff in this one aren't a bunch of crazed assassins.' Auron smirked.

Shift in the saddle and shook their head at Auron in disbelief. 'Did you *have* to say that out loud?'

The spirit shrugged.

'It's really odd hearing you all talk to a g...spirit,' Billy corrected himself quickly.

Suddenly, Auron was no longer smiling, his mouth pursed in annoyance.

Sometimes, Nicolas found himself envying those who couldn't hear Auron, especially when it was story time.

But now isn't story time. It's lunch time.

'Let us hope that this tavern contains the knights we are looking for.' Garaz's tone almost made it sound like they'd forgotten the purpose of their quest. Nicolas certainly hadn't, but between adventuring and training for said adventuring, he was learning quickly that when you had the opportunity of a good meal, you embraced it heartily.

The tavern was a lot smaller than The Merry Ogre, which had offered overnight accommodation to travellers—who might well find themselves killed in their sleep. Still, its thatched roof and the smoke rising from the chimney gave it the same homely quality. The tantalising smell from inside teased some delicious food to come. His stomach growled again.

Though I'm not sure I'd care much about the quality of the food right now. Within reason.

His best guess was that it was another stew of some sort. That would be very welcome. He'd been craving stew all morning after the delicious-smelling concoction the chef of The Merry Ogre had created, now forever sullied by having its creator's face dunked in it.

'What do you reckon for the daft tavern name?' Shift asked the group as they studied the wagons lined up outside. 'Whoever gets it closest doesn't have to chip in for food.' They scrunched up their face in thought. 'I think it's troll related.'

'Something about dwarves,' Auron suggested. Like he would eat or pay anyway.

'I think *Gold* something,' Nicolas guessed.

'Bulls,' Silva said. Was that a guess or was she just saying random words?

'I reckon a dragon-themed name.' Billy smiled.

'Maybe something to do with wizards,' Garaz suggested.

Billy was on the money. The sign above the door read *The Dragon's Tooth.*

'Well played,' Shift said, their voice betraying a hint of annoyance at losing.

'Cheers.' Billy smiled, either missing or ignoring it. 'But I have to forgo my winnings. You guys saved me from who knows what. Least I can do is buy you all lunch by way of thanks.'

That's really good of him.

'I humbly accept the free meal.' Shift grinned.

The group tied their horses to the hitching post and walked to the door.

'You know,' Auron said, almost dreamily, 'I always thought that if I didn't go into hero work, *this* is what I'd do. Tavern owner. Greeting weary travellers, telling stories...' *Oh so many stories.* '...and offering hospitality.'

Shift looked at Auron then at the tavern. 'I can see that.'

Nicolas could too.

If only our lives had taken different paths.

As they entered The Dragon's Tooth, Nicolas frowned in confusion. Turning his head, he looked outside at the wagons hitched in place, confirming that he hadn't been seeing things. His gaze returned to the tavern, and his brow furrowed again.

Where are the customers?

Because they sure weren't in the tavern. The tables were all clear—there was no sign of a plate, half-full tankard, or even some errant crumbs.

Well, at least it's clean.

Even if moving around was difficult. The owner of the tavern had elected to make the most of his small space, filling it with more tables and chairs than was really comfortable. If this place got busy and he needed to relieve himself, he'd have wet breeches well before he managed to get to the door. Even the idea of the tavern being full caused a pang of claustrophobia to run down his spine.

Carefully, he made his way down what little walkway there was. Auron contented himself with walking through the tables as he studied the room curiously.

Another interesting choice was the wall décor. They were practically covered with paintings, which ought to look nice, but the mishmash of styles made it slightly nauseating to take in as a whole. Old portraits sat next to bright landscapes, which were themselves surrounded by bowls of fruit. Part of Nicolas itched to reorganise them, putting them in some kind of order that made sense to him. But he wasn't about to give up chasing Tavish to do some redecorating.

Worse still was one wall given over to a detailed mural of a great, red, fire-breathing dragon that was such a blast of colour it was hard to look at directly. Nicolas had never seen a dragon, thank the Deities—although he *had* ridden a cow-dragon—but he'd heard them described, and this looked accurate.

'Welcome to The Dragon's Tooth, folks,' the serving maid behind the bar cried cheerfully. It seemed the lack of customers was echoed by a lack of staff. 'Take a seat, and I'll be right with you.'

The group took a table, and the maid practically skipped from behind the bar to stop alongside them, hands on her hips and a beaming smile that showcased her dimples. She was cute, with a freckled nose and long brown hair, but she had an eerily intense way of staring at him, almost like she was trying to look right through him. Nicolas looked away uncomfortably, but when he peeked up, she was still staring. The fact that the stare seemed reserved for him doubled his discomfort. He was awkward enough when he thought someone was casually glancing at him.

'So, what'll it be, handsome?' she asked with a broad grin.

Handsome?

'Handsome?' Shift whispered, their lip curling.

Billy frowned at the serving maid, his lips pursed in thought. After a moment, he shook his head and spoke. 'I'll have some food and drink for my companions, please.' Seemed he planned on being as good as his word about taking care of the bill. Always an endearing quality.

'It is quiet in here,' Garaz noted as he took in the room. 'Quieter than the wagons outside suggest.'

The serving maid laughed. 'Must've heard an orc was coming.' The chuckling stopped abruptly at the look of offence on Garaz's face. 'Meaning no insult, sir. We don't get many orcs around here, that's all.' The unspoken part of the sentence was that the ones they did see were trying to burn the place down.

Garaz responded with a grunt and found a painting to interest him on the wall. The orc was prone to bouts of sullen silence lately, and when he did interact with the group, there was always that edge of sadness to him. Nicolas knew he had to try and talk to Garaz, but there was just so much going on that finding the right time was difficult.

It's Garaz. I need to make the time.

'Sorry about that,' the barmaid whispered. 'I didn't mean to—'

'It's fine,' Nicolas said. 'Really.'

She seemed happy enough about this, save for one last wary glance in Garaz's direction. Quickly, she trotted to the bar and poured out their drinks. Returning, she set a pitcher of ale in front of each of them.

'Shame you're late,' she said conversationally as she served them. 'You're missing the festivities.'

'Festivities?' Nicolas asked.

The girl grinned in a way that made him question her sanity a little. 'There's a travelling show in the village nearby. It's got firebreathers, jugglers, the works.' A sad slump curved her shoulders as she let out a longing sigh. 'I'm sad to miss it, truth be told. But one of us had to mind the place whilst my brother took the customers to go see it.' She rolled her eyes theatrically. 'He gets the silly notion that tiring them out by taking them on a tour will encourage them to stay longer when they return and therefore make us some coin.' The maid leaned in uncomfortably close. 'Let me ask you, does it look like we're making any coin now?'

'You are off us,' Nicolas replied sheepishly, very aware how close she was but unwilling to ask her to step back.

Suddenly, her hand was on his shoulder. But what he thought would be a pat turned into a lingering touch. 'You're a smart one, aren't you?'

'From the way she's looking at you, kid, I think you could've charmed us into a free meal.' Auron sniggered.

He didn't dignify that with a response. Anyway, doing so would only lead to questions from his new—and very unsubtle—admirer.

I'd be flattered if she wasn't so unnerving.

'I'll go and sort your food out,' she said, hand still on his shoulder. 'Once you're done, I can point you in the right direction, if you like. Maybe you can go enjoy the show and send my errant brother back here with some more paying customers?'

'I don't suppose there were any knights amongst them?' he knew the question was a stretch. If Billy's escort were here waiting, they wouldn't have buggered off to check out the local fair for an hour or two. That wasn't knightly at all.

'Knights?' the girl said thoughtfully before shaking her head. 'No. Sorry. I haven't seen anyone like that.' The hand on his shoulder squeezed slightly. 'Are you sure I can't tempt you...' Her pause was long and deliberate. '...with the fair? I am due a break sometime soon.'

It didn't take a scholar to work out the invitation was not being extended to his companions too.

'Sorry,' Nicolas replied quickly, 'but we don't have time.'

'Fair enough.' The girl smiled, finally releasing him. 'I'll be back with your stew in a minute.'

'Enjoying your visit?' The venomous tone in Shift's voice was echoed in their expression.

I'm not dignifying that with a response.

Any one he did give would come across as petulant. He found the question more than a little insulting. Shift had kissed him, slapped him, then pretended it never happened.

And now they act...what...jealous? That's a bit rich.

'It's a nice enough establishment,' he said finally, and carefully, knowing that not responding would ultimately just goad Shift more. 'I don't care much for the décor though.'

Neither did Auron, judging by the way he was pacing the room with a furrowed brow.

'You all right?' he asked.

'Hmm.' The spirit turned to look at him. 'Just wondering how blind the guy who decorated this place actually was. The state of the walls makes it hard to concentrate.'

True enough. Nicolas was doing his best not to look directly at them. He was sure doing so would lead to a bright colour induced headache.

'We should go to this fair,' Shift said after a sip of their drink. 'I think we could all use a bit of time to relax after this morning's antics.'

'It would be hard to keep Billy safe in such a crowded environment,' Silva answered.

'We've passed lots of people on the road,' Shift replied, frowning.

'It is a different kind of crowd.'

'How so? Surely, a crowd is a crowd.'

Silva's mouth opened, then closed abruptly. 'Save your games for Nicolas. I am not playing.'

'I don't know what you mean.' The sly smile as Shift took a sip of their drink suggested otherwise.

'If it's all the same to you,' Billy began tentatively, 'I'd rather not be out there wandering about when there are people looking for me. I know you ran Tavish off, but he's sure to come back.'

Though if Billy was out in the open, then Tavish –

No. That was wrong. Very wrong. The implications of that thought were shocking. That wasn't how he did things. Ever. For a moment, Nicolas had the very strong urge to slap himself for such thinking.

'Strapping man like you gets served first,' the maid said as she put a bowl of stew in front of him with a playful wink. 'Here you go, folks,' she said louder as she served the others. 'A beautiful plant-based stew for you today. I don't want to give you high expectations, but some locals come here *just* for this stew.'

Across the table, Shift's lips were moving in a petulant manner, as if copying what the girl had just said. Nicolas couldn't help but enjoy their reaction to the maid's obvious flirting. But he tried not to dig any deeper meaning from it. All he'd end up digging up would be disappointment and embarrassment.

Focus on the food.

Warm steam rose to his nostrils, filling them with the smell of cooked vegetables. Food was very welcome right now, as was sitting on something that didn't bounce under his ass. As the others were served, he picked up his spoon expectantly, ready to dig in the minute the last bowl had been given out. As soon as it was, he ate heartily.

Across from him, Garaz looked forlornly into his bowl as he slowly brought the spoon up to his lips, emptied it, and returned it slowly, as if it weighed a ton.

'Are you okay?' he asked in a faux whisper, knowing how private the orc liked to be.

Garaz looked surprised to have been spoken to at all. 'I am well,' he replied finally. 'I have not been sleeping properly of late. That is all.'

Really? You've been snoring loud enough.

'And...sometimes the looks from people take a toll,' the orc admitted. 'The fear and hostility.'

'Your people have gone to great lengths to earn their reputation.' Even Nicolas winced at Shift's poorly timed remark. It was meant as levity, but Garaz certainly didn't take it that way. Shift quietened as the orc stared at them.

'Well, you shouldn't judge everyone based on a few bad eggs,' Billy cut into the awkwardness breezily. 'All orcs can't be bad.'

'Quite,' Garaz said coolly, giving Shift the evil eye again. 'So what will you do once we find your escort, Billy?' Garaz's attempt to change the subject was blatant and clumsy, but necessary.

'It's pretty straight forward I think,' Billy shrugged. 'Go to the city surrounded by knights. Hand over the jewel. Take pride in a job well done. Then...continue with my life as usual, I suppose.'

Damn. I didn't get that option after my first adventure. Hopefully it works out better for Billy.

'We need to find the escort first,' Silva noted. 'There are many taverns along the trail. So who knows how long it will take to find them.'

'Hopefully they're patient knights,' Shift added. 'Though waiting for the person you're meant to protect to come to you instead of going to get them is a bit lazy.'

The notion of how long this could take was not lost on Billy, who stared into his stew, his mouth a thin line.

'We will protect you until we can find your escort,' he said, hoping to reassure his companion. 'And if not, we will take you to the city ourselves.'

Billy gave him a warm smile and nodded thankfully. 'That's really kind of you.' The bushy-haired man clicked his fingers and shot him a wink. 'As long as you aren't using me as bait to get that black knight guy.' Billy laughed.

'I...Well, no, of course not,' Nicolas said before coughing awkwardly.

I wasn't going to do that. I'd never...

'What Nick means to say,' Shift spoke for him, 'is that we just want to see you safe, and will be by your side until you are.'

He was reminded of his earlier thought, the unwelcome one. *Bait* was such a loaded word. That wasn't what he was doing. He just wanted to protect Billy, and get that jewel locked away where it could do no more harm.

I mean, I wouldn't be upset if Tavish did come for him. It would give us a chance to grab him and learn where my parents are. But I would never knowingly use Billy as...that word.

Sullenly, he looked at his bowl. His appetite was quickly dwindling. But he needed to eat, so he gobbled the stew down greedily before he couldn't anymore. Besides, there was no room for his foot in his mouth when there was already a spoon in it.

'I think we will be safe enough if we keep to the main road,' Silva said between mouthfuls. 'Kidnappers do not generally like lots of witnesses. With the high level of traffic, Tavish is unlikely to try anything.'

Good. Because Billy isn't bait. Never.

'And at least we are facing humans this time,' Shift said, waving their spoon as they did. 'After all the shenanigans with sea monsters, vampires, zombies and strange creatures, I think this will make a refreshing change of pace.'

The humans we've met so far have been pretty deadly.

'Though we may come across a giant,' Billy chuckled nervously.

'At least we will have plenty of warning if one is coming,' Nicolas offered. 'I know I'm not the most worldly of us, but even I know a giant cannot sneak up on you.'

'You'd be surprised kid.' Auron's contribution was not helpful.

'If we do, then we have a way to control it and guide it somewhere it can do no harm. I would imagine discerning how to use the jewel would be quite straight...' Garaz's sentence was interrupted by a *splat* as the orc fell face first into his stew.

Why isn't he moving? Actually, why is the tavern moving?

It was becoming hard to focus. A bout of furious blinking and then rubbing his eyes didn't seem to remedy the problem.

Splat. Now Shift had done it.

'Guys?' Auron's tone was full of concern.

Splat. There went Billy. Silva managed a single expletive before her eyes rolled back into her head and she toppled forward, into her food. *Splat.*

Nicolas laughed. This was an odd game. He tried to stand, but the walls of the building seemed to be moving in and out. He leant back as they came closer and forwards as they retracted. One of the murals winked at him.

That doesn't seem right.

He was vaguely aware that he was swaying from side to side. His head was full of fog as the lights dimmed. Then his stew was coming towards him...or was he going towards it?

Splat.

CHAPTER 9

A room blurred into reality around him. Everything was rocking, as if he were still at sea on Captain Ramirez's ship, the *Irresistible Amora*. The dull ache in his neck suggested that his head was lolling to the side, and had been for a while now, which would explain why he was looking at the floor. And possibly the sharp throbbing in his head. He wouldn't have been surprised if there were dwarves mining in there. Raising it took a ridiculous amount of effort and created an unpleasant *click*. His mouth was dry and itchy. Opening it several times, he poked his tongue out, as if the nasty feeling would be carried away on the air.

'They're coming around,' a familiar voice nearby declared with a giggle.

Was someone clapping excitedly? He was still having trouble focusing on the blurred shapes around him.

'Good,' came a moody reply. 'I thought you'd overdosed them.'

There was a gasp of shock. 'You question my dosing? I'm offended, brother!'

'Would it be the first time?' came the snide reply.

The familiar voice sounded almost petulant now. 'You keep saying that, but the man just had a weak constitution. Not my fault.'

'You say *weak constitution*, I say *you gave him too much and he started spasming on the floor so hard that he broke his own back*.'

'He died, didn't he? Contract completed.'

'Well, yes,' the second voice snapped testily. 'Technically, you're right. But we were supposed to make it look like natural causes. The way his body was contorted when he died looked anything but bloody natural. There was an investigation and—'

'Oooooh.' The first voice chuckled disdainfully. 'Humblest apologies for disappointing you. I'll endeavour to do better next time, *father*.' There was a loaded pause. 'Oh, but wait, you are neither my mother *nor* my father.'

'And yet, in their absence, you still need parenting.'

'Are you still upset Daddy said you had to bring me? Is that why you're being such a giant ogre gonad?'

'Don't call me that. And don't call him *Daddy*. He isn't that, and you aren't a child.'

'Oh, sorry, *Lord Serious*.' There was sniggering. 'Behold, my serious face.'

'Will you stop that?'

The conversation continued devolving into a snappy back and forth, but their words were drowned out by a person speaking closer to him. Nicolas squinted into the bright light stinging his eyes.

'Kid, you need to come around quicker. You're in a bit of a situation.' Auron's aura, which emanated from his smoke-based spirit form, was great in a dark cave, but not so good when he was just waking up...or struggling into consciousness.

Needing to wipe the bleariness from his eyes, he brought his hands up. They stopped short with a metallic clink. Focusing, he finally saw the shackles around his wrists. A thick metal chain ran from them around the pillar they all seemed to be tied to. Auron hadn't exaggerated. They were in trouble.

Shit.

Glancing around, he saw that the tables had all been pushed back, creating an open space in the room. Two figures stood in the centre of it, but he still couldn't make them out.

What in the Under… What's going on?

Though everything still swayed, he could see his companions coming around too, each looking bleary-eyed and confused. Garaz was groaning as his yellow eyes opened slowly.

A boot kicked Nicolas's foot. 'I said you were strapping, and look, the first to come around.'

The serving maid stood over him with a wide grin on her face. Her dimples didn't look so damned cute now. Behind her stood another figure in black leather armour with a long cape and serious face that was the polar opposite of the grinning barmaid. In his belt were a pair of nasty-looking scythes, but he didn't appear to be any sort of field hand. In fact, now that Nicolas really examined him, he was similar to the barmaid, after a fashion. Nicolas's eyes flicked between them, noting the similarities and differences. The man stared just as intently as the maid, though his gaze appeared to be more of the *'I'm calculating exactly how long it will take to skin you'* variety.

'You two look alike.' Nicolas's voice was a bit slurred, as if he'd been drinking.

I wish. At least then I'd have earned this feeling.

'Are you saying I look like a girl?' the man snarled, face darkening. His hands went to his scythes.

'Or that I look like a boy?' The serving maid – though she clearly wasn't that – seemed equally offended, putting one hand to her heart and the other to her forehead as if to swoon theatrically.

'I'm saying you look identical.'

The serving maid crouched in front of him, holding his cheek and jiggling it slightly. 'That's what twins do, silly. They look alike.' *Silly?* She patted him twice then began to laugh. It was...maniacal. And her wide eyes were downright frightening.

I don't think she's entirely right in the head.

'Will you calm down?' the man snapped. 'You're making a fool of yourself, as usual.'

The serving maid rose, poking her tongue out at the man. 'You're my *brother* not my *mother*,' she said in a singsong voice.

The male pursed his lips, massaging the bridge of his nose as he huffed. He was muttering under his breath. All Nicolas caught was '*...drowned you at birth.*'

That gives me an idea.

'That's not a very nice way to talk to your sister,' he said.

The pair looked first at him then at each other and burst out laughing.

'Trying to play us against each other.' The man laughed. '*That's* the best you've got?' He scratched his chin in mock thought. 'I suppose that would be an ingenious plan...for a moron.'

Is he saying he'd have to be a moron to fall for it, or I'm a moron for trying it?

Either way, he was offended. 'Hey—' His words were cut off by the serving maid's finger on his lips. She was fast.

'Shhh,' she soothed. 'You're handsome, but please don't push it. It'd be a shame to rob the world of such handsomeness.' The finger on his lips moved across and stroked his cheek slowly, and weirdly. Was he somehow supposed to find pleasure in a compliment paid to him by someone who was clearly not sane?

'I will remove the pair of you from the world,' Silva snapped, announcing her return to consciousness as she struggled against her bindings. 'And mark my words, it will be violent.'

The twins looked at each other again then let out a hearty chuckle.

'Oh, please have mercy,' the male commented dryly, shaking his head as he walked over to Billy and crouched in front of their new companion. 'Hello, Billy.'

'Hey, Alexi,' Billy replied with an awkward nod, before glancing at the serving maid and sighing. 'I thought you looked familiar, but I just couldn't think how. Now I see your brother it's...'

'You *know* these two?' Shift said incredulously.

'Yeah, they're members of the Assassins Guild.'

There was a stunned silence.

We're at the mercy of professional assassins?

Great.

Hang on, shouldn't we, therefore, be dead? Do assassins take prisoners? Why would they?

The potential answers to those questions were quite worrying.

'Yes, we are,' Alexi said coolly. 'And you *were*, until we excommunicated you.'

'Oh.' Billy sounded almost disappointed. 'They excommunicated me? That's a bit rude.'

Nicolas looked at Billy wide-eyed. 'You're an *assassin*?'

Billy shrugged, the motion awkward with his hands shackled. 'No, I'm not. I'm just a member of the guild. Like I said, I have a weakness for joining things. I met a guy, we got chatting, I gave him some helpful advice, and I ended up joining the Assassins Guild. You know how it is.'

'No,' Nicolas scoffed. 'I really don't.'

'I was more of an *'honorary member'* really,' Billy smiled nervously. 'I've never actually assassinated anyone. Or was even asked to. Can you imagine?'

'Hence the excommunication,' the male assassin, Alexi, said flatly.

'What?' Garaz snarled, his hackles obviously rising. 'How can you be an assassin and not kill anyone? That doesn't make any sense.'

'Truth.' The serving maid giggled. 'He tells the truth. No blood on his knife. Old Billy comes to the meetings, talks, and makes friends.' Then her face dropped. 'But then he left us and got himself in some trouble.'

Leather creaked as Alexi moved closer. 'Yes, Billy. We hear some people are after you. We don't know why, but the Council has decided it'd be better to silence you for good, lest guild secrets fall into the hands of outsiders.' He rose again and began to trace the blade of one of his scythes with his finger, making a very unsubtle point. 'But first, we need to be sure you haven't told anyone anything already. We also need to know whether this is part of an attack against the guild itself. So what I'm going to do is, for every question you refuse to answer, one of your new friends dies. If you're still tight-lipped after you run out of friends, Emelina will put her poisons to work.'

'Please don't talk.' Emelina pouted playfully. 'I have some brilliant new ones I've been dying to try, and Alexi keeps telling me no. Spoilsport.'

Alexi seemed unbothered by the accusation. 'There's this one, I call it Dragon's Breath, that makes you feel like your whole body is aflame. Not like, passionate aflame, but really on fire. It's so neat.'

'It is, actually,' Alexi added grudgingly.

'Alexi and Emelina,' Auron mused as he searched the room, probably for some way to help. 'Never heard of them. I knew something was off when I saw the empty tavern, but I was too distracted by all that crap art on the walls.'

We all have off days. Though yours may get us killed.

'Alexi and Emelina,' he found himself saying. 'Never heard of you.' In his limited experience of the world, some people didn't like not being heard of.

Like Auron. And he was quite verbose about it when he found out. Maybe this pair are too?

He was hoping to buy the spirit some time to produce a miracle. Though all Auron could do at the moment was throw things. His abilities had yet to graduate to beating up a pair of assassins and undoing his companions' shackles.

Alexi stomped over to him indignantly, leaning in close. 'Well, of course you haven't, fool. We wouldn't be very good assassins if everyone had heard of us, would we?' The man scrutinised him. 'You know what? I don't like you.'

'The feeling is mutual.'

'You can die first.'

'You can kiss my ass.'

Eyes wide, Alexi reached for one of his scythes, only to be stopped by his sister. 'We haven't asked any questions yet. We should really do the questions first.'

Reluctantly, Alexi rose, keeping his gaze on Nicolas as he ran his finger slowly across his throat. Nicolas responded with a finger of his own. He'd had to bring his hand up to make the gesture, and his shackles caught his eye.

Oh. An idea.

'Shift,' he whispered. 'Remember the vampire cave, when we first met?'

Shift's sly smile suggested they very much knew what to do. In fact, it kind of suggested they'd already thought of it.

Nicolas nodded to Auron, hoping to impart with a single gesture of his head that he needed to create a distraction. Judging by the spirit's impressed nod, he got the point.

Walking to the bar, Auron used his finger to knock a bowl off the counter. He was getting better at that all the time. It barely looked like he was trying anymore. The bowl hit the floor with an echoing thud. Alexi and his sister spun around. Alexi had scythes in hand and Emelina pulled two needle-like knives from her dress. It didn't take a wise man to guess the blades were poisoned somehow. The assassins looked at each other meaningfully before the pair advanced on the bar from both sides in as wide a circle as they could manage in the small room. Despite the clutter, the twins moved silently. It was actually quite impressive.

Beside Nicolas, Shift changed form, shrinking to the body of a child, just as they'd done when he'd first met them shackled in a vampire cave, before slipping their tiny hands from their bindings and lowering them to the floor carefully, so their captors weren't alerted by clattering. Then the loose-looking clothes filled out again as they returned to their preferred form, rubbing their wrists and glaring a hole through the oblivious twins.

Nicolas raised his wrists and gestured to the shackles. He wanted out, and Shift had a magic key, but they waved him away. Before he could ask what they were thinking, Shift got to their feet, an almost-evil grin on their face. His companion flexed their wrists a couple of times before they changed again.

The sound of tearing clothes made the twins turn back to their captives. By the time they did, a large and very angry-looking bear awaited them.

Emelina screamed, as the bear roared in fury. Nicolas tried to cover his ears, but with his hands bound, he had to settle for just the one nearest Shift. Alexi made to raise his weapons, but the bear swatted him aside, launching him across the room. The crash as he hit a pile of stools was most satisfying.

As Emelina backed slowly toward the door, paling as she stared at Bear Shift in shock. Her brother scrabbled forwards and grabbed his dropped weapons from the floor. Judging by the half-crouch as he rose, he was unsure whether to fight or flee. Shift made the decision for him, roaring again before surging forwards.

Emelina cried out and fled the tavern, her brother on her heels. A second after Alexi disappeared through the door, the table Shift had launched at him hit the frame, shattering into pieces. Bear Shift growled toward the now-open door, which they were unable to fit through in their current form, before one final roar, the point of which was clear.

Don't come back.

'Brilliant.' Nicolas smiled. 'Can you let us out now?'

Shift's snout jiggled as they shook their head before pointing a clawed paw at their torn clothes on the floor.

Oh.

Shift's clothes didn't change with them, so they'd be naked when they returned to their preferred form. But that didn't necessarily mean they had to wait.

'The key,' he said, gesturing to the magic key that hung from their neck, the rope also magic and changing with them.

Shift looked at him, snorted derisively, and padded off to the back of the tavern.

Looks like we're waiting then.

It wasn't like they were going anywhere. And Alexi and Emelina would undoubtedly be fleeing for a good while yet.

CHAPTER 10

S ilva was seething as she strode back into the tavern, her face set in a snarl that would've given a charging dragon pause. She slammed her sword back into its sheath as she glared toward the door. 'They have vanished.'

'You keep losing the bad guys lately,' Shift said, after sucking their teeth. 'It's starting to become a habit.'

It has happened twice in a short space of time.

Not that he'd openly agree with Shift. He wanted no piece of the glare they were currently getting from Silva.

'I doubt they'll have gone far,' Auron said as he entered after the warrior, snapping Nicolas back into the moment. 'Assassins are known to be good at hiding, but they aren't known for giving up on contracts easily. They'll be back.'

'That's a shame.' Nicolas sighed. 'I'm quite comfortable with them never returning. Ever.'

Auron gave him a sympathetic half-smile. 'Sorry, kid. In this game you collect enemies like a witch's nose collects warts. The real trick is to make sure they don't stay alive long enough to be a problem.'

Why is Auron looking at me like that?

'So, this one time...' *Ah.* 'Six of my old enemies, survivors, decided to team up and try to take me down. The theory was sound, but the execution was piss-poor. They couldn't agree on how to attack me as a group, so they decided to do it one at a time. Which completely defeated the point of teaming up in the first place. But then, when they finally confronted me, they couldn't decide who would get the first shot at me. A discussion became a heated debate, which quickly became an argument, and soon swords were drawn. I literally stood there and watched them kill each other.'

'Do you think they could have defeated you had they worked together?' Silva asked.

The spirit shrugged. 'Who knows? But they gave me a fantastic idea. After that, every so often, I would take the identity of someone I'd killed, and use his connections to create a gathering of my surviving enemies on the pretext of coming together to defeat me. Once they were all in the same room...' Moment for dramatic pause. '...they never walked out again.'

'That is pretty ingenious,' Nicolas said with an impressed chuckle.

'Maybe we could gather all our enemies in a tavern and have Garaz burn the place down?' Shift ventured.

Might be the only way to defeat K...the demon.

'I doubt gathering them will be an easy task,' Garaz said quietly as he worked on the herbal concoction he was brewing for them. 'But I suggest we do not dally here too long discussing the finer points of the idea.'

If Nicolas had had his way, they would've already been out the door, but whatever they'd been drugged with was unwilling to let them go so easily – it was more stubborn than Auron when it came to finishing a story. Mostly, it was just small bouts of disorientation, but when riding a horse, that could turn out to be pretty fatal.

Especially when I don't have someone's leg to grab on the way down.

Silva was suffering too, her skin a little paler than usual, but she'd been determined to try to run the assassins down—despite Nicolas's hesitance. Auron had assured him that most assassins weren't up to much in a straight fight. As their prey were normally dead before they had a chance to fight back, most assassins didn't bother training for real combat.

'A little fact that's saved my life more than once,' the hero had told him smugly.

Luckily, Garaz had the ingredients to create a brew to chase away the stubborn aftereffects. Whatever he was cooking up would almost certainly taste foul, but if it stopped him feeling like he was walking through water, he was all for it.

'For what it's worth, I'm really sorry about this,' Billy said sheepishly, holding his forehead tenderly. 'I make friends easily then I just can't say no when someone asks me to join something. It's a very bad habit.'

At least it explained what Tavish had wanted with him, though the Maestro wanting leverage on the Assassins Guild was very worrying indeed. Taking the wet cloth he'd been using to soothe the pounding headache Emelina's poison had produced, Nicolas thought about the twins. 'Who are they?'

'Alexi and Emelina Cladovich are two of the guild's best assassins.' Billy sighed. 'They may not look it because of the bickering, but trust me, if they'd just wanted us dead, we would've been.' *I can believe that. Thank the Deities they aren't fond of angry bears.* 'They call Alexi The Reaper. He takes great pride in his work...'

'Runs around wearing black, carries scythes, and calls himself The Reaper. Subtle.' Auron scoffed, shaking his head.

'His sister, Emelina, is known as The Deadly Flower. She can do all sorts with poisons and toxins. And she's a little...unhinged.' Billy let out a sorrowful groan. 'I'm in trouble, aren't I?'

You've been in trouble since we met you. It's just getting worse.

Thoughtfully, Nicolas took the cup Garaz handed him. Things were becoming more complicated by the moment.

I hope when we find those knights there's a whole troop of them. Billy may need it.

Though Nicolas knew it was more than likely he'd stick with Billy until he was safely in the city, and the jewel was locked away in a heavily guarded vault. Until then, their new companion would need all the help he could get, and he was happy to provide it. Besides, there was still a chance Billy knew something about Tavish that he didn't know he knew. A titbit of information that would make hunting the black knight down much easier once they came to it.

Hopefully, it shakes loose when we're on the road again. Which we will be once this poison loses its hold over me.

He drained the cup in one swig. The wincing and gagging afterwards took longer, but once it passed, the disorientation was gone.

Reassuringly, he patted Billy on the shoulder. 'You don't have to worry.' He smiled. 'We're going to keep you safe. We promised to get you where you need to go, and we keep our word.'

'Thank you,' Billy replied with feeling. 'Hopefully, it goes a bit smoother from here on out.'

'Smooth or not, you're in good hands with this team.' Shift flexed their body as they tried to break in their new leather outfit, which creaked and groaned with each move. Judging by their displeased face, it wasn't the best fit.

Nicolas had to disagree. In fact, he was making a concerted effort not to stare, lest he get slapped again. He wouldn't think about the kiss. He refused. If he started, he'd overthink it until he caused one of the embarrassing moments that were becoming standard in his life.

They were just relieved to see me alive. That's all.

'And when I say *team*,' Shift continued, 'I'm the one who does all the hard work. Once again, I saved the day when the rest of you got yourselves in trouble.'

'As I recall, you were bound like the rest of us,' Silva countered sourly, just regaining her composure after retching from drinking Garaz's herbal tea.

'And yet I was the one who freed myself, chased away our enemies, and let the rest of you out.' The thief shrugged.

'Hey,' Auron cried, 'I provided the distraction.'

'Thank you, Auron,' Nicolas said, before catching Shift's eye. 'And thank you for bailing us out again. It must be a real burden, but you wear it well.'

Shift winked at him. 'It's a responsibility, but someone's got to look after you, Nick. And I think you'll agree I wear *everything* well. It's...' Stopping mid sentence, Shift sighed and suddenly found the taverns door very interesting. 'I need to put the rest of this in my saddlebags.' Quickly, they picked up the pile of clothes they'd taken from the back room for spares and left the tavern.

'I think you've done something to upset them,' Billy whispered with a grimace.

His ire rose as he tried to think what he could have done to upset Shift. If anything, he ought to be upset with them. There was enough upheaval – and evil – around right now that he shouldn't be dwelling on a kiss. That wasn't going to help him find his parents. Awkwardly, he took his hand away from his mouth. He'd been brushing his lips.

'It was a good distraction, wasn't it?'

'What?' He squinted up at Auron.

'The distraction, kid,' the spirit huffed. 'It was good, wasn't it? I got them to turn right round whilst Shift did their thing.'

'It worked like a charm.'

'I mean, if you'd let me possess you, I'd have been able to pick the lock, and the twins would both be dead by now, but it's still a victory.'

Oh, for Deities' sake. 'You did great.'

'I mean, I wish I could be more useful.' The spirit drew his ghost sword, or whatever it was Sha'then had gifted him along with the horse. Holding it aloft, he looked at it as if it were a mouldy cucumber. 'Stupid useless blade.' He sniffed before thrusting it into Nicolas repeatedly to prove his point. 'Stab, stab, stab.'

Seeing the sword enter his body, even though he knew it wouldn't hurt him, made him queasy. With a flash, the sword was replaced by the image of an arrow sticking out of his chest. 'Stop it!'

'I wasn't doing anything,' Billy said next to him, looking around warily.

Letting out a deep breath, he shook his head. 'No, it's... Never mind.'

Auron looked taken aback then made a big show of sheathing the blade. 'Sorry, kid. I didn't think.'

'It's okay,' he mumbled, just wanting to forget it.

The door of the tavern darkened, drawing his attention. Shift stood in the doorway. 'I've found the patrons.'

CHAPTER 11

With a sinking feeling that he was about to find a pile of dead bodies, he made for the door. Considering the urgency of the situation, he was surprised when Silva blocked his way.

'Everything okay?' he asked, slightly nervously.

'I have failed, again,' the warrior said bluntly.

'Ummm...have you?' Silva could be very intense when the mood took, and right now her stare was making Nicolas feel like *he* was in the wrong, when that was clearly not the case.

If only I could train myself to be less oversensitive.

'Twice now, I have allowed our enemies to slip away,' the warrior said, in a tone that sounded more like she was telling Nicolas off, rather than admitting a mistake. 'It is unacceptable, and I apologise.'

'Like Auron says, they always come back. Don't be too hard on yourself.'

'So...you are not upset with me?'

What?

It took him a moment to properly understand what Silva had just asked him. The consideration that the warrior may be bothered by his opinion of her had never crossed his mind. Nicolas shook off his awkwardness and met the warrior's gaze.

'No. Not at all,' he said firmly. 'I wish you'd caught Tavish, of course. But he got away. It happens. I can hardly be angry with someone over that. I've made enough mistakes myself.'

Silva studied him for a long while. Nicolas got the impression she was trying to discern whether or not he was speaking the truth, which he was.

'There are a pile of bodies outside that we shouldn't really keep waiting,' he said with a half chuckle, praying that this conversation ended soon.

'Of course,' the warrior said. 'Let us...' Silva was about to step aside, but she stopped suddenly. 'I would never let any of our enemies get away without doing everything in my power to run them down. I need you to know that.'

Does that need saying?

'I...'

'Excuse me.' They both looked at Billy, who was holding the table for support. 'I don't think the orc's potion completely worked for me. Can someone give me a hand, please?'

Silva looked at Nicolas again, sighed, then went to help Billy. There was a pang of worry as he watched the warrior walk away. It wasn't like her to be so...he supposed *emotional* was the right word.

Well, emotional for Silva.

'Kid, hurry up,' Auron shouted through the door.

'Coming.' Quickly he left the tavern, following the spirit's voice around to the side of the building.

The others were stood beside a small shed at the back of the tavern. The wooden door bulged, as if great pressure was being put on it from the other side. The thick metal chain around the handle seemed to be the only thing keeping it shut.

'I heard a groan from inside.' Shift eyed the door warily.

'What kind of groan?' Auron asked. 'Zombies groan.'

Their companion considered this for a moment. 'It was less of an *'I'm hungry for fresh flesh'* groan, and more of a *'oh Deities, my head'* groan,' Shift replied finally.

'Then why did you not open the door before calling us?' Garaz asked.

'Just in case I was wrong, and they are zombies,' Shift replied, shaking their head as if the question was daft.

'Hold on then.' Auron walked up to the shed and put his head through the door. 'Huh.' Drawing it out again, he turned to the rest of the group. 'No zombies, just a heap of semi conscious people. My guess is they were drugged and shoved in there. Be careful when you open the door. They're all piled against it.'

'Noted.' Shift approached and began working the lock.

Shift's skill as a lockpick made the magic key they carried seem a little redundant.

Still a nice gift though.

Within a second, the lock clicked and Shift pulled it off the chain. Instantly, the door swung open, several people rolling out onto the dirt. There were more inside. Fitting that many people into such a small shed was, admittedly, impressive. It must've taken a lot of work.

Why not just kill them?

It seemed like a lot of extra work for the assassins to put themselves through. But the pair were clearly mad, so Nicolas wasn't about to try to delve into the thought process behind their actions.

It might make me the same way.

'They will live,' Garaz confirmed as he crouched beside the nearest bodies. 'Let us move them out of here so I can check them over properly.'

'Damn, they fitted all those people in *that* shed?' Billy looked bemused as Silva leant him against the wall, before the warrior came over to help them.

Nicolas glanced from his new companion to the pile of people. Sorting this out would delay their journey, but it wasn't even a question. He wasn't about to just leave these people before ensuring they were all well.

The knights can wait a bit longer. They'll be in a tavern anyway, so they can hardly complain.

Dragging all the bodies out into the open was a laborious task, though they were all in various stages of coming around, they were also dead weight. A lot of huffing and puffing, and sweat was required to get them all laid neatly together on the ground. Once the last one, a slight fellow with straw like hair, was in place, Nicolas took a moment to catch his breath.

'Are you okay?' Shift was smirking as they asked the question.

He quickly realised he was the only one sweating and out of breath. The others – Silva and Shift – barely appeared to have exerted themselves. He responded to his companion's question with a nod. If he talked, he may betray his ragged breathing, which no doubt would invite commentary from the shapeshifter.

No one said my fitness would improve overnight.

Garaz got out of the hard work by brewing up some more of his cure-all. The group all helped ensuring each of the people from the shed got a dose. It did its work quickly, and soon all of them were coming around properly.

The side effect of such a large group of people waking up at the same time was a lot of groaning. All of them seemed to be suffering terrible hangovers as the poison slowly left their systems. Then there was a fair amount of screaming.

'*Orc. Orc,*' one woman cried as she opened her eyes to see Garaz standing over her.

That roused the others quickly enough, and soon they were all scrabbling back into the shed, closing the door behind them with a heavy thud.

Garaz put his fingers to the bridge of his nose and huffed. Aggravation emanated from beneath his cloak.

'All that work to get them out of there, and they run straight back in,' Shift remarked dryly, shaking their head.

Inside the shed, people were crying and shouting and generally talking about how they were about to die.

'Hey,' Nicolas shouted, trying to get their attention. '*Hey*.'

'*Quiet*,' Silva roared.

Silence was instantaneous.

Taking a moment to ensure that everyone was staying quiet, Nicolas addressed the shed. 'You're all safe now. We're here to help.'

'Orc.'

'Yes, we have an orc with us,' he replied levelly. 'But he's a good orc.'

'Ain't never heard tell of no good orc,' came a petulant reply.

Garaz huffed again.

'That doesn't mean there aren't any.'

'Also doesn't mean there's one outside the shed right now. It's just your say-so, and we don't know you.'

Now it was Nicolas's turn to pinch the bridge of his nose. 'Look, I understand you've been through an ordeal, but—'

'Such an ordeal,' a woman's voice piped up. 'There I was, preparin' the stew and this woman in a mask strolls in, lights this powder, and next thing we know, we're waking up outside.'

'They were assassins,' Nicolas replied. 'They were laying an ambush and—'

'Orc.'

Worried muttering came from inside the shed.

Biting his lip, Nicolas looked at the sky. It was starting to get dark. It'd been a long day, and they had nothing to show for it. No Tavish, and no sign of Billy's escort. He was quite surprised to find himself getting angry.

They've been through an ordeal. They can't help it.

'I think we've got off on the wrong foot.' Nicolas raised his voice to be heard. 'I'm Nicolas Percival Carnegie and...'

The sudden silence from inside the shed made him stop talking.

'Nick Carnage?'

Now it was his turn to huff. 'Yes.'

The shed burst open, and smiling faces appeared. 'Why didn't you say so?' A grey-bearded man beamed at him, taking his hand and shaking it. 'If we'd known it was you before, we'd have known how safe we were.'

What?

'Oh, Deities be praised, it is you,' the woman said, clapping her hands together.

What's going on?

'We've heard tell of you,' the man said as they all gathered around him, staring at him as if he were some curiosity in a travelling show. 'Saviour of Sarus, stopping the war in Merida. We heard you helped King Eldric stop the vampires in the city as well.'

'Well...I... Yes,' he stammered.

How are these people hearing about my...exploits, I suppose is the right word?

'Do these people travel with you?' the man asked as the crowd shuffled closer. More than a few cast wary glances at Garaz.

'Um...yes.'

'Looks like the legend of *Nick Carnage* is growing, kid,' Auron said as he looked at the awestruck crowd.

Nicolas ignored the remark. There was no legend. He wasn't that guy. He wasn't even sure he was *him* anymore.

'You've heard of Shift the shapeshifter, of course?' Judging by the expectant look on his companion's face, Shift was hoping to hear some epic song written about their part in his adventures.

The group looked blank. Though a couple nervously muttered, *'Is she human?'*

'They are part of my group. Shift has been a part of all my...adventures.' He wouldn't have Shift disrespected like that. The shapeshifter gave him an appreciative glance.

Slowly, the crowd took it in turns to shake his hand. He didn't want it. He hated being the centre of attention at the best of times. Now they were, what, looking up to him? He was no example to follow.

I'm just a village boy doing...the right thing, I suppose. I mean, I hardly had a choice.

Except I did, didn't I? There are about a thousand times when I could have just turned and run away, or curled up in a sobbing ball and stayed like it.

'Bless the Deities for you.' The barman clapped. 'Who knows what those ruffians would've done to us had you not happened along? The legends are true.'

He didn't have the heart to mention the fact that the *ruffians* had only been there to ambush them.

'Please, come in and stay the night. We don't have rooms, but we have a roof, a fire, and some good food.'

As long as it isn't a plant-based stew.

A glance from the owners made it clear Garaz was less welcome than the rest.

'That's a kind offer and all—' he began.

'We aren't going yet,' Garaz interrupted. 'These people still need ministering to. They were poisoned.'

Several did appear a little disorientated, yet they were still standing and smiling. Good of Garaz to want to continue caring for them after...their reaction. But if they aren't happy with him being here then Nicolas wasn't sure he wanted to stay.

Besides, we need to get Billy to safety. Then we can continue our hunt for Tavish.

'But—'

'Do not question me.' The sharp retort stunned him. That wasn't how Garaz talked. In his peripheral vision, Billy backed away from the orc nervously.

Garaz's jaw set as his yellow eyes flicked down.

What in the Underworld?

Nicolas's hand was hovering near the hilt of his sword. It must have been some odd reflex action. He'd never really draw his blade on Garaz. His mouth opening and closing, hoping to come up with the perfect apology, Nicolas awkwardly put his hand to his side. The hurt in the orc's eyes before Garaz turned and walked away stung him.

'One night won't hurt,' Auron interjected, eyeing the pair oddly.

Nicolas watched his red cloaked companion disappear behind the tavern in confusion.

What just happened?

CHAPTER 12

After an hour, he finally managed to slip outside. Though he had a fairly sizeable history of getting attacked when he strolled around alone at night, the adulation being piled on him was unbearable. From the thanks for saving them, to the congratulations for his previous deeds—each piece of praise made the room a little smaller. Shift hadn't helped, starting to tell the tales of their exploits at Auron's excited behest. His anxiousness had become so bad that at one point he swore some of the paintings on the wall were smiling at him, ready to start heaping praise of their own.

Taking in the cool night air, Nicolas stood by the side of the tavern, bent over with his hands on his knees to support himself. He was just trying to breathe, which should've been easy after so many years of practice. Everything was starting to become so overwhelming of late. Not just events themselves, but his reactions to them.

Perhaps I'm not dealing with all of this as well as I'd thought.

'Mind if I join you?'

His instinctive reply of *bugger off* was stopped short by the sight of Billy with two drinks in hand, covered in shadow due to the less than adequate lamps around the tavern. He nodded, taking one of the offered cups and draining it. 'Thanks,' he managed once he'd wiped his mouth clean.

Billy came and leant against the wall beside him, taking a thoughtful sip of his drink before speaking. 'So you're a bit of a big deal then?'

'No,' Nicolas scoffed.

Billy didn't seem convinced. 'They seem to think so.'

'*They* are wrong.' *They got my name wrong, for starters.*

'Oh.' His companion looked taken aback. 'So you didn't do what they said then?'

'Well, yes,' he admitted. 'But I more survived it than really did anything.' Nicolas chuckled dryly. 'Besides, it was a group effort.'

Billy seemed thoughtful for a moment. 'Forgive me for saying this, but you don't seem like the adventuring...type. The others, of course. But you...I get the impression you're more of a homebody.'

Nicolas let out a single bitter laugh. That was the truest statement in all Etherius. 'I got swept up in events, I guess,' he replied. 'I got chosen to go and deliver a message, and things just...happened. One after the other until I ended up here.'

'I know that feeling well,' Billy said, shaking his head. 'I come from a big family. They can be a bit much sometimes, so I decided to get away and see the world. I suppose having all those siblings made me a people person.' The man looked at his tankard. 'I found it quite lonely, on the road by myself. That's why I have a tendency to join any group that'll welcome me, I guess.' Billy frowned and turned to him. 'If you don't want to be here, why don't you just go home?'

'It isn't that easy,' he replied slowly, staring at his own tankard. 'My village was taken in retribution for interfering in someone's plans.'

Billy let out a long whistle, shaking his head. 'You must've really interfered to warrant that kind of response.'

'I suppose so,' he said thoughtfully. 'I keep waiting for them to come at me again. I wonder what will happen when they do. Can I defeat them? Can I get my people back?'

Can I defeat it. *The demon.*

Mentally, he tried to force himself to say it's name, but he just couldn't. Fear grabbed the word before it left his lips and dragged it back into his mouth.

The bushy-haired man smiled at him. 'At least you have good people around you. Though they're certainly a mismatched bunch. You must be quite the guy to bring them together.'

He thought about his companions. They *were* a strange bunch.

Billy put a hand on his shoulder. 'Hey, buddy, don't be hard on yourself. You have a shapeshifting thief with you. An orc. I mean, man, an *orc*, of all things and...well, I've heard a thing or two about Silva, and they weren't good. But you brought them together. That's great.'

Did I? We were just thrown together, really.

The thief, the orc, the spirit and the mercenary. Truth was, he still barely knew any of them. But they had fought together, and saved each other. So he trusted them.

'They've saved me a few times.'

'So they're the reason you're here.' Billy smiled. 'The reason I got saved.'

If I hadn't met them then would I even be here?

Nicolas's had to admit that things would be very different if he hadn't met any of them. Right now he would be home, in bed. Same as all the people of Hablock. Same as his parents. Instead they were all...somewhere. He tried not to dwell on specifics, to visualise their possible fate. He knew it wouldn't be a nice place, and that was enough.

That's even if mum and dad are still...

Emotions surged in him. Worry. Frustration. Fear. Uncertainty. Maybe grief, if the worst case scenario he refused to acknowledge turned out to be true. His tankard shook with the force of his grip as he stared into the night, trying to push it all away.

At least I don't have to do it alone.

'They're the only family I have left.' He was saying it more to himself than Billy. 'Besides, like Auron would say, *'Kid—'*

'He calls you kid?' Billy chuckled. 'That's sweet. A lot of people would find that sort of thing condescending, but it's great you've got that relationship.'

Actually, it is *a little condescending sometimes.*

'Billy,' Shift called, popping their head around the corner. 'I'm running out of stories. Come back in and tell us tales of your exploits as a master assassin.'

Billy shook his head with a smile as he rose. 'I wasn't even an amateur assassin. I'm sure I can make something up, though.' He gave Nicolas a cheeky wink. 'Wouldn't do to let the crowd down.'

That wouldn't do at all.

As his companion loped away, Nicolas was alone. Or thought he was.

'The adulation is deserved, kid.'

He nearly jumped out of his skin, and he'd only just gotten back in it. How long had the spirit been standing there?

'You've done some great things. And some terrible things have happened to you.' Auron gave him a sad smile. 'For what it's worth, I'm sorry it happened to you. But you've stood tall in the face of some very bad stuff, and still do. Maybe one in a thousand would do what you're doing right now. The rest would have fled, or been broken.'

'I know,' he said quietly. 'Though I don't really feel like I've ever had much choice in the matter.'

'You did,' the spirit replied. There was a moment of hesitation before Auron continued. 'There weren't any bodies kid. Right now, your parents are most likely alive.'

'I'm trying really hard not to consider the alternative.'

'You know what's good for taking your mind off of your ills?' Auron asked, leaning in and dropping his voice to a conspiratorial whisper. 'Some training. I think a lesson would do you the world of good right now.'

'Yes. Please.' Having something to focus on right now would be most welcome.

Auron led him behind the shed, into a small clearing. It was dark, but the light of the moon, coupled with the light from Auron, was enough to see by. Besides, as the hero had said to him before, *'Sword work isn't always about seeing. It's about feeling.'* He wasn't sure exactly what that nugget of information meant, but it would surely become apparent in time.

Standing in the centre of the clearing, as Auron directed, he quickly checked for any logs or stones. Tripping in the dark whilst holding a sword was a recipe for disaster.

'Draw,' Auron said as he watched, arms folded.

Nicolas wrapped his hand around the hilt of the *Dawn Blade* and drew it from its sheath. The sword's reflective blade shimmered slightly as it caught Auron's light. He took the ready stance the spirit had taught him, sword held in front of him in both hands and his legs shoulder-width apart. That last part had taken a long time to perfect. Apparently, he thought his shoulders were a lot wider than they were.

'Hey, you're learning your correct proportions.' Auron chuckled as he noted the stance. 'It's about time.'

The spirit walked around him. There was nothing more nerve-racking than having someone appraising him closely, but he kept it in check. This was no time for nerves.

Finally, Auron walked in front of him, but slightly to the side. Turning his back, the spirit drew his own sword.

'Just like before,' he said. 'Go through the basic lines of attack. Follow me. Slow and smooth, but with purpose.'

The pair went through the set he was becoming so familiar with. First came the cuts from each shoulder to hip, each hip to shoulder then to each side, followed by straight down and a thrust. The last move was to spin the sword into a reverse grip and thrust it behind, each with a number attributed to it by the spirit. Nicolas copied Auron, repeating the set over and over, each time getting faster until the movements were a fluid flurry of attacks. Nicolas lost himself in the ritual, shutting his mind off as the blade danced in his hands.

'Enough,' Auron said as he sheathed his blade and turned. The spirit gave him a half-smile. 'You're getting it. Let's see if you can do them out of order.'

Auron shouted out random numbers relating to the attacks he'd taught Nicolas. Some of them he got instantly, but for a couple there was a moment of hesitance as his brain engaged and cut off his natural flow. For the most part, though, he was pleased with his progress. They hadn't been training for long, but he knew the importance of it, and he was dedicated now. It had a purpose.

'Time to change it up again,' the spirit said. 'I'll shout out combinations of numbers, and you step forward with each attack.'

And so they moved into the next phase. Auron would call out four or five attacks, and Nicolas would perform them. Soon enough his arms ached and his body was covered in sweat, but he persevered. He didn't have the luxury of rest or weakness anymore.

I need to be ready.

'That'll do,' Auron said after a while. 'Sheath the blade.'

Nicolas gave Auron a bow, which was returned, and then did as he was bade.

'You didn't drop the sword once,' the spirit remarked glibly. 'If we can get you doing that in an actual fight, we're halfway there.'

Though the compliment was hidden in a jest, he'd take it. There was definitely something more natural about having the sword in his hand, and his confidence about using it was growing. It was hard to believe there was a time when holding the *Dawn Blade* had made his wrists ache. Still, swinging it around in a clearing was a lot different than using it to take someone's life. And he wasn't sure he'd ever be comfortable with killing.

'Before you give in to whatever doubts are causing your brow to knit like that,' Auron remarked, 'it's time for the next part of your training.'

He followed the spirit's pointing finger to Silva, stood by the wall of the tavern. Who knew how long she'd been there for? This was how it had been since Hablock. Auron would teach him the way of the sword and Silva would spar with him and teach him hand-to-hand combat. In the mornings, fitness training. In the evenings, how to fight. It was rigorous, but again, necessary.

'Are you ready?' Silva asked as she strode into the clearing. She'd removed her armour plates and was dressed in a simple leather tunic. That was an adjustment they'd made early on, after she'd used her chest plate to intercept one of Nicolas's punches and nearly broken his knuckles. Shift had been highly amused by his howl of pain.

He replied to Silva's question with a nod. Undoing the clasp on his belt, he removed the sword from his hip, placing it gently on the ground next to the nearest tree before returning to the centre to face Silva.

'We will pick up where we left off last time,' the warrior said. 'With some gentle sparring. You are improving with your striking, but you need to learn to be more fluid when flowing from one strike to the next.'

What I need is a magic lightning bolt that smites my enemies wherever they are. But until I nab one of those, this'll do.

Silva took a fighting stance. 'When you're ready.'

I'm ready.

With a deep breath, he swung a right hook at Silva. The warrior stepped back, using her hand by his wrist to guide the punch away from her. Remembering what he'd been taught, he drove in with his body weight, turning the failed punch into an elbow strike to the chest, which, unsurprisingly, Silva parried in the same manner, stepping to the side. Turning, Nicolas dropped his right hand and swung with a left hook.

'Better,' Silva said as she took his punching arm and turned her hips, causing him to stumble forwards. 'You're improving.'

'And yet you still can't land a hit,' Shift said from...wherever they'd appeared from, sucking their teeth. 'Maybe one day, if you find a genie and wish really hard, you'll manage it.'

Nicolas hesitated briefly as he looked at Silva and instead saw the demon. Blinking it away, he readied himself.

I can hit her.

Turning, he threw a kick at Silva, immediately driving in with another punch as it was batted away.

'Slow down,' Silva told him.

I can hit...

Instantly, he drove forward with an uppercut then a cross, a kick, another elbow. Each time Silva parried his strikes, he got a little faster.

'Slow down,' the warrior repeated firmly.

I can hit the demon.

'Kid, calm down,' Auron said.

He barely heard it. All his focus was on the demon stood before him, the creature that had taken his parents from him. Right now he ought to be terrified, but some deep well of rage drove him onward as he launched strike after strike at air. He may as well have been trying to punch Auron. Vaguely, he was aware someone was talking to him, but it was a whisper lost in the space between their lips and his ears.

I can defeat the demon. I can beat it.

'Arrrggggh,' he cried, focusing all his frustration into his balled-up fist.

This time he hit something: Silva's open hand. He let out a gasp of surprise. Her fingers closed around his in a vice-like grip before she stepped to the side, turning his elbow up and over and throwing him to the ground. After crashing in a heap, Nicolas went to scramble to his feet when a boot pressed him back to the floor.

'What was that?' Silva asked, furious gaze burning him like dragon fire.

He didn't have an immediate answer, so he lay on the ground, panting.

What just happened? It's Silva, not...the demon.

'Sorry,' he said between breaths. The warrior glared down at him and he quickly realised he was frowning at her.

The frown was confusion. I wasn't glaring at her. I wasn't.

'I know you are in pain,' the warrior said, her face softening a little. 'But do not take it out on your allies. Save it for those responsible.'

He took her offered hand, and Silva began to haul him to his feet.

I'd know for sure if my parents were alive now if you hadn't let Tavish go.

His fist, almost with a mind of it's own, sailed toward Silva. Her slap across his cheek struck first, stunning him out of his involuntary action. The hand holding his released, and he fell back to the floor, boot on his chest once again forcing him to the ground.

Silva looked enraged. 'Do not try me,' she hissed, pointing a threatening finger at him.

For a moment, as he looked up at the furious warrior, he was reminded of the old Silva, the one who had tried to kill him.

That's not her. They are two different people.

'I'm sorry. I don't know what happened.'

I really don't.

Silva removed her boot. 'You can get yourself up this time.'

As he rose, brushing debris from the floor off of himself, the warrior left. He wanted to go after her, but he didn't know what to say to make it better.

'What was that?' Shift asked.

He opened his mouth, but all he could do was shrug.

'I know you've been through a lot, but we are all here beside you,' the shapeshifter said. 'Don't forget, we've all been through a lot too.'

'Yes. Deities, of course I know that.'

'Good.' Shift folded their arms. 'I want to hear you say the demon's name.'

'What?'

'I get the impression that wasn't Silva you were fighting then. You were fighting the demon,' his companion continued. 'You need to say it's name and break this hold it has over you. You need to scream into the night and just let it all out.'

'I...don't think I can.' It was more than just saying a name. The demon had become the living embodiment of everything bad in his life right now.

'Say it.'

Nicolas shook his head. Even the idea of it terrified him. If he named the creature, he had to name what it did. He had to fully grasp the possibility that his parents may be...

'Nick, there's a lot of uncertainty right now. You need...'

'...an explanation about you kissing me and walking away.'

Instantly he clasped his hand over his mouth. He'd had no intention of saying that, it'd just come out, and right now, he had no idea what else he may accidentally say.

Shift stared at him. Their indignation rose above them like a giant waking up from a nap. But they said nothing. Instead, the shapeshifter turned and left.

In his peripheral vision he could see Auron shaking his head. 'Kid...'

Nicolas waved the spirit away. The urge to leave became very strong, and he gave into it.

He'd nearly made it around the corner when he bumped into Billy.

'Are you okay?' his companion asked.

'No.' Before he was asked to elaborate, he continued on his way. Right now, he couldn't trust his mouth or his mind.

What's happening to me?

CHAPTER 13

Having drawn the last watch gave Nicolas a chance to gaze at the sunrise, albeit through tired eyes. Over the course of a few hours the darkness of the night gradually lightened. Then the golden rays of the newly rising sun peeked over the horizon, bringing with it a new day. Which was very welcome after the previous one.

That time had also given Nicolas a chance to think. Though him having ample thinking time wasn't always a good thing, he had put it to good use. He still had no clue why he had acted the way he did the previous night, but he knew it was wrong. A slew of negative emotions were forcing him to behave in a very uncharacteristic way. And he wouldn't have it.

'New day, new Nicolas,' he promised himself.

Well, not a new Nicolas. *But a return to the regular one. Or as regular as I get.*

Blinking from staring for too long in the general direction of the rising sun, he turned his attention to the camp. Stubborn spots of light refused to leave his eyes, but they would fade over time. Mixed amongst them he could see his sleeping companions. His eyes flicked to Garaz, and he was suddenly amused at how the orc's snoring had once kept him awake all night long. Now he barely even registered it.

'You're lucky I'm here to keep watch with you,' Auron remarked as he approached. 'Because I'm pretty sure you've been daydreaming for the last few hours.'

'I would have known if there was trouble,' he replied defensively.

'Of course you would, because I would have been standing right in front of you, waving my arms and shouting *danger, danger,*' the spirit chided. 'Even you could pick up on that hint.'

'You don't have to be an ass.'

Auron smiled at him in that fatherly way he did on occasion. 'So, what is the sum total of your contemplations then?'

'That I was an absolute dickhead last night,' he shrugged. 'I can't explain it, beyond…everything that's happened to me. Though it's not an excuse for the way I behaved. But I'll make damn sure it doesn't happen again.'

Auron circled his hand, prompting him to continue.

'And I'll apologise to the others.'

To make things right with himself, he would have to make things right with them too. It was going to be awkward, and embarrassing, and Shift would no doubt make some remarks. But it had to be done.

'Please,' Shift grumbled from beneath the fur pulled tightly over their head. 'Keep having a conversation at normal speaking volume. No one here is trying to sleep.'

'It's morning,' Auron said in a faux sweet voice. He approached Shift and dramatically yanked the fur off of them. 'Rise and shine.'

What *rose* was their middle finger. But it didn't shine.

'You're getting much better at grabbing objects,' Nicolas congratulated the spirit.

'Of course, kid. Another couple months and I won't even need to offer to possess you at every turn,' Auron winked.

'Don't encourage him,' Shift grumbled.

How does someone with such a bad attitude in the morning look so damned…

Nicolas quickly cut off that trail of thought as Garaz rose and stretched his thickly muscled arms in the air, unleashing a big yawn as he did. Silva shook herself, before standing and strapping her sword to her hip. Billy stirred with a groan that would impress the living dead.

No time like the present.

Giving a loud cough, he steeled himself. 'If I could have your attention please.' Five pairs of surprised eyes blinked at him. 'I acted poorly last night, to each of you. I could stand here and try to explain or justify it, but no matter the motivation, it was wrong. I'm going to do better. And I apologise. Sorry.'

The stunned silence that followed did not fill him with confidence.

'How long were you rehearsing that for?' Shift asked, frowning.

'I didn't. It came naturally. From the heart.'

'Are you sure?'

'Yes,' he answered coolly.

'Please Shift,' Garaz interrupted. 'I think we should be appreciative of Nicolas's intent. And the theatrical delivery.'

Oh, for Deities' sake.

'Just sorry would have sufficed,' Silva suggested as she checked her pack. 'It did not require a speech.'

'That was hardly a...' Realising he was rising to the bait, Nicolas calmed himself. 'The sentiment behind it was genuine.'

Shift lay back on the ground, tucked their arms behind their head and closed their eyes. 'If you want to earn forgiveness, go knock on the tavern door and scrounge us up some breakfast.'

'And after that it's time for your morning training,' Auron said sternly.

As Nicolas began to stroll toward the tavern, he stopped and looked back at his companions. Taking a moment to watch them, he couldn't help but smile.

This might turn out to be a nice day after all.

****

Leaving the small tavern had been a long process—the people wanted to show their gratitude until the end of time, it seemed—but they needed to get moving. Although the assassin twins had failed once, no one was keen to stay where their enemies knew they'd be. Well, except maybe for Silva...

There was still a little lingering tension in the group, focused in his direction, but Nicolas knew he deserved it, so he endured it. At least the road was nice and busy already, lessening the likelihood of them getting attacked.

Though it would be nice if Tavish did put in an appearance.

'Seems like the economy's doing okay after the vampire attack,' Shift noted, inspecting the goods on the wagons that passed a little too closely.

It seemed a lifetime ago that Nicolas had helped foil the scheme of a necromancer—the very one who'd sent him after Tavish—and his vampire allies.

Huh, a lifetime ago.

Of course it appeared to have been so long ago. That was the effect of having packed so much – mostly near death experiences – into such a short space of time. Yet they were all still here.

Well, maybe not me. Maybe I'm now some undead monstrosity? It may explain why I acted like such an ass last night.

His contemplation of his own existence was interrupted by the sight of something big on the edge of his vision: a large wagon in the road. That wasn't unusual—they'd passed plenty—but this one was piled high with furniture. There seemed to be no rhyme or reason to the way it had been stacked either, as though everything had been thrown on in a hurry. The load didn't look safe, and he didn't like the idea of passing it. The road wasn't that wide, and the cargo was listing threateningly toward them.

Just as they were passing the wagon, which was headed in the opposite direction, one of its wheels hit a pothole and several small chairs clattered to the ground, thankfully missing Nicolas's head. That they weren't broken was a minor miracle, considering the height of their fall.

As the wagon pulled to a stop, Nicolas brought his steed to a halt and dismounted.

'No, sir. No, sir,' cried a voice frantically, the owner approaching him quickly, waving hands. 'We don't need no help nor no trouble.'

The fellow standing nervously before him was short—smaller and slighter than a dwarf—with pudgy cheeks and a snow-white beard. A gnome?

'It's fine.' He smiled, extending his hand. 'And there's no trouble here.'

The gnome flinched as if he were about to be struck.

'Garod, leave the chairs and come back.' The gnome's wife was staring at him fearfully, a couple of small children cowering by her side. The youngest was obviously a boy, judging by the tufts of hair already sprouting from his dimpled chin.

Nicolas raised his hands. 'Sorry if I startled you. I just thought I'd help.'

Garod eyed him warily. 'That's mighty neighbourly of you.' The comment was laden with suspicion.

'He's a nice guy,' Shift called from their saddle.

That was debatable lately, but he did want to help. For the gnome to get those chairs back to the top of his mountain of furniture would require a ladder, and the only one he could see was stuck between some table legs and a foot stool.

Slowly, Nicolas bent down and picked up one of the chairs. It was hard to know where to put it in the mass of furniture, but he managed to wedge it in well enough that it wouldn't fall back out until the next pothole. This seemed to soften Garod, and the pair had soon picked up the other chairs and placed them back on the wagon nearly securely.

Afterwards, Nicolas offered his hand again. This time, Garod shook it. 'Nicolas Percival Carnegie.'

'Garod Grasshill.' The gnome nodded amiably. 'Sorry about that just then. We can't be too careful lately.'

'Careful?' Shift asked.

Garod seemed hesitant to reply. 'Well, a lot of your...type...of folks can be quite unwelcoming of late. It's better to just assume the worst.'

'Someone has been harassing you?' Garaz asked, a slight growl on the edge of his tone.

'I wouldn't say harassing, exactly.' Garod shrugged sadly. 'But making it damn clear that we ain't welcome. That's why we're upping and moving. Going to find somewhere with a few more of our own kind.'

It was only then that Nicolas realised that the stuff on the back of the wagon wasn't just a load of bric-a-brac but their worldly possessions.

Something about a whole person's life being loaded onto the back of a wagon cut him deeply. Or maybe it was the fact that he, too, had just lost his home.

'You must've been in a rush to go,' he noted, looking at the way the pile had been assembled.

Garod coughed awkwardly. 'Well, we gotta be quick, before them new laws come in.'

'Laws?'

'The Un-Native Tax.' The gnome's face contorted in disgust. 'Anyone who's not considered a *Born Citizen* of Yarringsburg has to pay extra taxes. What it really means is anyone who's not human. Also means we get charged extra at the stores. Then I get laid off at the mill. *'Human jobs for humans,'* apparently.' Garod seemed to have some fire in him now, spitting on the ground. ''Tis ridiculous. I'm the fifth generation of Grasshills to live in Yarringsburg. I'm as native as anyone. But those Helstrum people say we can't possibly be native 'cause we ain't like them. So they make it so we gots to up and leave. Disgusting, is what it is.'

Helstrum. A disturbingly familiar name. The man wrote crappy, hate-filled pamphlets that knew a little more than they ought to about already unfolding events. And now he had *people;* that was disconcerting. But what right did they have to drive this pleasant family out of their home? Why would the king allow it? Okay, so King Eldric, the High Marshall of the Kingdom when they'd met him, had some racist tendencies, but he'd fought for his kingdom. Surely, he hadn't fought to allow this kind of persecution?

I have a mind to walk right up to that castle and ask him what in the Underworld's going on.

But he wouldn't. Not now. Get Billy to safety first. Secure the giant herding jewel. Then once Tavish and the Maestro were dealt with and his family were safe, he would go and bend the king's ear.

Though if we end up seeing Billy to Yarringsburg with his escort, I'll make sure to call in on the king about this nonsense.

'I'm sorry for your troubles,' he said. It was an empty gesture, but it was all he had. 'I hope you and your family find somewhere nice to settle.'

One of Garod's children got brave enough to give him a little wave, so he put his hands to his ears and poked his tongue out, wiggling his fingers. The child giggled then whispered to his mother, who smiled warmly.

'He says you're silly,' the mother said warmly.

'I am.' He chuckled. 'More often than I intend to be.'

'Well, it's nice to know there are still some decent folk about.' Garod smiled. 'I haven't got much, but my wife baked some fresh bread 'smornin' and—'

'No, no. You keep it,' Nicolas interrupted hastily. 'You'll need it for the journey.'

Besides, the tavern owner of The Dragon's Tooth had given them enough provisions for days.

Garod seemed almost overwhelmed by emotion. For a second, it appeared the gnome was about to hug him, but finally he nodded appreciatively instead. He held out his hand, and Nicolas took it. Garod held his hand in both of his and shook it passionately. 'Thank you.' Judging by the emotion in his voice, this family hadn't seen kindness in a while.

Nicolas watched the family leave, waving. Judging by the state of the load they carried, they'd be stopping again before long.

'That was odd,' Auron remarked thoughtfully.

'Sounds typical of human behaviour.' Garaz remarked sourly. Frowning, Nicolas looked up at the orc, only to find Garaz glaring at him slightly. What had he done to deserve that? He'd been the one to help the gnome.

What, just because I'm human, I get tarred with the same brush? I didn't notice Mr Green High-and-Mighty getting down off his high horse to lend a hand.

Nicolas couldn't help but glare back.

'It was really nice of you to help them.' Billy smiled.

'Yeah, well...' Nicolas didn't have an end to that sentence. Instead, he got ready to remount his horse.

Putting his leg in the stirrup, he kicked up with the other one. It fell back to the ground. He tried again. And failed. Then the horse plodded off, and he found himself hopping along with it thanks to his trapped foot.

His companions were sniggering.

'Yeah, all right,' he said testily as he lulled the horse to a stop.

He'd just helped some stricken travellers—surely that had earned him some good karma?

With one last kick, he made it onto the saddle, to a round of applause from Shift.

They were *so* funny.

CHAPTER 14

The gnome family had disturbed Nicolas greatly. Not because they were gnomes and he was bothered by short people or anything like that—though no one could blame him after his last encounter with a dwarf—but because of what their leaving Yarringsburg represented.

How can good people get driven out of their homes?

Since he'd left his village the first time, he'd heard an increasing amount of *us* and *them* talk, all of which was stoked by the incidents he'd somehow managed to find himself part of. Was it creating some kind of sickness in Etherius, or just feeding something already there?

Where does it end? Do...? Oww.

Not paying attention to where he was guiding his mount turned out to be a painful experience as Vigour stepped off the bank at the side of the road, making his testicles bounce painfully against the saddle. Bringing his horse to a halt, Nicolas sat up with his hands on his hips, fighting back tears.

'Are you okay?' Silva called back, once the others realised he'd stopped.

'Of course,' he said with fake casualness. 'Just taking a breather.'

'From being carried around on a horse?' Shift asked suspiciously.

'Just...letting Vigour have a breather,' he corrected quickly.

'Have you seen the size of yourself, kid? You're hardly a burden.' Auron frowned.

'I'll catch up.' It was all Nicolas could say. A wheeze of pain wanted to escape his lips, and holding it in was killing him. If he said any more, it would slip out, and questions would be asked.

Turning their backs to him, the others carried on down the road, and he sagged forwards in the saddle until he was practically lying on the horse's neck. Only then did he let out his wheeze.

Danger?

Some instinct honed by his adventures told him something was wrong. He looked up.

'You sneaky bastard,' he cried.

Reaching up, he grabbed the dangling noose that would've been around his neck and choking him to death by now had he not fallen suddenly forwards. With a single heave, he pulled Alexi out of the branch directly above him, where the assassin had been perched, holding the other end of the rope. With no time to react and counterbalance himself, the assassin toppled out of the tree with a cry, landing in a heap beside Vigour.

Quickly, Alexi scrabbled to his feet, but his cape had flicked over his head during the fall, giving Nicolas a moment of entertainment as the assassin fought his own garment.

'Back again so soon?' Nicolas asked casually as he watched the flailing assassin.

'Ah-ha,' Alexi pronounced as he freed himself and drew his scythes.

Nicolas kicked him in the face. Arms flailing, Alexi stumbled backwards until his foot found the bank that had caught Vigour, and he tumbled down it and into the brambles that lined it.

'Ah.'

Nicolas flinched as a fist closed directly in front of his face. Deities knew how she'd approached without him noticing, but Silva shook her head in disapproval as she opened her hand. In her palm was a single dart that must've been meant for him.

After flicking the dart up and catching it between two fingers, Silva threw it back to its owner. The dart hit Emelina, concealed in a nearby bush, in the back of the hand. The assassin jumped up, urgently removed the dart, and sucked at the wound before spitting onto the floor. By this time, Silva had dismounted and rested her sword against Emelina's neck.

'I yield,' the assassin yelped as Silva dragged her from her concealment and onto the road.

'Do I care?' Silva asked with a furrowed brow.

'Yes, you do,' Nicolas said. 'She yielded.'

'She tried to kill us, twice. Are we to just let her live for another attempt?'

'Not everyone who tries to kill us is necessarily a bad person. Some can be saved.' Nicolas regretted the words as soon as they left his lips. There was an implication in them that he hadn't intended to make.

Shame covered Silva's face as she looked away, sheathing her sword. 'Is this okay?' Venom laced the edge of every word as she sent Emelina rolling down the bank to join her brother with a single punch.

'That's fine,' he confirmed with a sigh.

Can't begrudge her that. Emelina did poison us.

Below them, Alexi got to his feet, furiously pulling his arms away from the thorns that had caught in his clothes. A coming bruise shadowed the assassin's chin, which Nicolas found most satisfying.

'You'll pay for that,' Alexi snarled, rubbing his chin.

As the assassin's eyes lowered, Nicolas followed them. At the edge of the bank lay Alexi's weapons, which he must've dropped due to the boot to the face. Alexi licked his lips, clearly weighing up his chances of retrieving them and finishing what he'd started.

'Don't,' Nicolas said firmly, drawing the *Dawn Blade*. 'Between the bank and my horse, I have all the high ground. You're outmatched.'

The assassin continued to eye his scythes.

'Don't...' Nicolas repeated threateningly.

Grinning sadistically, Alexi reached behind his back and drew a pair of long knives. 'Oh, I think I will,' the assassin snarled, before yelping in fear as a fireball exploded on the ground beside him, leaving small trails of flame on the nearest brambles.

'Don't,' Garaz said, smoking staff levelled at their attacker.

Pursing his lips, Alexi stared at the orc then at Nicolas, before finally dropping his weapons and raising his hands in the air. Though the look on his face wasn't exactly surrender.

'Say it,' Nicolas said.

Alexi frowned at him. 'What?'

Nicolas tilted his head slightly to the side and gave the assassin a *'you know'* look.

'*What*?' Alexi hissed, his eyes widening as understanding dawned. 'No. A thousand times no. My hands are in the air. Is that not clear enough?'

'Say it,' he repeated firmly.

Good thing Alexi wasn't a wizard, because if he had been, Nicolas would've been a pile of charred bones, judging by the assassin's rage-filled glare.

'I *yield*,' Alexi muttered finally, before quickly adding, 'For now.'

Beside him, Emelina jumped up, accompanied by a tearing sound as the thorns took their toll on the sleeve of her outfit, which was now very much the opposite of a welcoming tavern maid's. The assassin pouted as she regarded her damaged garment.

'We're in trouble, aren't we?' she asked her brother.

'It would appear so,' Alexi replied through gritted teeth.

'Before we tie you up, I've got to know something...' Nicolas began.

'Whether or not I am attached?' Emelina asked hopefully.

'What? No.' He quickly composed himself again. 'Back at the tavern, why did you go to the trouble of knocking out the patrons and staff? Why not just kill them?'

Alexi stared at him incredulously. 'Because I'm an assassin, not a murderer.' He scoffed.

'But you kill people.'

'Only the ones I'm paid to kill, you dick.'

Nicolas recoiled at the insult. 'You're a dick,' he spat back.

'*Dick*,' Alexi snapped at him, wide-eyed.

'Dick,' he fired back.

'Will you both cut it out?' Garaz rumbled.

'Let's just be clear,' Nicolas snarled, getting in Alexi's face, 'You sparing those folk is the *only* reason I'm giving you this chance now.'

'And what *chance* is that?' Alexi asked suspiciously.

'We're going to find a big tree to tie you to, then we're going to leave,' he explained. 'At some point, you'll free yourselves. But in the meantime, you can have a nice long think about whether you want to try this a third time.'

'So, you'll just leave us stranded, tied to a tree like a couple of damsels in distress?' Emelina gasped.

'*One* damsel in distress,' Alexi corrected irritably, before addressing Nicolas. 'There are two flaws in your plan.'

'Go on.'

'One. As soon as I'm out of here, I'm coming after you,' Alexi snapped defiantly. 'I'll kill you for free.'

'I thought you weren't a murderer?' Shift asked.

'I make exceptions,' Alexi snarled, glaring at Nicolas.

Nicolas turned to the others. 'Did I just speak dwarven or something? I gave him a free pass, and he's threatening to kill me?'

'You should be nice to your future brother-in-law,' Shift said with a smile.

'That will never happen.' Nicolas spun around, shocked that he and Alexi had said exactly the same thing at the same time.

'How rude,' Emelina pouted, squirming against the ropes.

'Top assassins, my ass,' Shift scoffed.

'I still think we should finish them now,' Silva counselled. 'He admits they will come after us again.'

'Try it, witch,' Alexi hissed.

The balls on this guy.

'Come on then.' Nicolas sighed. 'What's flaw number two?'

'This.' Before anyone could react, Emelina produced a small ball from her belt and threw it at the bank. A huge cloud of smoke appeared, causing Nicolas to cover his mouth, coughing. For a moment, all he could see around him was smoke. He readied his sword.

When the smoke cleared, the twins had vanished, along with their weapons.

Dammit.

'Fantastic,' Silva snapped, taking out her annoyance with a swing of her sword at a nearby bush. 'You should have just let me finish them.'

Maybe. But sometimes there's too much unnecessary death.

'They'll be back for round three then,' Shift noted, shaking their head.

'It'll go as badly as the first two.' Auron shrugged.

'Was I right to try to show mercy?' he whispered to the spirit beside him.

The spirit looked at him appraisingly. 'So, this one time...' *I guess I asked for that.* 'I met a troll that could talk. He was the result of some alchemical experiment or other. Of course, my first instinct was to kill him. My hand was stayed by my mentor. Turned out the troll wanted to do some good. I was less than convinced, but I went with it anyway.'

'And.'

'It didn't end well,' Auron answered grimly. 'Part of it set in motion a chain of events that led to my death. But I don't regret sparing him or trying to let him help. This world is a strange and dangerous one, and whatever decision you make in it has consequences that even great seers can't always know in advance. Sometimes you just have to go with your heart and hope for the best.'

'So instead of yes or no, I get a lot of words that can essentially be summed up as *'I'm on the fence*?"

'Exactly.' The spirit smiled. 'Just be you, and hope it works out.'

'I think we need to change the plan,' Shift said as the group returned to their original route.

Nicolas's back was instantly up. 'What do you mean?'

'What I mean,' Shift said, looking at him intently, 'is that time is moving on faster than we are, especially with the assassin twins slowing us down. How long do you think the knights will wait until they think Billy's dead and return to the castle?'

Nicolas turned his attention to the road ahead. Who knew how long it would take them to find the right tavern? 'We could just take him straight to the city ourselves,' he suggested.

'We could,' Silva agreed. 'But if the enemy know Billy's intended destination, then there will most likely be a well prepared ambush waiting somewhere on the road.'

That's not good. Though it does mean we'd come across Tavish.

'By that logic,' he began thoughtfully, 'even if we do drop Billy off with the knights, they will still walk into the ambush. Even if we pre-warn them, we don't know where, or what it will be?'

And I doubt the Black Knight will take any chances this time round.

'Exactly. That is why it'll be better to go in force, with the knights,' the warrior said. 'Once we find them, we join them. When facing the unknown it is better to have strength in numbers.'

Inwardly, Nicolas sighed. It would make the whole journey take longer. For a long moment, he looked at Billy. He was a decent guy, for a not-assassin. As much as he wanted to get back to hunting Tavish, Nicolas couldn't ignore that the stakes were higher now, and he wouldn't allow Billy to get hurt.

He's just a guy who got chosen against his will to do a dangerous task. I can certainly relate to that.

Nicolas wouldn't let Billy's task spiral the way his had. And he certainly wouldn't let anyone get their hands on the jewel so they could flatten any village they fancied. Or worse.

'Okay, we take him to the city after we find the knights.' Then the obvious flaw in the plan needed to be addressed. 'But like Shift said, what if we don't find them?'

'The Hall of Guardians,' Auron exclaimed with a smile.

Before Nicolas could question him, Silva chimed in. 'The Hall of Guardians is not too far from here,' the warrior began, her eyes refusing to meet anyone else's. 'If we get that far and still cannot find Billy's escort, we can petition Jerric to allow a cadre of heroes to accompany us to Yarrinsburg for extra security.'

'Jerric?' Nicolas asked.

'The Hall Master of the Yarringsburg Hall of Guardians,' Silva explained. She and Auron exchanged a tense look. Silva had been part of the Guild of Heroes before she became a mercenary, and the pair had known each other then. Yet neither of them spoke about what had occurred between them, nor how she came to leave the guild. Whatever it was, it still looked raw, and Silva didn't seem excited at the prospect of returning.

But it does make sense. What better way to protect Billy? And if Tavish does ambush us on the road to the city then the more swords – and axes, spears and maces – the better.

Yes, that fit together nicely. Then something clicked in Nicolas's head. 'Oooh, *Jerric*,' he said with a smile. 'Jerric Doomsword. The Saviour of Kal'ra. The Defeater of the Skinless Horde. It'll be great to meet him.'

His head turned as he caught Auron's expression in his peripheral vision. The spirit was slack-jawed. 'So let me get this straight.' Auron scoffed. 'You meet one of the greatest heroes of our generation, and you have no idea who I am. But mention Jerric, and you get all giggly and excitable, listing off his deeds like some wide-eyed child. Are you kidding me?'

Shift sucked their teeth beside him.
All he could offer in response was a sheepish grin.

CHAPTER 15

E ven as the sun hit its midday peak, there was a hint of chill in the air. Winter would be upon Etherius soon enough. Some of the trees were already beginning to brown, and soon they'd be covering the road with leaves, which crunched under hoof and wheel of those who travelled the Ale Trail.

What I wouldn't give for a hot meal and a bed.

He was exhausted, to his core. All this conflict—especially the number of fights they'd had in a short time— and the increasingly constant struggle against the emotional turmoil making him say and think nonsense was making it harder and harder for him to function.

I won't let it stop me.

Though he was after Tavish because of his family, he couldn't deny the wider picture. Bad things were happening in Etherius, and it was spreading. This Maestro was playing games with people's lives, and things were changing. Yarringsburg used to be such a nice kingdom; now natives were driven from their homes, and assassins and villains – and the occasional giant – roamed freely.

Or maybe it was always like this?

His entire life to this point had been sheltered in the peaceful village of Hablock, so he really had no reference for how the world should be. Maybe this was the norm? But the others seemed to think things were getting worse, and they were much more worldly.

Either way, it's wrong and needs fixing. Find Tavish, find the demon, and hunt down the Maestro. The world would certainly be a better place with all of them gone. Nicolas scoffed to himself. *Listen to me. I go from, 'Oh Deities, I've killed a faun in self-defence,' to making a list of people I want to kill.*

His brow knitted together at the possibility that the Oracle's Choosing Stick had actually picked him on purpose, that maybe this had all been pre-ordained. The Deities had actually chosen him, knowing what he would have to try and endure.

Please.

He couldn't help laughing. As if the Oracle's ridiculous choosing ceremony was anything other than random.

'Something amuses?' Garaz asked beside him.

Nicolas thought before replying. 'At the moment, it's a choice between laughing and crying. Today, it's laughing.'

'What a world we live in where those are our choices.' Garaz shook his head ruefully.

Considering this was the most the orc had said in a while – in fact, this was chatty for Garaz – Nicolas decided to take advantage of it. 'Are you okay?'

Garaz frowned at him. 'What do you mean?'

'Well...' He stumbled over his words under the orc's harsh gaze. 'You just haven't been...yourself...lately.'

'*Myself?*'

Nicolas was going to have to tread carefully. 'Yeah, you know. Normal.'

Garaz stared at him levelly. 'What would you know about what is *normal* for an orc?' The wizard urged his horse forwards.

Apparently, I didn't tread carefully enough.

'We've got another one,' Shift called from near the front of the group.

Up past the curve of the road was a building. Shock, horror, it was a tavern. And one with a pleasing amount of noise coming from it. At least this one's patrons weren't all unconscious in a shed. Hopefully, the staff weren't trained killers either.

Hopefully the knights are there.

'Even if the escort isn't here, we'll stop here for food,' Silva declared. Then the warrior looked back at him. 'If that is okay with you?'

'Yes, it's fine,' he answered when he finally realised the warrior was actually waiting for one.

Strange for her to act so petulantly.

...and also, why is everyone getting so damned sensitive lately?

If he'd just waited a moment, his stomach would have answered for him, as it suddenly growled like a snarling troll.

'One of the good things about being a spirit,' Auron smirked as he pointed at Nicolas's stomach. 'No more hunger pains.'

'All right, it wasn't *that* loud,' he muttered, before returning to his normal tone. 'I suppose that's something to envy you for.' As if awoken by his comment, his stomach growled again, something inside him vibrating uncomfortably as it did.

'I have been the envy of many, kid.' The spirit said solemnly. 'I'm used to it.'

'Can you stop that?'

Auron looked confused. 'What?'

'Calling me *kid*. It's a little condescending.'

Ethereal eyebrows rose slowly in surprise. Finally, Auron spoke. 'So this one time.' Nicolas hadn't realised the comment warranted a story. *Any excuse.* 'There was this new blood in the Heroes Guild called Auron of Tellmark. He'd done a few great deeds, but when he came to the guild, that's what they called him: *new blood*. He had to work hard to earn people's respect, but this young, talented, and handsome fellow was no stranger to hard work. It took a long time, but when he finally did, he shed the name *new blood*—which was a bit like *kid*—did many, many, great deeds, and bedded innumerable women. The end.'

Innumerable women. How had an arrow killed him before the pox? But that was only a sidenote to the real takeaway from the story. 'I think I've done enough to earn your respect by now.'

Auron laughed. 'Stop dropping your sword and then we'll talk.'

Nicolas looked away, mainly because he didn't want Auron to see the flash of annoyance. Everything he'd done, everything he'd been through, and everything he'd lost...and he was still just *kid*.

Now who's being over sensitive?

The group didn't play the naming game as they approached this tavern. They were all too weary. Besides, Shift, who'd initiated the game, was chatting away to Billy. Either way, this one was called the Buried Nugget.

Dammit, if we'd played and I'd guessed gold again, I would've won.

After dismounting, the group secured their horses and entered the tavern. It was bustling...or had been until they opened the door. Now everyone was silent and staring at them. The customers did not seem hospitable.

'What's the problem with this lot?' Shift asked, looking warily back at the crowd.

'I don't know,' Nicolas replied, but he did know that swords might be drawn at the slightest provocation.

Can we please just walk into one *tavern without things getting out of hand?*

Billy looked awkward. 'Um, guys. I think the problem is *him*.'

Their new companion was referring to Garaz. Now that his attention had been brought to it, none of the patrons' eyes were on him, Shift, Silva, or Billy. And definitely not Auron. All were on the orc, who matched the glares and returned them with interest.

'Can we get a table?' Perhaps Billy was asking to break the tension, but Nicolas wasn't sure it was the wisest move.

'You can,' the landlord, a stout man with a long, drooping moustache, shouted from the bar. 'But we don't serve *those* here. Nor any o' the like.'

Nicolas looked at Garaz with wide eyes. He wanted to tell the barman to stick his cloth where the sun didn't shine and storm out...but he'd hesitated too long.

'Bring me my meal outside,' Garaz snarled. 'I will not set another foot in this *establishment.*'

'Garaz—'

The orc rounded on him. 'Maybe there is a trough out there you can put it in so I can eat with the rest of the animals. I highly doubt the barman would want me using his plates.' And with a swirl of his cloak, the orc stormed from the tavern.

Nicolas wanted to run after him, but Garaz didn't seem in the mood for company. The others' glances seemed to agree.

'Okay?' Shift asked the landlord, more than a pinch of sarcasm in their voice.

'Aye,' the landlord replied warily. 'As long as there's no trouble from the rest of you.' Judging by his suspicious glare, he considered it very possible. 'Take a table, and I'll send the girl over to take your order.'

The group exchanged rolling-eyed glances as they took their seats at a well-worn wooden table. Nicolas flicked a Helstrum pamphlet to the floor and scrunched it up subtly with his boot as he sat. Instantly, the patrons relaxed and returned to their conversations, thank the Deities. The place was filled with a wide variety of folk, but there was no sign of Billy's escort.

'What can I get you?' asked the serving maid after pushing through the patrons to reach them. Judging by the flat nose and pudgy cheeks, she was the landlord's daughter.

'Just a round of ales, and a plate of anything that's hot and delicious,' Shift answered with a smile. 'Same for our friend outside.'

'I'm sure I can rustle up something,' the girl replied, with a fearful glance at the door. She smiled at them, but it was guarded. She wasn't about to relax around them anytime soon.

'Do you think he's okay?' Nicolas asked.

'It is unfortunate he is treated like that,' Silva said, looking at the door. 'But orcs do not usually make themselves welcome.'

'We haven't exactly been welcome many places of late.' Shift chuckled, but it was cut off as their shoulders sagged slightly. That half-joke had a little too much truth in it.

Everywhere they turned lately, someone was trying to kill them, or plotting to kill a lot of other people and they were in the way. It was taking a toll on all of them. Except Billy, who was positively chirpy as he looked around the room.

Billy should be more worried than the rest of us. He has assassins, and Tavish, after him. But then he does have us to protect him.

He found himself yearning for the days when all he had to worry about were vampires. Those undead creatures seemed almost a side quest by comparison. In the last two days, they'd fought in a tavern, chased down a villain, taken part in a battle (somewhat) on horseback, been drugged and imprisoned, escaped, and then ambushed on the road.

And not exactly much to show for it.

That wasn't true either. They had Billy. And whilst Billy – and his jewel – was with them, no one was using giants to pound villages to the ground. That was something.

Now to just complete the task.

'At least we know the food isn't poisoned here,' Shift said, glancing around at all the people eating. 'Or has just had a chef's head dipped into it. That makes a nice change.'

'Sometimes the small victories are the best.' Billy chuckled.

Small victories. They had Billy. And it still wasn't clear why Tavish had abducted their new companion. Surely Billy knew something, anything that could help them.

'So Billy,' he began, 'you have no idea why Tavish wanted you? None at all?' He was being heavy handed, but he had nothing but bluntness left in him right now.

At least I'm not shaking him for the information.

Billy shrugged. 'All I really got from him was, *'Move,' 'Get on the horse,' 'Keep moving.'* Didn't seem the charismatic sort, if you know what I mean. They treated me more like cargo than anything else.'

'*Black knight.*' Auron scoffed, shaking his head. 'Only thing about them of note is their armour. So this one time, someone with delusions of being a mighty warlord forged himself some black knight armour. It was huge, covered in spikes and bat wings. Really had all the intimidating trimmings. Of course, he'd been so focused on making it big that he'd not thought about function. When I fought him, he could barely move in the thing. It was a bit of a hollow victory, truth be told.'

I doubt that was reflected in whatever sonnet had been written about it.

That was all well and good, but off topic. 'So they didn't give you a sense of destination at all?'

Billy shook his head apologetically.

'Nothing?'

'Let him be,' Shift said. 'It's been a tough couple of days.'

'I know,' he said with a sigh. 'I was just hoping we'd be at least a bit closer to Tavish by now.'

'He got away,' Billy said in a conciliatory tone. 'It was no one's fault.'

Nicolas found himself shooting a glare at Silva. The warrior noticed it and stiffened. 'Is there a problem?' she asked. For a second, he was sure he heard the word *sir* muttered under her breath.

'Actually—'

'Your drinks, folks. Food will be a few more minutes. But trust me, it's worth the wait.' The serving maid seemed to sense the tension at the table, placing down the whole tray of beverages instead of serving them their drinks individually. She then took her leave politely but quickly.

'Thank you,' Nicolas called after her as she practically fled. Then stared into the foamy liquid in front of him, having no clue what he would have said just then, but knowing it would have been unkind.

For Deities' sake man, pull yourself together.

'I think a nice ale will do us all the world of good right now.' Shift lifted their tankard. As they took it from the tray, there was a slight ripping sound. A piece of paper was stuck to the bottom of the flagon. Peeling it from the beneath the cup Shift went to throw it aside but stopped. Instead they held it up, frowning at something before unfurling the paper. The frown deepened.

That can't be good.

Casually, they put the piece of paper on the table and slid it to Nicolas.

Table left of the door. Trouble.

Raising his own tankard, Nicolas tried to casually glance at the table in question. Around it sat a group of seedy men who were obviously trying not to draw attention to themselves. They talked in muted whispers, and the beer and food in front of them was untouched. A couple of them were armed, and it didn't take a scholar to surmise that the rest would be as well. His free hand rested on the hilt of the *Dawn Blade*.

One of the men facing him looked up and caught his eye. As their gazes met, the man sat up straight then urgently whispered something to his companions, who all turned to look at him. Slowly, he returned his tankard to the table.

Bugger.

The men rose together. Nicolas caught the flash of a knife being drawn before it was hidden behind one man's forearm, the motion so smooth only someone looking directly at him, like Nicolas, would've noticed. The group stalked forward, weaving through the tavern, eyes fixed on their targets.

'They're coming,' he whispered to his companions.

'Of course they are.' Shift tutted. 'Because you decided to start a staring contest with them.'

'Sorry.'

The tavern was crowded. Briefly, he glanced at his sword. He could hardly go swinging it around without the worry of beheading some innocent wagon driver. That made things more complicated.

The group pushed through the last of the patrons and surrounded the table. One of the men opened his mouth to speak.

'Now,' Auron said calmly.

Silva, who'd been sat with her back to the men as if paying no attention to them, rose and turned in a very fluid motion, her fist sailing through the air. The blow caught the lead man in the cheek, sending him reeling and stumbling until he ended up crashing over a nearby table, spilling drinks and food everywhere. The tavern went silent again.

A large, hairy, and very angry-looking man with a soaking wet lap rose like a minotaur rearing to charge. Grabbing the thug by the back of his shirt, the man hauled their attacker's face out of his wife's ample cleavage, where it'd come to rest, and dragged him to his feet, where he lolled drunkenly. Holding him by the shirt still, the man lifted him from the floor to bring them face-to-face.

'Them's be mine,' he rumbled angrily. 'Ye don't go puttin' yer face in them, boy.'

With a hand the size of a dinner plate, the hairy man cracked the thug across the cheek, struck him again with a backhand blow before throwing him across the room as if he were lobbing a pillow. The flying thug crashed into his second table of the day, spilling the food and drink upon it over it's occupants as they scattered in all directions. The leader of the men, who Nicolas guessed were caravan guards, glared at the big hairy man as liquid from his drink ran down his leather armour to drip onto the floor of the deathly quiet room.

'You bastard,' he snapped finally, pointing an enraged finger at the hairy giant.

And from there, the fight spread through the tavern like wildfire. As their would be attackers watched the scene unfold, Shift and Silva used the distraction, wading into the group.

Pushing Billy behind him, Nicolas used his forearm to parry a stab from one of the other thugs then punched him in the face with two fierce hooks. When he staggered back, Nicolas kicked the man into the only table left in the place that hadn't got involved in the fight. Turned out, they didn't need much incentive to join in.

Shame for them to get left out, I suppose.

'You okay?' he asked Billy, ensuring he kept himself between his new companion and anyone else.

Instead of answering, Billy pointed past him. Turning, Nicolas was just in time to catch the fist with his cheek. Forced back by the impact, he landed heavily in his chair and sat there as his skull vibrated and he tried to blink off the sudden dizziness. Still, he somehow managed to duck his head to the side just in time, and the knife stuck in the headrest of his chair. Thrusting himself out of the chair, he landed a flurry of punches on his would be killer. The man initially staggered back under the onslaught but recovered quickly, though he'd lost his knife. Lashing out, he grabbed Nicolas around the neck and forced him backwards towards the door. Thick fingers closed around his throat as he fought to breathe and stay standing. Then a fortuitous tankard hit his attacker on the side of the head, breaking his concentration and giving Nicolas a moment to act. Nicolas drove his fist into the man's stomach, doubling him over, then grabbed his shirt and ran forwards, taking the thug with him. Stopping abruptly, he launched his attacker out through the tavern's window with a sharp smashing sound.

A second later, the door burst open, and Garaz entered, accepting the invitation Nicolas had given him. Several patrons decided to take the opportunity to have at an orc. Something they quickly regretted as Garaz piled into them the way a healer very much ought not to. The orc bounced one attacker's head off the doorframe even as he kicked a second away.

Nicolas ducked as a stool was swung at him, rising with an uppercut that sent his attacker reeling. But at least the man had given him a good idea. Grabbing the stool, he smashed it over the back of a man attacking Shift. The thug lolled drunkenly on the spot for a moment, until Shift headbutted him and he crumpled to the ground.

'Billy,' Shift cried, pointing to the door.

A large thug was dragging Billy towards the door of the tavern, and Garaz was too swarmed with opponents to help. Taking a run up, Nicolas jumped onto a table and launched himself onto the back of the thug, pushing him forwards and into the door frame. The man grunted in pain.

'You okay?' he asked Billy, who nodded in reply. 'Get over there, under the table.'

Billy obliged, crawling under the table and ensuring that as little of him could be seen as possible, save tufts of his overly large hair, which would look almost comical, were he not in the middle of a fight. The man whose back he'd jumped on elbowed him in the stomach. Winded, he couldn't defend himself from the oncoming punch. The crack to the cheek drove him to the floor, where the yellow-toothed man stood over him, grinning, with knife in hand. Before he could use it, Shift grabbed him and rammed his head into the door frame, four times. His eyes rolled into his head as he slid to the floor.

'We're even now,' Shift panted.

Shift was about to help him up when someone seized them around the waist and lifted them into the air. They kicked and thrashed as Nicolas tried to get up, but his lungs still burned and his legs were like jelly. All he could do was watch helplessly as the man released one of the arms restraining Shift to slip another knife from his belt. The man's body suddenly went limp, releasing Shift before he fell to his knees and then crashed to the ground. A hand belonging to someone familiar was held out toward him.

'Rex?'

The young thief smiled as he hauled Nicolas to his feet. Rex was about to speak when he was unceremoniously yanked by his hair back into the swirling melee engulfing the tavern.

A cry got his attention. Some eager fighter was charging him. The man was bulky, and Nicolas doubted his chances of standing his ground. Instead, timing it perfectly, he gripped the man by the collar as he got into arms reach and fell backwards. As he did, he drove his foot into his attackers gut and used it to propel him overhead. There was a satisfying thud on the ground behind him.

Getting to his knee, he turned just as the bearded man did. Nicolas snatched a tray from the floor and swung it furiously, smashing it across the man's face. As he swayed, Nicolas picked up a discarded tankard with his other hand and hit him again. That did the trick.

Stealing a glance at the table hiding Billy, he could no longer see the tell-tale tuft of hair.

No.

Shoving two men aside, he ran to the table, practically sliding to his knees and peering underneath.

Billy waved back at him fearfully.

Thank the Deities.

A cry made him turn. A man was running at him with the jagged edge of a broken bottle, ready to inflict some nasty wounds.

'Finger poke of doom,' Auron said as he drove his incandescent finger into the man's eye. It was one of the things he could do now, besides throwing things and telling incessant stories.

After catching the falling bottle, Nicolas smashed it over the thug's head then kicked between his legs. The thug collapsed to his knees then the ground.

'Nicely done,' Auron said before something caught his attention. 'On your left.'

There was no time to even say *thanks*. A knife flashed towards him. Quickly, he grabbed the attacking arm, pulling it forwards and driving his knee up into the elbow joint. There was a snap and a cry of pain. Before his attacker could get too distraught, Nicolas punched him square in the nose and sent him flying over the nearest table.

The fight was beginning to peter out, mainly because most of the fighters were unconscious. Garaz traded a final blow with the big hairy man who didn't care for people intruding on his wife's cleavage, and he fell back onto a chair then toppled off it to the floor. The fight had been fast and furious, and the tavern was a mess. No piece of furniture was still in place. Food and ale covered the walls and floor. Debris from smashed trays, plates and glasses littered the ground.

As chaos became calm, Nicolas found he still had his fists raised and tried to shake off the rush of the fight. His companions and Rex all seemed well, thank the Deities. In fact, Shift and Rex were hugging each other.

Huh.

'They must be close,' Billy noted as he got up from under the table, brushing himself off.

Nicolas tried to ignore the pang of jealousy. Instead, he turned away, looking at the slack-jawed landlord as he and his daughter surveyed the destruction to his establishment from behind the safety of the bar.

'Can I just say—'

'*Get out!*' the barman roared. '*Get out and never come back!*'

And there went his chance of a hot meal.

CHAPTER 16

The landlord's curses dogged their steps as they quickly vacated the wrecked tavern. Well, as quickly as they were able when they had to step over groaning bodies in various awkward positions. Tentatively, and with one last sheepish smile at the proprietor, Nicolas pulled the door, which Garaz had kicked open, shut. Just as the handle clicked into place, the latches gave, and the door crashed to the ground, the loud noise and ensuing awkwardness making Nicolas wince.

'Don't come back,' the landlord screamed, futilely balling up his rag and throwing it in Nicolas's direction.

He wanted to apologise profusely. They hadn't had a choice about fighting, but they had thrown the first punch, so technically, had started it. But he doubted his explanation would be gratefully received. What was more important now was getting some distance between themselves and the tavern before the occupants woke up and decided they fancied round two.

'Three taverns,' Shift said in disbelief. 'Three taverns and three fights. What are the odds?'

'None I'd care to bet on,' Auron said, shaking his head.

'Are we all okay?' Nicolas asked, searching the others for cuts or broken bones. He flexed his jaw, which was tender but nothing that required Garaz's ministrations. All his companion's had were a few superficial bruises. Thank the Deities they were all okay. It could've been so much worse.

'Looks like,' Shift answered. 'That escalated quickly.'

'Tavern fights often do,' Silva remarked with a nonchalant shrug.

'Billy, are you well?' Nicolas asked, needing confirmation of what his eyes were telling him, that his companion was unharmed.

'I think so,' their new companion said. 'A little shaken, but no harm done.'

Thank the Deities for that too.

'Are you lot still here?' the landlord roared from the doorway, scrunching up his rag and throwing it in their direction again. 'I told you to *get*.'

Before the dirty towel could be launched at them a third time, the group mounted and took to the road. Thankfully, Rex's horse was close to theirs, and the young thief joined them.

'Thanks for the note,' Shift said as the group of horses moved away. 'If we weren't pre-warned, that could've gone very badly.'

'That was intense,' Rex said with a long sigh. 'But you're welcome.'

The last time they'd met, Nicolas had gathered that Rex was a companion of Shift's from the Thieves Guild. They'd worked together a few times, but he wasn't exactly sure of the nature of their relationship. What he did know was that Rex had been there to help the group whilst he was dead, and they were ambushed by...

What was it? Jace? Mance? Mace?

Either way, Rex had helped his companions, and he was thankful for that.

Shift, who rode beside Rex, leant across their saddle and gave the young thief another hug.

Oh.

'Lucky you were there and noticed those guys,' he said once the hug broke. His voice sounded funny, but he had no idea why.

'It wasn't luck.' Rex smiled. 'Those guys in the tavern were from the guild. They'd been sent after your friend there.' A jerk of his thumb indicated Billy. 'Their orders were to grab him and kill anyone who was with him. I was quite happy to stay out of it, but then he comes in with you lot and...' The thief shrugged.

'You couldn't help but come to my rescue.' Shift fluttered their eyelashes like a hero-struck maiden. 'Gosh, I am honoured, good sir.' They fanned themselves with their hand, smirking.

If I did that, all I'd hear would be, 'I don't need saving, I can save myself.'

'Great,' Billy said with a sigh. 'More people after me.'

'Silva,' Auron said from his ethereal mount. 'Ask the guy who looks like a piece of broccoli why the Thieves Guild are after him.'

Broccoli?

Now that Auron had said it, Nicolas saw it—the big bushy hair, the skinny frame. All he needed was to be green and the picture would be complete. He struggled not to snigger. Shift was giggling behind their hand. Garaz was smirking, and Silva's face was neutral, but its redness hinted that she might be suppressing laughter too.

'Wh-why are the Thieves Guild after you?' Yup, definitely holding in a laugh.

'When I spoke to the guys in the tavern,' Rex answered instead, 'they said the Council had sent them personally. Apparently, they reckon Billy knows a few things about the guild and wanted to get to him before anyone else did.'

'Sounds familiar,' Silva growled, the trace of mirth vanishing completely.

In fact, it sounds exactly like the reason Alexi and Emelina are after him.

'Why do the Thieves Council think you have information about them?' Garaz asked, his mirth vanished, to be replaced by sullenness.

Billy shrugged. 'Probably the same reason as the assassins. I'm a member of the guild.'

Shift and Rex swivelled in their saddles so quickly it was a wonder they didn't fall off. '*You* are in the guild?' they both scoffed as one.

Billy smiled and nodded.

'No way.' Shift laughed. 'You're no thief. Or if you are, well done for pulling the wool over my eyes.'

'Okay, so I don't actually *steal* things, but I am a member,' Billy confirmed.

'That doesn't make any sense.' Shift snorted in disbelief. 'How are you a member?'

Billy shrugged. 'Same as with the assassins. I met a guy, we got chatting, I gave him some advice, and we hit it off. He practically dragged me back to the guild and asked me to join. When someone invites me to join something, I just can't say no. It's almost an addiction.'

That, and attracting trouble.

'Preposterous,' Garaz snarled under his breath, just loud enough for Nicolas to catch.

Their new companion looked sheepish. 'If I'd thought it'd get me in this much trouble, I would've politely declined. All of them.'

'It's worse than that,' Rex said. 'About a half hour before you showed up, some big, bearded guy walked into the Buried Nugget asking about you. I mean, he was huge, and certainly not the kind of guy I'd like to mess with.'

Oh good. Another one to add to the list.

'Anything else you can tell us about him?'

Good old Silva, always wanting to be prepared.

Rex thought for a moment. 'He carried a big battle axe. Um...he had lots of scars. He bumped into one of the other patrons on the way out and called him a whore-something or other.'

'*Whoreson?*' Silva asked.

'Yeah.' Rex clicked his fingers. 'That was it. He called the guy a whoreson. The other guy didn't look happy about it, but he wasn't about to challenge that giant.'

Auron and Silva looked at each other pointedly.

'You know him?' Shift asked, clearly noticing the same cue.

'Gornak.' Silva said the name with distaste.

'You're going to hear the word *whoreson* a lot,' Auron added with a slight smile.

'Who's Gornak?' Nicolas asked, though he could vaguely recall Auron mentioning that name before.

'Gornak is a member of the Guild of Heroes,' Silva said. 'And quite the formidable warrior.'

Brilliant.

'And he's looking for you, Billy, because...?' Nicolas could pretty much guess the answer.

'I'm a member.'

'*What?*' It was strange seeing Auron, usually so calm and collected, aghast. 'He's a member of the guild?' The spirit shook his head. 'Nope. No. That can't be right.'

'How is that even possible?' Garaz snapped. 'You display no heroic qualities or skills.'

Ouch.

'I-I...' After a couple of attempts, Billy found his voice. 'I met this travelling hero once. Sir Everheart the Chaste...'

'That guy was a barrel of laughs at an orgy.' Auron scoffed.

'He was liberating some artefacts from a powerful wizard but needed help transporting them. I helped him, and they made me an honorary member of the guild,' Billy said. 'I mean, I'm downplaying it. It was a pretty dangerous trip.'

Auron shook his head. 'Sounds like Everheart. Never one to get the job done solo. This one time—'

'So you're an assassin, a thief, and a hero?' Nicolas asked, cutting Auron off.

'Don't forget an enjoyer of magical antiquities,' Shift added.

'And yet I'm none of those, really.' Billy laughed. 'I'm just a guy who makes friends easily. Like with you guys.'

'Ridiculous,' Garaz snarled, suggesting they weren't *all* friends with Billy.

'Will Gornak be a problem?' Nicolas asked.

'He is a mighty warrior,' Auron replied. 'A bit slow on the uptake, and not one for asking questions, but once you point him towards something, he doesn't stop until it dies.' The spirit laughed, possibly at a funny memory of his comrade.

'I don't see how that is funny,' Nicolas said. 'We now have *another* person after us, and he's a giant with a battle axe.'

'I can handle Gornak,' Silva replied, though she didn't sound entirely certain.

'One does not *handle* Gornak,' Auron said haughtily. 'You usually just die by his axe. And you're the last person who should be near him. If we cross his path, I'll do the talking.'

'Does this not change our plans?' Garaz asked, eyeing Billy angrily. 'Now we have yet another guild hunting Billy, delivering him to them might not be the best course of action.'

'Don't worry about it,' Auron said with a confidence Nicolas really wanted to feel himself. 'I can talk Jerric round through the kid. Once that's done, he'll call Gornak off. If we haven't already talked some sense—or at least what passes for sense with Gornak—into him too.' The spirit thought for a moment and smiled. 'Actually, he will be the ideal person to have with us to take Billy to the city. Gornak is a beast in a fight.'

'You assume he will stop and allow us to explain,' Silva said, pursing her lips. 'Those we have come across seem desperate to get to Billy. I doubt the Guild of Heroes will be any different.'

'Hey,' Auron snapped. 'It's different. You, of all people, ought to know that.'

'There are certainly a lot of people keen to get him,' Shift added.

Tavish should be first on the list, yet we still haven't seen a trace of him.

Nicolas looked back down the road longingly. He *had* to be coming soon.

Chapter 17

The next leg of their journey could be summed up by a single word: tension. Who was going to come at them next? Would they have to wait for the next tavern to get attacked? Why was everyone *but* Tavish coming for them?

This damned road is making us all act crazy.

At first, he'd thought it was just him. But everyone had begun acting off. Garaz's quietness was becoming a general ill temper. Silva had a wall around her with the words *leave me alone* painted upon it in huge letters. And Shift seemed to have forgotten they had any companions other than Rex. Nor did it help that a headache was starting to constantly buzz in Nicolas's head, most likely brought on by the combination of all this turmoil, that was piling on like a gnome piled furniture on his cart.

At least Billy is okay. That is the point of all this, after all.

Though it wasn't for a lack of trying on behalf of everyone who crossed their path. Which begged a question.

'Guilds,' he began quietly to Auron, not wanting the others privy to his continuing naivety about the world. 'I don't understand.'

'Neither do I sometimes,' the spirit said with a chuckle. 'It's one of those things that always starts out well enough. A group of people with a common interest or cause get together and say, *'Let's form a guild for people like us.'* They gather others then they decide they need some rules to keep things running smoothly, which means leaders.' Auron sighed. 'Then they just keep getting bigger. They start creating their own traditions and codes. More like tribal customs, really. Soon the need to protect themselves starts to seep in, lest other people learn their precious secrets. It quickly becomes us and them. If you ask me, it all got out of hand a long time ago. There are guilds for everything nowadays.'

'None of that sounds fun,' Nicolas remarked, scrunching his nose. 'I would've thought people who got together due to a mutual interest would do it to have...fun.'

'Most of them forgot to do that a long time ago, kid,' Auron scoffed. 'All they see around them is other guilds, peering curiously in their direction. And when you're surrounded, you get paranoid, close ranks.'

Suddenly, something made sense. 'That's why Tavish wants Billy then. If he's a member of a few key guilds, he may know some interesting stuff.'

'That was my theory,' the spirit agreed. 'And guilds keep their secrets more fiercely than a dragon protects its gold. This situation could escalate and turn really bad.'

'Worse than it already is?'

Auron pursed his lips thoughtfully. 'Guilds are so deeply woven into our society now, that any turmoil in them would ripple outwards. It could cause chaos.'

'And the Maestro likes a bit of chaos.'

'Exactly.'

Somehow, what was in Billy's head now seemed of more importance than a crystal that could control giants. Was information really a greater weapon than a giant?

It won't matter when we get Billy to safety. Then...

A hearty laugh from ahead broke his concentration, the kind that was becoming quite commonplace between Shift and Rex since the young thief had joined them.

'Kid, calm down.'

Nicolas looked at Auron in confusion.

The spirit nodded towards Rex. 'You looked like you were about to ride over and kick him off his saddle.'

What?

'I did?'

Auron nodded slowly. 'You certainly did. In fact, you're all getting like that. We can't protect Billy properly if we aren't acting like a team.'

Thank the Deities I'm not the only one noticing it.

'I never thought you were one for teamwork,' he replied jokingly, hoping to deflect from the spirit's worrying point.

'With *this* many people after Billy, we need all the help we can get.'

'Up ahead.'

Silva's warning call shooed away Nicolas's calculations as to how many other enemies they would face, and who they would be. Of course, his imaginings would err on the side of the overly dramatic, just as they always did.

In the road ahead was a young woman. Hands clasped together, she was trying to get the attention of any passing wagon or rider, all of whom were doing a fantastic job of pretending she didn't exist.

So much for human kindness.

Not that he'd seen much of that on this journey so far. In fact, it was getting to the point where he found himself missing facing cow-dragons and minotaurs.

'Are you okay?' he asked as the group came to a halt.

'Oh, bless you, kind sir, bless you.' The poor woman looked frantic. Her face was pale and her eyes filled with worry. 'Are you a group of travelling heroes or something?'

'Close enough.'

'Please, sir, our village needs help. Can you help us please?'

There's a request I can never say no to.

'Of course we can,' he said with a reassuring smile. 'What's the problem?'

The woman opened her mouth, then looked behind her. When her gaze returned to Nicolas, she appeared gripped by uncertainty. 'It's probably better if I show you.'

Before he could press the matter further, she darted down a side track and into the forest.

'I guess we'll just follow you then,' he muttered in confusion.

****

Nicolas sighed and let his head hang forward. 'For the fourth time, I don't think this is a trap.'

'I never asked if you thought it was,' Silva replied cooly. 'I simply said that if it *is*, I will make sure she dies first.'

'She's a frightened villager,' he cried. 'No one can act *that* well. Garaz, help me out here.'

The orc appeared both uncertain and unhappy that he'd been put on the spot. 'She does appear in genuine distress,' he began. 'However, you do have a kind heart, which could easily be taken advantage of. I am happy to help her, and I am equally happy that Silva avenge us should this be a trap.'

Nicolas exchanged an eyeroll with Silva. At least they could agree that Garaz's fence-sitting was irksome.

In truth, it could be a trap. The woman had been frustratingly vague about why she needed help, answering all their questions with, *'Please come. I'll show you. This way.'*

She'd led them off the main road to a track she said led to her village.

'Hey, Nick,' Shift called from the back of the group. 'Your new love interest best not be leading us into a trap.' The shapeshifter grinned at Rex, who appeared amused by his companion's antics.

My new love interest? That's rich.

'We're just discussing that,' he replied dryly. 'Don't worry. If she is, Silva will kill her.'

He quickly turned his eyes to the front, realising that the woman may've heard that. If she had, she gave no sign. He sighed in relief.

Suddenly, she came to a stop and turned. 'I'm sorry I didn't really say what we needed help with,' she said nervously. 'I just didn't think anyone would believe me.'

Gesturing ahead, Nicolas spurred Vigour on, and he entered the clearing in which the village lay.

What in the Underworld?

Ahead of him was a small collection of homes made of wood with straw roofs, all very usual for a village. What was unusual was the giant curled up around several of the homes, sound asleep. It was big. Bloody big.

They're called giants for a reason.

Beside him, Billy was gawping at the monster, eyes wide with surprise.

'Is that the same one you saw?' Garaz asked.

'Ummm...' It appeared their new companion was dumbstruck. Nicolas probably would've been, too, had he seen the destruction the thing was capable of unleashing. 'Yes.'

The giant was...it was hard to describe it without using words like *huge*, which seemed a little redundant. Its general appearance was humanish, but maybe a less evolved-looking human. Its bald head was resting on the thatched roof of a house, the structure visibly buckling under the weight. The monster's clothing was restricted to a single loin cloth big enough to cover a barn.

Thank the Deities it's covering something.

A large club, which was just a tree minus the branches, rested at its side.

Keeping one eye on the giant, as if it might somehow wake and run at him if he took his gaze from it for even a second, Nicolas turned to Auron. 'Advice?'

'This is definitely one of the bigger ones,' the spirit remarked, scrutinising the giant. 'But despite the popular myths—and a few of my own tales—giants are usually relatively peaceful. They don't attack unless provoked. But when they do, they pretty much embody the phrase *cross me and die.*' Auron frowned for a moment. 'Unless you're me, of course. I am the slayer, as opposed to the slayed, in those situations.'

'Well, I'm not you, so what do *I* do?'

'Nick.' Shift put a hand on his shoulder, causing a slight thrill to flash through him even in the midst of his concern about the giant. 'As usual, you miss the obvious. We have a jewel that controls giants, remember?'

All eyes turned to Billy.

'We do,' their new companion began slowly, face paling. 'But I don't know how to use it.'

'You said the faun who used it spoke some magic words,' Garaz said. 'What were they?'

'I said he said some words.' Billy shrugged. 'I couldn't hear any of them over the approaching giant. I couldn't tell you if that was because of the noise of its footsteps, or because I was too busy trying not to crap my breeches in terror.' He sighed heavily. 'I'm not really comfortable waving that thing around. Especially if I don't know what I'm doing.'

'I could approach and stab it in the throat,' Silva suggested.

'No,' Nicolas said quickly. 'If it was being controlled by the jewel when it smashed that village, then it didn't mean to do any harm. And it hasn't attacked this one. It's just having a nap.' Regarding the creature, he tried to imagine actually fighting it. 'Besides, if you don't finish it off quickly, and it wakes, we'll have a lot of trouble on our hands. And there are people around.'

The people of the village on which the giant had chosen to sleep were—understandably—giving it a wide berth. They huddled at the edge of the tree line, watching the sleeping monster with fear.

'Please, sir,' the woman who'd brought them here begged. 'Please help us.'

Nicolas looked at Billy who shook his head slowly, eyes wide. He held his hand out. 'Okay, give me the jewel, please.'

There was a moment of reluctance then Billy raised his foot. Halfway up, he realised it was the wrong one and grabbed the other boot, opening the secret compartment in the heel and passing the yellow gem to Nicolas. Holding it in his hand, he steeled himself and approached the giant.

Hopefully there are no magic words, and the faun had just been raving. I suppose I'll just wave it a little bit and see what happens.

'Be careful,' Shift called after him.

Like I'd be anything but careful. It's a Deities-damned giant.

As he got closer, the monster let out a long breath that blew his hair back and made his eyes water. Slowly, Nicolas raised the jewel. His hand was shaking slightly, as he was well aware that the previous user of this magical item had managed to get himself killed when the giant he was stood directly in front of squashed him.

I don't want to end up like that faun. And if I don't start adjusting my thinking soon, I'll end up like another faun I met. A nasty little piece of work with no friends.

Making no sudden movements, he waved the jewel in the air. For a long moment, there was nothing. Then the sun caught the yellow gem, and it reflected a speck of light onto the eyelid of the giant, which danced as Nicolas waved it.

First, the monster frowned then a bleary eye opened and regarded the little man stood before him.

'Afternoon,' he said nervously, gesturing away from the village with the jewel. 'If you could get up and go that way, please. There's a good fellow.'

Though it gave no sign it understood him, the giant rose, stretching its long arms and letting out a yawn that sounded like a battle horn. Nicolas took an involuntary step back as it stood to its full, imposing height. But he kept waving the jewel in the direction he wanted the giant to go. The faster it did, the better.

Still paying no attention to Nicolas, the giant scratched its chin, then its ass, and then simply left. The ground shook slightly with its footsteps as it lumbered away. Once he was sure it was set on its direction, Nicolas finally let the jewel drop, his arm suddenly limp as he let out a sigh of relief.

That was a lot easier than I thought it'd be.

Chapter 18

Having come close to being crushed by a giant, there was elation in the village as the sun set on another day in Etherius. This thankfulness to be alive took the form of a party, the villagers lighting a bonfire and breaking out food and drink, whilst a fiddler played jaunty tunes. It'd be business as usual tomorrow, but tonight was time to celebrate.

And the group themselves had a lot to celebrate. They'd been attacked four times, and survived, and they'd saved a village. Nicolas was also personally happy that they'd spared the giant and the assassin twins. Their deaths were unnecessary. There was plenty of that in the world already, without him adding to it.

He'd been slightly concerned the giant would just go and menace another village, but Auron reassured him that giants weren't natural in this area—in the kingdom of Yarringsburg at all, actually—and that without the jewel, it would just return home.

And as for the assassins...their deaths just didn't feel necessary. Nicolas would kill now, but not gratuitously. He just hoped they'd learnt their lesson and didn't try again.

Too many people are dying lately.

The worry that his parents may be amongst them still nagged at him. But he had to use hope to armour himself against that, lest despair take him.

A small stone hit him on the arm. 'You need to lighten up,' Shift declared, pointing an accusing finger at him. 'You faced a giant today.'

'*Herded* a giant would be more accurate.' Garaz chuckled.

'*That's* your heroic middle name,' Auron cried, clicking his fingers. 'Nick *Giant Herder* Carnage.' Now it was his turn to throw the stone, which passed through the spirit's chest. 'Nice shot, kid.' Auron grinned.

'I think you deserving it for coming up with that terrible name somehow improved my aim,' Nicolas grumbled.

'No, no, no,' Shift said, suddenly jumping up. 'I can hear the stories now.' They looked around the area dramatically. 'Did you hear the tale of the great, scruffy-looking Giant Herder? If you have a giant problem, he shalt appear and wave a little yellow stone in the air. And lo, your giant shall bugger off.'

'Substitute *scruffy-looking* for *muscular and dashing,* and I'll allow it,' he replied with a nod.

'You have a lot more training to do before you achieve either of those.'

Shift stared at Silva, from whom the comment had come, in wide-eyed admiration, before turning to Nicolas with a big grin. 'That must've stung.'

He shrugged. 'I'm getting used to the abuse I have to suffer from you lot on the road.'

'You'll need to with Shift. I think it's the only thing they're better at than stealing.' The comment earned Rex a playful punch on the arm from Shift, Nicolas averting his eyes from something that could be interpreted as *flirty.*

If they're going to do that right in front of me then—

Deities.

It's a punch. Calm down.

'If you take it as another form of training, your self-esteem will be harder to break than a fortress wall.' Garaz chuckled. 'No one will ever be able to insult you again.'

'See,' Shift declared, pointing a finger at the orc. 'I'm doing you a favour really.'

'Thank you so much,' Nicolas said with thick sarcasm. 'How lucky I am to have you around.'

'Don't you...' Shift trailed off and coughed slightly.

'My takeaway from today is that if you can herd a giant, you can fight the demon.' It was classic Silva to think of practicalities, but he appreciated her not saying the demon's name. All his companions had been good about that. Whilst they didn't necessarily understand *why* he couldn't say it, they respected it.

Though I don't think fighting a demon and entrancing a giant with a magic stone made specifically for that purpose are equal.

'We can worry about the demon after we get Billy to safety,' Nicolas said thoughtfully. 'All we've got to do is make it to the Hall of Guardians then things should be much smoother.'

Especially as we've made a couple more enemies today. I just hope if we cross Gornak's path, we can convince him to play nice.

'We will most likely find his escort before then,' Garaz said. 'We can travel with them. Assuming they have no problem with me.' A dark look crossed the orc's face, but with a furrowing of his brow, it vanished just as quickly.

'Assuming they aren't camped on the other end of the Ale Trail,' Auron said with an eyeroll. 'Which I'm starting to strongly suspect is the case.'

'Yeah, Shift mentioned the knights,' Rex began nervously. 'Are we sure they can be trusted?'

Rex was referring to a man called Sir Gerran. The knight had been part of a troop dispatched to investigate the reported raiding of Hablock. Whilst the majority of the knights in the troop were true, Sir Gerran had been seeded amongst them to ensure that Shift, Silva, and Garaz died in the aftermath. Apparently, the blame for the attack would've been laid on his companions and it would all have looked very neat. Unfortunately, all the knights, save Sir Gerran, had been killed by a necromancer's shade thralls. The knight himself had been cooked to death in lava, thanks to Shift.

'Even when we reach them, we'll stay with Billy until he's safe in the city, and we'll remain vigilant the whole time.' Auron gave Nicolas the nod to repeat his words for those who couldn't hear, so he did.

'A group of heroes may be more trustworthy,' Shift suggested. 'Assuming we can stop them from attacking us long enough to get them to help.'

'That will be fine,' Auron said dismissively.

'I am sure it will be.' Nicolas was sure he'd known Silva long enough by now to pick up the faint hint of old regret in her voice.

'Must be difficult, going back to the guild after...' Not knowing how best to finish that sentence, Nicolas let his voice trail away.

The warrior frowned, her mouth a thin, angry line. *'After the things I've done?'* she finished for him. 'Am I to be constantly reminded of my wrongdoing?'

'Not at all,' he replied hastily. 'I was just worried about you.'

Silva closed her eyes and shook her head. When they opened again, the anger had passed. 'I appreciate the thought.'

This trail is winding us all up a little too tightly.

'I think we all need to lighten up a bit.' Nicolas smiled. 'Which should be pretty easy when there's a party around us.'

'I would quite happily help these people celebrate their village not getting crushed under a giant's foot,' Shift mused as they watched the dancing villagers, before rising.

As his companion approached him, elation gripped Nicolas. He prepared himself to get straight to his feet when the question was asked.

I'm not missing out again.

Shift opened their mouth before an aura of awkwardness fell around them. Finally, they turned to Rex. 'Care to dance?' they asked, extending their hand.

'Love to.' The young thief grinned, taking Shift's hand and being hauled to his feet before the pair disappeared into the crowd.

'For Deities' sake,' Auron muttered with a sigh.

Nicolas yelped as he was grabbed by the elbow and unceremoniously pulled up from the floor.

'I think dancing would be nice, considering we have fought so many battles of late,' Silva announced as she dragged him toward the dance square the villagers had made.

Nicolas had little experience of dancing, but he was sure what happened next was not it. Silva made fierce, jerky motions, pulling him in her wake. Most of the time he could barely keep up with her and ended up stumbling around, or being thrown around. It was only slightly less painful than their sparring sessions.

In between the blur of the people around him, he caught sight of Garaz. The orc doing a poor job of holding back a smirk, which he guessed was brought on by his current plight on the dancefloor. Beside him sat Billy, brow furrowed thoughtfully.

I'd be worried too, the number of people after him. Maybe I could convince him to cut in with me and Silvaaaaaaaaaaaa?

The world spun as he was swung violently around in time with a rise in the tempo of the music. In between that he caught a glimpse of Rex and Shift dancing together. The young thief was talking, but the shapeshifter was staring at Silva with indignation.

What's that abooooooooooooout?

CHAPTER 19

'**K**id? Kid? *Kid?*' The voice started sweet but quickly became insistent. 'Wake up.'

In truth, he could've kissed Auron for waking him—though any attempt would've proved pointless for both of them—as the spirit had dragged him from a truly terrible dream.

Yet I can't remember what it was.

He was slightly surprised to hear stirring around him. All of the others seemed to be having an equally difficult nights slumber.

At least I tried to rest, I suppose.

'Are you getting up or what?' the spirit asked testily. 'You asked me and Silva to train you. The minimum commitment we expect is for you to be awake during said training.'

'I'm up,' he whispered, careful not to disturb the others slumber more than it already was.

'If you don't want to train, I can just possess you during the next fight.' The comment was clearly intended as a threat.

'I'm up. I'm ready to train.'

Auron gazed down at him. 'You're *ready to train*, yet you're still lying down.'

'I wasn't staying there,' he muttered as he rose.

It was still night, but a faint light on the horizon promised the dawn to come. He really wanted to remember the dream. He knew it'd upset him, but not knowing why was oddly frustrating.

'Are your eyes watering?' Auron asked.

Blinking, he was surprised to find tears in his eyes.

'Yours would be too if someone woke you up by doing the equivalent of holding a lantern directly above your head,' he countered quickly.

The spirit nodded sagely. 'I get that. You want to talk about eye-watering, though. I'll tell you about the Witch of Granthom Canyon. She was ugly as f—'

The story was interrupted by a stick being thrown through Auron. 'Some of us are trying to sleep,' Garaz grumbled before turning his back to them.

'Normally, he could sleep through a dragon attack,' Auron said with a wink.

Nicolas stretched the lingering tiredness from his limbs before taking a swig from his canteen. The water was as cool as the early morning air. He was awake, thank the Deities. Without a word, Auron led him towards the woods.

At the border of their camp, Shift was standing watch by a tree. Nicolas had taken the first watch. He'd hoped for one in the middle, so he wouldn't have the opportunity to fall into a deep enough sleep to dream, but like so many things lately, he hadn't gotten his wish.

'Managing to stay awake.' He smiled.

'Just about.' Shift smiled back. The bleary look in their eyes confirmed their statement.

'Still, you being the first person I see in the morning is quite nice.'

'The first person you saw was Auron,' Shift replied quietly.

Well, that got awkward quickly.

'Does he count? He isn't technically alive, so you were still first.'

Why am I persisting with this?

'He counts,' was Shift's flat response.

Embarrassment gripped him roughly before changing to annoyance. Of course he would try to flirt with someone who'd kissed him. How could Shift expect anything else? How could they be so cold? He rubbed his temples, anger rising, and turned away.

Calm down.

Seeing Billy with his eyes open, having witnessed the whole thing, did nothing to help him remain calm.

Auron gave an impatient cough, reminding him why he was up at this hour. 'Ready?'

He nodded. His mouth had gotten him in enough trouble for one morning, so he'd only use words when really necessary.

'Okay then.' The spirit smiled and led him into the forest a little way from the camp, before suddenly speeding up. 'Go!'

It took Nicolas a second to process what'd happened as Auron darted into the forest—and then he was in pursuit. The sun was just rising, so although long shadows covered the ground, there was enough light to run by.

Nicolas dashed through leaves and hopped over logs as he pursued the spirit. It was getting easier. Not so long ago, he would've been falling against the first tree to catch his breath, so something was working. Not that his lungs weren't still burning, and there was an echo of a stitch in his side…but only a few days ago, that would've turned him into a stumbling mess.

Huh. I might actually be getting fitter you know.

Leaves rustled as sweat-soaked hands pushed them aside. He took comfort in the sweat and the pain—they were pretty convincing evidence that he was, indeed, alive. Although being dead had its advantages, as Auron literally breezed through every obstacle.

'Are you back there, or did you stop for a breather?' the spirit taunted.

'I'm here,' he replied between pants.

Finally, the tree line broke, and he saw the spirit waiting at the edge of a bridge. He slowed to a jog and forced his protesting muscles the last few feet, determined not to lose face by stopping when he'd come this far. He did, however, double over against the bridge as soon as he'd finished. He was half-tempted to throw himself into the water to cool down.

'Nicely done, kid,' Auron said with an impressed nod. 'Faster *and* less complaining. Plus, you aren't falling to the floor when you stop anymore.'

'You can compliment me without reminding me of my mistakes, you know?'

The spirit grinned. 'Yeah, I know.'

When he finally hauled himself upright, he eyed the bridge nervously. It was an old-looking thing made of tied-together logs with rope handholds on the sides. It didn't strike him as sturdy, and he was wary of bridges anyway. Being attacked on a bridge by a hammer-wielding maniac was where this had all really begun.

When his lungs finally settled into a normal rhythm, energy coursed through his body.

I think I could actually do that again.

Not that he was about to test that theory out.

A rustling from behind him brought his attention back to the forest. His second training partner was early for the rest of his session.

I hope Silva goes easy on me this morning. I don't think I've fully recovered from that dance.

The giant man with the equally large battle axe who emerged from the trees most definitely wasn't Silva.

'Hello, little man,' the bearded giant greeted with a smile. Actually, giant might've been an understatement. His chest was so broad Nicolas could've probably curled up and slept on it, though all that hair would've made him itch. In fact, he was covered in hair, which Nicolas knew because all he wore was a cloak, some furred pants, and straps criss-crossed over his chest—most likely a harness for his axe.

How is he not frozen right now?

'Gornak,' Auron said with a broad grin.

'Sorry to interrupt your morning,' the man rumbled amiably. 'I wonder if you have seen a around these parts? He is lean with great, bushy hair.'

'I'm not letting you take Billy.'

Why, Nicolas? Why? You could've said you don't know him, but ooooh no...

'Ah,' the big man replied with a nod. 'I see. You are one of whoresons who escort and protect him. Gornak understands.'

I'm a what now? 'Well, I wouldn't say—'

'Kid, be careful,' Auron warned. 'Let me do the talking, through you. Repeat after me...'

'Gornak—' Nicolas began, following the spirit's directions.

'Ahhh, you have heard of me,' the mighty warrior interrupted, not picking up on the fact that he'd just said his own name. 'This is good. That means you will not waste time drawing puny sword and tell me what I need to know.'

'Hey,' Auron shouted. 'Don't disrespect my sword.'

Gornak may have taken pause then, if he could've actually heard him.

'Now, Gornak—' Nicolas persisted.

'Yes, yes.' The giant warrior dismissed him with a wave of his hand. 'You begin to beg for mercy. All whoresons do.'

Okay, that's twice he's called me that.

'Please listen—'

'Are you going to tell me location of skinny, big-haired man?'

As much as Nicolas didn't like the idea of earning Gornak's ire, he had to answer, 'Well, no.'

'Then I don't listen to words of whoreson.'

Three times.

'Kid, you need to tell him to just—'

Nicolas raised his hands in a conciliatory gesture. 'If we could just—'

'The only *just* for a whoreson is *just* dying at the hands of mighty Gornak.'

Okay then, big man.

He drew his sword from the sheath, holding it before him in hands trembling with rage. 'Let's get one thing straight,' he snarled. 'My mother is no *whore*.'

Taking no notice, Gornak instead stared at the sword for a long moment, evidently dumbfounded. 'Gornak knows this sword. That is the *Dawn Blade*,' he rumbled in awe. 'Where did you get this?'

'Oh crap,' Auron said at his side. 'Kid, listen—'

'I...well...I...' He tried to find the easiest way to explain it, but his brain and mouth completely failed him.

'No, no,' Gornak said, reaching behind him. 'Gornak understands. You are grave-robbing whoreson. This makes me very angry. It makes Sasha very, very angry.'

Oh crap.

The warrior produced a giant, double-bladed battle axe at that proclamation, which could only mean he'd named the weapon Sasha. Somehow the fact that he'd named it after a lady made it all the more menacing, but he had no idea why.

'You will die in dishonour like you lived, you grave-robbing whoreson,' Gornak said matter-of-factly. 'Please try and put up fight. Gornak does not care for easy kills.'

That's five.

With a cry, somehow Nicolas found himself charging Gornak. The big man stood still as he fell on him. 'My mother is no *whore!*'

'Kid, wait—'

He swung his sword.

Clang.

The vibrations travelled up his arms to his shoulders as he fought not to drop the blade. How could the giant swing his axe so fast?

'There you go,' Gornak said. 'I let you take one swing, so you do not feel death is pointless. Goodbye, grave-robbing whoreson. I will kill you now.'

The warrior came at him with a speed that defied logic for someone his size. Nicolas ducked and dived as the axe swung at him, though he was barely able to pre-empt Gornak's attacks. This had gone badly really quickly.

'Kid, just tell him—' Every time Auron tried to speak, it was drowned out by Gornak's grunts.

'Ah,' Gornak said in a voice that was annoyingly not out of breath. 'You dodge well, little grave-robbing whoreson, but you just prolong the inevitable.'

What's that? About seven times now? Eight?

'Rrrrrraaaaaagggggghhhhh.' The world around Nicolas went red as he attacked, his limbs moving as if he were a puppet—or possessed by Auron again—unleashing a frantic flurry of blows on his opponent.

The big warrior was smiling as he batted them away. 'Yes, yes. Fight, little whoreson. This makes battle all the more glorious for Gornak.'

Nicolas redoubled his efforts. His form and stance went to the Underworld as he blindly threw strikes at the larger warrior.

'You have fire, whoreson.' Gornak nodded, seeming impressed. 'It is cute. Pointless, but cute.'

'Kid, your form,' Auron called. 'Remember your form. Or you could try listening to me and *bloody well talk to him.*'

He remembered nothing, knew nothing. Only anger. Which he poured into his blade.

He was brought back to reality sharply when Gornak stepped back from a sideways cut then stepped forward again and planted a boot the size of a tree stump directly into Nicolas's chest. His heart skipped several beats and his eyes bulged as he was sent sprawling to the grass.

Every time his chest rose to take in a breath, he was stabbed by a spear of pain. Part of him was sure his rib cage had been kicked clean out of his body.

I...he...Gornak... Do something.

Drunkenly, his head lolled to the side. He saw his hand beside him, but he couldn't tell it to move. Not that it mattered, because the sword wasn't in it anymore.

Cra... Bug... Fu... Dammit.

'Kid,' Auron cried with exasperation.

'My turn,' Gornak bellowed, bringing his axe overhead with a grunt.

Adrenaline flooded through Nicolas like he'd been struck by lightning. Using it, he crawled back just in time, the thick axe blade throwing up dirt and taking a chunk from the grass instead of permanently separating his testicles. Nicolas scrabbled to his feet. Unable to see the *Dawn Blade* around him, he had no choice but to use his other strategy: calling for help.

A backhand from Gornak put paid to that idea. He was vaguely aware of the axe rising again as he spat blood from his mouth.

'What sorcery is this, whoreson?' Gornak's cry made Nicolas look back.

Auron was pelting the large warrior with any rock he could find, making Gornak gaze around in confusion. The spirit's other hand was pointing to the grass. The sword.

Quickly, Nicolas grabbed the weapon. Problem was, would it be of use? Gornak had him outmatched. And he couldn't even run for help, as the mountainous warrior was between him and the camp. Stumbling backwards, he instead made for the bridge. Auron ran out of rocks a moment later.

'Kid,' the spirit called. 'Tell him—'

Whatever Auron said was drowned out by Gornak's roar as he charged. It made him almost nostalgic for the minotaur.

The ground under his feet became hard. He was on the bridge.

Brilliant.

CHAPTER 20

Only having a fifty-fifty record when it came to fighting on bridges, Nicolas backed away from the oncoming man-mountain. The wooden bridge groaned as if in pain as Gornak set foot on it. He wanted to turn and flee, but turning his back to his opponent would be suicide. If he'd learnt anything from Auron and Silva, it was that. Instead, he tried to stand his ground, and Gornak slowed, frowning and looking past him.

'Right, kid,' Auron said quickly. 'Now there's a lull, tell Gornak that—' The spirit caught Gornak's look and followed it. 'Oh shit.'

Sensing danger, Nicolas swung around.

Oh, for Deities' sake.

'Where in the Underworld did you two come from?' Nicolas shouted. 'How did you even manage to catch up with us, let alone get ahead of us?'

'We're assassins.' Alexi grinned menacingly. 'Appearing from places no one expects is what we do.'

'I will always find you,' Emelina said dreamily, doing a strange little dance on the spot, her wide grin displaying her dimples to full effect.

'Can't you see I'm busy?' Nicolas asked in exasperation, gesturing to Gornak.

'Who are these whoresons?' the warrior rumbled, pointing a thick finger toward the assassins.

The twins raised their right eyebrows in unison. 'What did he just call us?'

'He's called me that, like, twelve times now.' Nicolas sighed. 'I think he just says it by rote.'

'No matter,' Alexi said, brandishing his scythes as he eyed Gornak warily. 'We aren't here to trade barbs. We're here for Billy.'

'Do you see him around?' Nicolas asked, theatrically scanning the banks of the river. 'Because I don't. So you're in the wrong place.'

'Oh no.' Alexi smirked. 'I think killing one of his protectors is a fine step toward our goal.'

'This one is mine to kill,' Gornak interjected.

'He's ours,' Alexi snarled at the warrior, pointing one of his scythes at Nicolas.

'I wish he was mine.' Emelina giggled unnervingly.

'I disagree,' the warrior rumbled simply, as if that were that and it was the end of the matter.

'Noted.' Alexi sneered. 'And ignored. I hope you aren't too disappointed when you wake up.'

Should I be flattered that they're arguing over me?

A dart implanted itself in Gornak's broad chest. The warrior looked down at it in surprise. For some reason, he chuckled heartily at the sight of something sticking out of his chest.

Two more joined it. Then a fourth.

'Gornak does not succumb to tickles.' The big warrior shrugged. 'Nor does he have patience for pricks.'

'Well?' Alexi asked testily, looking at his sister.

Beside him, Emelina let the blow gun fall from her lips, which were pursed questioningly. 'I... But...that should be enough to knock out an elephant,' she muttered in disbelief.

Gornak's laugh was hearty and booming. 'Gornak has better constitution than common elephant, silly little whoresons.'

Isn't Emelina a whoredaugh— Actually, forget it.

'Well...' Alexi had clearly seen this going a different way, but he wasn't about to give up just yet. 'We're still taking him.'

'I think we can resolve this without violence,' Nicolas protested. 'You don't even have a contract for me.'

Alexi shrugged. 'True, but you're escorting Billy, sooooo...'

Nicolas got the impression the assassin was just looking for an excuse to kill him.

'Shame to waste such a handsome man.' Emelina giggled. 'But work comes first.'

No charming my way out of this either then, eh?

So he was on a bridge again. Assassins on one side and a warrior who might as well be a giant on the other. This was going to be tricky. Briefly he looked over the side of the bridge, considering jumping over. The water looked pretty rapid today. So what could he do?

'Help?' he asked Auron.

'I could poss—' The spirit changed tacks at Nicolas's look. 'Take the twins first. Try to keep your distance from Gornak as you do then keep dodging. Wear him out. He's fast, but his stamina is shit.'

Sounded simple enough, but the execution would be insanely difficult. Then a sudden resolution hit him, a lesson from some of Auron's recent tales. It was simple, elegant, and might just see him walk off this bridge alive. Carefully, he sheathed the *Dawn Blade* then strode to the side of the bridge and folded his arms.

Alexi eyed him with suspicion. 'What are you doing?'

'I'll tell you what I'm *not* doing,' he replied casually. 'I'm not engaging in *this*.'

'Huh?' Gornak was as confused as the assassins.

'You both want me, so fight it out amongst yourselves.' He shrugged. 'I'll take on the winner.'

The assassins looked less than enthusiastic about that idea. Gornak more so. 'Good, good. I shall kill these whoresons then finish my business with you.' He smiled genially.

Auron stared at him with a furrowed brow for a moment then smiled with comprehension. Nicolas gave his companion a slight nod, and Auron sprinted away to get help whilst Nicolas's opponents were occupied. Hopefully, by the time Gornak was done with the twins or vice versa, the others would be here to turn the tide in his favour.

Gornak stood ready with his axe. 'Come then, little whoresons. Sasha is waiting to meet you.'

'*Stop* calling us *that*,' Emelina cried, stomping her foot.

'Our mother was no *whore*,' Alexi snarled.

See, nobody likes being called that.

'Do not try to run, grave-robbing whoreson,' Gornak rumbled at Nicolas. 'If you try, you die with axe in back.'

Noted.

The twins stalked forward as did Gornak, moving to either side of the bridge to make best use of the advantage of their numbers. Not that it mattered to Gornak, who took up most of the walkway anyway. Nicolas kept himself ready as the warrior passed, silently keeping an eye on the forest, willing the others to appear.

The fight began. Both Alexi and Emelina were quick, he'd give them that. They ducked and dodged the mighty battle axe as it swung at them at speed. Gornak proved equally light on his feet, stepping away from the scythes, despite the fact that Alexi had apparently had chains fixed to them so he could swing them out over distances. He must've done that after dropping them earlier.

Maybe I should do that with my sword?

Emelina only had a pair of little—and most likely poison-tipped—knives and was having trouble closing enough to use them.

Auron had once told Nicolas how much fun it was to get your opponents to kill each other. He was right. It was actually quite nice sitting back and watching his enemies taking care of eachother. Perhaps he would try to do this more often.

Gornak swung his axe at Alexi, who jumped back, and the blade took a chunk out of the bridge. Seconds later, it fell into the water with a splash.

Oh, another idea. Two in one day. Not too shabby, Mr Carnage... Carnegie. Dammit.

Nicolas strolled lazily to the far end of the bridge as Alexi took Sasha's hilt to the chin. The assassin stumbled back a few paces, before falling to his rump, dazed. Emelina used the moment, as Gornak's attention was fixed on Alexi, to drive one of her knives into Gornak's side. The big warrior looked down at the wound as if he'd been pricked by a thorn. Emelina's face went from victorious, to surprised, to disappointed, to horrified.

A large hand shot out, grabbing Emelina and hauling her into the air. Her eyes bulged from either the grip or fear. Most likely both.

'That was silly, little girl,' Gornak said. 'Gornak must now snap your neck.'

Nicolas could've waited a moment or two until the assassin had died, but for some reason, he wanted her to live. He grabbed a rock and hurled it at Gornak's head. It struck him in the dead centre of the back of his skull. There was a moment of loaded silence then Gornak slowly turned, dropping Emelina.

'You say you let us fight it out then attack me from behind,' the large warrior said slowly. 'That is not honourable, little grave-robbing whore-son.' He looked shocked. That wasn't the emotion Nicolas needed; he needed angry.

'I don't waste my honour on giant hairy whoresons.' He shrugged.

Apparently, Gornak didn't like being called that any more than anyone else. Slowly, his face reddened as what Nicolas had said sank in. 'Gornak's mother was virtuous woman.'

'A virtuous whore is still a whore,' Nicolas retorted with a wide grin.

That did it. With a roar, Gornak charged him.

Crap.

Maybe this wasn't so smart, after all? The axe came down. He dodged it. *Crack.* A piece of the bridge fell into the water, the piece that Nicolas had been stood on seconds before.

'Missed,' Nicolas said glibly.

With a mighty bellow, Gornak brought the axe down again, and again and again. Each time, Nicolas wasn't there. And the effect was the same. *Crack. Crack. Crack.*

When he heard a deep groan beneath his feet, Nicolas took a single step back onto the grass and firm land. Gornak looked down at the source of the groan then up at him in surprise. 'You crafty whoreson. You—'

The large warrior's words were cut off as the bridge gave out beneath him with the loud splintering of wood. Gornak dropped from sight as the end of the bridge collapsed into the water below. Unable to take the sudden jarring impact, the other end of the bridge snapped away from land, and the whole structure dropped into the water.

In the split second before it fell, he saw Alexi, staring at him, aghast and enraged. Then he too disappeared.

As the bridge crashed into the water below it sent up a mighty spray that covered Nicolas. It was kind of refreshing.

Looking out over the edge of the bank, he watched the remnants of the bridge float downstream. He couldn't see Gornak, but the twins were clinging to pieces of wood for dear life. It was petty, but he couldn't help waving goodbye.

Stepping back, he breathed out a large sigh of relief.

Did I just best three deadly opponents in one go?

He most certainly had. And he'd done so unscathed. Was it a miracle, or was he just getting better? Either way, he was in the mood to celebrate.

Rasing his arm to cheer, he stopped dead when he saw the dart sticking out of it.

He only managed to say one thing before he passed out. 'Oh, come on.'

CHAPTER 21

T he ground kept jumping up and down, and he wasn't entirely sure why. It was very hard to focus on anything. He was sure he was moving but also sure he wasn't moving himself. He tried to remember what had happened.

The big hairy man fell into the water.

He chuckled. Only when the person holding him gripped him tighter did he realise there was actually a person holding him. His head lolled back, and he looked up, blinking to focus. The person holding him was a woman, and she had a very serious face. Vaguely familiar.

Scowling. Scowler scowler. Try smiling. I bet you have a pretty smile.

The woman glanced down at him in surprise, and he chuckled. His head lolled again, and he watched the ground moving beneath him. It was nauseating, so he stopped that quickly. It occurred to him that being carried by a woman might not be very manly. Not that he had any illusions about his manliness.

Am I a manly man? I want to be a manly man. I could be the manliest man, I think.

Suddenly, the movement stopped, and he looked up at the woman carrying him. Her eyebrow was raised. A strange thought occurred to him. *Am I saying things out loud?* Of course he wasn't. He knew the difference between thinking and speaking aloud.

As the woman started moving again, his head lolled to the other side.

Oooh, look at all the muscles she has. I wish I had half the muscles she has. Not the breasts though. Those wouldn't look good on me at all.

Again, the woman stopped. This time she was glaring at him. Could she read minds?

Maybe she's in my mind right now, reading my thoughts. I need to stop thinking about her boobs. Oh for Deities' sake, why is this suddenly so hard? Let me think of something else. Castles. Castles are neat. I've seen some magnificent boobs...castles!

Roughly, he was hefted into the air and over the woman's shoulder. The sudden movement nauseated him. When she continued, he threw up. For a moment, he thought he heard something like, *'For Deities' sake, Nicolas.'*

I think I got some on her boobs...boots!

The woman began to move faster. Grass, bushes, and trees flashed past him as he bounced up and down, desperately trying not to be sick again. For some strange reason, it made him want to sing...in his head.

Oh, the grass is green, the woman carrying me is mean. She's covered in muscle, and makes the leaves rustle. The way she throws me around has me miffed, but she's not my type because I think I'm in love with...

Coming to a sudden halt, he was lifted off her shoulders and stood face to face with her for a moment.

Hey, I know her. Silva. She looks angry. She's always angry. Good thing I didn't say anything out loud about her boobs. She'd have killed me. Oh shit, I think I was sick on her boots.

Silva's face became gradually redder for reasons he couldn't understand. Finally, he was lowered to the grass, which was a good job, because his legs weren't working, and he needed help. He was vaguely aware of people around him talking. Glancing around, he saw a guy who he could see through. That was odd. Picking up a stone, he lazily threw it. It passed through the man's shin, and he turned and looked at Nicolas.

Shiny light man. So shiny...and light. But not really there.

Reaching out, he moved his hand backwards and forwards through the man's leg. He didn't look amused. Nicolas didn't care; he was too busy giggling.

Rrragggh, angry shiny fellow.

'Is he okay?' Was that voice in his head? Or had he heard it? Surely a voice he'd heard was therefore a voice in his head because it entered through his ears.

Deities, things are entering my head through my ears?

He tried to slap his hands over his ears before more things entered them. Maybe insects. Missing, he ended up slapping himself across both cheeks.

Keep your words out of my head.

'He has been drugged,' Silva answered, arms folded, 'And it is making him...well, you shall see for yourselves.'

A figure loomed over him, a big green man with big white teeth. What was he looking at? Was he...?

Oooh, look at that orange hair hanging down. I'm going to flick it.

The green man eyed him suspiciously as he slowly reached up. For a second, Nicolas let his hand hover beside the hanging orange ponytail, before he pushed it and quickly retracted his arm. He snorted with laughter at the incredulous look on the green face as his hair swung from side to side. Then he repeated the process, but this time, he gently tapped the green man on the nose.

Boop snout.

He rolled around in laughter at his own antics. His hand was swatted away as he tried to make the hair swing again.

Green man have no fun, rah rah rah.

Wow, that was quite the stink eye he was getting. Wouldn't it be awkward if he was actually saying these things?

Wow. That's bigger hair.

There was a man standing close by that looked like a tree. Or was he a broccoli? Did he remember someone saying he was a broccoli? Yes...broccoli man, that was it. No, that was silly. No one was a broccoli. So why was the guy pretending to be a broccoli?

Hey, silly broccoli head man. You aren't real. You don't exist. Take that broccoli off your head and stop pretending to be a vegetable.

Maybe he ought to get up and rip the broccoli off his head? He still wasn't in full control of his body. This would be tricky. But that broccoli didn't belong on his head, so it was coming off as soon as...

You're so pretty.

The green eyes of the person beside broccoli man widened in surprise. Was their face going red? Why had he thought *their*? That was clearly one person. No, *they* was right. He didn't know why, but it was right.

No, you're not pretty.

An eyebrow was raised.

You are a deity of beauty made flesh. You're what poets mean when they write about love incarnate. Yours is a face I could wake up to every morning. You are...I don't know. I need more words to describe your beauty. Can someone get me a poet? A poet, please. I need words. What rhymes with beauty...? Fruity, booty, hooty...

'Oh, for Deities' sake.'

Hey, you need to give me a minute. When my legs start working again, I'm going to get up, take you in my arms, and marry you. Yup. How many children are you going to bear me?

'Nick!'

Yeahhh, that's right. Nick. Nick Carnage. The Nick Carnage. Big scary warrior guy. Behold, my muscles! I don't have as many as Silva, but gaze in awe at these mighty biceps.

What was the see-through guy laughing at? Could he read minds too?

You disrespect my muscles, shiny man? Fine, I have more. I'll show you all my muscles.

'Nicolas, stop trying to take your trousers off.'

I will not. He needs to see my big muscle. Muscles.

'Kid, nobody wants to see that.'

Beautiful one does! Get off me, angry green man. I'll bite you.

'Garaz, can you just knock him out already?'

'Very well.'

****

Nicolas edged slowly forward and risked a glance out into the abyss that surrounded the small, circular patch of rock he stood on. Below him, above him, and all around him was blackness. As dizziness took hold, he quickly stepped back.

'Well, I think it's safe to say this is a dream.'

He remembered being knocked out, but he couldn't exactly remember why. The fact that every time he tried to bring the memory up, he shuddered with a pang of embarrassment wasn't a good sign.

The dream became a nightmare.

From the darkness, a gigantic figure emerged. Nicolas took an involuntary step back. A small stone was dislodged by his heel and fell silently into the abyss.

'Y...you.' Terror was robbing him of his ability to speak as he stared up at the giant horror. 'W...what are you d...doing here?'

Koth tilted its unnatural, half-goat-skulled head. 'Silly human. You just said this is a dream. And now you believe I am really here?'

'Stranger things have happened.' His voice was meek and quiet. He couldn't even force himself to talk in a normal tone.

'They have,' the image of Koth agreed. 'And that is why I am here. You deny your fears. All of them. That is why your mind has chosen to confront you with this form.'

'You want me to what...apologise to myself for not wanting to say the name of the creature that killed me?' he muttered. 'I think I am well within my rights to be scared of him.'

Wetness on his chest made him look down. Blood seeped through his shirt where an arrow had once struck him. Ripping his shirt off, he saw the wound, and something else. A giant demonic handprint burned into his chest.

Koth's.

Desperately, he ran his hands across it, as if he could just wipe it away.

'My mark does not come off so easily. Things are not so easily undone.'

There was something in the demon's tone that made him frown. 'What do you mean?'

Koth tilted its head. 'Your soul was banished to the Underworld and was then brought back. Do you not think a toll is incurred for such a thing?'

'The thought hadn't occurred—'

'Liar.'

Nicolas crouched and covered his ears as Koth's roar echoed all around him.

The tip of a large claw touched his chin delicately, raising his head to face the demon again.

'You have wondered on the toll it took on your soul,' Koth purred. 'Are you some form of zombie now? Is your anger because your soul is tainted? You cannot lie to me, for I am you. You cannot lie to me about yourself, or about your doubts about 'them'.'

'My parents...' Instantly, tears stung his eyes. 'They're most likely dead. Aren't they? I keep trying to hope, to just keep going. But how can I keep denying what's most likely?'

'That is true.' Nicolas could sense Koth's satisfaction. 'But you jumped ahead of me, Nicolas. Your parents are not the 'them' I referred to.'

The realisation set in instantly. 'No.'

'Yes,' Koth whispered. 'Your companions. Your so-called friends*. The niggling voice in the back of your mind, the questions it has been asking. You have tried so hard to ignore it. Now, it is time to face it. To listen to it. If you don't pay attention now, it may be your final undoing.'*

Nicolas couldn't respond. He just shook his head.

'You've noticed the change in all of them of late. Or was it a change?' Koth's stare intensified. 'How well do you really know them? Any of them?'

'Stop it. We've fought together. Saved each other's lives.'

'Will Auron ever stop treating you like a...kid?'

'Stop.'

'How did *Tavish get away from Silva? Did she* let *him get away?'*

'Stop it.' Nicolas shook his head fiercely.

'Why does Garaz's mood change so quickly? Typical of an orc, wouldn't you say?'

'Stop it.' He tried putting his hands over his ears.

'How can Shift kiss you and then pretend it never happened? How can they ask Rex to dance, right under your nose?'

'Stop—'

'How can you face attacks on all sides, when you can't even trust your so-called companions?'

'St—'

'Do they even really like you? Or are you just a fool to them, here for their amusement?' Koth leant in close to him, dropping its voice to a whisper. 'What would your life have been like if you'd never met them?'

The frustration built in Nicolas, and he leapt to his feet and screamed into the abyss. 'Stopppppppppp...'

CHAPTER 22

Coming too with a cry, Nicolas turned on his side, panting heavily. Nearby, he saw Billy frowning at him. His new companion got up and went to come and check on him, but Nicolas waved him away. Instead Billy walked to the other side of the tree he had been lying in front of, toward the sound of the others.

He was aware he was surrounded by people, yet right now he had never felt so alone. The only thing keeping him company right now was the voice of the demon in his head, repeating the questions it had asked. The ones he didn't want to answer.

Oh crap.

Nicolas threw up passionately and suddenly. It was that nasty kind of being sick that kept going even when there was nothing left to unleash, so he spent a good few moments dry heaving, his stomach burning with every contraction.

Groaning, he noticed a cup next to him. Greedily, he drank the water, washing the foul taste from his mouth. If only his memory of the dream could be so easily washed away. But he knew it wasn't going anywhere, and the uncertainty it stirred in him made him shiver. As did the returning memory of how he was knocked out.

After forcing himself to his feet, he stumbled over to the nearest tree, walking like a new-born deer. When the memories returned, a little clearer this time, he eased himself into a seated position and stared at the grass, wishing the ground would open and swallow him whole.

'Now we know we're really on an adventure.' Nicolas looked up and smiled thinly at the spirit stood over him. 'You've dropped your sword *and* thrown up.' A slight look of concern creased Auron's brow. 'How you feeling, kid?'

Don't call me that.

Closing his eyes, he fought the surging anger back. He had more important issues right now. Including answering the spirit's question. To answer that, he had to ask one of his own. He didn't want to ask it. Well, truthfully, he didn't want the answer, but he needed to know exactly how much of an ass he'd made of himself.

'How much of it did I say aloud?' His voice was a whisper, as if his mouth were still on the fence about asking.

'I can't say for sure,' Auron said sympathetically. 'I mean, you said a lot of stuff. Apparently, you considered how Silva's breasts would look on you.'

'Shit.' He hung his head, sighing heavily. 'And I tried to take my clothes off?'

'Yup,' the spirit confirmed. 'You were quite resolute about showing us *little Nicolas.* The sight of Garaz trying to wrestle your breeches back on is without doubt one of the funniest things I've seen in my life. And afterlife.'

'Dammit.'

'Somehow, even after he'd knocked you out and was trying to give you his herbal drink to flush out Emelina's poison, you reached up and started jiggling his cheeks.' Auron badly suppressed a laugh. 'Garaz's face...'

I really am the fool, aren't I? Why didn't the demon just finish me when it had the chance?

Nicolas couldn't help but chuckle. He'd dreamt of the demon, yet still couldn't bare to even think of it's name.

Mum and dad...

Looking away from Auron, he rubbed his face, removing the tear from his eye. What the demon had suggested couldn't be right. He couldn't think that. He couldn't believe it.

I need to find them. I need to find all of them.

But how? When all of his companions had been behaving strangely of late. He couldn't deny it. And the tension developing in their group wouldn't be helped by his drugged nonsense. Plus, he'd made a colossal ass of himself. This was becoming as much a staple of his adventures as the constant danger.

If I ever see Emelina again...

On the other side of the tree, his companions, if he could still call them that, were bustling around. Briefly, he considered running back to the river and throwing himself in, but the last time he'd been washed down-river, his life had just gotten worse, and it wouldn't help him get Tavish. He needed Tavish. Only he would have the definitive answer about his parents' fate. To get him, he'd need their help, which meant right now he had to pick up the smashed shards of his pride and apologise.

'Sorry,' he said to Auron as he rose tentatively.

'Don't worry about it, kid,' the spirit said reassuringly. 'Just don't throw stones through me again, please.'

'Understood.'

Taking a few deep breaths, he steeled himself for what would come next. Then he took a few more deep breaths. Then one more, just for luck. Though embarrassment threatened to paralyse him, he stepped around the tree.

Instantly, the conversations stopped, and all eyes were on him. The urge to jump back behind the tree was hard to fight off. No one looked particularly pleased to see him, save Billy, who appeared as amiable as ever.

Oh Deities, I tried to pull his hair off.

'So,' he began with an awkward cough, 'I owe you all an apology for my behaviour.'

Garaz rose from his cross-legged position. The orc didn't look happy, but when did he of late? 'You were poisoned. The effects were understandable.'

Nicolas's eyes were drawn to the hair that hung over the orc's shoulder. Garaz noticed it and pushed it back with a slightly annoyed growl. His eyes flicked to Silva instead, and he instantly wished they hadn't. She looked *pissed*.

'Sorry,' he said meekly.

Before he could say any more, an arm grabbed him and pulled him back around the tree. 'We need to talk,' Shift said firmly.

Oh shit. This was probably the worst of all.

'When you came back from the Underworld, I kissed you,' they began bluntly. 'I did that because I was relieved you were back. I'm not used to letting people in and I'm certainly not used to losing people. So I reacted in a very strange way. Nothing more.' Shift's eyes softened a little before they continued. 'I need to know you understand that. There will never be anything more between us. Friends. That's all. So please, for the love of the Deities, no more trying to write sonnets about my beauty.'

It felt like being punched directly in the heart, by a burly man wearing spiked knuckles. He'd known this would be the worst of all, but he'd had no idea how much their words would sting.

'You understand?'

'Yes,' he said firmly. 'I was drugged. That's why I said all that nonsense, nothing more. Whatever Emelina stuck me with made me say some crazy things. But we're just friends. You've made that very clear.' He hoped he hid the petulance from his tone.

'Good.' Shift gave him a firm nod and walked away, leaving Nicolas to slump heavily against the tree, trying to remember how to breathe.

Why were their words affecting him so badly? At least now he knew where he stood. No more confusion. His eyes shifted to Rex, sat casually on the grass.

Maybe it would be different if he wasn't here?

Maybe it would be different if none of them were here?

Nicolas became entranced, wondering at the possibilities of where his life would have gone had he not met any of them. All he could see was him, at home with his parents, living his life. No battles, no near death experiences. Just living.

No. No, no, no.

Closing his eyes, he forced himself back to reality. Because this was his reality now, and he needed to accept it. He needed to focus on his quest. The people of Hablock were out there.

And my parents.

They all needed rescuing, and he was the only one who could do it. But to do it, he needed to find Tavish. Quickly, he quashed the glare in Silva's direction.

For all we have done so far, really, we have nothing.

All they had to show for the fighting, for their effort, was Billy.

He must *know something about Tavish.*

His hands clenched as the urge to stomp over to their new companion and shake him until some nugget of information came loose was nearly overwhelming.

Stop. Billy is the key. Tavish will come for him. I need to be ready when he does.

But how could he really be ready when he was no longer sure of anyone around him?

CHAPTER 23

Nicolas had spent the next half hour in a quiet daze as they packed up their camp and set out for another day on the Ale Trail. Though no one spoke, their judgement was a giant standing right in front of him, pointing a tree-trunk-sized finger in his direction and shaking it's head. It just served to widen the gap between them all. To reinforce his isolation. Part of him wanted to turn Vigour around, kick him into a gallop, and leave his companions, and his shame, behind.

But we have a job to do. And I can't do it alone. Besides, where would I even go?

'We can't go to the Hall like we planned,' Shift said as they messed around with their saddlebag.

'Why not?' Auron's reply was both quick and defensive.

'Because you said you could talk some sense into Gornak,' the shapeshifter said testily. 'And when the opportunity came, *he* was nearly killed.'

Do you have to say he *like that?*

'Well, the kid should've talked faster.'

'So this is *my* fault?' he snapped bitterly.

'Shift is right,' Garaz cut in before the argument could escalate. 'Who knows how many of the guild we will encounter before we get to Jerric?'

'And it is best not to have to fight our way through them,' Silva added.

The spirit mused on this a moment. 'Fine. You make a good point,' he said grudgingly. 'I don't think fighting our way through my peers is the best idea. There will be a turn off from the trail soon enough. If we haven't found Billy's escort by then, we should just chance going to the city by ourselves. Besides, the sooner we leave this damned road the better.'

Isn't that the truth.

The idea they were heading, potentially, right toward Tavish should have elated Nicolas, but his mind was a swirling mess of emotions that he could barely contain right now. Between recalling his drugged antics, replaying the conversation with Shift, and the implications of everything the demon had said, it was hard to think straight.

'Psst.' Snapped out of his moping, he saw Rex looking at him as he rode past. 'Don't worry about it. We've all made fools of ourselves from time to time. Usually, it's the drink that makes me do it.'

'Thanks,' he muttered back through gritted teeth.

Despite the fact the thief was clearly trying to be sympathetic, a flash of rage gripped Nicolas. In that moment, he wanted to pull Rex down from his horse and beat him to a bloody pulp. Tightening the grip on his reins, he tried to pour his aggression out through his whitening knuckles. The previous flashes of annoyance were becoming sudden rages. And they were getting harder to control.

'Try not to let it get to you,' Billy said at his side. 'Like Shift's fella said, we all embarrass ourselves sometimes.' *Shift's fella?* The rage flashed again. 'They'll get over it. Personally, I thought it was funny, so don't worry so much about other people's opinions, they vary.'

Slowly, he turned in the saddle. 'Why? What have the others been saying?' His voice was a low, almost feral, growl.

Billy's eyes widened. 'I...well, they...' his new companion stammered. 'Look, I spoke out of turn. Forget it.'

How?

His eyes flicked to his *companions*, and he could almost see the wall rising between them. How close were they, really, if they couldn't just shrug off some drugged ramblings?

But isn't that my place amongst them? The fool of the group? Good ol' Nicolas, throws up, drops his sword, makes an idiot of himself. This isn't the first time they've all laughed at me or been annoyed with me as a group. Maybe it's going to be the last...

The sound of annoyed voices ahead brought him back to the moment, banishing the whispering in his mind. There appeared to be something blocking their way forward.

Keeping one hand on the hilt of his sword, the group spread out, ready for anything.

A tree lay directly across the road. In front of it was a giant shape covered in a huge blanket. On the other side of the tree was a queue of wagons, their occupants shouting curses as if it would somehow encourage the tree to politely move aside.

'Well, this is just a classic ambush, isn't it,' Auron scoffed, shaking his head. 'A log in the road. Where's the creativity?'

'I'm more concerned with how well the ambushers can fight, than giving them advice on their ambush technique,' Nicolas said as he made sure Billy was safely behind him.

That's all this road is. Attack, after attack, after bloody attack.

For a brief moment the forest on either side closed in on him. Surrounding and isolating him as his paranoid eyes flicked from bush to bush, trying to find signs of their imminent attackers. Would this be enemies they had faced already? Or maybe a new group of foes to add to the ever rising list of people who wanted them dead?

Enemies everywhere. Everyone wants to fight. Everyone wants Billy. Yet no Tavish. Never bloody Tavish. Never the one man who can give me answers.

He only realised he'd growled aloud when he saw the others looking at him in confusion.

Dismounting his horse, followed by the confused looks of his companions, he took a few steps toward the roadblock and drew his sword. His eyes caught movement beneath the sheet. Something was breathing.

And it won't be if it comes at us.

'To whoever's waiting to attack us,' he declared in a loud voice, 'Make yourselves known and let's get this over with.'

And woe betide whoever answers the challenge.

After a few tense moments, the bushes on the side of the road parted, and eight men strode out, flourishing their capes behind them. They were...fancy. Each had flawlessly quaffed hair and pale faces. On closer inspection, they all appeared to be wearing powdered make-up, with bright red circles on their cheeks. They wore elaborate tunics with fine gilding and thick capes, all of which were quite nauseatingly colourful. Even at this distance, Nicolas coughed slightly at the overwhelmingly sweet scents coming from them. Forming a parallel line to their group, the men stood around haughtily in a manner that screamed of the overly dramatic. Were they about to be attacked by travelling fools?

'*Bards...*' Auron said through gritted teeth.

I thought he loved bards?

They did have a habit of writing songs about him, and if the spirit liked anything, it was having a song written about him. Looking back at Auron, he raised his eyebrow quizzically.

'I like bards...singularly.' Auron snorted. 'Collectively, they're unbearable. They become a bunch of mooching fops. Each trying to outdo the other about how much of a *tortured artist* they are...or getting ideas above their station.' There seemed to be a story there. The spirit thought about it for a moment. 'If they start anything, can I possess you so I can kick their asses?'

Nicolas shook his head, 'I don't want you inside me.'

Auron screwed his face up. 'Why do you have to make it sound so weird?'

'What?' He scoffed. 'I wasn't.'

'Greetings,' a melodious voice cut in. 'Your arrival is fortuitous, as we prepare to unleash the violence most gratuitous.'

There was a stunned silence. Nicolas looked back at his companions uncertainly. Each of them was wide eyed and unsure.

From the group of bards, one—presumably the leader—stepped forward.

How did you curl a moustache that many times?

'Welcome, dear travellers, to our roadside trap,' the man said with a flourish. 'But please, do not our humble troupe clap. For today we are here on business most grave, so your fond applause you must save. For you see, you have something we want this day. Hence us impairing your way.'

'By the Deities,' Shift exclaimed, aghast. 'They talk in *rhyme*!'

'Bards.' Auron glowered. 'Told you.'

'Please know that you may yet live,' the leader continued. 'If over to us, your charge you do give. Surrender the one they call Billy, and, we beg of you, do nothing that could be considered...silly.' The last bit was followed by a self-indulgent titter.

This was ridiculous. He wasn't about to fight a load of rhyming guys. Especially such a...delicate-looking group of fellows. Though the rhyming was irksome, there was no way they could put up any kind of fight.

'I suppose you are a member of the Guild of Bards?' Garaz asked Billy in a low growl.

'I'm a joiner.' Billy smiled with a shrug.

How many bloody guilds does Etherius have?

'Can you even sing?' the orc snapped, then replied to Billy's sheepish expression, 'This is so foolish I have no words for it.'

Garaz looked like he was about to rip someone's head off.

I know the feeling.

Yet Nicolas needed to diffuse this situation. These weren't fighters. Idiots, yes. But that didn't mean they should die today. 'Look, we don't want any trouble, okay?'

'What you want is neither here nor there,' the leader retorted melodiously. 'Stand between us and our quarry, and we'll dispatch you with flair.' He punctuated the end of his sentence with a flourish of his small cape before taking another step forwards. 'Ye knave shalt suffer at the point of my blade. From Etherius, your memory shalt forever fade.'

'None shalt stand between us and our prey,' spoke a more falsetto bard. 'Unless atop a funeral pyre they wish to lay.' They'd already done a *'stand between'* one. And it should be *lie*, not *lay*. This was getting tiresome.

'Surrender to us our errant guild member,' sang another. 'Lest our anger grow from an ember.'

A larger bard stepped forward, got to a single knee, and pronounced in a deep bass tone, 'Cross us and thou shalt dieeeeeeeeeeee.'

Nicolas struck his idea about not fighting these guys out of his mind. Now he really wanted to kick their heads in.

'I have no patience for these buffoons,' Silva snarled. 'Can we have at them?'

'This is the silliest thing I have seen in my life,' Garaz muttered.

'Told you.' Auron sighed.

'Hey, Nicky,' Shift said from their mount. 'Maybe you should try to out-sing them?'

Slowly, he turned to look at the sniggering shapeshifter. 'No thanks.'

'Nicky?' the leader of the bards said with a raised eyebrow. 'As in Nick Carnage?'

Oh, that's it. They're going to die now. 'Near enough,' he replied through gritted teeth.

'Ah ha,' the leader exclaimed. 'There is a hefty purse on your head. Either alive or dead. Once your death at our hands is told, we shall be able to afford new harps of gold.'

The rest of the bards giggled, clapping their hands in a very foppish way.

'I've had enough of this.' As Nicolas took a step forward, the bards all leapt back, drawing thin, pointed blades in unison and holding them ready.

'Are those swords?' Nicolas asked Auron. They didn't look like any kind of sword he'd ever seen. They seemed too...fragile to be swords.

'Kind of.' The spirit shrugged.

'And now they threaten us with toothpicks.' It appeared Silva's warrior sensibilities were greatly offended by this whole confrontation.

'Are you sure you want to come at *us* with *those*?' Nicolas asked, very aware that his companions were now dismounting. This would be neither long nor glorious.

The leader gave him a self-satisfied grin. 'To our blades, you need not beckon. For we have a secret weapon.'

Maybe they were going to melt his brains with their shitty rhymes? It was most likely already happening.

The leader gave a little cough then uttered a single high-pitched note. Soon the others joined in, harmonising with their leader one by one. The sound was irritating. As he watched, the bards went purple, even behind their make-up, with the effort of holding the note. Somewhere ahead he was sure he heard the sound of shattering glass.

Screaming started behind Nicolas. When he turned, Billy and Rex were on the floor, their faces contorted in pain, teeth clenched and veins popping on their temples as they clasped their hands over their ears and writhed on the ground. Shift, Garaz, and Auron looked at them in surprise. It appeared to be having a similar effect on the people in the wagons on the far side of the roadblock too. The sheet behind the bards began to jerk fiercely.

Finally, the bards could hold the note no longer, each doubling over, panting heavily. Billy and Rex continued to groan on the floor.

'I...don't...understand,' the leader of the bards said between panting breaths. 'That...should've...incapacitated you. Yet you seem unaffected, how is this true?'

It took him a moment to find the answer. 'We were on a ship once, and it was attacked by a siren,' he explained. 'Now that thing could make some noise. Sorry, guys, but you're amateurs by comparison.'

There was a lot of offended scoffing amongst the troupe. The leader held out his hand, and there was silence.

'In that case, it's time for a dramatic reveal. Away this sheet, we shall peel.' With a wave, he gestured to the object behind him. 'Since you have gone and forced our hand, it is time to unleash our monster on your merry band. '

With unnecessary theatrics, two of the bards pulled the sheet off of the large shape, revealing a large, muscular ogre standing in the road. Suddenly, the wagons on the other side of the roadblock decided they were urgently needed elsewhere.

What's wrong with...

The ogre's eyes were wide and empty. Blood trailed from the monster's ears down it's neck.

That is not a merry ogre.

Slowly, it toppled forward before crashing to the ground. Dead.

'Bloody bards. The idiots killed their own monster.' Auron began to laugh heartily as the bards milled around in confusion, muttering worriedly.

'They can't have had much faith in their singing ability, if they felt the need to bring an ogre too,' Shift smirked, much to the troupe leader's ire.

Nicolas took another step forward and raised the *Dawn Blade*. 'So, about that fight then?'

The bards didn't just withdraw, they fled, clambering over each other in their desperation to get as far away from him as possible. It was quite gratifying, really. Several dropped their swords, which would've been funny if Nicolas didn't do it so much himself.

'And don't come back,' Shift shouted after them as they helped Garaz tend to the others on the floor.

Oh, look how tenderly they help Rex to his feet. Very sweet.

Reflexively, he shivered. He was not about to start rhyming. 'Bloody bards,' he muttered.

Thankfully, they recovered quickly. Wishing to get as far from this annoying encounter as possible, the group circumvented the roadblock and continued on their way.

Just around the corner was a tavern. The quaint place looked more like someone's cottage than an alehouse. The outside had been over decorated with plant pots and hanging baskets that had bright flowers sprouting from them. Nicolas guessed it's windows had once housed beautiful stained glass mosaics. Now they had been reduced to shards of coloured glass on the floor, being swept up by a furious looking woman in a shawl.

'Are you lot responsible for that racket?' she snapped as they approached. 'The one that smashed all my beautiful windows?'

'Not exactly...'

Her face reddened, the vein on her temple suggesting it was from anger. 'So you are at least partly responsible then?' She brandished her broom like it was a spear. 'Sling your hook. You ain't welcome at the Golden Wand, and you never will be. Now get gone before I summon the local militia.'

For Deities' sake. We can't even make it as far as the tavern door now.

CHAPTER 24

A head of him was the Ale Trail. Behind him was the Ale Trail. The damned road seemed to stretch on forever, the monotony only broken by attacks in, or in the vicinity of, a tavern. There was no camaraderie in the group anymore. How could there be when the threat of constant—and increasingly ridiculous—attack loomed over them like a storm cloud, waiting until they let their guard down to unleash a torrential downpour.

Nicolas was struggling to comprehend how so many people could be after the same person. How many secrets did Billy actually know? Were there any or were the guilds—so many bloody guilds—just being overly cautious? And where in the double damned Underworld was Tavish? It wasn't like they'd been proceeding at a decent pace. They were stopping for a fight every other hour. Tavish could be on foot and would have caught up to them by now.

Or he's waiting in ambush on the road to Yarringsburg and has died of old age.

The world had gone insane, and he was one more tavern away from joining it. Dreamily, he had a fantasy that the next tavern would contain the elusive Maestro. Just sat there, ready to be brought to justice. Of course, the minute he saw Nicolas, the Maestro would beg for mercy, telling him exactly where to find his family so he could go home and get on with his normal life.

I'll have to kick him right in the balls first, mind. Actually, I might just unleash Silva on him. Provided she isn't—

Quickly, he banished the thought. He couldn't give in to suspicion now. Not after everything Silva had done. They'd just nearly fought a group of bards together, after all.

A knight, Sir Gerran, was above reproach too.

'I trust Silva,' he muttered to himself, trying to fan away his rising anger as he opposed the whispering in his head. 'I—'

'If it helps, I'm really sorry about this,' Billy offered, breaking the silence.

'Hmm.' Nicolas had been so lost in his own thoughts he wasn't really paying attention.

'All the guys after me,' Billy said. 'I'm sorry this has landed in your laps.'

Nicolas smiled back at him wearily. 'Don't be. It isn't your fault.' As long as he got Tavish, this would all be worth it.

I have to get him.

Billy gave him a sympathetic smile. 'I'm sure you're used to this anyway. For me, it's all new. I never thought joining up would get me in so much trouble. Who knew being friendly could be so deadly?'

'This hasn't been my life for very long at all.' Nicolas thought back. 'It's only been a couple of months.'

Billy looked surprised. 'Oh wow, I'm sorry. I know what you said the other day, but I didn't think it had been such a short time.'

Despite himself, Nicolas laughed. 'And yet it seems like an eternity.'

'Forgive me for saying,' Billy began hesitantly, 'but considering how much of the *stay-at-home type* you claim to be, you've taken to this pretty well.'

Finally, someone who got it. He sighed. 'I just got caught up in a chain of events that led me here. There's no going back now.' Deities, that was hard to even say aloud. For a moment he became hollow inside as he considered how true those last five words could be when he finally discovered the fate of his parents.

I need to know. *I need* to find Tavish. He began to cast longing glances at the roadside, as if he could simply *will* the Black Knight into appearing.

Billy looked away and shook his head slowly. 'It must be terrible to be stuck in a life you don't want. I mean, you actually died once already.'

'Technically,' he said quietly.

'Close enough, by the sound of it,' Billy replied. 'I doubt many get to walk away from Koth.' Nicolas winced at the name, letting out a gasp of shock at finally hearing it said aloud. 'And now you're forced to jump from battle to battle, trying to find your people. Trying to find a semblance of self, I suppose. You must feel so lost.'

Emotion welled inside him. 'I really do. Hablock was my world. All I ever really knew. Every time I left it, I wanted to go straight back, even when I was excited to leave. And now there is no going back. My bubble has well and truly burst. And my parents...'

'At least you have some good companions,' Billy ventured. 'Must've been comforting that you didn't venture out alone that first time.'

'We actually haven't been travelling together for long.' That seemed strange to admit. It felt like a lifetime. 'I met them just *after* I left my home.'

'Oh, so they were part of the events that led to…you know.' Billy looked almost unwilling to continue, but Nicolas nodded for him to continue. 'Your parents.'

Resentment surged in him, along with the question that had been stalking the ruins of his peaceful mind. The question posed by the demon in his dream.

Would any of this have happened if I hadn't met them?

If he'd washed up on the riverbank alone, he would've just run home, and his family would still be alive. But he *had* met Auron, who'd convinced him to go chasing hostages. Then one by one, the group had grown, until, eventually, his whole life fell apart.

Looking around, he saw Auron riding next to Billy. The spirit was frowning, his mouth half open, as if ready to say something. Instead, Auron looked away, deep in thought.

Billy wouldn't look directly at him, as if guilty. 'Sorry if I—'

Nicolas held up his hand. 'Don't worry about it.'

His trust in the others was slowly slipping away as the resentment built. He wanted to stop it, to tell it to bugger off. But it wasn't going anywhere. The whispers nagging him were not so easily silenced anymore.

And then there's that.

At the back of their group, Shift and Rex rode together. They seemed deep in hushed conversation, as per usual, interspersed with the occasional laughter. Very cosy.

Shift had been clear that the kiss meant nothing. But it was a *kiss*. How could something like that be meaningless?

'You seem angry.'

Nicolas started and nearly fell from his horse. He hadn't even realised that Silva was beside him, replacing Billy, who'd hung back and was now with Shift and Rex.

Good. He can be the third wheel that—

Silva was studying his face in a way that was very uncomfortable.

'Who do I need to kill for upsetting you?'

Without thinking, Nicolas glanced at Rex. Then he realised Silva had been joking. It was always hard to tell with her as she barely ever did it, and when she did, the delivery left something to be desired.

'No one,' he answered finally.

'Hmm.' The warrior considered this for a moment. 'When I am mad, I take out my aggression on my enemies. When there are no enemies, I chop things.'

'*Chop things.*'

'Yes,' Silva replied. 'Wood. Bad men. It is good for chasing away sadness and anger.'

His brow furrowed. He'd never considered Silva someone overly burdened by sadness. Anger, obviously. But beyond that... Though her idea actually had merit. Maybe later he'd find a tree or something and work out his issues. He needed to, before they spilled over and caused him to say things he might regret.

****

After putting some distance between them and their latest ridiculous fight, the group took a break by a stream to allow the horses to rest.

Looking at the horses lapping up the cool water, Nicolas found himself envious. Animals didn't have to worry about the mass of fear and doubt and anger besieging him right now. He had more troubles than he could count, to the point where the world beneath his very feet no longer felt right. It was as if he were Auron, walking across the ground but not touching it.

'Hopefully, we get off this damned road soon,' Shift said, lying back in the grass.

'Before we get attacked again?' Silva remarked. 'Unlikely.'

'Maybe we should leave the road completely before the next attack comes and go cross country,' Nicolas suggested. 'I'm not sure trying to find these knights is worth the hassle.'

'Hmm,' Auron said thoughtfully. 'I wouldn't. My gut is still telling me Tavish will be waiting for us, no matter what route we take to Yarringsburg.'

'Why is that a problem?' The spirit frowned at the challenge in Nicolas's voice. 'We saw him off once. I don't think it'll be a problem a second time.'

'Kid...'

The volcano of anger inside him began to rumble. 'Nicolas,' he said firmly. 'That's my name. Not *Nick*. Or *Kid*. Nicolas.'

Well, I assume I'm still Nicolas. I barely know anymore.

Shift opened their mouth to speak and Auron gestured for them to stop. Nicolas could have kissed him for that. Judging by the look on their face, he wouldn't like what was about to be said.

'Look,' Auron said softly. 'Tavish is a smart man. Ninety percent of the black armoured idiots I faced would have charged us once their minions were run through, out of some over inflated belief at their own prowess in battle. I'm not sure if it's an effect of wearing the stupid armour, or people who declare themselves *black knights* are just prone to having egos that don't match their skill set.' The spirit pursed his lips thoughtfully. 'Not Tavish. He fled. And he did so with the knowledge that we have no trouble tearing through four of his men. A smart man like that...next time he brings forty.'

'Does it make a difference?' Nicolas asked, an edge of desperation in his voice. 'We're going to get attacked again in the next hour anyway. They are literally lining up to get Billy. What are our options?' He gestured in the direction they planned to head. 'We either get ambushed again by some random idiots who may get lucky. Or we go directly toward Tavish, the enemy we actually know is coming, and we need. We use Billy to draw him out and we can finally grab him.'

Though really, we don't know anything. If he wanted Billy so badly, then why isn't he here? Why hasn't he shown up already? We could be half way to finding my family by now if he pulled his finger out of his black armoured ass.

Problem was, Billy was a beacon for trouble, and their luck would only hold out so long. So many people wanted the easy-going guy and weren't shy about coming for him. Yet the one person he wanted to come for Billy was nowhere to be seen. Surely Tavish knew that every guild and its mother was after them by now? So why wasn't he racing to claim his prize first?

'I think facing forty men without help would be quite reckless,' Garaz said.

'Hardly,' he scoffed. 'We can use the jewel and summon a giant...'

'I would be hesitant in using a magical weapon we have little knowledge of,' the orc counselled. 'We do not even know if it summons giants, or if we would need to find one first. It would be highly reckless to play with it. You of all people should know the dangers of misusing magic by now. The Big Boss gave us a prime example of that.'

No one was calling me reckless when I was using it to shoo the giant away. But when it's my idea to use it, and not theirs, suddenly it's a bad idea.

His hands began to clench and unclench as desperation to find some sort of solution burned inside him like fire in a dragon's gut. 'Well...We have Silva.'

'It is true. I am just a weapon to be unleashed. Nicolas points and tells me who and who not to kill.'

It took Nicolas a good couple of seconds to get over the surprise of Silva's words.

For Deities' sake.

They were getting attacked left right and centre, and instead of coming together like they had in the past, the group seemed to be fracturing more and more. With every passing hour he felt more alone. The doubts and suspicions that he had initially written off as nonsense were becoming a constant and insistent chatter in the back of his mind.

But I need Tavish. It's the only way I can be sure. I need to know if they're alive, or...

For a moment time slowed and the world around him became disorientated, as if he randomly entered a trancelike state. Images of everything that had happened flashed before him. There were surrounding him. Closing in on him. Beyond them he could see his companions through the haze, distant, and growing more so.

If I don't get Tavish. I don't get my answers. But we can't walk into a battle outnumbered. What do we do? What do we do? Please...I need an answer...

'Nick...' Shift's voice was distant.

'Silva knows.'

The voice of the demon came to him, inspiring an idea. One that may help them get his answers *and* save them having to fight forty odd enemies – or whatever random nonsense the Ale Trail threw at them next.

CHAPTER 25

Reality slid back into place, but the idea still clear in his mind. It was perfect. He could get the answers he needed, or at least find another path to take to get to them, and they wouldn't have to fight an army to do it.

And it's right here in front of me.

Silva frowned as he stared at her. 'What?' she asked in her usual blunt manner.

'Your mind,' he said absentmindedly.

The warrior looked confused.

'A lot of people have come for Billy, but Tavish isn't amongst them,' Nicolas began. 'Finding him was the whole point of this. But maybe we don't need to. The answer we need could be right there, in your mind.'

On the list of nefarious deeds Silva had been part of in her shadowed past, one of the most prominent was being in the service of the necromancer, Avus Arex. Except she hadn't been. Instead, she'd been in the employ of whatever organisation was causing all this mess in Etherius. She claimed her memory had been damaged due to drowning, which had happened because of Nicolas, but he'd recently learned that part of the warrior's mind had been magically sealed—the part that contained the information about her employers. She knew something that might be the key to all of this.

Silva seemed unusually uncomfortable. 'I...don't know.'

I beg your pardon?

'What?' He knew his tone was snappy, but he couldn't help it. 'I thought you wanted to help?'

'I do, but—'

'But what?' He scoffed. 'After you let Tavish escape, I thought you might want to do something else to actually help our quest?'

The warrior squared up to him, but he didn't back down. '*Let* him escape?' Her tone was filled with warning. Too bad.

'I thought you wanted to atone for your sins?'

Her gaze was furious, but then, so was his.

'Guys, let's calm down.' Shift got themselves between Nicolas and Silva, pushing them apart.

'No, actually, I won't,' he said. Shift looked at him in surprise. 'I need to find my family. I need to know if they're alive or dead. She knows something and is reluctant to share it. Suspiciously reluctant.'

Shift glared at him indignantly. 'Now, wait a—'

'Kid, no one said your family's dead,' Auron interrupted. 'There were no bodies.'

'Why burn down the house of someone you aren't killing? Maybe they got away and were hunted down and killed? What do you know for sure? Or do you have some kind of story that's relevant?'

Auron's brow darkened. 'Kid—'

'It is okay.' Silva put a hand on Shift's shoulder and held the other toward the spirit to calm him. 'He is right.'

As satisfied as he was at the validation, he couldn't ignore the guilt. He knew exactly why she was hesitant. The warrior was concerned that unlocking that memory might somehow unlock her past self. But he had no other hope. This had to work.

'I will do it,' Silva confirmed.

A big part of him wanted to tell her not to. Instead, he said, 'Okay then.'

Garaz, who was watching the conversation carefully, raised an eyebrow as Nicolas gestured for him to come over.

'You summoned me?' It was delivered in a very snide tone. Yellow eyes regarded him from beneath a furrowed brow. What was his problem?

Actually, he didn't care. Whatever it was, it wasn't productive, and he needed Garaz productive. 'I need you to do your thing.'

'*Do my thing*?' the orc repeated as if somehow confused by quite a simple sentence.

Or maybe I've just started speaking dwarfish?

'Silva has some information in her brain, and we need it,' he continued. He wasn't about to let a snarky tone put him off. 'So you need to use your magic to unlock it.'

'Just like that.' *Was* he speaking a different language? 'I would advise against it.'

'Why?'

Garaz pursed his lips. It looked like he was summoning his patience. It was nice he had some left. 'Because part of her mind has been closed off by some very powerful magic.'

'And it's the mind. Just heal it.'

'*Just heal it*?'Garaz scrunched his face up. It could either have been through confusion or annoyance. 'I forget that you do not know how magic works.'

Why was this so difficult? 'Look, if you would just stop sulking for ten minutes—'

Garaz looked affronted. 'I beg your pardon?'

'Kid—' Auron began warily.

'I'm not a kid. I don't know how many times I need to repeat it,' he cut in sharply. 'And no, I don't know magic. But I know when someone is prepared to try.'

The orc closed his eyes and took a deep breath before he spoke again. 'If I just go poking at whatever spell has been cast on her, I may inadvertently damage her mind.'

'That's a risk I'm willing to take,' Silva said solemnly. 'Apparently, some trust needs to be earned, and if this helps our quest then so be it.'

'Hey,' Shift said, 'you don't have to do this.'

'I am willing.'

I'm getting what I want, so why does it feel so wrong?

Without further comment, Silva sat on the grass. With a huff, Garaz walked behind her, shaking his head and muttering to himself. Nicolas caught the word *idiot*. Undoubtedly directed at him, and possibly deserved.

Moving with petulant slowness, Garaz lowered himself to the ground in a cross-legged position behind Silva.

The orc held Nicolas's gaze with disappointed yellow eyes. 'I will say one last time that I disagree with this.'

Nicolas wanted to scream at the orc, but just managed to close his lips before the words spilled out. Instead, he took a moment to compose himself before answering. 'Noted.'

He looked at Silva. If the warrior refused, called it off, his rage would be overwhelming. Yet part of his mind begged her to say *no*, because he couldn't.

Silva looked away from him and closed her eyes. 'Begin.'

His stomach sank, but still he said nothing.

Garaz closed his eyes too and chanted under his breath. Slowly, his hands glowed with white light as his magic manifested. His bright palms were interspersed with yellow twinkling lights, almost like small shooting stars, there one moment and gone an instant later. The orc placed his large green hands on either side of Silva's head, looking like he could squash it like a grape. Nicolas hoped nothing went wrong. He was not at all proud of himself right now.

For a few moments there was nothing then Silva's face twitched uncomfortably.

Come on.

Beads of sweat formed on her brow, and Garaz's lips moved as if he were reading something he didn't like.

Come on.

Silva let out a sudden gasp of pain, echoed by a wince on Garaz's face.

Come on.

Slowly, the warrior's face contorted as if she were in terrible pain. Her teeth clenched and her face reddened under the strain, and thick veins appeared on her temples. Garaz's face creased with determined effort, beginning to show the same signs of discomfort as Silva's.

Come on.

Silva screamed.

'Enough.' Shift grabbed Garaz's hands and pulled them away. The spell broken, both the orc and the warrior fell to the ground, panting heavily.

Nicolas ran to Silva, reaching out for her arm to help her. She jerked it back from him, avoiding his eyes.

Garaz, however, had no trouble glaring at him with red tinted eyes.

He needed to ask a question. He really didn't want to, but this couldn't have been for nothing. 'Anything?'

For a moment, Nicolas was certain the orc was about to jump up and rip his head from his shoulders. But instead Garaz shook his head slowly.

Why is everything failing? Why is every opportunity to find the information I need slipping through my fingers?

Somehow, that desparation became anger, and he rounded on Shift. 'What did you do?' he cried. 'If you hadn't interfered, it might've worked.'

'What did *I* do?' Shift scoffed. 'What are *you* doing? They were getting hurt.'

'We were about to get answers.'

'Not like that.' Shift gestured to their two companions. Both seemed weak as they lay on the grass.

'Maybe you—'

Rex took a hesitant step forward. 'Perhaps if you calm down a minute—'

Nicolas had a moment of confusion. *Who asked Rex a Deities' damned thing?* 'I'm sorry, who are you again?' he asked incredulously.

Rex raised his hands in peace as Shift got in Nicolas's face. 'He's my friend,' they told him. 'That's all you need to know.'

Oh, friend, is it? He bit back the words before they left his mouth.

'And Silva is your friend,' Auron said at his side.

The warrior was rubbing her temple tenderly, her skin pale and drenched in sweat. The arm she'd used to prop herself up was shaking.

'Happy?' Garaz asked as he rose with difficulty and went to the warrior's side. Even as he looked away from Nicolas to check on Silva, his disappointment was clear.

As the orc checked on Silva, Nicolas stared at the warrior. Usually so mighty and proud, she was now drained and hurting.

Because of me.

He took an involuntary step back as he replayed the last few minutes in his mind.

What did I just do?

All the times Silva had been there for him, saved him, and he was happy to question her, to put her in a position that caused her pain.

This isn't me.

A voice in his head insisted that he'd been right. But he hadn't been. Not at all.

What did *come back from the Underworld?*

He quickly dismissed the thought. He was responsible for his actions. He couldn't try and blame it on some notion that he may be a zombie, or had lost his soul. He'd spent all this time doing the right thing. Yet somehow he acted like *this*.

'I'm...sorry.'

'There are only so many times you can say sorry,' Shift retorted angrily. 'It's starting not to mean anything.'

No one seemed open to accepting his apology. Silva met his eyes—only for a second, but the look of sadness and regret she'd given him lingered. Nicolas wanted the ground to swallow him whole.

'Don't worry,' Shift hissed in his ear spitefully. 'You've still got your *bait*.'

His mouth opened and closed like an aghast fish. 'I'm...I...you what?'

The shapeshifter shook their head. 'You said it yourself. We can *use* Billy to get Tavish. That is pretty much the definition of bait.'

Billy? Bait? No, that's not right at all. That isn't what he is...

He shook his head. What was he becoming? What were they all becoming?

I really am alone, aren't I?

CHAPTER 26

She may still look pale, shaky and weak, but Silva was her usual determined—or stubborn—self and insisted they continue. Though her logic couldn't be faulted. It didn't pay to dally when half of Etherius was after them. And only a couple of days ago, capturing Alric Tavish had seemed so simple.

At least they'd be off this thrice-damned road soon enough, knights or no knights. With so many people after Billy, the castle was the best option for his protection, and Auron had assured them that a major road leading to it was close. The general hope was that everyone would assume they'd keep following the Ale Trail, and they could lose some of their pursuers or dodge the upcoming ambushes. That would let them focus on the black knight. If they could pull themselves together enough to fight him and whatever he had in store.

Once – in reality *if* – they made it to Yarringsburg, King Elric would keep Billy and his jewel safe, surrounding both with an army. Of course, with their luck, it would turn out that Billy was a member of the Guild of City Soldiers, or something equally ridiculous, and they'd end up having to fight off the whole army. Most likely in a tavern.

Maybe we should get the bards back. That last stand would make an epic poem.

No, they were jackasses.

And all of that assumed they made it that far, as the Ale Trail appeared never to end.

Maybe I am still dead, and this is Sha'then's torture, making me ride eternally up this bloody road, picking fights in taverns and falling out with my friends.

Friends. Were any of them that anymore? They were still travelling together, but that was about it. The discord in the group was a giant blanket, smothering them. The only time they seemed to come together was in a fight. Billy was the exception, of course, currently riding beside Silva, chatting away merrily.

I wish I was as oblivious to it all as he is.

He took in each of his companions in turn. Whatever turmoil had gripped him earlier was loosening its hold. Sadness and shame crept in, and a longing to reach out to them, to make things right. But every time he opened his mouth to say something, the whispering voices grew louder, drowning out thoughts of apology.

'Another tavern up ahead,' Silva called from the front.

There were several groans from the group, Nicolas's included.

The warrior looked back and caught his eye briefly. Despite the brave face she was putting on, it was obvious she was still suffering the effects of Garaz's spell.

Nicolas was too, but in a different way.

With their recent experience in taverns so fresh in all their minds, the group all drew their weapons. Though *tavern* was a stretch. It barely looked like a building at all. The shack was slightly askew, as if one half-assed gust of wind might blow it over. The wooden walls were pockmarked with gaps, mould and cobwebs. *Rickety* was the best way to describe it. A mangey old nag surrounded by flies was hitched to a worn post outside. Eating in this *establishment* was right out of the question. And with recent events, even entering it was right out of the question. Nicolas was sure no self respecting knight would be caught dead here.

'Let's keep going,' Nicolas called.

The group had agreed to avoid these places like the plague...something it looked like you might actually catch if you dined here. The only exception would be if there was a hint of the waiting escort that Nicolas was now sure was a figment of all their imaginations.

'As you wish.' Silva's tone made him frown. It had hardly been a command.

'The Rat's Tail,' Shift read from the sign as they rode past. 'Even the name of the place doesn't sound inviting.'

Sounded accurate, though.

The group kept a suspicious eye on the tavern as they continued onward, muscles tense and prepared for the inevitable demon horde about to pour from it because Billy was a member of the Demons of Etherius Guild. The thought of a demon sent a shudder down Nicolas's spine, remembering the abomination who'd killed him.

Light flashed, and he winced reflexively closing his eyes. He managed to pry them open again in time to see The Rat's Tail explode in a ball of blue flame. His horse reared, throwing him from the saddle just as the concussive force of the blast reached him. A vertical trip through the air became a horizontal one as he was caught mid-air and propelled backwards, surrounded by jagged shards of wood, any one of which could impale him at any moment.

Gravity reasserted itself, and he crashed to the ground, rolling heavily across the road before ending up staring at the sky. His ears rang and his eyes struggled to focus. Blurred images slowly pressed together to become one, and his sense of self returned, along with the realisation that he had just been thrown from his horse. With an anxious cry he patted himself down, expecting to see at least one shard of wood jutting out of his body. What followed was a heartfelt sigh of relief.

I got lucky.

Which is more than could be said for the tavern. The Rat's Tail was a smoking ruin. Several blackened stumps of wood protruded stubbornly from the ground where it had once kind of stood. A couple were still edged in blue flame.

'Oh, come on,' he faintly heard himself cry. 'We weren't even going *in* that one.'

Hang on...the others...

His desperate attempt to search for his companions was hampered by the fact his head moved as if it were underwater. But his worry for them made him push through the feeling. Bodies lay on the ground around him. Auron, a blurry light to Nicolas, was moving from one to the other. Some were stirring. As the spirit's form finally became clear, he looked directly at Nicolas, his ethereal features creased with concern. Nicolas held up a thumb, and Auron smiled with relief. Nicolas cast a gaze to the others, and his companion confirmed with a nod that they were well.

Thank the Deities, if I lost them...

Shaking off the last of the dizziness, he forced himself to his feet. Every single joint protested the motion, but otherwise, he appeared unscathed.

Where's my sword?

Luckily, it hadn't gone far. He picked the *Dawn Blade* up, shaking off the dirt and debris that'd covered it. This one he surely couldn't be blamed for. He'd been blown off his horse, after all. As he rose, he took one last look at the destroyed tavern, saying a prayer for any souls that'd been in there. Judging from the state of the place, he doubted they had many customers, but any loss of life was a tragedy. Then his eyes caught the old horse that had been tied up outside. The poor creature got a prayer too. As far as he could tell, their mounts had bolted when the place exploded. Thank the Deities.

Then a realisation hit him.

Taverns don't spontaneously explode.

Instantly, he was in a fighting stance, sword ready.

There was a flash of light. It passed me.

It had been quick, but he remembered it, and the direction from which it'd come. Tracing it back, he saw four figures emerging from the bushes on the far side of the road.

Long robes. Stars and runic symbols. Oh crap, wizards.

That was a whole new type of opponent and potentially much more dangerous. One could throw lightning or whatever that had been, but what about the other three? Wizards specialised in schools of magic and right now he had no idea what they could do, making them potentially more dangerous than the lightning thrower.

'Hang on a minute,' he said, shakily pointing the *Dawn Blade* toward the centre of the quartet. 'I know you.' The name wasn't coming right away, but it was on the tip of his tongue, but seemed to dance away the moment he tried to say it. It still wasn't easy to think straight. Though he did know this was a bad guy.

Now I remember. The faun's ship.

'Hello, pest.' The wizard sneered.

Oleg Hobrath.

The name came to mind the minute the wizard spoke, as did the memories. He was part of the same organisation as Tavish. They'd crossed paths when Oleg had been part of the faun's plan to start a war between the Kingdom of Merida and the undersea Tidal Kingdom. That plan had been foiled and the faun killed, but Oleg had somehow gotten away. But Nicolas had been aware of the wizard before then. When first captured by the insane necromancer, Avus Arex, he was due to be tortured by a man called Old Hob, which, according to Garaz, had been the wizard's nickname at the Academy of Magic, due to his hair greying at such a young age. Now it appeared to be retreating from his forehead. And that wasn't the only thing different about him.

'Didn't you have two eyes the last time I saw you?' Nicolas asked, squinting at the wizard in confusion. 'We only met briefly, but I'm sure you had two.' Not that he really cared, beyond possibly wanting to congratulate the person who'd taken it.

Oleg gently caressed the skin around the milky orb that had once been an eye. 'This was because of you,' he snarled. 'Penance for Merida. The Maestro doesn't take kindly to failure.'

Maestro.

Suddenly, Nicolas's senses were fully restored, as if a lightning bolt had struck him. Of course. This guy knew the Maestro. He could lead Nicolas to him. This was his chance. No more worrying about where Tavish was. Oleg was here. Now.

'I was told you were off limits at the moment,' Oleg continued. 'But when I heard that the great *Nick Carnage* was escorting Billy…Well, I just couldn't resist a little payback. I'll do penance for it later.'

What? Off limits? What does that mean?

'Are you sure, given your last…penance?'

'I'll just make sure I enjoy this enough to *make* it worth it.' Oleg smiled evilly.

Okay, Nicolas had a massive opportunity here. But he was also facing four wizards. This was going to be tricky. Or, more likely, pretty damned deadly.

Luckily, he wasn't alone.

'Oleg!' came the menacing rumble of a familiar voice behind him.

Garaz was rising, framed by the remnants of the burning building, and he was mad. The pair had been feuding since their time together in the Academy of Magic. Apparently, Oleg took exception to non-humans entering the Academy, an orc worst of all. The white-haired wizard had made it his business to try to drive Garaz out.

'*You*,' Oleg sneered. 'You're as persistent as a tick on a troll, aren't you?'

Garaz smiled, though there was no happiness in his red-tinted eyes. 'If by that, you suggest that I do not allow myself to be pushed around by low men with small-minded ideas, then you are correct.'

'I should've just killed you when I had the chance.' The wizard snorted.

'That would require bravery beyond a hedge-born knave such as your-self.'

Whoa. That was a verbal slap to the face. Oleg flinched, and even Nicolas felt dirty hearing it. It wasn't like Garaz to talk like that. He must *really* hate Oleg.

'How dare you?' Old Hob looked flustered. 'You…you…green monstros-ity.'

'I think you broke him with your words,' Auron said from Nicolas's side.

'And now I shall break his body as well.' With a roar, Garaz dropped to a knee, scooping up his staff and swinging it forwards. When it was level with Oleg, a bright fireball launched in the wizard's direction. It passed so close to Nicolas that hairs were almost certainly singed.

What happened next was so quick he nearly missed it. At the last second before the fireball hit home, Oleg put his hands out before him, creating a shield of energy. The fireball struck it and exploded in a bright flash. Once the flash receded, though it left its imprint on Nicolas's retina, all that stood where it had hit was a smoking crater. Oleg and the others were gone.

No. They can't be gone. I need Oleg. He has to be here somewhere.

'On your left,' Auron shouted.

The spirit was right. The group of wizards were somehow down the track a little way from where they had been.

Nicolas looked around in surprise. 'How did they manage that?'

'It's called *magic,* kid,' came the response, with no shortage of sarcasm.

There was another flash, and Garaz threw himself aside. The fork of lightning only missed the orc by a split second. Smoke trailed from the earth where it had struck.

This was the problem. How was he going to get Oleg alive when he could lob lightning all over the place and miraculously transport himself? The solution came to Nicolas so quickly that he surprised himself. Garaz had taught him that magic wasn't an inexhaustible or far-reaching power. Indeed, it was limited by the amount of energy a wizard could produce, which was why most wizards specialised in just one or two schools of magic. Over-exertion with their powers required them to recharge.

All they had to do was keep this battle going long enough, and Oleg would wear himself out. But there was another concern...

'Don't kill him,' Nicolas shouted to Garaz. 'We need him alive.'

'Then you had best get to him before I,' the orc retorted, throwing another fireball. Why was he being such an ass?

Oleg turned towards him, arms outstretched. The time for questions was over. Nicolas dived aside at the last second, lightning scorching the dirt where he'd stood.

'Die,' Oleg screamed, eyes bulging as he tracked Nicolas's rolling body with several more shots, until Garaz got the wizard's attention with a near-missing fireball.

As Oleg and Garaz duked it out with elemental powers, Nicolas ran a wide circle around the wizard, intent on striking him from behind.

He was just passing Silva, who was groggily rising to her feet, when a flash of movement in his peripheral vision caught his eye. Instinctively, he grabbed Silva's head and forced it down. The sword passed where her neck had only just been.

The turbaned wizard hissed at him and exclaimed something in an unfamiliar language that was clearly a curse. Then, with a puff of smoke, he vanished, just as Nicolas was about to run him through.

Unsure where the wizard had gone, Nicolas spun around fearfully. As he did, the tip of the *Dawn Blade* slashed a sword-wielding hand just as it re-materialized at his side. The turbaned wizard cried out in pain before vanishing again, minus his curved blade, which now lay on the floor. Nicolas kept turning, looking for the next attack. This was getting old fast.

'I will—' Silva's words were cut off as the wizard appeared again and struck her in the back of the head. The warrior fell to the ground.

'Ha-ha.' With a puff of smoke, the teleporting wizard appeared at his side.

Nicolas didn't block the punch to his jaw quickly enough. The wizard disappeared again even as he reeled from the blow, staggering to the side as the turbaned menace appeared on his other side and punched him again.

Thank the Deities he practised his magic more than his punching.

Aware of smoke to his left, Nicolas swung his sword, but the wizard was gone as quickly as he'd appeared. A blast of smoke directly in front of him stung his eyes, blinding him. The fist emerging from it made his face sting even more. Nothing was broken, but it hurt like crazy as he stumbled backwards.

'Kid,' Auron shouted in a commanding voice. 'Position nine.'

Letting his training take over, Nicolas obeyed the command, switching the *Dawn Blade* to a reverse grip and thrusting it under his arm just as the wizard appeared behind him. The sword didn't stab the wizard. Instead, he appeared *on* the blade. As Nicolas turned slowly, the wizard stared down at the sword protruding from his stomach with wide eyes, realising that he was dead. The turbaned head shook in disbelief. The wizard held a raised knife in his hand, ready to cut his throat.

He was a bad guy, and he was going to kill you, he told his rising panic.

He was only just getting used to killing, but he understood the necessity now. There were too many bad people out there for him to keep staying his hand. And any ally of Oleg's *had* to be bad.

Slowly, the wizard pulled back his knife hand, as if he thought he could still kill Nicolas before his death finally caught up with him.

With one fluid motion, Nicolas withdrew the sword. The wizard grunted in pain, spitting blood onto Nicolas's cheek as it also poured freely from the now-open wound in his stomach.

I'm not going to throw up. I'm not going to throw up.

He was successful...just. The wizard collapsed.

'Teleporters,' Auron scoffed. 'Always think it's original to appear directly behind you...'

'Dathran!'

Nicolas fought the urge to apologise as he saw the third wizard staring in disbelief at his dead companion. He had to stop saying sorry to the bad guys. The wizard looked down grimly. When he looked back up again, his eyes were green and animalistic. He opened his mouth, displaying rows of thick fangs, and he began to change. Hair sprouted from his body. Bones snapped. Muscles expanded. The sound of clothes ripping was just about audible over the ongoing duel between Oleg and Garaz. As the last of his ruined clothes fell from his body, the wolf stood on four legs, fully formed, before unleashing a feral howl.

That's a big wolf.

The creature snarled at him, clearly readying itself to strike. He didn't want to fight a wolf. Looking back, he saw Silva still unconscious on the floor. Garaz was busy, and Deities knew where the others were. So...he was fighting a wolf. Shakily, he readied himself to stand against the creature, almost jumping when a hand touched his shoulder.

Behind him, Shift looked battered and bruised and, most of all, angry. 'I've got this one,' they said confidently, before turning toward the wolf wizard. 'Big wolf.' They nodded with pursed lips. 'Decent, but still amateurish. Allow me to school you in the art of shapeshifting.'

Nicolas looked away as Shift's clothes tore apart, unable to contain the muscles growing beneath them. By now he'd seen Shift change enough times to know when it was safe to look back. What stood beside him now was a giant, slavering wolf monster that made the other wolf look like a puppy. Fangs like daggers were displayed as wolf-Shift snarled at their already whimpering opponent. The wizard tucked his tail between his legs and fled, badly out-wolfed. Shift charged in pursuit.

A flash of movement caught his eye, and he blocked the incoming blade just in time. Another wizard was coming at him, and this one had a twirled moustache and four arms of blue energy growing out of his back, to add to the two the Deities had given him. Each was holding a sword. All six blades stabbed at him as one. He intercepted three of the swords, and Silva was kind enough—and timely enough—to block the other three.

'Go,' she said firmly, keeping her eyes on the wizard. 'This one is mine.'

Good, I can focus on Oleg.

That turned out to be quite difficult, because of the fire versus lightning light show. Garaz was using the staff gifted to him by T'goth to great effect, casting shields of flame he'd never seen before. It must've been an equaliser, because Garaz was still a novice when it came to combat magic, and fighting a well-trained battle wizard had to be a struggle.

But they were both tiring. He could see the effort it was costing them to throw their spells and defend against oncoming ones.

We're going to get him.

Nicolas started slightly as a wolf's head appeared at his side.

'That was quick,' he remarked, trying not to focus on their blood-covered snout and whatever was between their teeth. They were a great ally but damned terrifying all the same.

Silva appeared at his other side, rubbing the back of her head and looking ready to tear someone else's off. Shocked by how quickly she'd dispatched her multi-armed opponent, he couldn't help but look. The wizard lay dead on the grass. He'd gone from six arms to none.

We're definitely going to get him.

Oleg glared at each of them in turn, most likely coming to the same conclusion as Nicolas. The wizard was pale and shaky from the exertion of the fight. In fact, he looked close to having a heart attack. Not wanting to give him the option of dying before he got some answers, Nicolas charged, the others following in his wake

Oleg hurled one last lightning bolt at Garaz before stretching his hands high into the air, fingertips splayed. Despite his need to get Oleg, he found himself stopping. The wizard's arms shook as if he were holding a giant log over his head.

With a cry that was half exertion and half pain, Oleg threw his hands forwards. A wall of lightning struck the ground around them, blinding them with light and knocking them backwards, sending a tsunami of dirt over them all.

As the light receded, Nicolas jumped up, dirt crumbling off him.

Oleg was gone.

'Noooo!' Nicolas and Garaz cried in unison.

CHAPTER 27

Despite looking as if he could barely stand, Garaz did an excellent job of hauling Billy from the ground and slamming him into the nearest tree, one-handed. The orc glared at Billy, looking even more menacing with the smoke rising from his singed cloak.

'*You* are part of the Guild of Magic?' he snarled right into the skinny man's face.

'I...I...like to sign up for stuff.' Billy looked terrified, and he was right to be.

'Preposterous. You don't even know magic. *Do you?*' It was an accusation, not a question.

Still, Billy shook his head in response.

Garaz looked even more riled up, though he must've known the answer. 'How dare you sully the guild with your presence, *layman.*'

Silva and Auron seemed too dumbfounded by what they were seeing to act, and Shift had disappeared somewhere. Someone had to step in before things got worse.

'Hey.' Nicolas grabbed one of the orc's arms. As Garaz's face swung towards him, Nicolas became less clear about his course of action. 'Just...um...calm down.'

From the look in the orc's eyes, that was entirely the wrong thing to say. 'No,' Garaz rumbled from beneath a hooded brow. 'I am tired of this assassin beacon and his nonsense. He brings all Etherius down on us because he likes to *join things*. Ridiculous.'

'You can't go acting like—'

'*An animal?*' Garaz snarled furiously. 'Why not? That is what you all think of me. Just another orc animal. Violent and primitive.'

'What? No.' Nicolas scoffed. 'I don't even know where you got that stupid idea.'

'You deny it?' the orc challenged.

'I certainly do,' he protested. 'I also challenge your treatment of Billy.'

'He can't help it that people are after him.' At least Auron was finally backing him up. 'Are you really going to blame him for something that isn't his doing? Besides, this isn't about him. This is about you and Oleg.' The orc snorted at the name. Auron continued, 'You'll get another chance. Don't let that dick of a wizard make you do something you'll regret.'

Garaz met Nicolas's eyes, and he could see the orc's mind working, coming to see his reasoning. Finally, with a roar of frustration, he let Billy go and stormed off. 'This is not what I was supposed to be doing.' Garaz appeared to be talking to himself more than anyone else.

What in the Underworld was all that about?

'Oi.' His attention turned to Shift, who was half-concealed behind a thorny bush. What were they doing over—? 'Clothes, please.' Never mind.

He looked around for Shift's horse. Unfortunately, it had bolted, just like the others, taking a portion of their supplies with them. At least they had their discarded packs, one of which had some of Shift's spare clothes in it.

Once that was done, he turned his attention to Billy. 'You okay?'

'I think so.' Billy smiled nervously, rubbing his neck. 'That was intense.'

It certainly was. 'I'm sorry about that... He isn't normally like that.'

His companion didn't seem convinced.

'He's more like that lately.' Wow, Shift could get dressed quickly.

They seemed to pick up on Nicolas's expression. 'Putting clothes on in a hurry is a well-practised skill.' Their face wrinkled in disgust as their tongue played around their teeth. Eventually, they spat out a tuft of fur. 'I hate fighting as an animal,' they declared. 'Too much biting.'

Between the pair, they helped Billy to his feet. 'I know you said Garaz had been acting weird lately,' Nicolas began, keeping one eye on the orc, 'but I didn't think he was that bad.'

'He's getting worse,' Shift said grimly. 'I don't even know about the animal stuff. But he's been off ever since that business in Hablock. In truth, he hasn't been himself since the freighter.'

'What do you mean?' At least he finally had a good excuse for his ignorance, having been dead at the time. Someone had mentioned...something, but he'd been attacked, like, seven times since then.

'Remember I said a group of orcs came after us in Hablock?' Shift said in a low voice. 'Well, it was Garaz specifically. It looked personal, a grudge of some kind. Garaz seemed reluctant to fight, but when I was in danger, he finally went for the lead orc, Shagraz.'

'Did Garaz kill him?'

'No, the zombies—'

'Shades,' Nicolas corrected.

Shift's eyes told him their opinion of his interruption. 'The *shades* from our old buddy Avus did. I never thought I'd be thankful for the necromancer.' Shift looked hesitant for a moment, as if unwilling to continue. 'But what he did kill was that toad butler that hung out with the faun.'

Just the memory of the—now-deceased—faun sent a tingle through the lash marks on Nicolas's back. He clearly remembered the toad butler that had followed the faun around, but he'd lost track of it when fighting the faun one-on-one.

After a moment's thought, Shift continued. 'Garaz didn't just kill it. He ripped it in two. I...I was surprised.'

'It was a bad guy in a fight,' Nicolas offered. 'He ripped the head off a vampire before.'

'True.' Shift looked annoyed, as if frustrated they weren't getting their point across. 'Don't get me wrong, I'm all for making sure my enemies don't have the chance to demand a second round, but I've not seen *him* like...*that* before. It was different.'

'Perhaps doing what we're doing is changing him.' Nicolas stopped himself before he said, *'Just like me.'* Just like all of them, in fact.

For a moment, Shift held his gaze, giving him a sympathetic smile that said they'd heard what he hadn't said.

'Orcs really don't have a good reputation.' Billy was looking fearfully towards the red-cloaked orc, who was now leaning on a tree, muttering to himself. 'And for plenty of good reasons. But, I mean, you guys can vouch for him, right?'

Could they anymore? Nicolas wasn't sure; he was just glad Silva was keeping herself casually between Garaz and the rest of them.

He certainly acted like an animal just now.

As much as he hated the idea, Nicolas had to admit that Billy had a point. How well did he *really* know Garaz? Auron came to stand beside him, looking thoughtfully, not at Garaz but at him. He gave Auron a questioning look, but the spirit moved away without answering.

'I think we need to be careful from here on out.' Nicolas hoped his implication wasn't lost on Shift. From the look on their face, it wasn't.

As he turned back to Billy, his hand accidentally brushed Shift's. They yanked their hand back as if he'd set them on fire. He closed his eyes for a second, not wanting to watch them walk away.

Just friends. I get it. I don't have the plague.

'That was awkward,' Billy said, sucking his teeth slightly.

That was certainly the truth of it. Part of him wished he could turn back time and stop the kiss before it happened, but he knew he would regret it if he did. He also knew that if he did turn back time, that wasn't the point he'd go back to.

Billy put a hand on his shoulder. 'I don't have much experience with women—'

'Shift isn't a woman,' he cut in quickly, and defensively enough that it surprised him.

What have they told me about defending their honour?

Personally, he doubted Billy had much experience with women. Though if a group of prostitutes with knives appeared saying that Billy was part of the Whores and Lap Dancers Guild and they wanted to stop him revealing their secrets, he wouldn't be even slightly surprised.

'Sorry,' Billy continued. 'But they're probably just making sure he doesn't think you two are up to anything.'

Who?

Frowning, he turned toward Shift, who punched Rex playfully on the shoulder, exchanging some joke or other. His fist closed as he imagined punching Rex himself.

How can they be so blatant about it after they kissed me?

Anger at Rex became anger at Shift. They were playing games with him, messing with his head. He'd been through enough already without being made a fool of by them. The sudden thought of redirecting the punch his mind had thrown at Rex to Shift shocked him. So much so that he forced his clenched fist open, splaying his fingers and trying to calm himself before he did something stupid.

Which is getting increasingly harder of late.

****

After half an hour, everyone seemed to have calmed down slightly. Nicolas was trying his best to put it all down to the stress of the previous fights, and this ridiculous situation. But it sounded hollow. It just wasn't him...and yet it kept happening.

Hanging around the site of our recent fight probably isn't helping either.

Truthfully, they should've left earlier. The column of smoke thrown up by the ruined building had basically been a giant beacon calling to all those after Billy. It was only a matter of time. Nicolas didn't know who would come, but he highly doubted it'd be Tavish.

Unfortunately, they were now horseless—their attempts to track down their mounts had proven fruitless—so wherever they went, it'd be at a slower pace. As uncomfortable as he'd been at the start, he soon found himself missing Vigour.

There were plenty of passers-by, but, unsurprisingly, no one was open to offering a lift to the six battered people sat in front of a ruined tavern surrounded by bodies.

'We can't stay here any longer,' he said as another wagon made a show of not speeding up as it sped up to pass them.

'True enough,' Silva confirmed. 'As much as people are keeping away from us, there are some out there who actually seek us.'

Too many, in Nicolas's opinion. Garaz had been right about one thing: Billy's guild memberships were ridiculous. Their need to get to Yarringsburg became more urgent every time another random group came out of the woodwork.

'To the Underworld with it,' Auron said. 'We need to get off this road now. The escort can go hang. They're probably back at the castle by now anyway. Or dead in some daft tavern fight.'

Getting off the Ale Trail would be nice. It was fast becoming the trail of death. Plus they may actually come across Alric sodding Tavish.

Whatever he brings with him can't be worse than this lot.

Nicolas had faced a lot of crazy magic and a lot of monsters on his short adventuring career so far. But humans were turning out to be a greater threat – and more irksome – than any of them.

And I fought the legions of the dead.

'Cutting across country would be best,' Shift said. 'We go across the fields and break out on the main road to the city. I know we said we'd be more likely to walk into a bigger ambush on the way to the castle, but,' they gestured to the ruined tavern, 'it isn't like we aren't getting ambushed already.'

The side-eyed look Shift gave him that contained an unspoken *'but you'll be happy about that as you're getting exactly what you want'* drove a sword of guilt right into his gut.

'Let's just go for it.' Auron nodded.

'Hopefully, everyone will think we're sticking to the main route.' Nicolas was very close to never going into another tavern again. Ever.

I'm definitely giving this bloody road a wide berth in the future.

'Maybe we'll stick out less walking,' Shift suggested. 'And at least we don't have to hear Nick's grumbling about being on a horse.'

'I haven't been grumbling.' He was sure of it. He'd been careful not to.

'Some do not need to speak to make their views clear.' He detected a slight smirk from Silva.

I really need to do something about my facial expressions. It'd be nice if everyone didn't know every *thought in my head just by glancing at me.*

Taking a breath, he attempted to make himself look neutral. That was the wrong word. *Casual*, was the look he was going for.

'Ah,' Auron said, studying his face with a grin. 'Not looking forward to walking again then?'

The moment of warmth, of camaraderie briefly silenced the whispering voices and for a moment, he completely forgot why he was upset with the others. Instead, he remembered what they had been all this time. His companions.

Pains in the backside though they are.

He was about to respond, most likely with a curse word, when Garaz re-joined the group. There was a tense silence. The orc's yellow eyes were firmly on his feet. His skin was a paler green and his face weary.

With an awkward cough, Garaz finally spoke. 'I am sorry.' Another cough. 'My behaviour was...unbecoming.'

On the surface, their companion appeared genuinely contrite. However, he could sense some repressed aggression beneath the words. He looked at Auron, who seemed to have noticed it too. The whispering voices returned. The only time they ever seemed to stay silent was when the group were in danger.

Shift was the first to answer. 'Don't worry about it.' They smiled. 'We all lose our head from time to time.'

'Quite,' the orc replied. 'But I should not have taken it out on Billy.' Finally, he looked at their new companion. 'You have my sincere apologies.'

'No worries, man.' Billy smiled genially. 'We all have our crazy moments.'

'Indeed.' Garaz sat heavily on the grass. 'And crazy times like these make them more frequent.'

'True enough,' Nicolas said, shaking his head. 'But you're okay?'

'I am.' The orc gave him a nod. 'Thank you.'

If we can just stick together for now, we may just make it out of this alive. What happened beyond that, he couldn't say.

CHAPTER 28

The gentle shushing noise the corn made in the light breeze was kind of calming. Or maybe it wasn't the shushing. Maybe it was the fact that no one had attacked them in the last half hour? Either way, Nicolas had almost forgotten what calm was like. If they continued this way, they might achieve some kind of milestone. No doubt the universe would fix that for them before long, when the Guild of Corn Farmers appeared with their farming implements in hand, ready to claim Billy.

At least Billy and Garaz made amends.

Or if not exactly amends, Billy was walking beside Garaz chatting away, and Garaz hadn't ripped his head off yet. As the corn husks parted in the large orc's wake, Auron, who walked beside the pair, passed right through the corn. Occasionally, an ear of corn appeared through his head, giving him, for a second, the most bizarre hairstyle.

To his left, he caught a glimpse of a face in the corn. He should've drawn his sword, but he knew who it was. To his right, another face appeared and disappeared in the waving corn. Suddenly, it was like he was moving through mud. The two faces were on his left. Part of him didn't want to look.

What if I never see them again? What if I forget their faces?

So he forced his head to turn. Through tear-filled eyes, he tried to sear their faces into his brain, so he'd always remember them, so that nothing, not even old age—if he ever reached old age—would cause the memories to fade. It was all he had left. Any trinket that might have a fond memory attached to it was reduced to ash with his home.

He had used hope to force away the grim predictions about what had happened to his parents. But the longer they travelled, and the more they fought, the more that hope was being gradually eroded, to reveal the most likely scenario. His house had been burnt down. No other home in Hablock had been. The fact there were no bodies was a mystery, but he couldn't help but believe the worst when the evidence pointed to it. It was almost like the demon had been told to do it as a warning to anyone else who would cross the Maestro.

The demon. It angered him how much power that name had over him. It angered him that these things existed at all. He'd just gotten used to a world of fauns and minotaurs and dwarves when he'd been introduced to demons.

How can the Deities allow such creatures to exist?

How can they allow tragedies like the destruction of my village?

Where was the message to the Oracle, warning me of the impending attack?

Clasping the hilt of his sword tightly, he tried to stop himself spiralling. The rage was so close to boiling over that he didn't think he could fight it back.

Shut up, Nicolas. There's nothing but sadness and anger if you let your mind wander down that road. Go somewhere better...

He couldn't immediately think of anywhere better to go. But he did remember a piece of advice that Silva had given him.

The others were ahead of him, engrossed in the way forward. Keeping his eyes on them, to ensure that no one looked back, he drew the *Dawn Blade* and cut the corn at his side. The sword whistled through the air and the stalks cracked under the force of the strike for a millisecond before they were severed in two. The husks fell to the floor beside him even as he sheathed the sword again. It helped a little, for now.

Touching his cheek, he took the tear from it onto his fingers, holding it in front of his face.

'That corn will think twice before crossing Nicolas Percival Carnegie again.'

Embarrassed, he quickly wiped his hand on his tunic. Blinking away the last of the tears, he turned to Auron. How could someone whose face was made of smoke be so expressive? Nicolas squirmed under the sympathetic gaze.

'Grief can eat you up if you let it.'

Eat what up? There wasn't anything left of him. He kept his gaze on his feet. 'I don't want to talk about it.'

'At the moment, we don't know anything for sure,' Auron said. 'But if I were you, I would probably be thinking the worst too.' That was actually comforting.

'I'm torn,' he admitted. 'I want to believe they're alive, but it's getting harder and harder. I'm already starting to grieve.'

'So this one time.' *Oh Deities, I've earned a story.* 'I was given a task I didn't want. I was asked to train some kids, some kids with skills, to become the *new generation of heroes,* or something like that. One of them was Silva.'

Despite his dearest wish that Auron would go away and leave him alone, his curiosity was piqued. Neither of them talked about their past, though it hung over them constantly.

Auron chuckled. 'They were a strange bunch. They had that troll amongst them, the one who could talk.' Nicolas wasn't used to seeing Auron so forlorn. 'I didn't want to train them. It was stupid and a waste of my time, but I didn't have much choice. So I got to work.'

'And?' Dammit, Auron had him hooked.

'I got kind of fond of them. It was only a handful of weeks, but they were an endearing bunch.' The spirit looked away. 'And when you peeled back the nonsense, their hearts were in the right place.'

'What happened to them?'

Auron's ethereal mouth became a thin line, his eyes focusing on something distant. On the past. 'They died. Vargas Quell lured them into a trap and slaughtered them.' Nicolas remembered that pony-tailed ogre's anus. Good riddance to him.

'I'm sorry.'

'They died bravely, saving some trapped villagers. In my mind, they earned their place in the guild as much as any twenty-year veteran.'

Something occurred to him. 'But Silva's still here?' Then again, the warrior wasn't easy to kill. He'd tried.

'Silva was...with me...when the group slipped away and ran off to face Vargas.' Nicolas understood the connotation of *with me* very clearly. 'By the time we got there, it was already over.' Auron's face was the very description of sadness. 'They were all dead.'

'What did you do?'

The spirit's face became grim. 'I spent four years tearing apart Vargas's network, until I got to the man himself and finished it. I did that not for me, or necessarily for them...it wasn't vengeance, you understand. I made sure that the bad people who killed them never got to hurt anyone again. I honoured their memories by defending what they stood for in life.'

'And Silva?'

Auron chuckled harshly. 'She took a different path. The guilt consumed her. She became hard and uncaring and did a lot of bad things. Ultimately, that village four years ago led to my death. If I'd only known it then...' The spirit looked Nicolas right in the eye. 'Point is, grief can affect people differently. At the moment, you're on a fence and could tip either way. You're a good kid, and a terrible thing happened to you. Terrible things are still happening to you. Don't let all this make you something you aren't. You don't think you have anything right now, but you've got us.'

Auron's words brought a very unwelcome memory to mind: the last conversation he'd had with Avus Arex, in a dream. Avus had left a message, part of his own essence, in Nicolas's mind in the event that he died, in order to point him in Tavish's direction so that the necromancer could ensure he was killed. But that wasn't the only thing he'd left there. A memory had also passed between them—the memory of Avus's great love, her mystery illness, and his desperate work to save her. His failure to save someone he cared about had taken him from the path of the healer and put him firmly on the road to becoming a maniacal necromancer.

Will I let my grief corrupt me like Avus? Like Silva?

No.

He wouldn't. He couldn't. If he became like them, it would sully the memories of those he loved, of those he was fighting for. This anger had to go. He was only hurting those around him. To the Underworld with the whispering voices.

'Okay,' he said slowly.

'Good,' Auron smiled. 'Now, as much as I appreciate what you were trying to do by cutting a swathe through some innocent crops. You know what you really need to do. You need to say that name. You need to scream it into the air and let it all out.' The spirit pointed an ethereal finger at his chest. 'Because right now, it's all in here, brewing away and making you act like a royal ass.'

The spirit had not told a single lie, and he knew it.

You can do this.

Nicolas took a deep breath.

'K—'

Ahead of them, past the closing tree line, a flock of birds rushed into the air, their noisy, urgent caws echoing across the fields. There was a bright flash.

Was that...lightning?

'Oleg,' he whispered, already running through the corn, sword drawn.

CHAPTER 29

The rest of his companions had come to a stop at the sight, save for one. As Nicolas ran through the corn, Garaz was charging forwards to his left, face set in a murderous scowl.

You aren't killing him. You can't. I need him.

And so it became a race. With Silva's calls for him to stop barely registering, he redoubled his efforts, determined to get to Oleg before Garaz.

Who's he fighting?

The thought was as faint as Silva's summons and just as easily dismissed. It didn't matter. Oleg was close, and he was occupied. That gave him a chance, and by the Deities, this time he'd make good on it.

The cornfield broke into open grass. Ahead of him, a line of trees separated their field from the next. Between the trunks, he could make out movement.

Maybe I'll be too late?

He forced his legs faster, despite the warning in his mind that if he kept up this pace he'd be in no fit state to face a rabbit, let alone a battle wizard. The tree line grew closer. He was nearly there.

As he closed on it he began to frown, his hero instincts – for want of a better term – warning him of danger. Almost in slow motion he watched the foliage ahead of him bulge, as if something was pushing against it. Reacting, he threw himself to the side just as the large figure burst through it, scattering leaves and branches everywhere in his wake as it flew through the air. Rolling on the ground, Nicolas blinked as the large shadow passed by him, before the inevitable crash to the ground, sliding as it did and tearing up the grass as it created a visible indent in the ground before it finally came to a halt.

Rising, sword ready, he looked at the smoking figure.

'Gornak?'

The warrior was unconscious, thankfully, though the heaving of his voluminous chest suggested he was alive. His skin was blackened and his chest hair singed, creating a most unpleasant odour. Deities, he had an impressive amount of chest hair.

On the other side of the warrior, Garaz caught his eye. Both of them looked towards the hole in the treeline before looking back at each other.

'Alive,' Nicolas said with determination.

The orc's answer was a snarl, which wasn't inspiring.

Will I have to take on Garaz too?

The orc still looked drained from his last encounter with Oleg, his green skin a few shades lighter than usual.

But if he's still weak then so is Oleg.

He looked back at Gornak. Surely felling that mighty warrior had required some power? There was a chance.

Provided I get to him first.

He could see the look in Garaz's eyes as they met his. The orc wanted his pound of flesh. Somehow, his companion appeared rejuvenated, and Nicolas was sure that was because Oleg, and the chance to finally defeat him, was near.

I don't think I can trust you not to kill him, can I?

At the same time, he and Garaz ran for the tree line. He was surely faster than Garaz, but the orc had no intention of playing fair, barging straight into him and knocking him back to the ground. He cursed, a lot, picking himself up even as the orc jumped through the hole.

'*You!*' The sneering exclamation came just before the first bang, which backlit the trees like a rising sun.

He was just about to get up and throw himself into the fray when a groaning from behind him caught his attention. Gornak was stirring.

Dammit.

As much as he wanted to get to Oleg—he found himself jogging over to the semi-conscious warrior.

'Gornak?' he asked softly. Really, this man wasn't his enemy, but...a rival? He didn't really know him at all, but he couldn't just leave him.

Gornak's dazed eyes opened slowly. After several blinks, the warrior focused on him, and there was a frown of vague recollection. 'Grave-robbing whoreson?'

Bastard. At least he's okay.

Rex and Billy went to the warrior's side as the others caught up. 'We'll look after him,' Rex confirmed. 'You go.'

I'm sure Shift will think that's lovely of you.

Shaking off his pettiness, he turned, but a hand grabbing his shoulder stopped him.

'We do this sensibly and together,' Shift said firmly.

Behind them, Silva's facial expression showed that no nonsense would be tolerated.

And she's usually so open to nonsense.

But if they were the ones cautioning *him* to be sensible, perhaps he'd lost his mind? Beyond the hole, light flashed and explosions boomed.

'I cannot protect you if you charge off like that,' Silva said quietly as she passed him.

Auron raised an eyebrow at him. 'I'd rather face a pissed-off wizard than *her* in a bad mood, kid.'

'Okay, point taken.' For a moment he couldn't help but smile at his companions.

Moving as one, the quartet approached the edge of the treeline as further blasts of blue energy and yellow and red flames illuminated it.

The sight on the other side was almost comical. Both Oleg and Garaz looked to be on their last legs. They listed drunkenly from side to side as if standing on the deck of a ship in a storm. Hands were raised with what appeared to be enormous effort before spells were flung. Their aim was poor, despite neither really presenting a moving target. Even the power itself looked to be fading. The lightning was less tangible than Auron and the fireballs didn't even look hot. Still, the field they stood in was already pockmarked with smoking craters.

What the...?

There were other figures in the field. Several bodies lay in the grass, the powder on their faces now covering the pale skin of the dead.

'The bards,' Shift said. 'What are—?'

Another large explosion got their attention. Garaz's fireball blew a charred hole in the grass, but missed its target. Panting, the orc slumped to one knee.

'Ha! Weakness,' Oleg gloated. 'I knew you were a lesser wizard than me. No non-human can wield power like we do.'

'You...' the orc replied between exhausted gasps. 'Speak as if...you are greater, but every word...shows how lesser you are.'

Oleg snarled and sent another bolt of lightning from his hands. This one didn't even cover half the gap between them before evaporating completely. The wizard collapsed onto all fours, panting just as heavily as his rival.

Finally, an easy victory.

'It's over,' Nicolas declared as they all emerged onto the field. 'You're coming with us.'

The wizard looked up in surprise. His sweat-drenched face contorted into an exhausted snarl. He raised his hand, but all that came from his fingertips were sparks.

'Seems he can't perform.' Shift smiled.

'Must be terrible,' Auron added. 'Not that I'd know.'

He allowed himself a chuckle, caused partly due to his companions, and partly due to relief. They had him. No need for Tavish anymore. They had Oleg. 'Like I said,' he reiterated, taking a step forwards. 'You're coming with us.'

Oleg glanced behind him. What was he thinking? He didn't seem like a natural sprinter under the best of circumstances. And if he tried, Nicolas would bet good money he'd trip on that garish robe. Those facts made it even more frustrating that he'd gotten away the first time, souring his victory slightly.

The wizard's face became panicked as the group took another step forwards. 'No, no, no,' Oleg stammered. 'It can't be over. I won't let it.' He fingered a small pouch around his neck. 'Maybe I'm not done. Maybe *they're* done.'

'He's talking to himself,' Shift said. 'Never a good sign, especially in a wizard.'

'I met a wizard who talked to himself once,' Auron began. 'Turns out—'

'Not the time,' Nicolas said.

Something about that pouch wasn't good. Nicolas broke into a sprint as the wizard opened it. Oleg brought it up to his face, shoving his nose into it and inhaling so deeply Nicolas could hear it from where he was. As the pouch came away, the wizard's nose was covered in red powder. His mouth opened and his jaw worked, but no sound came out. Oleg's head shook, and soon his whole body joined in.

Everything that happened next happened very fast but seemed to occur in slow motion. Oleg sat bolt upright, screaming in pain before his teeth clenched. The wizard's eyes bulged, and his neck muscles tensed as deep red veins appeared across his skin. His pupils went from black to bright red then a surge of power emanated from the wizard like a wave, throwing Nicolas backwards until he rolled to the ground next to Garaz.

Shaking off his sudden and painful meeting with the ground, he looked up just in time to see Oleg levitate above the grass. Directly above the wizard, the sky was broken by a swirling black cloud that formed from nowhere. Forks of lightning struck the ground around Oleg as well as the wizard himself, the power coursing through his body. Several nearby trees were destroyed outright, ancient trunks cut into two blackened and burning splinters.

'I will not leave here unavenged.' The wizard's voice betrayed a new-found insanity. Or maybe it had always been there and whatever that red powder was had just unlocked it? Either way, they were in trouble.

With a crazed laugh, Oleg pointed at various members of their party. 'I wonder which of you I shall kill first?' Then his eyes settled on Garaz. 'No, I don't actually.' The wizard laughed maniacally.

Crying out, Oleg released a bolt of energy from his fingertips.

Before he even had the sense to question the action, Nicolas put himself in front of Garaz, sword up.

Ah, so you plan to cut the lightning in two with a sword. Genius.

He winced, ready for his inevitable cooking.

As the lightning impacted, he grunted in pain, his entire skeleton shaking as his body was pushed back, cutting deep divots into the dirt. After a moment, he opened his eyes with the stunned realisation that he wasn't dead, just very close to it. He pushed fiercely against the force being exerted on the *Dawn Blade*, which glowed brightly as bolts of crackling lightning gripped it. Somehow, the sword was holding out against the energy.

Does Auron know it can do this?

Now was not the time for questions. He poured all his might into his shaking arms.

'*What?*' Oleg screamed from the other end of the lightning chain. 'That can't be. It's not possible. It's impossible. It can't be possible. Surely, it's an impossibility.'

What was worse: holding back the lightning or having to listen to Oleg's numerous variations of *'it's not possible'*.

One of the forks of lightning flicked from the blade, singeing his face. For a second, his concentration wavered. Between the bright sparks of light, he could just about make out Oleg's face, contorted in fury as he pressed forward with his hands, pouring more energy into the beam. The pressure against the sword was enormous, his wrists near the point of breaking as the grass all around him burned. It was like trying to take a leisurely stroll through a hurricane that was a second away from blowing him into the sky.

He almost fell forwards as the lightning suddenly ceased, only managing to keep his balance by flapping his arms in a semi-bent-over position. Oleg's attack had been interrupted by his need to shield himself from an incoming fireball.

'A poor attempt by a poor excuse for a wizard,' Oleg snarled as his shield dissipated and the last few embers of the fireball continued their winding dance to the grass.

A large green hand grabbed Nicolas's shoulder and turned him around. 'Run,' Garaz shouted.

But Oleg...

He looked back.

Ah.

Okay, he really needed to run. The wizard was holding his arms over his head, working them in a circular motion to form a giant lightning ball above him. Nicolas did not fancy trying to bat that away with his sword.

He ran at full pelt for the treeline, where his companions were already waiting for him. All around him, forks of lightning struck the ground, throwing up mounds of dirt. As he grew closer, the others' eyes widened before they all ducked, suggesting that the lightning ball was incoming. He pushed himself harder, leaping through the hole in the foliage a mere second after Garaz. The force of the blast behind him propelled him a good few extra feet and ensured that his landing was minimal on grace and maximum on pain. His bones hurt, but at least he was alive.

Raising his head, because he wasn't sure his body was ready to get up just yet, he looked back to the treeline—or where it'd been. Now there was a smoking hole of charred stumps.

Aren't wizards supposed to get less powerful the longer they fight? What's in that red powder?

'Are you okay?' Shift said, crawling to his side and checking him over. Their face was covered in small abrasions, most likely from flying debris.

He raised a thumb, though considering how much his arm was shaking, it probably wasn't convincing.

Shift grabbed his head in both hands and moved it until he was looking straight at them. 'You're okay, right?' they asked, their eyes frantic. 'Tell me you're okay. I need to hear the words, *I'm okay.*'

'I'm okay,' he managed finally. 'But you're hurting my neck.'

Shift looked away as they let out a huge breath they must've been holding in. He was about to ask if they were okay when he was interrupted.

'Revenge,' Oleg cried. 'Revenge on all of you.'

The wizard floated through the giant hole he'd made in the treeline. Stood between Nicolas and Oleg, Silva was ready to fight, though how she intended to fight a floating lightning wizard was beyond him. Oleg began to work his hands again, creating another giant ball of lightning.

With difficulty, Nicolas looked around him for the *Dawn Blade*. Maybe if he had it, he could—

'You bastard,' came a shrill cry from beside the wizard.

Straining to focus, he made out a figure crawling towards Oleg, who looked thoroughly bemused by the interruption.

'You killed my troupe,' the lead bard wheezed, a small flame still on the tip of his singed cape. 'All that talent, gone. You shall pay for this.'

As the wizard raised his hand to smite down the foppish man, the bard did one of those high-pitched notes he'd tried to use to subdue Nicolas and the others. Oleg covered his ears in annoyance as the note became shrill, before casually blowing the bard to pieces with a nod of his head.

'Stupid man.' Oleg shook his head as he floated towards them. 'Now for you. I shall burn you from Etherius. Not even dust will remain once I am finished—'

Oleg cried out suddenly, his body convulsing as if he'd been punched in the gut. The ball of lightning he was conjuring vanished. The wizard clutched his ribs, eyes bulging with the agonised cry his lips unleashed. Whatever force was keeping him aloft disappeared, and Oleg dropped to the ground.

Nicolas smiled.

'What's going on?' Silva asked, taking a few steps back.

'I don't know,' Auron said. 'But I suggest you all get down.'

With a scream that could've been the howling of a wolf, Oleg got to his feet, his body vibrating fiercely. Even from here, Nicolas could see the red veins in his face growing bigger, glowing as the wizard held his head in both hands.

'All of you, *down*,' Auron cried a second before Oleg Hobrath exploded in a ball of red light.

The wash of the explosion pushed Nicolas back to the ground as he used his arm to shield himself from the light. The sound of the blast, coupled with the wizard's ungodly death scream, left his ears ringing.

His head pounded, as if there were an orc in his brain banging a battle drum, as he opened his eyes and rose, brushing off dirt and grass chunks. The only sign that the wizard had ever been there—aside from the giant, smoking crater in the ground—was a finger near his foot that he was trying really hard to ignore. And, of course, the blood splatter arching out across the grass in all directions from where Oleg had...exploded.

Closing his eyes, he let his head drop. They'd been so close.

So damned close.

Every time he seemed to have a link to this Maestro in his grasp, it slipped through his fingers. Needing some way to expend his building anger, he kicked a nearby tuft of grass. The fact that it looked pathetic only served to annoy him more.

Hands grabbed him and turned him around. 'Are you okay?' Billy asked, showing more emotion than usual. 'Are you hurt?' His new companion studied him with as much enthusiasm as Shift had.

I didn't know he cared that much.

Looking over himself, nothing seemed broken, though he was a mess of cuts and bruises, and he had pins and needles in one of his feet. Nothing Garaz couldn't help with.

'Yeah,' he replied finally. 'I'm okay.'

Billy patted his shoulders with a big smile. 'Thank the Deities.'

This is getting awkward. I really hope he isn't sweet on me or something. I've had enough of that with Emelina.

'Wizard battles are messy things,' Auron commented.

Nicolas followed the spirit's gaze to the ground. A finger hadn't been the only part of Oleg to survive the blast. There were...chunks...everywhere. Suddenly, the sky became very interesting to him. Although, he did have to look down again. Completing his search as quickly as he could, Nicolas found the *Dawn Blade* and retrieved it, shaking a bit of...something...off it before cleaning it on the grass.

'Did you know this could absorb lightning blasts?' he asked, holding the sword aloft and studying the reflective blade, and his filthy face reflected in it.

Auron shrugged. 'I don't ever stand in the path of lightning blasts, kid. I'm adventurous, not crazy.' The spirit eyed the blade in an almost dreamy way for a moment before snapping out of it. 'Though I've got to say, I'm impressed.'

Only then did it actually occur to Nicolas what he'd done—he'd thrown himself in the path of lightning to save Garaz. Judging by the solemn expression on Garaz's face, that wasn't lost on him. Despite their fallings out, he was still ready to sacrifice himself to save the orc. The notion was comforting.

'Thank you, Nicolas.' For a moment, he thought the orc wanted to say more, but instead he rose, groaning.

'Happy your nemesis is dead?' Shift asked, kicking an Oleg chunk away from them in disgust.

'I...would have been happier if I had been the one to do it,' Garaz replied honestly. 'But Etherius is a better place without him in it.'

'We need some help over here.' They all turned to Rex, who was still kneeling beside Gornak. Instantly, Garaz hurried over to the warrior's side.

Nicolas was about to join them, but he turned back to where Oleg had died. The wizard had had them at his mercy, so what'd happened?

Maybe he'd never know. At least they didn't have to worry about the wizards or bards, for now. The guilds were sure to send more, if they wanted Billy so badly, but hopefully by the time that happened, they'd have thick castle walls and an army around them.

As long as we get Tavish before that happens...

Another groan emanated from Gornak.

...and he doesn't kill us when he comes to.

CHAPTER 30

'All the healing magic in the world isn't going to help him,' Shift remarked with a shrug as they inspected some of Oleg's strewn remains. Reaching down, they picked up the small pouch Oleg had worn around his neck, opened it and peered inside. How that'd survived was anyone's guess.

'Be careful with that,' he said quickly.

His companion frowned at him. 'I think I can look after a small pouch.' They then proceeded to pretend to drop it three times, smiling each time he flinched.

'Funny,' he remarked dryly.

Shift gave him a slight bow then walked over to Garaz. Nicolas followed, finally noticing a cut on his arm—not deep but bleeding—most likely due to all the shards of exploded tree that had just been flying around.

He would ask Garaz to look at it, but he was busy tending to Gornak—and considering the volcano's worth of fire he'd been flinging around recently, the orc needed to recharge as badly as Nicolas did.

'Here you go,' Billy said, offering him a strip of cloth.

Nicolas tried to tie it around his arm himself, but it was awkward, so Billy helped.

'I thought that was going to get ugly back there,' the bushy-haired man said as he worked.

'Thank the Deities Oleg just exploded.' In truth, Nicolas was only half-thankful for that.

'No, I meant with you and Garaz,' Billy said. 'The way you two were glaring at each other, I thought you were more likely to fight each other than the wizard.'

'Oh, that.' Nicolas winced as Billy tightened the cloth around his wound. 'It was a tense situation. We're fine now.' He could hardly doubt his faith in his companion when he'd nearly sacrificed himself to save the orc. A half smile teased on the edge of his mouth as he realised he couldn't hear the whispering voices any more.

Billy gave him a short smile. 'That's good then. All the tension here lately, I don't want you guys having at each other. You're good people.'

'Don't worry.' Nicolas smiled reassuringly. 'We'll get you to safety.'

Billy patted him on the shoulder thankfully.

Nicolas went to check on Gornak but stopped as he saw Auron watching him. 'What?'

There was a long pause. 'Just thinking how brave you were back there,' the spirit answered finally. 'You're taking to this hero stuff well.'

Somehow, he didn't think that was it. He got the impression Auron was concerned about something, but another groan from Gornak got their attention.

'How is he?' Nicolas asked Garaz.

The orc sat back on the grass, paler than ever. 'He will live.'

'But will we, once he wakes up?' Shift asked.

That was a real concern. Not only were they escorting Billy, but Gornak thought Nicolas was a grave-robber. And considering how close the warrior and Auron seemed to have been, Nicolas doubted Gornak would take kindly to seeing Silva with them. But he wasn't about to leave the warrior in this state, and the others wouldn't either. They'd just have to talk fast when he woke up. Silva had already made sure his battle axe was far out of his reach.

'Whoreson,' Gornak moaned quietly.

'He took a mighty blow,' Garaz said. 'But he is tough. I have ministered to him the best I can. The rest is up to him.'

'Old Gornak isn't so easily felled.' Auron chuckled. 'So, this one time, me and the big guy are out hunting this giant. Big old bastard had a thing for eating kids. You'd think it would be easy hunting a giant, because…giant, as we now all know. Though it was smaller than the one we saw, the thing was bloody elusive. We track it to a forest and we're moving nice and quietly when *wham*, a club the size of a tree trunk comes down on Gornak.' Auron shook his head, smiling. 'Of course, I think the big guy is done for, and so does the giant. The monster chases me through the woods, trying to turn me to paste on the side of its club. It corners me in a ravine. I won't lie, I was a little concerned, but suddenly the thing topples over, a battle axe sticking out of its heel. Old Gornak is there, looking worse for wear, and goes, *Ambushing whoreson*.' Then collapses. I finish the giant then have to drag his heavy ass out of the forest.'

'Ah, the real reason you worked alone.' Shift nodded knowingly. 'Not having to carry your companions around after a battle.'

'Have you *seen* the size of him?' Auron chuckled, gesturing to Gornak.

Nicolas flinched suddenly as Garaz grabbed his arm and undid the dressing.

'You are injured,' the orc said, studying the wound. 'Why did you not tell me?'

'Because you had bigger concerns.' It was his turn to gesture to Gornak. 'Besides, you look pretty drained.'

The orc let out a single chuckle. 'Considering you tried to sacrifice yourself to save me, I think I can find the energy to heal this.'

Nicolas wasn't about to argue. Garaz took his arm and one of his palms glowed. The orc laid his green hand on the cut.

Ow. Owww. Owwwwwwwww.

Something was stinging, badly. It was all he could do not to yank his arm away. Within a moment, Garaz pulled back. The cut was closed, a slight scar marking where it'd been.

'Thank you.' Nicolas didn't feel massively thankful. Curiously, he stared at his arm, not entirely sure what'd caused the stinging sensation. He was under the impression he'd been getting stronger, and now he was nearly crying over a simple cut?

'Hey, big guy. What do you think of this?' Shift tossed Oleg's pouch to Garaz.

The orc opened it curiously then put his nose in it.

Instantly, Nicolas's mind was off his arm. 'Stop,' he cried. 'Don't snort that!'

Garaz looked at him with a furrowed brow. 'I was sniffing it not snorting it,' he rumbled in reply. 'I am curious.'

'Well, don't be,' Nicolas shot back. 'You already know what it does. We're surrounded by the proof of that.'

The orc looked unimpressed. 'Please credit me with some caution, Nicolas.'

'I do,' he protested. 'But then you put that up to your nose.'

Garaz made a big show of taking the powder away from his face. Too much of a show.

'So,' Auron asked, 'what are your thoughts?'

Garaz looked at the pouch and rubbed his chin. 'It evidently gives a wizard a temporary boost to their power. I assume small doses are required, as opposed to shoving your nose in it as Oleg did, because it appears highly volatile. I would hypothesize that he overdosed and paid for it.'

'Volatile is an understatement,' Silva said, looking at the ground in disgust at what Nicolas could only assume was another far-flung piece of Oleg.

'Hopefully, I can find out more in Yarringsburg,' the orc continued, most likely talking to himself. 'I am sure I can make use of an alchemical lab to discern its ingredients and origin.' The orc loved a good mystery, be it science or magic. And he hated not knowing things.

'If anyone can solve the riddle, it's you, big guy,' Shift said.

'As long as you don't accidentally snort any,' Nicolas reiterated.

The orc's mouth creased as if he were biting back a retort, and when he replied, it was clear he was controlling his temper. 'I am aware of that and will treat it with the utmost caution.'

'Now we've established that no one is sniffing anything,' Auron said jovially, most likely attempting to lighten the mood, 'we need to think about our next step. I do have a story about a guy sniffing the wrong stuff, but I don't think this is the time. Remind me later.'

Nicolas had no intention of doing that. 'How far to the main road?' he asked instead.

'Can't be far,' Rex said, looking at the horizon. 'I reckon we should make it before the evening. Maybe we can find a tavern—'

Six voices cut him off simultaneously. 'No.'

'No more bloody taverns.' Shift huffed. 'I'm fed up with wanting hospitality but finding hostility.'

'Good one.' Rex sniggered after the surprise wore off.

Okay, mate, calm down. It was just a joke.

Silva glanced over at the bards' bodies. 'It seems Auron's stories about the enemies taking care of themselves are— *Urk.*'

Before he could question what *urk* meant, Nicolas threw himself flat as Silva was launched over his head. The warrior struck the ground with a force that made him wince.

'Filthy whoreson,' Gornak growled. Then the bearded beast looked confused. 'Or is it whoredaughter? No. Whore...just whore will do.'

How in the Underworld did he recover so fast?

'Filthy whore.' Then he spat on the ground, before turning to him. 'And you, you grave-robbing whoreson. I shall have that sword *and* your head for desecrating the grave of my beloved comrade.'

Nicolas drew the aforementioned sword, keeping it ready, but also held up an open palm, to try to show he meant no harm. Unless he wasn't given a choice, Of course. 'Now hang on a second, you have the wrong end of the stick here.'

'Says man who travels with murdering whore,' Gornak replied, indicating Silva. 'Gornak knows which end of stick is which.'

'Gornak, calm down,' Auron cried, before realising the warrior couldn't hear him.

'Let us just be calm...' Garaz rose and made to soothe the giant warrior, only to be batted aside with a slap that made Nicolas wince again.

'And you other people,' Gornak bellowed. 'Protecting this little whoreson with the big hair. Gornak shall makes chunks of you like the wizard. Gornak kills bad guys.'

Nicolas was quite passionate about not becoming *chunks*, so, shaking off his aching limbs, he put himself between the warrior and Billy in his guard position. The equivalent of a cat standing in front of an elephant.

'You are a smart grave-robbing whoreson.' Gornak nodded. 'And brave. But there is no river to drop Gornak in this time. And no silly assassins to distract Gornak from chopping down evil.'

What *had* happened to the twins? Chances were, when this was done, they'd jump him at the next bush. If he survived Gornak, of course. The big man might not have his axe, but Nicolas doubted it made him any less dangerous.

'But,' the warrior continued, scratching his chin thoughtfully, 'you and your companions did help me when stupid wizard knocked me out. You could've killed Gornak. So I will give one chance. One. Step aside. Surrender sword. Surrender Billy. And surrender murdering whore.'

That was quite the list of demands, and he couldn't agree to a single one. Maybe this was the right time to run for the hills? No. Gornak may be a giant, but it was still six on one. Good odds. 'I can't do that,' he replied with finality.

'Very well.' The warrior nodded. 'To be fair, Gornak would've killed you anyway for stealing sword.' Gornak looked pointedly at the *Dawn Blade*. 'At least you can die with more honour than you lived, grave-robbing whoreson. In fact, you can die first.'

Gornak reached down to pick up Silva's discarded sword then charged. Nicolas didn't even try to intercept the incoming blade. Instead, he ducked aside, rising just in time to get cuffed across the cheek, though it felt more like a rock had been hurled at his face. Once again, he was spinning through the air before a short and painful drop to the ground. All his aches reasserted themselves, and a few of his teeth screamed in pain. His bell had been really rung.

He was vaguely aware of the big warrior bearing down on him when he heard Auron's voice. '*Luna Tellgood*. Tell him *Luna Tellgood*.'

The sword came down. Nicolas flinched backwards, closing his eyes and bringing up his own blade in what was most likely a very futile gesture. '*Luna Tellgood*.'

There was darkness, and silence. Slowly, he opened his eyes. A sword hovered a foot away from his head, suspended in mid-air by a surprised-looking warrior.

'*What* did you say?' Gornak asked slowly.

'Luna Tellgood,' he repeated uncertainly, hoping he'd remembered the name correctly.

The sword blade withdrew.

Behind Gornak, Nicolas could see Billy helping Garaz up as Shift and Rex circled the mighty warrior. He gestured for them to hold.

'What do you know of that name?' Gornak asked suspiciously.

What did he know? Nothing. He had a name, that was all. He looked to Auron for help.

The spirit gestured for him to get Gornak away from the others.

'Can we talk *over there?*' Nicolas suggested. 'You may like some privacy.'

The warrior looked back at him awkwardly. 'Yes, I think discretion best.'

Nicolas got up and made a big show of sheathing his sword. Gornak made no such gesture himself. Nicolas indicated a direction for them to go, away from prying ears.

'Nick?' Shift asked warily.

He gestured that it was okay as he followed Gornak to a side of the field where they wouldn't be overheard. 'What do you know of Luna Tellgood?' Gornak asked urgently when they were out of earshot.

'Okay, kid,' Auron said with a smirk, 'repeat after me.'

As Auron spoke, Nicolas echoed his words. 'You have a scar on your neck.'

Unconsciously, the warrior brushed the scar.

'You told everyone it occurred in a fight with a vicious vampire lord, which Auron backed up. What really happened was that the pair of you were in a brothel. Once it came time to pay up, you realised you were short of coin. The woman didn't take too kindly to that and attacked you. She bit your neck open. You then rose, slipped on your own blood, and crashed to the floor, knocking yourself unconscious. When Auron burst in, she was about to beat you to death with a wooden leg. He paid your tab, and you made him swear to tell no living soul it'd happened.'

'The shame,' Gornak grumbled. 'Mighty warrior Gornak bested by a one-legged whore.'

'One-legged?'

'Leave it, kid.' Auron smirked.

'And he broke his oath.' Gornak looked sad. 'I thought him so honourable.'

'He's only breaking it now to stop you killing us all.'

The warrior's brow furrowed. '*Breaking?*'

'Yes, he's here.'

'Auron of Tellmark is dead.' Gornak grunted. 'What type of jest is this?'

This was going to be tricky. 'That's true. He is dead, but he's also here.'

'A ghost?' Maybe not that tricky.

'Yes, a ghost.' Nicolas smiled. 'He died and came back as a *ghost* and is *ghosting* around.'

'Be careful, kid.' Auron's face was stern. The spirit did *not* like being called a ghost.

'That's how I have the sword,' Nicolas continued. 'He passed it to me.'

'Let you borrow it,' the spirit mumbled.

'And you expect Gornak to believe this?' the warrior asked. 'Yes, you have sword. But you may have tortured the information out of him.'

Yes, I tortured Auron to learn your weird prostitute story. Come on.

'Hey,' Auron protested. 'I've been tortured before and not given up more vital information than that. And you certainly couldn't get me to talk, kid.'

'Sometimes I can't get you to shut up,' Nicolas said with an annoyed smile.

'Yes,' Gornak said. 'Your show of talking to air is very impressive. But Gornak needs more proof.'

'Fine.' Auron picked up a stone and threw it across the field.

'Could be magic,' Gornak countered.

Sigh.

'Hmm,' the big warrior continued. 'If you really see Auron, he should be able to tell you what he has tattooed on his left buttock.'

Nicolas turned to Auron, wide-eyed.

The spirit looked back at him with exasperation. 'I don't have one.'

'There isn't one,' Nicolas told Gornak.

Gornak smiled, resting his large hand on Nicolas's shoulder. 'Then you must be worthy. Auron was always a worthy companion too.' The warrior stroked his beard thoughtfully. 'I remember Effingham affair when we fought manticore together. Auron fought like demon that day.'

Beside him, the spirit scoffed. 'He's testing you again, kid. It was a gorgon, and it was half-asleep when we fell on it.'

He's craftier than he looks.

'Don't you mean half-asleep gorgon?' Nicolas asked.

The giant warrior's beard broke in a broad grin. 'That I do.' Suddenly, Nicolas was grabbed in a hug so tight he had half an idea Gornak was trying to kill him after all. 'Then we are allies.'

Gornak put him down. 'What is your name, successor of Auron?'

'Say *Nick Carnage*,' Auron whispered in his ear. 'Say it. You know you want to say it.'

'Nicolas Percival Carnegie,' he said instead, casting an irked glance at the spirit.

'Good to know you, Nicolas.' The slap on the arm nearly sent him reeling. 'There is one thing, my new friend.' The warrior became solemn for a moment. 'Please tell Auron Gornak is sorry such a great warrior passed. He was a legend, and my friend.'

Nicolas looked at the spirit and saw the expression on his face. 'He heard you.'

The warrior glanced back at the others, all of whom were watching the exchange with great interest. 'So, Gornak must not kill Billy fellow then?'

'No,' Nicolas replied. 'Somebody has made him a target, and we need to keep him safe.'

The big warrior stroked his beard. 'It goes against grain, but Gornak will trust Auron's judgement.'

'Just like in Teritha?' Auron asked with a half-smile.

Nicolas repeated it.

'Ha, ha.' Gornak laughed ironically. 'You are still funny man, even when dead.'

Unwilling to stand there being a conduit for their banter, Nicolas walked back to the group, Gornak and Auron following. As they returned to the others, Nicolas signalled that all was well.

As he approached, Shift looked at his face. It stung fiercely where Gornak had struck him.

'Did you do that to him?' Shift snapped at Gornak, getting in the warrior's face as best they could given the size difference, pointing a finger under his chin.

Gornak laughed. 'Tiny girl has spirit.'

Shift flinched, their face going red. 'Keep talking, because I can get bigger. And I'm not a *girl*.'

'Gornak doesn't understand,' Gornak said.

'You'll hear that out of him a lot,' Auron commented dryly.

'Shift is a shapeshifter, and they don't identify with any particular gender,' Nicolas informed the warrior as the pain in his cheek begged for his attention. 'You have to refer to them as *them*, *they*, or *their*. Anything else could be considered an insult.'

Gornak scratched his bearded chin for a moment. 'Gornak doesn't understand, but Gornak doesn't need to. If this is how you wish to be known, I shall use these terms. Sorry for offence given.'

'Okay then,' Shift said, coming down off their high horse. They glanced at Nicolas for a moment in a manner he couldn't read before stepping back.

It seemed, then, that they had a new companion. Good. Nicolas would much rather have Gornak's axe working with them than against them.

'Uh, guys,' Billy shouted from the distant tree he was hiding behind, 'is it safe to come out now?'

Will it ever be safe for Billy to come out again?

Nicolas had no idea, but Gornak seemed to have been placated.

At Nicolas's gesture, Billy warily stepped out from behind the tree and returned to the group, doing that loping walk of his. 'I think I nearly soiled myself,' he said with a smile.

He looked like he nearly would again as Gornak approached, towering over him. 'The allies of dear friend say you are good, so I will not kill you. If you prove untrue, you die. Gornak will crush your head like grape.' The threat was accompanied by a mimed demonstration. '*Splat.*'

Billy gave a nervous grin, coupled with a nod. Nicolas might've had trouble forming words, too, if threatened by Gornak.

CHAPTER 31

'One thing Gornak doesn't understand.'

Nicolas winced. This was the fourth time he'd heard that phrase. The big warrior also seemed not to understand the word *one*.

'Go on.' He sighed.

Beside him, Auron sniggered. There'd been a lot of that since they'd set off again.

At least it's keeping me distracted from other things.

'Silva killed Auron, right?' Gornak said slowly. 'We all hear. So why do we travel with murdering bitch?'

'Why indeed?' Auron huffed.

'Because she wants to change,' Nicolas said, watching the warrior ahead of them. Billy was walking along beside her, probably staying close to the person he thought could best protect him from Gornak, if the warrior changed his mind. 'And she has proven herself a few times now.' A thought occurred to him. 'Plus, Auron forgave her. It was really emotional. I've never seen Auron like that before.'

Beside him, the spirit swore.

'Doesn't sound like Auron.' Gornak shrugged. 'But I guess death changes you.'

'Plus, he's really fond of me,' Nicolas said, suppressing the chuckle that would've given him away. 'He sees me as the son he never had and after Silva saved my life, he couldn't stay angry at her.'

'You wish.' Auron scoffed, shaking his head. 'Besides, I'm sure I have more than one kid somewhere.'

That wouldn't surprise me.

A thought occurred to Nicolas. 'Maybe you can tell *me* something?' he asked Gornak. 'Do you know *why* you were sent after Billy? I've heard a lot about the guilds worrying that he'll give away their secrets, but is there anything else?' In all honesty, he took the reason at face value, but it never hurt to check. Maybe some nugget of information about Tavish would fall into his lap.

The big warrior shrugged. 'I was told he was bad guy.'

How could Gornak be so wrong? Nicolas supposed he was just following orders, but Billy was the salt of the earth.

Behind Nicolas, Shift giggled. Oh great, Rex was being funny again. *Funny, funny guy. What a fabulous jester.*

'You need to stop letting yourself get uppity about that,' Auron remarked at his side.

Nicolas threw him a glare, warning him to stay away from that topic without saying an actual word.

Auron ignored him. 'Don't you think you have enough going on without obsessing over those two?'

Those two? They were a two *now? Since when?*

'And what would you like me to think about?' he asked, incredulously. 'Because given the circumstances, I don't see how I can think of anything that *won't* make me uppity, as you put it.'

'That's a fair point,' the spirit nodded. 'But there are always things you can be thankful for, if you look hard enough. For example...you're alive. You have us. Take solace in that, keep going, and soon everything else will fall into place'

'That's easy for you to—'

'So this one time.' Oh, he was getting another story.

A second passed, and the spirit said nothing. Nicolas looked over, and Auron was happily looking at the fields around them. 'Well?' he prodded.

Auron turned and smiled at him slowly. 'Gotcha.'

Despite himself, Nicolas laughed. It was the look on Auron's face that did it. He couldn't help but chuckle.

'By the Deities,' the spirit smirked, 'he remembers how to laugh.'

'Hey,' he protested. 'I've laughed a few times recently.'

'True,' Auron confirmed. 'But you're starting to become the *grim avenging* hero, and that's not you at all. You're usually more the '*so, do I really have to do this*' hero. If we're using the H word at all. Maybe under my tutelage—'

'I'll become the *cocky, self-aggrandising, promiscuous hero*?' he asked with a grin.

'Nope,' the spirit said, shaking his head. 'You could try to be *promiscuous,* as you so politely put it, but when you do, you'll just hear Rex and Shift giggling and get jealous again.'

Jealous? Me, jealous? Of them?

The concept was so ridiculous that he laughed again. His body shook as he attempted to fight back the chuckles. It was funny. Ever since he'd thrown himself in front of Oleg to save Garaz, he hadn't been so angry, so distrusting of the others. Something had changed, but he couldn't quite put his finger on what.

'Gornak thinks it strange you talking to someone I cannot see, little Nicolas,' Gornak remarked with a furrowed brow.

That made everything even funnier.

His laughter ended abruptly when Silva stopped to glare at them. Beside her, Billy was smiling.

'Noise discipline,' the warrior snapped.

Chuckles became outright laughter. Even Auron joined in as Nicolas doubled over, and Silva's expression went from annoyance to confusion. That made the laughter worse.

'You guys all right?' Shift asked.

'No, no, I am not.' Nicolas didn't know why that was so funny, but suddenly he was rolling on the ground. The others looked at him as if he were a madman. They were probably right. But you know what? He needed this. He gave into the laughter.

****

The bright afternoon sky gave way to the dusk as the group continued. Nicolas was thankful to see Billy chatting to Garaz again, and this time, it was a two-way conversation. Hopefully, they were making peace.

Progress had been slow—making their way through fields, stopping to climb fences, or slowing to cross streams. But it had been consistent, and they could now see the road ahead. And thankfully it wasn't the thrice-damned Ale Trail.

But...

'Please tell me that isn't another tavern.' Nicolas groaned as he saw the building ahead of them, sat to the side of the road.

'I believe it is,' Silva replied, looking at the ever-growing building cautiously.

'I've got a new game, people,' Shift declared with a grin. 'Instead of *name the tavern*, we're going to play *who's going to attack us in this tavern*.'

That was a game Nicolas didn't want to win. Though it was a moot point, because they were giving the tavern a wide berth. They still played, though.

Shift went first. 'I think scribes from the Guild of Accountants.' They smirked. 'They'll come at us with parchment and try to kill us with papercuts...or bash our heads in with abacuses. Is that the right plural?'

'Yes,' Garaz confirmed. 'I believe we will be attacked by the Guild of Waste Collectors, who will roll carts of flaming faeces at us.'

Considering all they had seen and done previously – such as cow-drag-ons and talking chickens – Nicolas would consider that a pretty normal experience for them.

'Both of you are wrong,' Silva said with an eyeroll. 'It will clearly be the Guild of Architects, who will attempt to gouge out our brains with hammers and chisels.' That was gross, but possible. From the look on the others' faces, they agreed with Nicolas.

'I reckon, the Guild of Farmers, who will attempt to make us eat rotten vegetables until we die from the shits.' Even as Rex spoke, Nicolas mim-icked the words in his mind in a petulant voice, before checking himself and fighting back the sudden burst of annoyance.

Nicolas decided to go for the stupidest answer he could think of. 'Gnomes riding war sheep,' he said with a snigger.

'That isn't a guild,' Shift corrected.

'It isn't funny either. That happened to me once,' Auron remarked seriously.

Okay, Nicolas needed to hear *that* story.

'Funnily enough, I'm actually part of some of those guilds,' Billy offered sheepishly. Of course he was. 'But I don't know any gnomes, if that helps.'

'Well, that's one less threat to worry about.' Shift snorted. 'Another thirty or so to go.'

Garaz shot Billy an annoyed look. Maybe they hadn't made peace *quite* yet. The orc shook his head and muttered to himself.

How exactly does Billy manage to find the time to join all these guilds? I can barely manage being a member of this group, whatever we are.

Cautiously, they proceeded in a wide circle around the tavern. It was a multi-levelled building with a thatched roof. Tons of space for assassins.

'Can you hear anything?' Auron looked toward the tavern with nar-rowed eyes.

As soon as he heard the question, Nicolas realised how wrong the place felt. A tavern that size should've been busy. Where was the sound of revelry? Where was the drunk staggering outside to relieve himself at the back of the building? It was quiet. Too quiet. Dead quiet. As they got closer, Nicolas realised there was no light coming from the place either.

'I really don't want to visit another tavern.' He moaned quietly.

'This place does scream *trap* at the top of its lungs,' Shift noted.

'No, it doesn't actually,' Auron corrected as he continued to scrutinise the building. 'If it was a trap, the place would look normal.'

'*Hero instincts?*' Nicolas ventured.

'Very much so, kid. Something is very wrong here.'

'Then we should give it a wide berth,' Silva suggested. Sometimes, she could be as wise as she was deadly.

'Agreed,' Garaz said.

Continuing with weapons drawn and always pointed towards the building, the group reached the edge of the field. Quietly, they slipped over the hedge and onto the road. Still, there was no movement from the building. Worse than that, now that they had a decent view of the front, Nicolas could see that the door of the building had been broken outwards and every ground-floor window was smashed. As ominous as the place looked, what he was about to say was going to be very unpopular.

'We need to check out the building.'

'We most certainly do not,' was Shift's knee-jerk response.

'We need to check it out,' he said more firmly. 'There may be people in there.'

'Yes.' Shift nodded enthusiastically. 'A lot of them. Ready to kill us.'

'Innocent people, I mean,' he persisted. 'Like, patrons and staff and...I don't know...a pet dog.'

'I'm not risking *this* amazing butt for a pet dog.' Shift said the words, but he didn't believe them. They were already swayed, they just didn't like it, and he was on the receiving end of the glare to prove it.

Nicolas looked at his other companions. Auron was smiling at him in a way that suggested pride. Garaz glared at the building before looking at him and shrugging. Silva seemed the most sceptical, until she finally said, 'You know I follow your example. Even if it is into a building like *that*.'

For a moment, Nicolas had a strange sensation. He wasn't like...a leader, was he? No, that couldn't possibly be the case. 'Okay, Rex, you stay here with Billy while the rest of us check it out.' Nice to have Rex out of the way, at least. 'Gornak, if you could look after these two until we find out what's going on, please.'

It was only when Rex gave him a strange glance that Nicolas realised he'd patronised the thief a little. He hadn't consciously meant to do that, but subconsciously...?

'Gornak will stand guard.' The big warrior nodded. 'And if I hear trouble in drinking hall, Gornak will come in swinging mighty axe and kill many whoresons.'

'That'd be pretty helpful.' He smiled.

Part of him questioned the logic of leaving Billy under Gornak's care, but the warrior seemed honourable enough. Auron vouched for him, and that was enough for Nicolas.

Despite his every urge to the contrary, he advanced on the tavern, his companions spreading out in a line to either side of him. There was no sign of movement inside and no premonition that they were being watched. That almost made it worse.

Above the door was a sign that creaked ominously from side to side, though there was no breeze. On it was a painting of a cyclops, who was holding what appeared to be an eye. The name written above it was The Cyclop's Second Eye.

Lovely. Well, this isn't going to get any more sensible.

CHAPTER 32

T he sense of wrongness increased tenfold the closer they got to the door. As did the smell of death. He looked at his companions, who all nodded that they were ready. As one, they moved across the road in a crouched run, weapons ready. No arrows flew at them.

After making it to the tavern, they arrayed themselves near the door. Silva peered inside the window before looking at him and shaking her head; she couldn't see anything. The only sound coming from within was buzzing.

Keeping tight to the wall so they didn't give away their presence to whoever might be inside, he gestured to Auron. Casually, the spirit strolled through the entrance. It was only after Auron had gone through the door that Nicolas realised they should've just sent the spirit to scout before they'd even crossed the road. At least it was a sign he was getting braver.

Seconds later, there was an impressed whistle from inside.

'You won't need your weapons,' Auron called out to them.

If it was all the same to Auron, he fully intended to keep his sword in his hand. So did the others, by the look of it. As they slipped into the tavern, Auron glanced disapprovingly at their still-wielded weapons. White eyes rolled.

The only light inside was the glow cast by Auron's aura, and it took several moments for his eyes to adjust. Judging by what he saw when they did, that was more than enough light. Garaz decided otherwise, and lit the lamps in the room, displaying the bloodbath in all its glory, the flickering yellow lamplight somehow making it worse.

Blood was everywhere. Over the floor. On all the broken furniture. Splashes decorated the walls like the worst abstract painting he'd ever seen.

How can there be so much blood?

Nausea rose, and it rose fast. Putting his hand over his mouth, he tried to fight it back, but the scene combined with the smell of decay was too much. The contents of his stomach emptied onto a nearby stool.

Wiping his mouth clean, he rose. Something caught his eye. Movement.

Are those…ghosts?

The thin smoky outlines of figures were there, but they weren't. The lingering spirits of the dead leaving a last imprint on the world before they faded into nothing. But they couldn't have been there. He couldn't have seen them. He tried not to notice Auron staring in exactly the same direction.

Not wanting to contemplate what had just happened, he looked at his other companions, who were all staring grimly at the scene. The tavern was a mess. No piece of furniture remained unbroken. Bodies lay in every corner, and not always fully intact. The buzzing…the buzzing was flies. Considering how *fresh* everything looked, the little carrion bastards had gotten here quickly. Beyond the buzzing was the tell-tale dripping of blood onto wood.

He wanted to say something, but he had no words.

'Deities,' Silva gasped finally.

'I do *not* want to meet whatever killed all these people,' Shift said slowly.

Now that was a terrible thought. Nicolas had been so focused on all the…death, that he hadn't even thought about what could kill a room packed full of people.

Could it be…the demon?

'I don't think you need to worry about that.' Auron sighed as he scrutinised the scene. 'Kid, look carefully and tell me what you see.'

Nicolas didn't really fancy taking a test in what was essentially an abattoir, but he was too dumbfounded to argue. He looked closely at the scene. Deities, he didn't want to look closely at the scene. But as he did, his brain started to connect some dots, and an idea formed. At first, it sounded too stupid to say aloud, but it nagged at him.

'They all killed each other,' he said hesitantly.

'That they did,' Auron confirmed grimly.

Now that he'd said it, it was obvious. The pattern of the bodies, the angles of discarded weapons. Nothing had come in here and killed these people; there had been a fight, and they'd killed each other.

How does it still smell so bad in here when the doors and windows have been broken open?

'Hey,' Shift said as she looked over one of the bodies. 'I know this guy.'

Nicolas walked over to them. For a second, he nearly slipped in a puddle of blood, stumbling but righting himself again.

'Smooth, kid.' Auron smirked.

Nicolas ignored the spirit. Instead, he focused on the body. It took a moment. In his mind, there was the initial, *yeah, I know him*. Followed by, *yeah, but where from?* Slowly, his brain connected to his memory. 'That's one of the thieves who jumped us in the tavern.'

There were certainly some familiar faces in the carnage. Looking around, he could see several others from that group.

'So what, they got here, laid in wait but started another fight?'

'The thieves didn't start it by themselves, kid,' Auron said. 'Look at these guys. They were all warriors or fighters of some kind.' The spirit gestured to a man in light armour, which had a sword sticking out of it. 'If that patch is right, he's a member of the Bounty Hunters Guild. And those two there look like caravan guards from the Guild of Merchants.'

Another two to add to the list. For Deities' sake Billy. Saying no once in a while doesn't hurt.

Shift looked around, their eyes wide. 'You don't think...they were all here for us? For Billy?'

'That's exactly what I think,' Auron confirmed.

'So...' Nicolas was still struggling to process this death and destruction. 'You think several groups hunting Billy all arrived here together and killed each other. Why?' He'd already guessed why, but it sounded so...stupid. So pointless.

'Because they squabbled over who would get Billy, and it ended up in a fight,' Silva said from across the room.

That was terrible. *What a ridiculous waste of life. And over what, some nice guy who might know some secrets? Why doesn't the world make sense anymore?*

'And now they're all dead,' Nicolas said grimly.

'This will be enough to spark a war,' Auron said. 'None of the guilds will take this lying down. Each will blame the other for starting it. It'll get a lot bloodier before this is over.'

A war starting...over Billy?

'But how are they all even here?' Nicolas asked. 'How could they know where we'd be? We barely knew.'

'They are tracking us somehow, or someone led them here,' Silva suggested.

A sudden and horrifying thought dawned on Nicolas.

Tavish.

What if the Black Knight was amongst the dead, and the one link to his people and his parents was gone forever. Frantically, he searched the tavern, the imperative to rule out Tavish's death overriding his horror. Resting his hands on his knees, he breathed a big sigh of relief when he found nothing.

'No Tavish?' Shift asked.

'No.'

'Odd,' Auron said thoughtfully. 'I'd have thought if anyone were here, it'd be him. There's something we're missing...'

'At least he isn't dead, like the rest of this lot,' Shift noted.

'They aren't all dead,' Garaz interrupted from across the room. 'There are two survivors. And you won't like who they are.'

After treading carefully through what could most politely be described as *the mess* that littered the tavern's floor, Nicolas reached a large, over-turned table and looked over it. 'Oh, it's them.'

Alexi and Emelina were out cold on the other side of the table. The sister had a nasty gash across her head whilst her brother was bleeding from a stomach wound.

'Shame that,' Shift commented insincerely.

'They aren't dead,' Nicolas replied.

His companion shrugged. 'Near enough.'

'That's why we're going to help them.' Why was no one getting this?

His companions all stared at him wide-eyed. Silva was the first to speak. 'You...want to *help* them?'

'Yes.'

'But they're assassins.'

'And?'

Silva looked at him askew. 'They kill people for money. Three times they have tried to kill you. Three times they have been spared. And here they are, ready to try again. Why would we help them?'

'We helped you,' he replied flatly. 'You tried several times yourself.'

The warrior scoffed, a flash of rage across her face. 'I *knew* you would bring that up.'

'What does that mean?'

Silva looked at him for a long moment then shook her head. 'Never mind.'

'You do realise that if we do this,' Garaz said, 'they may try to kill us again?'

Was he not making himself clear? 'Well, obviously. I didn't mean for you not to restrain them first.'

'You didn't say that,' Shift said.

'I didn't think it needed saying.'

They shrugged as if to say, *Well, it did.*

Garaz rolled his yellow eyes before crouching and getting to work on Alexi, the worst of the pair...both in personality, and severity of injury.

Something occurred to Nicolas as he looked at the bodies. 'Where's the staff?'

Every one of the dead was a combatant. There had to be at least thirty of them. But none of them were serving maids or barmen.

'I would imagine they got out the door pretty quickly when the blades started flashing,' Auron remarked.

An epiphany struck him. A sudden moment of clarity. 'Then all we need to do is wait here.'

'What do you mean?' Shift asked then stopped at his look. Slowly, they followed Nicolas's gaze to the purse in their hand, one of several they'd taken from the bodies of the fallen. 'Problem?'

'No,' he answered quickly.

Shift shook their head and pocketed the purse. 'Don't worry.' They scoffed. 'I'm just a low-life thief. I know what you all think of me.'

You what?

'Let's get back to the kid's suggestion, please,' Auron said with a sigh.

'Well,' he began slowly, eyeing Shift cautiously. 'If it were me, and my tavern became a battleground, I'd run straight to the nearest garrison. That means there are soldiers on their way here. All we need to do is wait for them, explain the situation, and have them escort us to the city.'

'...and have them listen with raised eyebrows before arresting us for massacring a tavern full of people?' Shift said, with raised eyebrows of their own.

'I don't think we need to bother waiting for an escort, kid,' Auron remarked as he stepped over a severed arm. Why do that when he could walk through it?

'What do you mean?'

'He means,' Silva cut in, 'that everyone who was hunting us is dead.'

Maybe his epiphany hadn't been so amazing, after all. Instead, it turned into a moment of relief. They were right. The bodies in this tavern *had* to account for the majority of those after Billy, including several that they hadn't even known about until now. That meant they could finally focus on Tavish.

'Plus, any soldier that comes to this butchers' shop and sees us hanging around outside may stab first and ask questions later,' Shift remarked, studying a ring they'd taken from a severed hand. 'Especially if we have certain company in tow.' With their head, they gestured towards Garaz. The orc noticed the gesture, and Nicolas could've sworn he heard a snarl.

His idea had seemed so smart at the time. *That'll teach me to pat myself on the back too soon.* 'Fair point,' he conceded. 'As soon as the twins are good to move, we'll make ourselves scarce.'

Turning around, Nicolas yelped as he accidentally kicked a severed head. He fought back his first instinct: to apologise. The head was probably too busy being upset that it was no longer attached to a neck to be concerned about someone bumping it with their foot.

Walking to the door, he gestured to Gornak and the others that all was well, kind of. Then he found himself looking up and down the road, one thought playing repeatedly in his mind.

'Where are you, Alric Tavish?' he whispered into the dark.

CHAPTER 33

Once Garaz had given the twins' wounds some superficial care and ensured their conditions wouldn't worsen, they moved the pair. Shift had grudgingly accepted the idea of helping the assassin twins but made it perfectly clear that said *help* would be of no practical value, leaving Silva and Gornak to carry one of the makeshift stretchers and he and Rex the other.

Awkward on both counts. I should've partnered with Gornak.

'I recognise these,' Gornak said slowly as they moved towards the door. 'These are whoresons from bridge.' His mighty brow furrowed. 'We are helping them?'

'Apparently, it's the right thing to do,' Shift said with thinly veiled sarcasm.

'It is,' Nicolas confirmed.

'Gornak is not used to giving enemies aid,' the warrior continued. 'But I shall indulge this. If they come to and start trouble, I cut them down.'

'Thank you,' Nicolas said nervously.

Carefully, he manoeuvred the stretcher. It was cumbersome, and he suspected a little too wide for the door. When he was proven right, the pair had to tilt the stretcher slightly, trying to ensure that the unconscious Emelina didn't fall off.

Garaz will have a fit if she does.

How closely the orc was watching them confirmed his suspicion.

As he shuffled forward, Nicolas's boot touched something that slid slightly underfoot, making a squelching sound that he refused to think too much about. The stretcher jinked as he tried to keep his balance.

'Careful, mate.' Rex smiled at him. 'The doorframe's tricky, and we don't want to lose our passenger.'

Mate?

'No problem, buddy,' he replied. Though Rex didn't appear to notice, he was surprised by the venom in his voice. 'I've got it.'

'Wouldn't need to worry about it if we'd just left them in the tavern,' Shift offered with a sarcastic grin, not missing an opportunity to make their displeasure known.

'We aren't leaving them.' Did he really have to repeat himself again whilst getting a stretcher through a door? 'Just because they tried to kill us doesn't make them *bad* people.'

Someone needs to survive this senseless massacre, even people who may be our enemies. Someone has to live.

Shift rolled their eyes. 'Look, you don't need to save their lives. They're assassins, for Deities' sake. They've probably killed more people between them than we've ever met. I get that it's important to you because of what may have happened to your parents—' The words stopped coming out of their mouth abruptly as his head spun toward them, but the sympathy on their face forced him to look away again.

I don't want sympathy. I just want to get this bloody stretcher through this sodding door.

The need to get out of this tavern suddenly became urgent, but one side of the stretcher angled back up again, caught against the door-frame, and wouldn't budge. Using his body weight, he pushed against the stretcher as Rex heaved on it from the other side. Nothing.

'I think it's stuck,' Shift observed unhelpfully. 'If only you two had some muscle between you.'

With the pressing need to defend their manliness, both he and Rex redoubled their efforts until sweat was visible on the young thief's brow and openly running down his temples. Still, it didn't move.

'Not to worry.' Gornak smiled from beneath his beard. 'Gornak has many muscles and likes to help.'

After handing his stretcher to Garaz, Gornak approached the door. Leaning across Rex, the warrior put his plate-sized hands on either side of the door frame. With ridiculously little effort, Gornak pushed against the frame, visibly buckling it and allowing the stretcher to slide free.

I'd be happy being even half as strong as him.

'Thanks,' he said in awe as he passed the big warrior, who smiled back amiably.

'No problem, friend.' Gornak beamed. 'Gornak has more uses than just chopping up whoresons.' Architectural redesign being one, apparently.

Nicolas turned to look back at the tavern. Maybe they ought to just burn the place down? After what had happened inside, it would never be the same again. But that wasn't his decision to make.

'Do you think the owners will abandon this place?'

'Are you kidding?' Shift replied. 'My coin is on this place becoming a tourist attraction. *'Come one and all to the site of the massacre at the*

Cyclops's Second Eye. Half price drinks on Wednesdays, with food purcha ses.' Nicolas really didn't know what to think about that; he just stared at Shift wide-eyed. 'You'll see.' They shrugged, before pointing at Billy. 'You'd probably get invited back as a special guest. *The man behind the massacre.'*

'I think I'd rather focus on surviving this, before milking it for fame,' Billy said nervously as he watched Alexi and Emelina. 'Are you sure about sparing these two?' Considering they were assassins bent on killing him, he was well within his rights to be concerned.

'It'll be fine.' Nicolas hoped he was right. At least they'd been careful to relieve the pair of their weapons. Silva had searched them herself, and if anyone knew anything about concealing weapons, it was her. 'I was right about Gornak, and I'm right about this.'

I hope.

The group settled just inside a nearby forest—not the ideal place for tending the wounded but better than a blood-soaked tavern. There, Garaz once again began to treat to his patients.

'The girl has a bump on her head,' Garaz said as he ran his giant hand over Emelina's skull, though Nicolas hadn't needed telling, he could *see* it, and it looked angry. At least the wound was closed. 'I detect no swelling on the brain, so there will be no lasting damage.'

Her brother, Alexi, had a wound that needed more care. Though Garaz's magic had done its job nicely, there was going to be a nasty scar.

'He will recover,' the orc said, pointing to Alexi. 'Though that is a minor miracle. The blow was only millimetres from his insides being outside.'

Nicolas cringed.

'What do we do with them now then?' Shift asked Nicolas in a very *'well, this was your stupid idea'* way.

'When they wake up, we explain to them that we are the good guys. That Billy is a decent fellow and urge them to abandon their...task.'

'I think you lack the persuasive ability for that.' Was Silva mocking him or being serious? 'Gornak is one thing. You had Auron to aid you. This pair will be an entirely different task. But at least they are bound and can do no mischief.' Indeed. Silva had been very enthusiastic when it came to binding the twins. They would need Auron's intangibility to get out of that.

'Good thing we didn't need to bind Gornak when he was out. We'd need some big old chains for that,' Auron noted over his shoulder. 'So this one time I was doing a job with Gornak...'

'That's, what, three stories about Gornak?' Shift asked, bemused. 'I can't believe you let someone share your glory that many times. That must've been tough.'

Auron's look suggested that he wasn't amused. '...and we get captured by this wizard. I think he was trying to enchant a dragon. Or maybe a basilisk. Whatever. Anyway, he manages to knock us out using a gas trap and secures us to some pillars in his throne room—'

'Why didn't he just kill you?' Nicolas asked.

Auron pursed his lips at the interruption. 'Because villains love bragging like I like telling stories of my exploits.' *That much then?* '*So anyway*, we are tied to this stone pillar. I can barely move. Gornak wakes up, and with a few jiggles, he actually snaps the pillar in half. It causes a crack in the roof, which spreads to where our wizard is standing. A brick comes loose. Bang. No more wizard. Can you imagine that? All that power done in by a falling brick.' That was a pretty spontaneous ending.

Nicolas hoped Silva's tying up of the pair was a little more effective. It was put to the test a moment later as Alexi and Emelina woke in perfect synch.

Once they realised people were standing over them, both tried to rise and discovered the ropes around their legs. When they noticed the bindings on their hands, they tried to struggle out of them, writhing on the ground like crazed worms.

'Ah,' Gornak bellowed. 'Tiny assassins are awake Gornak sees.'

'Stay back, barbarian,' Alexi snarled, bringing his feet up off the floor to ward off Gornak. What he hoped to achieve was anyone's guess.

'Do not worry, whoreson,' Gornak rumbled, pointing a finger at the pair. 'Gornak will not kill you. Even though that woman stuck me with darts.'

'Shoulda stuck you with more.' Emelina giggled from beside her brother. 'All the darts in the world.'

'Try and come for her,' Alexi growled, waving his legs in the air a bit. 'Just try it, big guy.'

For a second, he looked ready to. So, naturally, Nicolas put himself between the two groups. No. Not naturally. Not naturally at all.

What am I doing? Why is it so important to me that these two live?

Maybe because so many had died already, and many more still would? Or maybe if he could save their souls, he'd prove he was still human?

'I think we need to all calm down.' Though he doubted Alexi knew the meaning of the word *calm*.

'*You*,' Alexi said as he focused on Nicolas.

'Hello again,' he replied.

'I'm going to kill you,' Alexi snarled.

'I think he means it,' Emelina whispered, wincing.

'You've tried,' he replied dryly. 'Repeatedly.'

'Do I look like I give up easily?' Alexi hissed, struggling against his bonds again.

'Instead of talking about killing me,' Nicolas pressed on. 'How about we talk about why no one has killed you, again. In fact, the pair of you are alive because of us.'

Alexi looked down at his stomach wound. The assassin pursed his lips as he saw the fresh scar. Finally, he relented. 'I'm listening.'

'So,' Nicolas said. 'We found you in the tavern—'

'That got bloody quickly.' Emelina sighed. 'So bloody. So quickly.'

'Yes, because you're all after him.' Once Nicolas pointed to Billy, the twins' aggression towards him and Gornak calmed, but only because their aggression was now focused on Billy, who had the good sense to back away. 'No,' Nicolas said, repositioning himself. 'No, no, no, no. There's been enough bloodshed.'

'But our mission still stands. And our target is right there.' Alexi shrugged. 'You don't become assassins of our calibre by *not* killing the people you're meant to kill.'

'And are you in any state to get through all of us to get to him?' Shift asked, pointing first to his wound then to his bindings. 'In fact, are you in any state to even stand up?'

A fair point. The assassin still looked very pale, so Nicolas doubted he could've put up much of a fight even if he *was* armed and unbound.

'Our mission—'

'Why are you after him?' Nicolas asked. 'Can either of you explain why you've been sent to kill this man? Who paid you to come for him?'

Alexi and Emelina looked at each other briefly before replying. 'We were not paid for this contract,' Alexi replied. 'This is a service to the guild.'

'So there's no physical contract on his head?' he asked.

'Only one of honour for the guild,' Alexi replied defiantly.

'You can't spend honour.' Emelina smiled. 'But it's good to have.'

'And you didn't think to ask for more details?' Hypothetically, if he were an assassin, he'd want to know every facet of his target, including the exact reason someone wanted him dead.

Probably why I'm not an assassin.

'We don't ask questions,' Alexi hissed finally. 'Again, that wouldn't make us very good assassins. Someone pays us to kill someone, and we do it. We do *not* interview our employer and carefully weigh up the pros and cons.'

'Can't ask.' Emelina put her finger to her lips. 'Get a job, someone dies.'

'What a quaint philosophy,' Garaz muttered.

'All we know is that he has secrets that could destabilise the guild.' Alexi huffed.

'What *secrets*?'

After a moment, the assassin shrugged. 'I don't know. That's why they're secrets. Dumbass. Only the Headmen know.'

'Who?'

'The *Headmen*, the leaders of our guild,' Alexi snarled. 'And if only they know then the information is of the highest priority, and we can't just let some *guy* who somehow wandered into our guild go walking around with it. Do you know what'd happen if the Thieves Guild got hold of it? Or the Guild of Heroes?' The assassin shook his head. 'It may not surprise you to know this, but we aren't well-liked.'

'*Gasp,*' Shift said with a snort.

'Shhhhh, you,' Emelina snapped.

'What about you?' Nicolas gestured to Gornak. 'You don't know either.'

'Well, no,' Gornak admitted. 'But Gavron said he needs to die.'

'Who?'

'Hall Master of the Yarringsburg Hall of Champions.'

Auron's brow furrowed as he looked at Gornak. 'Jerric Doomsword is the Hall Master. Ask him what happened to Jerric?' The spirit sounded positively panicky, so Nicolas quickly posed the question.

Gornak looked at him suspiciously. 'You know of Jerric?'

He just gestured to where Auron stood. After a second's confusion, the warrior understood. 'Jerric passed away.' Gornak's tone was heavy, laced with grief that was still raw. 'His heart gave out when he heard of Auron's passing.'

Behind Nicolas, there were two gasps. One was from Auron, the other Silva. Both looked equally stricken. His heart went to them. Obviously, this *Jerric* had been important in their lives.

'I'm sorry,' he offered.

'Jerric trained me,' Auron said to no one in particular. 'He brought me into the Guild. He was my mentor. A lot more than that, truth be told.'

'He was a great man,' Silva said solemnly. 'I never knew him as well as I would have liked.'

Part of him wanted to hug Silva, but judging by past experiences with the warrior, it wouldn't be well received. But his heart went out to them both. Another body to add to the growing pile. At the rate this Maestro was going, he'd need a team of mountaineers to get to the top of that heap. And he wasn't about to let Billy end up on it. Or Alexi and Emelina, for some strange reason.

'But despite you being sent after him,' Nicolas turned back to Gornak, 'you see now that Billy is a decent guy, right?'

Gornak looked at Billy, who waved back awkwardly. 'You say he is good guy, then he is good guy. Gornak trusts new friends.'

'Okay, so if he can change his mind, so can you,' he declared to the twins.

'No,' Alexi replied flatly.

Time for a new tactic then.

'Has it occurred to you that someone is maybe…using you?' From the looks the twins exchanged, they clearly hadn't. 'How is every guild in Etherius suddenly after this *one guy*? Because he knows too much? Or are you all being played?'

'I'm listening.' Great, he had the pair thinking.

'Let me ask you,' he continued. 'Was everyone turning up at the tavern at the same time a coincidence? How did you even know we were going to be there?'

'We encountered a traveller on the road and questioned him,' Emelina said. 'He was very forthcoming. Said he'd spoken to you and told us where you were going.'

'We haven't talked to anyone,' Shift interrupted. 'And even if we did, do you really think we'd tell some random passerby our destination when so many people are after us?'

The twins were silent.

'Someone's playing a very unpleasant game with Etherius,' he ventured. 'Stirring up all kinds of trouble in the kingdoms. And now this happens. Doesn't seem like a coincidence, does it? All of this must be destabilising the guilds. How much chaos would happen if the guilds went to war with each other?'

'A lot,' Auron answered solemnly.

'They do all have an understanding not to interfere in each other's affairs,' Shift added helpfully. 'A mound of dead bodies in a tavern could lead to an open guild war.'

'I bet whoever's behind all this would benefit from that nicely,' Nicolas finished off.

The twins looked at each other for a long moment. They appeared to be discussing something without actually saying a word. Finally, Alexi turned to Nicolas. 'You may have a point,' the assassin said grudgingly. 'I don't like to be used, and neither does my sister. And we both love the guild.' The assassin grimaced slightly, as if finding the words he was about to say next distasteful. 'I offer you a truce. For now, we put our contract on hold and work with you until we find whoever's behind this. If you prove false, you all die.'

Maybe you'll do better than the other three times you tried.

Actually, I really hope not.

'That's a fair compromise,' he replied, ignoring the audible huff of disagreement from Shift. The twins were hardly the first deadly people they'd travelled with.

With a sigh of relief, he began to walk to the pair, intent on untying them. Then he caught a sparkle in Alexi's eye and stopped. 'Nice try,' he said, shaking his head and stepping back.

'Just so you know,' Alexi snarled, 'I would kill you for *free.*'

'Get in line.' *It's a long one.*

Looking at Silva, he nodded toward the assassin's hand, where the concealed blade was. The warrior roughly turned Alexi over, snatched the weapon, and threw it away. Standing again, she put the tip of her sword to the assassin's throat.

'That'll do,' Nicolas said quickly.

Silva sheathed her blade, staring at Nicolas the entire time. 'As you command,' she said sourly.

CHAPTER 34

The campfire roared happily—dispelling the darkness as the group rested—but that was the only thing happy about their camp.

Only Billy was making the most of their chance to rest, sat cross-legged by the fire, eyes closed and hands in his lap, just as Garaz did when he meditated. Nicolas couldn't deny these last few days had taken a toll on him. On all of them. Instead of jests and conversation, all Nicolas could see were distrustful glances.

We're still together, though. That has to count for something.

Yet the whispering voices, which had now returned, told him otherwise.

He tried to fight back against the rising ire, bringing up fond memories of the others, but it was like trying to stop a rockslide with an outstretched palm. Half of him hated them and the other half wanted to call out to them and make peace.

The fact that it clearly wasn't just him made it worse. Shift had their back to him, having a nice time by the fire with Rex. Garaz sat solemnly by himself, staring into the flames. Silva sharpened her sword aggressively. Auron stood back from all of them, arms folded, like a displeased parent.

Gornak sat chewing on a leg of meat from the deer Silva had hunted. In between bites, the warrior hummed happily to himself.

If only I could be happy so easily.

'You continue to impress me, kid,' Auron said as he walked up to him.

Nicolas wasn't sure why, but despite the kindness in the spirit's tone, it rankled. 'When are you going to stop calling me that. How many times do I have to ask?'

Auron paused briefly, before resuming his smile. 'You did good. Showing the twins mercy. They'll come round soon enough.'

'Thanks.' Again, his reply was short. Why was he so annoyed? Sure, he'd been through a lot, but this anger just didn't feel natural. He didn't want it to be natural. This wasn't him. He felt like he was in quicksand, struggling to stay afloat whilst some hand from below grabbed his ankles and pulled him further down.

I want to make amends with the others.

No, his mind hissed back. *You don't. Not after the way they treated you. Not after what happened to your parents.*

It's not their fault.

Cause and effect. You met them, your parents died.

They're not dead.

Oh really? Silly naïve boy.

'It's funny what you said,' Auron began, snapping him from his mental argument. 'About everyone being played. We need to be really careful who we trust right now. I don't think...'

'I think I'm really starting to understand who I can, and can't trust,' he cut in quickly. 'And when I do, and do not, need counsel.'

The only one I can really trust is myself.

The spirit looked at him patiently, opened his mouth, then closed it again. 'Just be careful what allies you make,' he said finally.

The hint of warning in Auron's tone cut through the fog around him like a ray of sunlight. Before Nicolas could question him about it, the spirit walked away, shaking his head.

****

Nicolas was the first to wake the next morning. Red clouded his vision as he opened his eyes and saw Rex's arm around Shift. The arm offended him, the person it was attached to offended him, and the fact it was around Shift really bloody offended him.

'You okay?'

Billy had this reassurance about him that Nicolas found so comforting. And he had some stuff he needed to talk about. 'Not really.' Billy gestured for him to continue. 'Shift kissed me. When I came back from the dead. They kissed me. But then they slapped me and now, everything is weird. Especially with *him* here. It's just not the same.'

Wow, just blurt it all out, Nicolas.

'Jealous?' Billy ventured sympathetically.

'What?' Nicolas scoffed. 'No. Not at all. I've just...lost everything I've ever known, and now I feel like I've lost them as well. It just isn't the way it was. It's too much.'

'I don't want to stick my nose in,' Billy was evidently hesitant to continue, 'but that does seem a bit cold. After losing your parents and everything. But people act strangely when they're grieving. I'm sure they weren't messing with your head intentionally, though.'

Or were they?

'I mean, you need to stay close to your allies, especially now,' Billy said. 'You trust them with your life, don't you?'

Nicolas was shocked that he didn't immediately answer *yes*. 'I want to,' he said finally. 'But it's hard. Garaz has been strange, and Silva, I can't shake the feeling she's hiding something.'

'Perhaps she's just used to being guarded after her shady mercenary past,' Billy said quickly.

The past in which she tried to kill me. The past in which she worked with Tavish. Funny how he just...got away.

'Look, buddy,' Billy said slowly. 'I'm only saying this because I owe you my life, several times over. You've got some new people with you, dangerous ones. You need to sort your group out so you can be strong. Anything else, and we all die. If it was just me, well, old Billy takes his chances. But I'm kind of fond of you, Nicolas.'

It made so much sense to him. Why hadn't he just spoken up before? Why was he keeping everything bottled up? That had never worked for him in the past. His *companions* were all acting suspiciously, and here he was, just eating it like a troll-dung sandwich.

No more.

The whispering voices grew louder, until they became overlapping shouts, spurring him into action.

Rising, deciding to get this done now whilst he still had the backbone, Nicolas stomped over to where Shift lay. Auron, who'd stood watch so the others could all get the decent nights sleep they desperately needed – yet which continually seemed to elude them all – started to approach him with urgency.

'Don't...' the spirit warned.

Standing over Shift and Rex, he kicked Shift's boot. 'Wake up.'

Their eyes opened blearily and looked at him, uncomprehending. 'What?' Their voice was slurred and drowsy.

'We need to talk about *that*.' Nicolas pointed at the arm that was offending him so.

Shift noticed the arm around them and shrugged it off. 'What are you...?'

'You kissed me.'

Now Shift was wide awake. They stood up quickly, stirring Rex. '*What*?' Shift asked, gaze fierce, looking ready for a fight. 'We talked about that. Did I not make it clear enough?'

No.

'You kissed me then said nothing.' He was aware he was raising his voice, but he couldn't help it. 'People don't do that to other people. Especially after they'd just died. Is it because of *him*?'

'I beg your pardon?' Shift matched his tone.

Around them, the others began to wake.

'Well.' He snorted. 'Come on. It's obvious you two are romantically involved. But to shove it under my nose so blatantly after you kissed me and then acted so cold toward me is just...'

'Just what?' they asked with narrowed eyes.

'...dirty,' he said finally.

'Firstly, I didn't talk about it because, *as I said before*, the kiss was nothing, and neither is that.' Rex, now awake, seemed offended to be referred to as *that* but had the good sense to keep quiet. 'I was relieved you were alive. That's *it*. I'm pretty sure I told you that already, so I'm unclear why we're having this conversation.'

'Is this how you get your kicks?' Nicolas scoffed. 'Messing with people? Making them think you like them just to chuck them off a cliff so you can move on to the next guy who laughs at your jokes?'

'Of course.' She laughed. 'Because that's all us *thieves* do, isn't it?' they snarled. 'Mess with people.'

No. Not you.

'You said it,' Nicolas shot back angrily.

Rex got to his feet, hands up in a conciliatory gesture. 'Okay, man—'

Nicolas shoved him. Rex stumbled backwards before falling to the floor. Now everyone was wide awake.

Shift shoved him back. 'What's the matter with you?'

I don't know.

'*You*,' he shouted. 'Nothing around to steal so you think you can get your kicks playing with me instead? I'm not some trinket for your entertainment, here to be the constant butt of your jokes.'

What in the Underworld am I saying?

Shift stepped back as if physically struck, looking at him in disbelief. 'Is that what you think of me?' Their brow darkened. 'Of course it is. I knew it all along.'

No.

The words were just spilling from his mouth.

Silva, who now stood beside him, put a hand on his shoulder. 'You need to—'

He shrugged the hand off. 'You need to convince me I can trust you before I take a single piece of your advice.'

The warrior glared at him. 'I beg your pardon?'

'You heard,' he snapped back. 'First Tavish escapes...or does he? Then Garaz can't break this imagined mental barrier of yours. Certainly some interesting coincidences.'

'You dare question my honour?' Silva's words came through bared teeth.

Why am I doing this?

'Do you *have* that much honour, though?' Shift asked. 'The number of people here you tried to kill, or *did* kill, outweigh the ones you didn't.'

Silva pointed a threatening finger at Shift, her eyes narrowed beneath a dark brow. 'Be careful,' the warrior warned.

'Leave them be,' Nicolas snapped.

Silva's hand clenched into a fist. 'You do not command me, child,' she snapped back. 'I follow your example to be a better person. I am not here to be treated as if I am some sort of lackey at your beck and call. *Silva, hit that guy. Silva, don't kill that guy.* It is getting tiresome.'

'What?' Nicolas cried. 'I order you around. I stop you killing random people. I'm hardly going to apologise for that.'

'No,' Silva snarled. 'Instead, you stand here and accuse me of lying to you.'

'The mental barrier could not be broken because it is deep magic,' Garaz interjected.

Nicolas rounded on the orc. 'Is it? Or did you not really try?'

He tried. They both tried.

Garaz was wide-eyed for a second then shook his head slowly. 'Meaning?'

'*Meaning* do I even trust you?' he asked. 'One minute you're acting nice, the next you're growling and violent. Maybe it's all an act? Maybe you're just waiting to lull us *humies* into a false sense of security.'

The orc squared up to him. 'You *dare*?' Garaz asked with a snarl. 'I knew this was what you all thought of me. I see your looks, feel your judgement. I am just another orc to you, am I not? No better than an animal.'

'Is he wrong, though?' Shift asked. 'I saw what you did to the frog creature, and you've been acting suspiciously.'

'This again.' Garaz snorted. 'I have explained that, repeatedly, and do not care to again. Do I need a lecture on trust from a thief?'

Shift exclaimed something very rude very loudly. '*Thief.* There we go. The common opinion. I'm just the slimy thief? After all I've done to help you guys, you're all, *'Yeah, that's nice, but they steal stuff, so does it count?'*'

'You do have a past,' Silva said flatly.

'*Really?*' Shift yelled. 'Coming from you? Really? Taken anyone hostage lately?'

The warrior looked at the very end of her patience. 'I have warned you—'

'Or what?' Nicolas rounded on Silva. 'You'll get your friend Tavish?'

No. That's not—

Silva's hand went to the hilt of her sword. Nicolas had already drawn his by the time it did.

'You don't trust me.' She almost sounded hurt, taking her hand slowly from her blade. 'Not truly. I knew it.'

She was never going to draw it. It was a test. What am I doing? Why can't I stop?

'Ah.' Garaz laughed. 'The boy finally draws his sword without dropping it. A true marvel.'

'What?'

'Give him a minute.' Shift scoffed. 'Then he'll drop it and need rescuing.'

'Of course.' He laughed. 'I'll allow my staunch allies *the thief*, *the murderer*, and *the orc* to come to my rescue. Well, my cup runneth over, doesn't it?'

Why won't this stop?

From there, the whole thing devolved into shouting as suspicions were vented and accusations thrown. Nicolas couldn't tell what he was saying any more than anyone else could. He didn't even know why he was saying it; the venom just kept pouring from his mouth. It was like he was no longer in control of his own mouth. There and then they were all amidst a storm. Red clouds of suspicion and distrust swirled around them, urging them to give a voice to their grievances. Nicolas could see it and knew it was wrong, but he was powerless to stop it.

Aaaarrrrgggggghhhhhh.

'Enough!' he screamed finally, silencing everyone. 'Look at us. Look at all of us. We aren't companions. We aren't a team. You aren't my friends. Do you know what you are?' He looked up at the sky and let out a single harsh laugh. 'You guys are my tragic backstory. You came into my life, and it burned to ash around me. My parents died. Have one of you tried to comfort me, at all? No. You're all lost in your own stupid shit.'

'Because there is no evidence they are truly dead,' Silva said quietly.

'Nicolas—' Garaz's voice broke.

'Do you seriously not realise we are all here for you?' Shift cried, interrupting the orc. 'Every single one of us, you ungrateful little piece of giant's belly-button fluff. We have been since we all met. And now you stand there, full of your own self-righteousness, and *dare* to suggest we aren't...'

They're right.

'Well, excuse me for not handling my parents' death well,' he cried. 'Maybe we can find a necromancer to resurrect them, get one of the crazy twins to kill them again, and then you can explain to me how to handle it better.'

Shift rolled their eyes. 'Don't be a dick. If we get proof that they are really gone, we will all be there for you.'

'Look,' Silva said. 'We are all sorry—'

This isn't right. Why am I...? I don't... No. I can't be around them. I can't trust them. This is all wrong. This is over.

'No!' he cried. 'No. You don't get to say sorry. You know what you get to do. You get to leave. All of you.'

'What?' Shift asked with narrowed eyes.

'*I'll* take Billy to Yarringsburg. *I'll* get the job done. Because I can't trust any of you, and if you aren't around, maybe I don't get beaten and drugged and lashed to posts anymore. Maybe my life will be...better.'

What am I saying?

'Nick...'

'No,' he said, falling to his knees. 'You all killed my parents, as much as if you'd set the fire yourselves. You all came into my life, and they died. If I hadn't met all of you, they'd still be alive.' In his heart he knew he didn't believe a word of any of this, yet he couldn't stop himself saying it.

'Kid...' Auron said from where he stood.

'Get out of my life,' he whispered. 'All of you.'

Don't go. Ignore me. Please.

Shift walked up to him, their lip trembling with anger. 'Don't pretend you're innocent in this, Nick. You've been using Billy as bait this whole time.'

'Bait?' he cried. 'How dare you?'

'Please.' Shift scoffed. 'You aren't helping him out of the kindness of your heart. You're just using him to get to Tavish.'

That's not who I am at all.

'Let's see how well you do when he finally shows up and we aren't here to protect you.'

'You wish to play at being a mighty hero?' Silva scoffed. 'Then I suggest you make your peace with the world before you die.'

He didn't need their protection. He'd been fine before them, and he'd be fine after.

'Leave,' he said firmly.

One by one, they did as he'd bidden.

Stop. Come back.

Shift stormed off cursing, dragging their *lover* with them. Garaz walked away with a distasteful glance at him. Silva looked ready to say more, but Nicolas turned his back on her. Her footsteps trailed away. All it took was one glare at Auron to get him to go. The spirit even had the nerve to chuckle before he left.

They were angry at him, he knew that. Well, screw them, because he was angry too, and he had more of a right to be. He was better off without them. He could do this alone. He could. He had to.

I don't understand what's going on.

'What about Gornak, little Nicolas?' the big warrior asked.

'Please leave,' he whispered. 'I don't need anyone.'

Gornak said nothing; he simply got up and walked away.

'Now we are alone, I'm going to—'

Nicolas cut Alexi off. 'If you don't shut up right now, I will kill you myself.'

****

For half an hour, Nicolas stood, staring numbly in the direction his companions had gone.

He'd commanded them to leave, and they had. And he didn't like it one bit. He wanted to run after them, scream for them to return. Yet he couldn't make himself do it. The anger clouding his mind bound him to the floor, refusing to let him budge. With no other recourse, he finally dropped to the ground and began to sob.

Angry voices still raged in his head, screaming of betrayal. But in the darkness, another voice cried in disbelief that he'd sent his friends away.

Friends. That's what they were. And I banished them. Why? Why did I say those things?

He couldn't fathom how any of this had happened. At least Alexi had shut up.

Through the haze of sadness and regret. he heard footsteps behind him. 'You okay?' Billy asked.

'Not even slightly.' He laughed. Was it a laugh or a sob? 'What did I do? I... Why did I say those things? It was all wrong.'

'Nicolas,' Billy said, sitting at his side. 'You know exactly why you said what you said, why you sent them away. I heard your arguments, and, my friend, they were sound. You were right to cut them loose.'

'But now I'm alone.'

And I wish I wasn't. I wish I could take it back. I need to get them back, to apologise and make it right.

He went to stand up, to run after his companion's, but Billy's hand on his shoulder eased him back down to the floor.

'You aren't alone. Old Billy will take care of you.' The assertion came with a reassuring smile, before Billy patted him on the shoulder and rose, walking behind him.

That's not the same. You're not them. They're my friends. How could I treat them so poorly?

Desperately, he tried to make some sense of what had happened. Where had the anger come from? After Hablock, he'd been fine. Obviously, he was upset about everything, but not once had he questioned his companions and their motives. And now everything had fallen apart.

Where did the others even get the nonsense they were spouting? None of it's true. I value them all. So why did I say it? My anger only started when—

The realisation struck him like a giant kicking him all the way to the moon. What had happened was so clear, so obvious, that it just had to be right. Slowly, his hand slipped towards the hilt of his sword as he stood, trying to act casually.

Turning around, he put on a false smile. Billy already was already swinging the rock he was holding towards his head.

The world went black.

CHAPTER 35

Coming around was, all in all, not his best move. His head throbbed evilly. Nicolas tried to recall some facts and dates to check for brain damage. Everything seemed in order, but how would he know if it wasn't?

Judging by the constriction around his body, he was bound, most likely to a tree. He'd been tied up enough times now to know the sensation without looking. With great care, he opened his eyes. The blurry world resolved into the clearing they'd camped in. His eyes sought help, but saw none. All he could see was Billy sat across from him, and Alexi and Emelina, still bound and watching both him and Billy with great interest.

'Hey, you're awake.' Billy beamed as he rose from the campfire. 'You've been out a while. I thought I'd hit you too hard.'

'You filthy bastard,' Nicolas snarled, straining against the ropes that kept him tied to the tree. 'It was you. All of this. It was you.'

With a broad grin, Billy nodded proudly. 'That it was,' he said. 'Old Billy, hanging around, dripping poison in everyone's ears.'

'I don't understand,' Nicolas said, giving up his fight against the ungiving rope. 'Why?'

Billy nodded wisely. 'You're confused. I get it. How to explain this easily...?'

The skinny man seemed to mull this over before clicking his fingers in the air in success. Carefully, he kicked off his boots, inside of which were hoofed feet. Then, he grabbed his large bush of hair and removed it, revealing a bald head save for two small, pointed horns. He pulled on his ears, which turned out to be long and pointed. Non-human. Dropping his breeches displayed fur-covered legs. Then Billy did a little dancing twirl for him.

What? Who? But? How? 'You're a *faun*?' he cried finally.

'Hey, well done, smarty pants.' Billy smiled. The smile dropped as the faun frowned at Nicolas. 'What? What's that look?'

'Well...' Shrugging was difficult when bound. 'I don't know. When I figured it out I suppose I thought you'd be a trickster god or something. Not...a faun.'

Billy approached him. 'Well, then you were wrong. And here's what you get for it.'

The punch struck him directly in the stomach. Nicolas would've doubled over had he not been tied up. Instead, he coughed up a glob of blood.

'Don't worry, that was the first of many.' Billy smirked. 'Well, I guess you should be worried about that, actually.' The faun cackled. 'See, you killed my brother, asshole. And now you're going to pay for it.'

'Who are you?' The words came out shakily after the punch, but he had to know.

'Name's Fo,' Billy said. Shift was right. Billy Bobknobs *was* a stupid, made-up name. 'And like I said, you killed my brother Ro. You remember him, right? Magic flute? Trying to start a war between Merida and the Tidal Kingdom? It was all going smoothly until you showed up and stabbed him in the throat. I assume you recall that? One doesn't generally forget someone he stabs to death.'

I remember vividly.

'But...why Billy?' he asked. 'Why the disguise?'

'Interesting you should ask,' Bill...Fo replied. 'I'm what you would call a *professional agitator*. I go places, ingratiate myself, learn secrets, and sow seeds of discord. Just like I did to you and your *companions*.'

The implications of that shamed and enraged him in equal measure.

'Mostly, I just listen and wait for a scab to pick at. Then I ask questions, make my little comments, and let people's brains do the work for me,' Fo continued. 'Though I'd be lying if I said there wasn't a *touch* of magic involved. I'm a bit of an empath, see? It's a subtle magic, but I can sense and manipulate the emotions of others. Especially the negative ones. I enhance those little slights, those whispering paranoias people normally ignore, churning them up beautifully until they finally overcome you,' the faun said with clear self appreciation. 'Just a small pinch to ensure you aren't quite thinking straight, that you get annoyed easily, react instead of think, whilst I plant my seeds of dissent. Then I watch them grow, watering them with dreams and fertilising them with my little comments until they bloom into wonderful chaos. Ro was good at casting illusions. I'm good at this.' The faun waved a finger at Nicolas. 'Though you lot were a challenge. Even you, who was the most weak minded of the lot. The bond between you was strong and it took much longer than I expected. Every time I thought I was getting somewhere we'd get attacked, or come across a giant and you'd all come together again in disgusting harmony.

Still, greater the effort, greater the reward.' Fo shot him an evil grin. 'And I'm bloody good at what I do.'

And once again, I'm a prize idiot.

'The giant story?'

'Utter bullshit,' Fo laughed. 'And pretty good bullshit even if I do say so myself. For a moment, when we saw an actual giant, I was worried you'd pick up on my surprise and it'd give the game away. But nope. You were too busy being surprised yourself.' The faun smirked. 'The knights were bullshit as well, obviously. I needed an excuse to prolong our time together whilst I sowed my seeds of discord.'

Crouching down, the faun unclasped the heel of his boot and produced the jewel, holding it up to the light. 'This thing is actually a recorder of sorts. It steals memories from people, memories of secrets and stores them.' Fo threw the jewel in the air and caught it, before, sitting down on the grass. 'I went around the guilds being Mister Easy-Going whilst I stirred up as much shit as I could and grabbed some juicy secrets. One of my favourites was convincing some of the top lieutenants of the Thieves Guild to ignore their leaders, because they were just shady businessmen who imposed rules, took their cut and did none of the work. It's all about upsetting the established order.' Fo plucked a blade of grass and chewed it thoughtfully. 'And what could upset the established order more than a guild war? You humans have woven these guilds into your society so deeply it's ridiculous. Everyone's a member of something nowadays. The word is put out that I have all this information a guild doesn't want getting out and that someone's trying to get me, and suddenly, all those fools are stumbling over each other to keep me quiet. Stumbling becomes killing, like in the old tavern back there, and then there's open war. Chaos reigns, and I dance.'

Nicolas gave in to the rage, lashing out furiously with his legs. 'I am going to—'

A rock hit Nicolas in the head before he could finish the threat. Fo shook his head and laughed. 'See? I'm good at bringing out the worst in people.' The faun got to his hooved feet and approached him. Fo gazed at his forehead, which Nicolas guessed was bleeding from the rock. 'I find a wound, and I poke it,' Fo said thoughtfully. 'Poke, poke, poke.' Each word was punctuated by him jabbing his finger into the wound on Nicolas's head, causing a flash of pain.

Clearly amused, Fo went and sat down again. But not before spitting in his face.

'The idea was that Tavish would spirit me away, and when the others couldn't find me, they'd all turn on each other, each thinking the other guilds had me. A rumour we would spread, of course.' Fo took the grass from between his lips and used it to point at him. 'But I'm making good my escape, and who do I see chasing me? The little human shit who killed my brother. Well, I couldn't resist the chance for some retribution. Besides, Mother would skin me alive if I had a chance and didn't take it. She was y pissed when you killed Ro.'

'I noticed.'

'Yeah.' Fo smirked. 'She was going to massacre the entire kingdom. But the Maestro doesn't like that. He likes things neat and tidy. He likes things quiet. So he sent old Koth to kill you and take the others as recompense for her loss.'

'And that's neat and tidy, is it? A whole village being kidnapped?' He scoffed at his captor. 'I know you planned to blame the others for it, but people would still be looking for the stolen villagers. It isn't as easy as that to make an entire village disappear.'

Fo shrugged. 'Of course eyebrows would be raised. However, conveniently, the wrecked ship of a known slaver was discovered just off the Meridan coast with a single survivor, who will confess that his master took the good, hearty folk of Hablock, who were then lost at sea.' The faun sucked his teeth dramatically.

'What? He'll just do that out of the goodness of his heart, will he?'

'The Maestro has ways of coercing people. The plan was sound, of course, except that your companions didn't die, and you didn't have the good sense to stay dead.' Fo smiled at him evilly. 'Unlike your parents.'

He stared at the smirking faun as the implication of Fo's words sunk in and the ground slipped away from beneath his feet. The hope he'd tried to armour himself with crumbled away, leaving him a numb shell as he desperately tried to picture his parent's faces, to burn them into his brain as he now knew he'd never see them again. For a moment, he was numb to his core as his body and mind rallied against the terrible news, shutting down lest they feel the deep pain they knew was coming.

Mother. Father.

Nicolas's body went slack in the ropes. 'They're dead.'

'Oh yes.' The faun chuckled. 'Seems old Koth got creative when he was told to make you suffer and killed them. Though I am a little confused why he did it *after* he killed you. I didn't know that little titbit until I travelled with you. Still, who knows the logic of demons, eh?'

Logic? Nothing makes sense anymore.

'You were tied up.'

'You thought you saw me and Tavish scuffling.' Fo smirked. 'But really, he was binding my hands. He wasn't keen on the idea, you guys having a penchant for screwing up carefully laid plans, but I was insistent. Needed to avenge Ro, you see.'

'So you put yourself in danger? You put the jewel in danger?'

'To get to you, oh yes, I did,' Fo replied. 'I was hoping the guilds would at least take out your companions, so I'd get this chance to have you to myself. You had me worried a few times there, with all the fights you were getting in. Still, you're tied to a tree about to be offered up as a sacrifice to Mother – which will curry some serious favour with her after you killed Ro – so all's well that ends well.' The faun pursed his lips in thought. 'And as for the jewel. Well…just because I work with Tavish, doesn't mean I trust him. I needed a little insurance the Maestro's followers would come and pick me up.'

'Your brother was an asshole,' he spat.

'Yup.' Fo nodded. 'So am I. Runs in the family, you see. You're going to meet them soon enough. And my, are we gonna have some fun with you. Mother, especially, is looking forward to seeing you. She'll tear you to shreds. Slowly. Then eat the shreds.'

'You aren't going to do it here then?'

'Oh, I certainly want to, but I can't deny Mother.' Fo shrugged. 'Oleg was supposed to be on hand to transport me back with his wizard mate so Tavish didn't have to trail us himself.' Fo's face darkened for a moment. 'But he had such a hard-on for that damned orc he couldn't resist attacking him and nearly screwing everything up. Good job he killed himself or the Maestro would've fed his soul to Koth.'

Nicolas shuddered at the name.

'Which still leaves us stuck in a clearing,' Nicolas remarked. 'No way I'm letting you drag me anywhere without kicking and screaming the entire way.'

Fo scoffed. 'Not a problem. I've summoned Tavish. He'll be here to pick us up soon enough, and he's bringing enough men to make sure no one gets in our way, if that's even an issue after that nasty tavern fight. Once I get you stashed somewhere safe, they'll go back out and hunt down your companions, who you've helpfully scattered for us. They will die one by one, alone and believing you hate them.' *Dammit.* 'Then you can weep for them like you weep for your mom and pops. Or maybe you can just moan about being kissed by a beautiful woman? What a sad little life you have.'

'Shift isn't a woman,' he snarled, struggling against his bonds but succeeding only in burning his wrists.

'Humblest apologies,' Fo said with zero sincerity before throwing another rock at him. This one hit him in the chest.

'You dirty low life,' Alexi piped up. 'You *dare* make sport of the Assassins Guild?'

Fo snorted and shook his head. 'I keep forgetting you two are here. Are you pair *really* the best the guild have to offer?'

'If we were untied, you would find out,' Alexi threatened.

'And watch you fail to kill me a tenth time?' Fo remarked. 'You're an idiot. This guy saves both you and your sister's lives, and is there any thanks?' The faun didn't wait for an answer. 'See, *this* is why humans are fools. Stupid and single-minded. But you keep talking whilst I cut your sister up. I'll enjoy that.'

'I'll bite,' Emelina threatened.

'You'll die screaming,' Fo shot back casually.

Nicolas struggled anew against his bindings. 'I'll kill you—'

'You'll die slowly and painfully,' Fo snapped. 'And I will love every second of it.'

'I respectfully disagree.'

Nicolas wasn't sure who was more stunned, him or Fo. Stood at the entrance to the clearing was...everyone. And none of them looked pleased with the faun.

'What...? How...?' Fo stammered, getting to his feet. The faun held out a hand. 'Why come back? Don't you remember what he said to...'

Cracking her knuckles with a look of pure fury, Silva advanced on the faun. Fo tried to flee, but Silva was on him in seconds and gave him a thunderous beating as Shift cut Nicolas's bindings.

Finally loose, he rubbed his sore wrists as he found himself echoing Fo's words. 'What...? How...?'

Auron smiled the smuggest smile in the history of smug smiles. 'Me,' he exclaimed proudly.

Nicolas repeated his earlier statement.

'Koth,' Auron said with a slight eyeroll at Nicolas's shudder. 'You can't say that name, and we have been damned careful about not saying it around you. Yet I heard Billy say it. It got me wondering how he knew it, so I started watching him closely. Soon enough, I saw a pattern forming. And once I knew what to look for, it was easy to figure out. He was going around planting all those seeds in your heads, and I was literally stood behind him, watching it happen.'

'Why didn't you warn me?' Nicolas cried. 'Any of us?'

'I tried.' The spirit shrugged. 'Last night, I started to try and tell you to be careful who you trust, but your head was already right up your ass, and you wouldn't listen. I tried the same with the others, but no one wanted to know, so instead I thought I'd let things play out until he revealed his evil plan.' Now the spirit turned to the others, addressing them like a disappointed tutor. 'Besides, I guessed some magic was involved, and I needed to wait until at least some of you were away from that broccoli-wig-wearing buffoon before I could try talking some sense into your thick heads.'

'But how did you convince the others?'

'Auron grabbed us on the side of the road and explained things,' Shift said awkwardly. 'You weren't the only idiot this time round.'

'Which none of you made particularly easy,' the spirit chided.

A small comfort, if any.

Deities, would he ever be able to look any of them in the eye again? How had he let this happen? Well, that was easy. He'd been so caught up in his own shit, for want of a better term, that he'd not really paid attention to much else. Plus, it was him.

Taking a deep breath, he walked over to Fo. Silva didn't look pleased to see him approach, and there was an awkward silence before she finally stepped aside. The warrior had really gone to work on the faun. Even his mother would have trouble recognising him. Slowly, the faun's blackened eyes opened, and the bloody lips curved into a sneer.

'I sense some tension,' Fo said weakly. 'I don't think your friend likes you very—'

Nicolas kicked him in the head before he could finish whatever vile sentence he was about to say. 'Asshole,' he muttered as Fo's head lolled to the side.

CHAPTER 36

He shook his head and blinked several times, like he'd awoken from a long dream. There'd been a cloud over him, and he hadn't even realised it. The voices in his head hadn't even been his. Part of him wanted to send Fo to meet his maniacal brother. But the faun was unconscious, and he was no murderer.

Maybe he is dead? Silva was hitting him quite hard.

In reality, he didn't have time to dally here wondering about the health of a truly terrible person. Not when they had more urgent business to attend to.

'Fo told me Tavish is on his way, and coming with a lot of company,' he told his companions. 'I don't know how long we have until he gets here, but I intend to be ready for him. I'm going to kill whoever he brings with him, capture Tavish, then use him and Fo to lead me to the Maestro. Then he dies too, along with his stupid pet demon.'

'Bold plan, kid.' Auron nodded. 'You know I love it.'

Nicolas glanced back at the faun and let out a dry chuckle. 'I suppose after all this I *am* using him as bait.'

'I can't believe we all fell for it,' Shift said. 'He just mentioned stuff so casually. He says to me, *'Well, at least Nicolas isn't using me as bait.'* And plop. The idea is in my head.'

"So, you're his servant then. No? Oh sorry, I just assumed from the way he tells you what to do'. 'It's nice you all have such a strong bond. Sometimes, ha, I swear looking from the outside in that he doesn't trust you. Good thing I know better.' Silva stared at the faun, breathing heavily. Picking up Fo's head, she hit him with one last wince inducing punch.

'He plies his trade well,' Garaz said with a snarl. 'Telling me how much you all look down on me and...'

But how much of the anger, the distrust was really Billy, and how much of it was me?

'Look, you know we're with you,' Shift said. 'But before we go fighting any battles together, we need to clear the air. Some of the stuff Billy planted, but other things... I think those were just issues we had simmering away anyway. All our hidden paranoias and crap.'

Oh Deities, this is going to be awkward.

The group stood in a circle, yet none of them could really hold the others' gazes. Save Auron, of course, who was a beacon of smugness. The silence between them was almost oppressive.

Who's going first? Please, not me.

'I never let Tavish escape,' Silva began. 'I would never have allowed that, and I need you to believe that.' The warrior's voice was almost emotional. 'I am truly dedicated to renouncing my former life, but I cannot do it without help, without all of you to steer me right. I know that I need telling from time to time in order to be kept in check. I am trying.'

'I believe you, truly,' he confirmed. 'I think I always did. I was just frustrated and, well...wrong.'

Silva's mouth became a thin line. 'And I wish I could remember something to help you. I would do anything for you. Any of you. But it is locked away beyond my reach. All I can do is offer you my sword.'

'I know,' Nicolas said quietly. 'I'm so sorry I didn't trust you.'

'She is still murdering whore,' Gornak muttered.

'What he said.' Auron smiled, looking away quickly at the four glares he received in response.

Silva pursed her lips in annoyance but continued talking to Nicolas. 'And I follow your lead. I know you act in my best interests and do not consider yourself my master.'

'I'm certainly not qualified to be *that*,' he replied with a thin smile.

'I am not so sure,' the warrior said flatly. 'You are starting to show yourself to be a fine leader.'

Nicolas was pretty sure he flushed.

Okay, my turn, I guess. 'I—'

'Shagraz was my brother,' Garaz's words came out choked and hoarse. Shift and Silva's jaws dropped. His too, most likely. 'I know, we are hardly alike, but we are...were...siblings, nonetheless. Shagraz was your more *typical* orc, as some of you can attest to. My more civilised leanings created a rift between us, as he believed that orcs were what they were. But I never knew it had become so bad he would try to kill me.' Shift put a reassuring hand on the orc's shoulder, and Garaz rested his own hand over it. 'I always knew he would die in combat, that was the path he had chosen, but I never thought I would see it, or be part of it. I have been trying to come to terms with what happened, but...'

'I am so sorry,' Nicolas said, his sentiment echoed by the others.

'I appear to have bottled things up,' the orc continued, before allowing a small smile to creep across his serious face. 'Maybe I have spent too much time with Nicolas.'

Does Shift need *to laugh that loud?*

'And as for the boat.' Garaz let out a sigh. 'I am not a man of violence. I have dedicated my life to healing. Unfortunately, in recent times, a certain amount of violence has become necessary.' *Isn't that the truth.* 'On the boat, when I saw the toad creature about to kill Shift, I lost my composure. I *may* have overdone things, but I would do it again to save any of your lives. Yet it is a concept I am struggling with. And seeing the savagery of one of my own family made me dwell on what was in me, and how you all saw me.'

'It got the job done,' Shift said. 'And it was very much appreciated. But I get what you mean. I've been struggling with whether this life was right for me. I thought I was over it then Billy made a remark about whether I think I belong with you all, and bam, here we go again.'

'Do not be too hard on yourself,' Silva interrupted. 'He said there was some magic at play.'

'Still.' Shift shrugged. 'I made a living out of conning people. I should've spotted it. I should've known better. Sorry.'

Garaz bowed his head in acceptance, which Shift returned with a faux curtesy, before looking right at Nicolas. 'You then,' they said with raised eyebrows.

If we must.

'Look, Nick.' Shift was somehow looking right at him and still avoiding eye contact. 'I don't let many people into my life. Trusting people isn't something I generally do, due to the thief life. Or former thief life. And now I have all these people I care about, and I guess I don't always know how to deal with it properly.' Now they looked away from him completely. 'When you died, I didn't know how to handle it. I've never had someone that close to me die before. And then when you came back, my relief manifested in a kiss. But that's all it was: relief. There's nothing more to it than that. So please, please, please, for the love of the Deities, can we never mention it again?' Right now, Nicolas would've given coin to never speak of it again. He would've preferred being tied up with Fo beating him. 'And as for Rex, he's nice and all, but he's like a kid brother. That's it.'

Nicolas looked at Rex, and the thief nodded in agreement.

He knew then that it was finally his turn to speak. Could he say the words that had eluded him for so long? A pressure built in his throat. The others looked at him expectantly as he took a couple of deep breaths.

'I... My...' *Come on, say it.* 'I... I...' *Seriously?* 'My parents are dead,' he finally blurted, as if throwing up. Forcing those four words out was exhausting. 'Fo told me so. I tried to save them, but I couldn't. I was too weak, and I let them die. I tried to face down the demon, I really did.' Already, the tears were streaming down his cheeks. 'If I had been better, more courageous, fought harder...'

It wasn't the hug that surprised him, it was who it came from. Silva held him tightly, her armour digging into his chest, but he wasn't about to complain. His hand shook slightly before he returned the embrace. Despite his dearest wish not to, he sobbed into her shoulder, letting out the days of frustration and pain.

Finally, Silva stepped back, taking his head in her hands and raising his still-watering eyes to meet hers. 'The fact that you stood down a demon host at all is a testament to your courage. You were prepared to fight, lay down your life to protect them. There is no shame in that.'

'But—'

'You are brave and true, Nicolas,' Silva interrupted. 'The rest you will learn. And then we shall rain vengeance on those responsible, me at your side.'

'And I,' Garaz added. 'Apparently, I am quite good at violence when it is called for.'

'You know I'm in.' Auron smiled. 'I can't do much, but any time you need a story that gives you an important life lesson, or someone needs poking in the eye, I'm your spirit.'

'I'm not leaving you to your own devices,' Shift said. 'We leave you alone with Billy for five minutes and you end up knocked out and tied up.'

Wiping the tears from his eyes, he couldn't help but laugh. But there was something else.

'I died.' Another tough thing to say aloud. 'And then I came back. But I don't know if I *came* back. I'm not even sure I'm human anymore. I don't know if I'm feeling the right feelings or that I even belong in this body. I...I think I should still be dead. Occasionally, I still want to be. Maybe then I wouldn't feel...this.'

'I can arrange—' Alexi's words stopped abruptly as Silva fixed the assassin with a death stare.

'Interrupt again, and I shall rip out your tongue,' Silva said through bared teeth, before turning to Nicolas. 'That is acceptable?'

He looked at the assassin. 'In this case, I'll allow it.'

Alexi glared, but his mouth slowly closed.

Garaz put a large hand on his shoulder. 'You are you, Nicolas. Trust me.'

'No one else could piss me off so thoroughly.' Shift smirked.

'And if you weren't human, you'd hardly show mercy to a pair of assassins,' Auron added. 'That's a very Nicolas thing to do. Besides, no undead creature could be so frightened of mounting a horse.'

'Okay,' he said when the group laughed enthusiastically. 'Very funny.'

'We're a family again then?' Shift asked after they'd stopped chuckling.

'If you'll all accept my apologies for being the biggest fool in Etherius.' Nicolas shrugged.

'Wasn't the first time.' Shift smiled. 'And if it's the last then I'm a dragon.'

'But you can turn into one...' Nicolas ventured.

Shift shook their head. 'Tried it once. Too big. I couldn't remember my own name for a day afterwards.'

'Besides,' Garaz began, 'I do not think any of us can take the moral high ground, when all of us acted so poorly to each other.'

Silence descended on the clearing. There was no indication that the group was going to hug, they just moved together as one, embracing each other warmly. Nicolas could almost see the pain numbing, as if Garaz were healing a wound. Speaking of which, he did have some sore wrists the orc could look at.

'Look at all my children getting along.' Auron smiled.

'You still going to call me kid then?' Nicolas asked with a half-smile.

Auron mused over this for a second. 'I don't recall actually stopping. Besides, it's a term of endearment, so you'd best get over it,' the spirit said, before adding, 'Kid.'

Nicolas could live with that. Having them all at peace again calmed him for the first time in a long time. But they did have other issues to attend to.

'So,' he said, turning to Gornak. 'Tavish is on his way. Up for a fight?'

'Now that feelings have been mended,' Gornak smiled, 'Gornak is eager to chop up whoresons. Too much warm and fuzzy gives Gornak belly ache.'

After patting the big man on the shoulder, he walked over to the twins, sitting on the grass next to them. 'What do we do with you two then?'

'We don't like being used,' Emelina said. 'There must be blood.' She almost looked like she was salivating at the idea. It was creepy.

Or maybe she's salivating at me, which is much worse.

'The way I see it...' Nicolas began. 'You were sent to kill Billy, and your contracts are sacred. So how about this? You fight with us and help me capture Tavish. Once I'm sure I have every piece of information I can get out of them, the faun is yours.'

The idea of handing over Fo to be killed didn't exactly sit well with him, but he also didn't want to make eternal enemies of the Assassins Guild, and Fo was a villain.

The twins looked at each other for a long moment. Again, creepy. Finally, Alexi spoke. 'Your proposal is acceptable.'

'And you'll honour your word?'

'Yes.'

'I don't want to be pedantic,' Nicolas said, 'but I'm actually going to have to hear you say it.'

Alexi fumed from behind wide eyes as Emelina giggled. 'This one's smart.'

'Fine,' the assassin said. 'You have my solemn oath that my sister and I will be your allies. We will aid you in securing Tavish in exchange for Fo.' Each word was enunciated slowly, just in case Nicolas wasn't aware how annoyed the assassin was. 'Does that suit, good sir?'

'That'll do,' he said, patting Alexi on the leg, which was not well received.

'Are you sure you'll get them to talk?' the assassin asked.

'She will.' He indicated Silva, who gave him a single nod.

'Oh, yes, yes.' Emelina chuckled. 'They'll talk all right. Sing like little birds they will.'

That's two more on side. And they seem genuine enough. 'Can you cut them loose?' he asked Silva. 'Please?'

As the warrior went to work unbinding the twins, Nicolas stood and walked over to Rex. 'What about it?'

'I'm in,' Rex said almost unwillingly. 'But after this, I really don't want to see any of you ever again. This is not my kind of life, *at all*.'

Nicolas couldn't blame him for that. 'Sorry for shoving you.'

Rex offered his hand, and Nicolas shook it.

Maybe he isn't so bad after all.

'So, what now then?' Shift asked. 'Go back to the tavern and make it defensible?' Their sceptical expression suggested what they really thought of that idea.

'Nope,' Auron replied. 'That place is a wreck. We make our stand here.'

'With what?' Nicolas asked.

The spirit glanced around the clearing and grinned. 'Nature provides, kid.'

CHAPTER 37

The rest of the morning had been laborious, but it had needed to be. They had an attack to prepare for, and for all they knew, Tavish could be bringing five men or fifty. Hopefully five, but with Auron's direction, they were ready for any eventuality.

Ahead of them, the smoke from the second tavern they'd burnt down in the course of a week rose into the sky. It had been the wisest move. Maybe it was too late to stop the guilds going for each others throats over Billy, but at least without a massacre to use as a call to arms, it may lessen the impact.

Nicolas sat on a log, drenched in sweat. How he was supposed to have enough energy left for a fight was anyone's guess.

When they come, I will be ready.

His resoluteness, even in his exhausted state, surprised him.

A water skin appeared in front of his face. Shift smiled at him. 'Drink.' It wasn't a question.

He took the skin with a smile. The water was cool and refreshing.

'If you want to *really* enjoy drink, try drinking from skulls of enemies,' Gornak bellowed from nearby.

Nicolas stared at the big warrior. 'How could you even...?'

Shift tapped him on the shoulder and gave him a slight shake of the head.

They're right. I probably don't want to know. 'Thanks for the tip.' Turning back to Shift, he wiped his mouth dry and handed the skin back. 'We good?'

Shift looked outraged. 'Of course we are. How could you think any different?'

'Just checking.'

'Besides, Nick, we both know you can't stay mad at me.'

'What about the other way around?'

'I'll let you know.' They gave him a cheeky wink before turning and walking away.

That's better.

'You're all done for?' the faun spat from far above them. 'You know that, right?'

'Quiet, shit stirrer,' Nicolas called back. 'Just hang there silently like good little bait.'

'She'll die.' Fo sneered, indicating Shift. 'Just like the rest.'

'*They'll* die,' he corrected patiently, looking up. 'If you're going to threaten us, at least get it right.'

High above him, Fo was dangling in the air. Ropes ran from his hands to the thick branches of the trees on either side of him. Wouldn't do to have Tavish miss the man he was coming to find. Their bait. The faun had been flitting in and out of consciousness after the beating he'd taken, but when he was conscious, he made sure to fling as many furious insults at them as he could before he passed out again. His impotent rage was kind of sad.

'You think pronouns will matter when she's in pieces?'

Fo cried out in pain as a rock struck him between the eyes. 'It's when *they're* in pieces, asshole,' Shift snapped.

'Tried to tell him.' Nicolas sniggered to himself, before nodding to Shift. 'Nice throw.'

'I have a multitude of skills.'

'Ah, another good reason to take the knee and pledge fealty to you again.'

Shift appeared flattered but shook their head. 'I think I know why you were an only child,' they joked. 'There is no way they could make another one of you.'

'My parents won't now.' He sighed.

To his surprise, Shift hugged him. Half of him wondered if he would get a punch in the gut afterward, but the other half was just enjoying the moment.

'I'm sorry,' they said when they broke the hold.

He didn't have words, so he just smiled thankfully. Right now he had to focus on the coming battle. He knew pushing his emotions aside wasn't always his best move, but weeping from grief during a fight was a sure way to get killed. There would be plenty of time later to grieve them properly.

'Remind me why we did not gag him?' Garaz asked, looking up at Fo with distaste.

'I thought he'd be out longer than this.' Silva shrugged.

'Nonsense.' Gornak laughed. 'It is good to hear mewling of defeated enemies. It feeds soul better than king's feasts.'

If you insist.

'I'll tolerate that this once,' Alexi warned from the tree he leant by. 'But if sh...they throw another rock and kill him before I can, we shall be having words.'

'He knows I'm stood right next to you and can hear you, right?' Shift asked loudly.

'Yeah,' Nicolas confirmed. 'I think he's just intimidated.'

Alexi used a very profane phrase to explain his thoughts on *that* idea.

'You are up for this fight, right?' Nicolas asked. 'I mean, you're assassins, not warriors, per se?'

Alexi answered with his middle finger.

From their open mouth, he guessed Shift was about to level a snappy retort at the assassin—Deities knew they could match Alexi's language when they fancied it—but they were interrupted by a thump as Rex jumped off the lowest branch of the tree he'd been perched on and landed in a pile of soft moss with a deft roll, before getting to his feet.

'They're coming,' the thief told them, the worry lines on his forehead indicating his lack of confidence in the upcoming battle.

This is it then. Tavish is finally here. Time to make our stand. Fight or die.

No, he corrected himself. The only dying will be done by anyone foolish enough to accompany Tavish here. Once they're out of the way, he's ours.

The group moved to the edge of the forest and looked out over the horizon, following the line of Rex's finger. At first, there was just the crest of a hill and the fields and sky beyond. Then movement caught Nicolas's eye. Riders came over the rise. Right now, they were only distant bobbing shadows, but unmistakable.

'How many?' Shift asked nervously.

'I'd say near thirty,' Auron answered.

'I didn't *really* want to know,' they replied, looking unhappier now they had a clearer number.

Definitely more than five.

The spirit shrugged. 'The plan's still good.'

'And you think these things we've built will work?' As much faith as Nicolas had in Auron, he still needed to hear some reassurance.

'Of course,' the spirit replied breezily. All right for him, he couldn't die. 'Trust me. I've done this before.'

'And the bear-folk knew their business, right?' Nicolas asked.

The spirit looked confused. 'The *who*?'

'The...bear-folk,' he continued. 'You said you were taught this stuff by little bear folk who lived in the woods.'

'Oh yeah.' Auron sniggered. 'So I did.'

Shift put his arm around his shoulder. 'You are so sweet when you're being naïve.'

He shrugged Shift's arm away. 'Oh, very funny. You mean I had to listen to a whole story about bear-folk that wasn't real?'

Auron turned away, but his ethereal shoulders shook with suppressed laughter. 'You even went all wide-eyed when I described how cuddly they were.' The spirit laughed. 'I mean, how would little bear people even get those huge logs up there?'

'You ass.'

'Oh,' Auron said, clicking his fingers, 'I forgot to mention. They even had these magic potions. If they drank them, they'd bounce around—'

'Enough,' Nicolas interrupted.

'I bet you wished you could meet one and hug it.' Shift sniggered.

'Can we *please* focus on the oncoming cavalry charge?' Alexi sniffed. 'I wouldn't care to be exchanging jests when they arrive.'

'Are you worried?' Shift asked with a half-smile. 'Being in a battle is a bit different than sneaking up on someone from behind and stabbing them.'

The assassin didn't deign to respond, his cold gaze saying what he wouldn't.

'He's not wrong,' Nicolas cut in before Shift riled him up more. 'Let's take our places.' He spared another look at the oncoming riders.

Wow, they're a lot closer already. They must be pushing their mounts hard.

Before he moved, a thought occurred to him. Reaching into the pouch on his belt, he took out the yellow jewel.

Controls giants. Deities I am gullible sometimes.

Placing it on a log, he unceremoniously smashed it with a rock.

'Just in case,' he shrugged in response to Auron's raised eyebrow.

As the group dispersed to their various spots, Nicolas stopped Garaz. 'I know I've said it already, but I'm sorry about your brother.' He kept eye contact with the wizened yellow eyes. 'I know it may be tough to talk about him, but any time you want to, I'll listen.'

Garaz looked like he wanted to say a lot, but instead, he gripped Nicolas's shoulder and bowed his head. 'We will both share our grief once this is done.'

'Looks like we're all friends again,' Shift ventured.

Friends. It disappointed him a lot more than he'd expected.

'I'm going to go behind the tree and get ready.' Meaning they were going to take their clothes off before changing. 'No checking out my butt when I'm walking away.'

'I'll try to resist.' Nicolas grinned.

'You'll fail.' They winked. 'You always do.'

He proved them right a moment later...and Shift was already looking back at him, waiting for it. But at least they were back to normal again, funny kind of normal though it was.

As the rest took their positions, he watched the riders. Now he could make out the varied collection of weapons they carried and those horrible masks they wore. In the centre of the formation was Tavish, just as he remembered him. The dragon-helmed warrior approached with resolution.

'You're mine,' Nicolas growled.

'Many whoresons will die this day,' Gornak added, his massive battle axe still slung behind his back.

'Except the leader,' Nicolas said. 'We need him alive, remember?'

The look on Gornak's face didn't inspire confidence.

'Tavish,' he said, pointing to the black knight. 'The guy in the black armour and the dragon helm. We need him alive. We discussed that. Remember?'

'Yes, yes,' the warrior said with a dismissive wave of his hand. 'Gornak remembers. I shall leave that whoreson alive.'

Still, might be better if I get to him before Gornak.

They were at the edge of the forest, but that wasn't where the battle would take place. This was just the starting point, so Tavish and his men could see their bait clearly. But it meant Nicolas could see them too. Standing down thirty odd warriors wasn't for the faint of heart, and Nicolas had to fight back his rising panic, controlling his breathing until it buggered off.

I will do right by my parents. I will do right by the people of Hablock.

At his feet, the ground tremored under the massed hooves closing on them. Mentally, he attempted to run himself through his fight training. Only to find his mind blank.

What are my sword positions? How was it Silva taught me to throw someone? Do I lead with the left or right leg in that sword stance Ramirez showed me?

His eyes shot open as something furry touched his hand. A great black panther was pressing its snout into his palm. He crouched beside it. As animalistic as the beast looked, those green eyes were unmistakable. 'Thank you,' he whispered. 'And be careful.'

The panther gave a derisive snort, baring its teeth. The message was clear. It was the enemy who needed to be careful. He gave the panther a rub behind the ear before it sloped off into the bushes.

'Ready, kid?' Auron asked.

Nicolas smiled uncertainly. 'As I'll ever be.'

'That's all I can ask,' the spirit said. 'Remember your training, and if you need me to possess you—'

'I won't. Thanks,' he cut in quickly.

Well, maybe in an emergency.

'I know, kid.' Auron rolled his eyes. 'Believe it or not, it took it out of me, too, last time. I know I've mentioned it a bit lately, but only because I had a taste of the good life again in the Underworld.' *That was the good life?* 'I'll try to tame it a little. But I'll still ask occasionally.'

Nicolas smiled at his companion-slash-mentor. 'I know. Maybe one day I'll need it.'

'I pray for the day.' Auron chuckled, lifting his crossed fingers. 'By the way, Gornak's not going to just wait for them to come to us.'

Nicolas looked at the huge warrior. He was glaring at the attackers from behind his bushy eyebrows. But why wouldn't he glare at approaching enemies? Other than that, he appeared to be fine. Sometimes, even Auron talked rubbish.

'He's fine,' Nicolas replied.

'We'll see,' the spirit said knowingly. 'Gornak knowing the plan and Gornak following the plan don't usually marry up too well.'

'I have faith,' he said, focusing on the oncoming enemy.

Tavish and his men were really close now, nearly to the edge of the forest, coming at them in a neat line. The tremoring of the ground became an all-out rumble. Looking to his sides, he saw his companions arrayed out in their places. All of them were back from the edge of the forest; that was essential. They needed the enemy to come to them, to be split up.

It'd be nice if we had an archer or two.

Bit late now, though. The enemy were upon them, and they had to use what they had.

Which is an orc who can throw fireballs.

'Garaz,' Nicolas called. 'Now.'

Six fireballs emerged from the forest, striking the line at different points. For the most part, they hit nothing, but two of the riders were thrown from their horses, the men now flailing infernos as they rolled in the grass, screaming. The point hadn't really been to hit anything—those were a bonus—but to make the enemy break formation, to split them into manageable chunks. To make them easier to kill.

'That's a good start,' he whispered as the line broke into several smaller groups. Leaves rustled as Garaz returned to the group and took his position. They exchanged nods.

'*Whoresoooooooons,*' Gornak's voice echoed from tree to tree as the big warrior charged.

'Told you,' Auron remarked casually. 'Not a *wait for the enemy kind of guy*, old Gornak.'

'No, Gornak, wait!' Nicolas was set to pursue their new companion, but if he left his post as well, the whole plan might go up in flames. And he couldn't allow that just because a certain warrior didn't understand the word *wait*.

'He'll be fine,' the spirit said breezily.

'He hasn't even unslung his weapon,' Nicolas cried.

'Just watch.' Auron smirked.

Gornak, who could move surprisingly quickly for a seven-foot man, met the enemy in the field just before they breached the forest. Meeting the first rider head on, the big warrior punched him clean from his saddle. Even as the surprised man flew through the air, Gornak yanked another from his saddle by the collar and headbutted him. The warrior was wearing a metal mask and helmet; Gornak was not. Yet the rider's body went limp as the big brute tossed him aside. Finally, he unslung his axe. A third rider charged, spear at the ready. When he approached Gornak, he was whole, but by the time he passed the giant warrior only a pair of disembodied legs remained in the saddle. The tree nearest the pair was flecked in blood.

'Okay then,' Nicolas said in awe, looking at the *Dawn Blade*. Could he do that?

Whatever happened to Gornak next, Nicolas couldn't see, because four riders formed up on the track before him, urging their horses to a gallop. Coming to ride him down.

'Now.' Even as Nicolas said the word, he turned and ran back into the forest.

A wise leader would've stopped the pursuit, but Tavish and his men had their blood up.

Running full pelt, Nicolas slid to a stop beside a tree, Auron beside him.

'So no bears then?' Nicolas asked as Tavish's men bore down on him.

'Nope,' Auron replied.

'Let's see if your tree-trunk sorcery is all you say.' Swinging the sword, Nicolas cut the rope he was stood beside.

The rope shot up into the trees as the weight it had been holding back for so long took hold. The log came down much faster than it'd gone up. Tied at each end, the log swung down in an arc from the trees above, colliding with each of the four riders simultaneously, knocking them from their mounts to the forest floor, accompanied by a loud crash.

With a single deep breath to steel himself, Nicolas charged. The first of the riders had barely made it to his knees and was looking up in shock by the time the *Dawn Blade* was swinging toward him. With a cry, he fell back, Nicolas already turning to the next opponent. Behind him, he heard two distinct thumps. He guessed he'd taken the man's head but had no inclination to check.

The second of the rider's eyes went from his dead comrade to Nicolas and then to his sword, which lay on the ground beside him. Nicolas was almost sympathetic; he'd dropped his sword enough times. As the man went for his blade, Nicolas dashed forward. Tavish's man had grabbed the hilt of the sword and was picking it up as the *Dawn Blade* swung in an upward arc. The rider fell back, an arc of blood spraying into the air.

'*Yaarrrgggghhhh.*'

Nicolas managed to parry the stabbing sword away just in time as the third rider came at him. The man brought his blade up to block Nicolas's downward strike. Metal clashed. The warrior pushed him away then swung his sword in a horizontal arc. He jumped back just in time, the tip of the sword missing his stomach by inches. The masked warrior circled him, looking for an opening as the sounds of battle echoed through the forest around them. Nicolas tried not to let worry about his companions distract him; that would be deadly here. At last, his opponent charged, thrusting his blade forward. Nicolas batted the weapon away before driving in with his own sword, running the man through. The grunt of pain as the sword pierced the warrior's stomach was almost as bad as the '*urk*' sound when Nicolas drew the blade out again.

What?

Somehow, his opponent wasn't quite done yet, drunkenly trying to raise his sword to attack. Nicolas cut him twice across the stomach before kicking him away. This time, he had the good manners to die when he was supposed to, blood pumping out of his wound and—

Is that intestine? Oh Deities, I just saw a bit of intestine.

Fighting back the urge to vomit, he saw the fourth rider getting up. Judging by the wheezing sound and how he clutched his chest, the log had struck him a lot harder than his comrades. Seeing Nicolas, the warrior drew an axe from his belt and advanced...but he didn't make it, first falling to one knee, then to both, and then face-down on the ground. Just to be sure, Nicolas finished him with a downward thrust of his sword.

Not a bad start.

But it wasn't over by a long shot. A blur of motion caught his peripheral vision, and he ducked just as a spear went to skewer his head. Reacting instantly, the rider turned his mount, and Nicolas was immediately struck to the ground as the horse bumped him. Reflexes kicking in, he rolled with the fall, managing to come to a standing position as the rider loomed over him. All he could do was watch in horror as the man changed the grip on his spear, ready to launch it.

With a feral roar, the black panther burst from the undergrowth, leaping onto the warrior's back with a single bound of its four muscular legs. The man only had an instant to cry out before he was knocked from his horse. The panther landed atop him, driving its thick fangs into his throat as the horses bolted. With a bloody snout, the panther growled at the now-dead rider, challenging him to try anything else.

I let that mouth kiss me...after a fashion.

'Thanks,' he said to Shift. 'It's a good thing you didn't leave. Saving my life is a full-time job.'

Green eyes locked with his for a moment, a glint of amusement in them, before panther Shift growled and bounded off to find another enemy. As they did, Nicolas's eye was drawn to the bushes beyond him. Rex fell from a tree onto the back of one of the horses, wrapping his arm around its rider's neck as he repeatedly stabbed him in the back. As the rider went limp, Rex brought his knife up and cut his throat just to be sure, before jumping off the horse and running away.

Somewhere ahead of him there was a bright flash, a *whumph*, and a scream.

I bless the day Garaz decided to learn fire magic. But I hate the fact I can tell someone's on fire by the pitch of their scream.

The thumping of hooves forced him to concentrate. Turning, he saw a warrior bearing down on him. The attacker thrust with his spear as he passed, but Nicolas parried it with the *Dawn Blade*. It all happened so fast that Nicolas didn't notice the rider following in his wake until it was nearly too late. The axe rose to strike, but the strike was never made. Instead, the rider suddenly went limp and fell from his horse, a long dart protruding from his neck. Emelina, blowgun in hand, emerged from a bush, grinning insanely, before blowing him a kiss and disappearing. Readying himself to face the spear-wielding rider, he turned to find him dead.

'I save your life as easily as I could take it,' Alexi sneered as he backed into the foliage.

'You tried and failed. Three times,' he snapped.

'Maybe the fourth time will be the charm?' The assassin smiled before vanishing from sight.

Beyond the battle cries and clashing blades, Nicolas heard an unusual sound: singing. At first, he couldn't place it, but as he listened, he made out the tuneless song.

'This whoreson dies. And that whoreson dies. This whoreson dies. And that whoreson dies.'

Gornak would never make it as a bard.

On the forest trail ahead, two sword-wielding riders charged him, blades high and ready. Not fancying taking both on at once, Nicolas fell back. It wasn't cravenness but a strategy. Before long, a pair of rocks swung down from the trees. One of the riders was knocked clean from his horse and the other was diverted by the blow, charging to the left. The horse saw the pit before the rider, coming to a sudden halt and throwing its rider overhead, right into the hole full of spiked sticks.

'Those little bears know their stuff.' Auron smiled, standing beside the tree where the ropes keeping the rocks in place had been tied.

Nicolas rolled his eyes. 'Very funny.'

Not being able to fight conventionally, the spirit's role was to run around and spring their traps. At least Auron was finding a way to be useful.

The sound of running got his attention. Rex ran by, pursued by a rider with a swinging morningstar, its spiked ball moving almost too fast to see.

'I'll help him,' Auron called, disappearing through the trees. 'He's going toward the spiked log trap.'

Looking around, Nicolas realised that he couldn't see his other companions now. But all in all, he thought the battle was going pretty well.

Right up until the moment Alric Tavish rode past him, grabbing him by the collar and pulling him in the wake of his horse.

CHAPTER 38

P art of him had to admire Tavish's iron grip. Only a small part, though, as the rest was concentrating on keeping pace with the galloping horse so his body wasn't dragged along the forest floor. Every so often, he'd stumble a step, his legs flailing as he desperately tried to right himself.

After what seemed like an eternity, the grip on his shirt was released, and he went rolling across the ground, his legs unable to counteract the sudden stop in motion. Finally coming to a halt, he lay on the floor, directly under Fo, trying to bring the world back into focus.

With a cry, Nicolas rolled to the side just in time. The stream of urine struck the ground like a gross waterfall, landing where he'd just been lying.

'Dammit,' Fo cried from above. 'So close.'

You dirty bastard.

Nicolas took his glare from the faun to Tavish, who sat atop his black mount, regarding him silently.

'Yes,' the faun shouted with glee, staring down at him. 'You're done for now, boy. Shame I missed. I'd love to strip you of your dignity before Tavish kills you. I'll have to settle for pissing on your corpse.'

Ignoring the faun, he pushed himself from the ground. His legs wanted to refuse his command, but he wasn't giving them a choice. Shakily, he stood tall. Thankfully, the dizziness passed quickly. His gaze was briefly drawn to his hand, and he let out an impressed chuckle.

Huh, I'm still holding my sword.

Swinging the sword in the air in front of him several times, he prepared himself. Part of him was glad this was one on one. He'd waited so long to get Tavish that it felt right the battle should be between them, even if he had no real idea who the man was. Besides, if the others got involved, there was more chance of Tavish accidentally being killed. In his fighting stance, he pointed the tip of his blade toward the black knight, feeling the intensity of his gaze from behind the visor of his helmet.

'Alric Tavish,' he said in his most commanding voice. 'Yield and tell me where your masters are.'

For a long moment, the black knight didn't reply. When he did, it was simple and to the point. 'No.'

Worth a try.

Maybe one day he'd meet a villain who would just yield? Somehow, he doubted it, but he made a note to ask Auron if it'd ever happened before.

'Come on then,' he challenged.

Tavish accepted the invitation. Drawing a long spear from his saddle, Tavish secured it at his side, tucked under his armpit, and kicked his mount, spurring it into a charge.

Horse and rider bore down on him, but he didn't flinch. He wasn't about to run from this fight. That wasn't him anymore. That Nicolas had been left behind a piece at a time—on a bridge, in an arena, on a ship, and in the land of the dead. Instead, he focused on his opponent, ready for battle.

Tavish aimed low, intent on not missing. As the spear tip came closer, he moved forward to meet it, to parry it away, but his legs were still not entirely right, and he stumbled. The knight tried to adjust the aim of his weapon, but it was too cumbersome to manoeuvre at speed. Yet the tip of the spear, instead of impaling him through the chest, cut a gash in his thigh. Crying out in pain, he staggered to a tree stump for support. The cut bled freely, but it didn't seem too deep.

How am I still standing?

A snort made him turn. Tavish was bringing his steed around for another pass.

As long as he's on that horse, he'll have the advantage.

Knowing that he couldn't face the mounted attacker head on, he rolled aside again, hoping for inspiration before the spear finally found it's mark. Tavish's head turned, as he rode by, watching Nicolas, but not where he was guiding his mount. The horse caught its leg in a rabbit hole, shrieking as it fell forward, flinging its rider off. The Black Knight went head over heels, slamming heavily into the floor with a thunderous crash that made Nicolas wince.

An actual piece of luck. Except for the poor horse.

As much as he wanted to feel for the animal that had just been hurt, he knew his opponent wouldn't stay down for long. He had to use that time. The battle echoed across the forest as he tore a strip from his shirt and hastily bound the wound. Tentatively, he flexed his leg. The wound looked bad, but he could still move it. Yet he knew even a slight disadvantage here could be disastrous.

The sound of metal grinding told him Tavish was rising. After pushing himself up from the floor, the knight wavered slightly, before unleashing a feral shout, as if commanding his body to do as he willed.

Slowly, his opponent turned to him. His armour was a mass of dents, and the head of the dragon atop his helm had been torn off. With a growl, he marched to the saddle of his crippled horse, drew a flail from the saddle, and used it to finish his mount with a wet thud.

I hope you find peace, and a better rider, in the next life.

Then Tavish came at him, swinging the flail wildly. The metal ball was a blur, hard to track. Attempting to do it soon became hypnotic, so he stopped and readied himself.

With a cry, Tavish charged, lashing out with his weapon. Nicolas brought the *Dawn Blade* up to counter. The metal ball struck the sword, knocking it aside and causing waves of pain to travel up his arms. How he managed to keep a grip on his sword was beyond him.

When it's sword versus flail, flail wins. Got it.

With a cry, the knight swung down. Nicolas jumped aside, and the weapon thumped into the ground, throwing up dead leaves and clods of earth. Turning, Tavish swung the weapon horizontally. The blow glanced Nicolas's left arm. He stumbled back, furious pain flashing up his arm like a lightning bolt. It didn't feel broken, but it might as well have been for how badly it hurt.

The pair got into a dance. Swing and dodge, swing and dodge. Nicolas had done this dance before with a hammer-wielding maniac on a bridge. It hadn't ended well for him. At least there was no water for him to fall into.

Actually, it worked out better the second time. Have some faith in yourself.

Tavish swung down again, and Nicolas stepped to the side. *Crunch.* This time, the flail stuck in the thick tree root it had battered with its strike. The flail refused to budge as Tavish tugged on it, which meant it wouldn't come away easily. That tug told him he had a chance.

Charging forward with a cry, Nicolas seized his opportunity. Tavish saw him coming, abandoning his weapon and drawing his sword just in time to counter Nicolas's attack. Blades clashed.

Sword on sword, that was more in Nicolas's comfort zone. As comfortable as he got fighting, anyway. But Tavish had clearly been doing this a lot longer than he had. The knight came in with a flurry of attacks, alternating between high and low strikes as Nicolas desperately intercepted each one with his own blade. The knight was forcing him back under his aggressive advance and greater strength. Several times, Nicolas almost fell, his weak leg betraying him. All the while, Fo screamed down at them, apoplectic, 'Kill him! Kill the boy.' Apparently the faun was no longer worried about taking him to Mother, and wanted more instant gratification.

He may get it too. There's going to be a point where I either fall or run out of room to retreat.

Between his sword training with Auron, Silva, and a certain Captain Ramirez, Nicolas was becoming pretty decent with the blade. Still, sword fighting was sword fighting. Nicolas dodged a cut too slowly, earning him a diagonal slash across his chest—enough to tear his clothes and mark his skin, but not enough that anything inside him ended up on the outside. It hurt, but he couldn't give in to the pain. He was still in the fight.

But the slight victory spurred Tavish on. Using his weight advantage, the black knight came in with strike after strike, battering down on his sword. Nicolas held his guard up, but the repeated strikes wore away at him, and soon his weakened leg gave out, and he was forced to a single knee.

Come on, you're better than this.

Focusing on what he'd learnt, he rolled to the side as the next strike came, forcing himself to his feet—despite the not-inconsiderable pain—as Tavish came in with a horizontal strike. Blocking the blow with his blade, he let the swords part, swinging the *Dawn Blade* around in an arc that brought it down on the knight's helmet. Tavish cried out in pain as he stumbled backwards, one of the dragon's wings on the helm missing to reveal a bloodied chin.

Enraged, the Black Knight charged. In a moment of inspiration, Nicolas crouched low at the last second, allowing Tavish to roll over his shoulders. Knight and armour together were heavy, but so was his motivation, and he drove up, ignoring the pain in his wounded leg as he threw the knight to the floor with another mighty crash.

Oh, he's dropped his sword.

Smirking at the irony, Nicolas grabbed the blade and threw it into the bushes.

Slowly, the black knight rose, using the body of his horse to push himself to his feet. Nicolas kept the tip of his sword pointed toward him. 'Do you yield?'

I really hope he yields.

The knight brought his armoured fingers up to his exposed cheek. When he took his hand away, there was blood on his finger. With s roar of rage, the Black Knight grabbed the crossbow from his saddle and levelled it at Nicolas.

Oh no.

Watching Tavish, he kept his sword guard up, looking for some sign that the knight was about to fire. He'd only have one chance to dodge the arrow, and even then, he wasn't sure he could.

'Why aren't you *killing* him, *idiot*?' Fo screamed down at them.

The black knight looked from him to the faun then raised his arm toward Fo and pulled the crossbow's trigger. The arrow launched.

'*Noooooooooo*,' he cried as it impaled Fo's throat. The faun's body spasmed then went limp. Blood rained down on them.

Why? Why not shoot me?

His ears told him the truth of it. The battle around them was dying, the sounds of fighting fading. Tavish couldn't kill Nicolas and get the faun down before fleeing. And the Maestro didn't care for witnesses.

But still. There's a chance.

Or maybe not. Already, Tavish was reloading the weapon. Acting on instinct, Nicolas grabbed a knife from his belt and launched it. There had been no plan, no aiming, but the knife struck the crossbow, severing the string and making the weapon useless.

Yes.

'Your weapon is spent. *Yield*, Tavish,' he commanded.

'You wish,' the knight spat back.

Deities damn it.

The knight pressed a concealed button on one of his gauntlets, and a half-sword-sized blade emerged from within it. Tavish held his new weapon up with a cruel smile.

'Oh, come on,' Nicolas cried. 'How many weapons do you *have*?'

Enough of this guy already.

He charged, throwing himself at the knight in fury. Though Tavish had the wrist blade, he couldn't match the reach or ferocity of Nicolas's attacks. One errant attempt to block, and the *Dawn Blade* sheared the dagger in two. Unperturbed, Tavish stepped back, drawing a pair of long knives from his belt.

'Will you just *yield* already?' Nicolas cried in exasperation.

The Black Knight did not. Tavish came at him with the knives. Parrying one, Nicolas removed the other, along with the hand holding it. The knight cried out and the stump bled freely, but the injury only seemed to egg Tavish on as he attacked with the other knife. Nicolas's hand was cut, the *Dawn Blade* involuntarily falling from his grip as blood poured from the wound.

Tavish kicked the sword away as Nicolas bent to retrieve it, slashing with the knife as he did. Nicolas just managed to avoid the blow, though the tip of the knife caressed his cheek. Ducking another slash from Tavish's weapon, Nicolas grabbed an old log from the floor, swinging it wildly. It struck Tavish's armour, making the knight stumble backwards. Nicolas pressed the advantage, coming in with blow after blow until the log snapped in his hands. All Tavish could do was reel from the assault.

Discarding his ruined weapon, he snatched a stone from the floor, intent on pressing his advantage and finishing this. One solid crack to the knight's exposed jaw would be all it'd take.

Tavish listed drunkenly but was certainly not out of the fight—or cunning. Flinging his handless arm, he flicked blood from the wound, right into Nicolas's eyes, blinding him. Stepping back and dropping the rock, he wiped his eyes, trying to get the warm liquid out of them.

Then there was pain.

The knife was embedded in his side. It should've been a killing blow, but the fight was taking its toll on both of them. Enough so that Tavish's aim was poor. Still, it was agony and bleeding freely. In his mind, he saw his hopes of finding his people, of avenging them, slipping away.

No.

His hand clasped Tavish's, the metal of the gauntleted hand cutting his palm as the knight tried to remove the knife. Nicolas kept it in place. The wound burned fiercely as the pair wrestled with the knife, each movement sending a lance of white-hot pain through him, enough that he thought he might pass out at any second. His energy was giving out, his body succumbing to his wounds.

No.

He hadn't come this far, fought so hard, endured so much to lose now.

'*Nooooo,*' he screamed in Tavish's face.

Acting on instinct, all thoughts of strategy gone, he reached out with his free hand, grabbing Tavish's broken helmet, yanking at it as the knight roared in anger. The jagged metal cut into his other palm.

Finally, the helmet came away. Before him was a thick-jawed, bald man, who scowled at him with absolute hatred. His head appeared to be covered in some kind of writing that Nicolas had neither the time nor the inclination to try to read.

Nicolas took the helmet he'd stolen and used it to batter his opponent. Again and again, he swung it, each time the helmet connecting with its former owner's face to the tune of a beautiful thud, until Tavish's face was a bloody mess.

Releasing his grip on the knife, Tavish staggered backwards, a nasty gash across his forehead making his face a crimson mask.

Nicolas swayed and nearly fell, the abuse to his body almost too much to bear. He held the knife, willing himself upright. This wasn't over. Not yet.

'Do...you...yield...?' he asked between ragged, painful breaths.

'No,' Tavish snarled in response.

'Can you just bloody *yield* now!' Nicolas screamed, his frustration getting the best of him.

Please, I don't know how much of this I can bear.

Tavish smiled menacingly then spat blood and teeth onto the floor. 'Never.'

'You're just a man.' Why wouldn't this guy give in already?

Tavish let out a harsh laugh. 'I am no mere man, boy. I am a chosen servant of God, destined to smite heathens like yourself and cleanse this world of the weak and impure.'

'I'm not taking a lesson in weakness from a guy with one hand.'

There was a click, and a small blade protruded from the tip of Tavish's boot.

Oh, come on. This is getting ridiculous now.

Quickly, he pulled the knife from his boot, just as the black knight aimed a kick at his side. Impressive, considering the amount of armour he wore. Nicolas grabbed the leg then drove his knife between the armoured plates and into Tavish's shoulder. As the knight grunted in pain, he released his grip on the blade and wrapped his arm around Tavish's waist. With his last strength, Nicolas hauled the black knight into the air and slammed him spine-first onto the forest floor, before collapsing beside the knight.

Both of them lay panting on the ground, looking up at Fo's dripping corpse, hung like a piece of meat in a butcher's shop.

Nicolas couldn't get up. All the fighting, the wounds he'd suffered. He was spent. He couldn't even wiggle his fingers. He really hoped Tavish was the same.

Damn it.

Rising to his elbows with the carefulness of someone in great pain, Tavish looked at him and laughed. 'That all your fight gone then, boy?' the knight asked. 'All that effort, and you still fail? Never mind. Won't have to live long with your shame.'

There was a rock in the knight's hand. Part of him couldn't believe that all of this, from the start with that bloody choosing stick, had led to him being bludgeoned to death with a rock on some forest floor. And there was nothing he could do about it. He couldn't move. He was done.

Tavish readied the rock, lifting it high...before crying out in surprise as a giant axe blade embedded itself in his chest.

Noooooooo.

'Whoresons do not hurt Gornak's friends,' Gornak declared as he pulled the axe out.

The black knight's eyes were wide then glassy and then they closed as Alric Tavish died beside him.

'We were supposed to take him *alive*,' Nicolas muttered weakly.

The giant warrior looked abashed. 'Oh. Sorry.'

All of this. For nothing.

Dammit.

CHAPTER 39

Everything was going dark then bright again, as if someone were blowing out a lantern on a dark night, only to light it again immediately. But there was no lantern. He was slipping in and out of consciousness because his body was a wreck. He was bleeding quite a bit, but he had no energy to do anything about it. Above him, the dead faun hung limply in the ropes that had been used to bind him.

There was another bout of blackness, and as the light returned, he started. Heads hovered over him. All his companions looked down at him, their faces grave with concern, save Alexi, who was grinning broadly.

Asshole.

Emelina was weeping freely.

Deities, I must be worse than I thought. Is this it then. My second death is going to be the one that sticks.

All his work would be left unfinished.

Oh crap, that means I'm going to come back as a ghost.

Though his companions would finish what he'd started. He trusted them, to his core. No idiot faun whispering poison would ever shake that trust again. Not that it mattered much now.

A glint caught his eye.

Is that a tear on Shift's cheek?

Nicolas was aware that Garaz was touching him, but only because he saw it. His body was numb. He was no healer, but that was a bad sign. Suddenly, his ears began to work again, and he realised people were talking to him.

'Kid? Kid?' Auron sighed with relief as Nicolas's eyes went to the spirit. 'You slayed your first black knight. Quite an achievement. You should be proud of yourself.'

'I thought you said black knights were all posers?' he replied weakly.

'Well,' the spirit shifted uncomfortably, 'they are, but you're quite inexperienced, and I thought a confidence boost would be good.'

Technically, Nicolas hadn't been the one to slay him, so it was a hollow gesture. Besides, Auron could've dispatched Tavish in a moment, whereas he was nearly dead. He still had a lot left to learn.

If I live.

'I will miss you, my love,' Emelina wailed. 'My only hope is that our souls meet in the next life, to renew our great romance.'

'Will you shut her up?' Shift snapped at Alexi.

The assassin shrugged. 'We have been together all our lives, and I've yet to learn how to do that.'

'Then you can at least stop grinning,' Shift said.

'I could, but—'

'Or else.' Silva's intervention made the smile drop from the assassin's lips and stay gone.

'Does it hurt?' Rex asked, looking him over.

'No,' he replied. 'I can't really feel anything.'

Garaz's eyes widened slightly, and he started moving faster, which was...concerning.

At least I'll die around my family. And two assassins, and a guy I'm still not really fond of.

'You are brave warrior, little Nicolas,' Gornak said brightly. 'You will survive. Gornak is happy. The blood of many whoresons decorates his axe this day. Thank you for allowing Gornak to join your fight.'

And Gornak.

'You're welcome.'

His eyes were again drawn to the dead figure above him.

'We lost Fo,' he moaned quietly. 'And Tavish.'

'Do not worry about that now,' Silva said, almost softly. 'Concentrate on healing. We shall find another way to track down your people.'

'Exactly.' Auron smiled. 'As much as they think they're all subtle and stealthy, these villains are actually quite loud. We'll pick up the trail again.'

'I hope so.' He sighed. 'I just need to live first.'

'You will,' Garaz said as he worked. Nicolas was quite pleased he couldn't move his head and see what the orc was doing. 'Especially if you quieten down, save your energy, and let me work.'

'Okay,' he said with a chuckle. 'I fancied passing out now anyway.'

And he did.

The field was very pleasant. It was comfortably warm, with a slight breeze. Sitting on the grass, his arms around his knees, Nicolas just took a moment to breathe.

'Hello, Nicolas.' It was his mother's voice. Someone had sat down beside him, but he didn't want to turn and look, just in case his mind was about to pull the rug out from under him and show him a hideous zombie.

'Nice day for it, son.'

Now he knew his father was there too, he had to look.

Thankfully, neither of them were hideous, decayed creatures. They were just his parents. He allowed himself a sigh of relief.

'You've been busy, I see,' his father said with a cheery grin. 'Plenty of battles.'

'There certainly have been,' he said with a derisive chuckle. 'I'm sorry.'

His mother furrowed her brow. 'What for?'

'Failing,' he answered honestly. 'All my efforts, and I'm still no closer than I was.'

'Nonsense.' His mother smiled, putting her hand on his. Though it was all in his mind, it felt real enough. 'You did so well. You did what was right—'

'Protecting Billy...Fo...certainly wasn't the right thing to do,' he interrupted bitterly.

'But you didn't know that at the time,' his mother retorted firmly. 'You followed your heart. That's what's important.'

'Besides, the world's full of sneaky little bastards.' His father grunted. 'You're still new to this. Things like this are going to happen.'

'Oh,' Nicolas said with a raised eyebrow. 'You make it sound like I'm continuing?'

'Of course you are.' His father chuckled heartily. 'You still need to find our people. Don't even pretend you're giving up. We are in your mind, you know.'

That was true enough. Though despair gripped him because he had no idea what to do next, he wasn't about to throw down his sword and go to what was left of home.

'I'm also sorry that you're dead,' he said sadly, turning from his parents.

'None of that was your fault,' his mother said.

Tears ran down his cheeks. 'I'll avenge you.'

'Nicolas Percival Carnegie.' His mother's firm tone snapped him to attention. 'You will not go off half-cocked on some vengeance quest. You do that, and it'll consume you, and that nearly happened without Fo's help.'

'I...'

'Fight the good fight for the right reasons,' his father added. 'To save those who still live. To stop evil from getting worse.' His father gave him a coy grin. 'But if you fancy giving this Maestro a kick in the balls in our name, I think the universe will be all right with that.'

His gaze fell to the ground. Grass had it so simple. Grow. Sway in the breeze. No commitments, no crusades, just the occasional ass plonking down on it.

'What if I can't do it?'

His mother put her hand on his chin and raised his eyes to hers. 'Of course you can,' she said softly. 'You have a lot to learn, but you have good teachers. Even with us gone, you have a family now. They'll help you, look out for you.'

'That they will,' he said with a smile.

He was about to say more, but the light brightened, as if the sun was growing, filling the sky. The heat became oppressive. His skin began to sweat then blister then burn.

He cried out in pain as the light consumed the sky.

****

'How long was I out?' Nicolas asked as he opened his eyes to Shift at the end of his bed, feet crisscrossed on his sheet as they leant back in their chair.

'About a day.' There was a glimmer of something in Shift's eyes before they settled to their usual casual-with-a-hint-of-mischief look.

That explains why I'm so thirsty.

Looking around, he reached for a cup on the table at his bedside. Before he could grab it, Shift did and carefully brought it to his lips.

'Where are we?' he asked after taking his drink.

'A tavern.'

'Oh shit,' he said, sitting bolt upright, a movement he wasn't sufficiently prepared for.

Shift put a hand on his shoulder. 'It's okay. This one's friendly. Some old comrade of Auron's put us up.'

That doesn't necessarily mean we're safe.

'What's it like out there?' he asked, nodding towards the window.

'Not great,' Shift said, their mouth a thin line. 'No one's saying anything about the tavern massacre, which is good. But now Billy's mysteriously vanished, accusations are being thrown everywhere and knives sharpened. The guilds are still on the brink.' Shift cast a look toward the window. 'We've tried spreading the word that Billy was a faun, but everyone is taking it as evidence that a spy was in their midst, and that he'd been planted there by the other guilds. Fo is still spreading paranoia, even in death.'

'So the world is worse off than when we started.' He sighed, lying back in the bed.

'No,' Shift said firmly as their gaze returned to him. 'Because each side thinks the other has Billy, none of them are making any moves yet. It will come, but at least we've delayed things. Hopefully, we can use that time to bring the Maestro to account and avert it completely.'

'Besides,' Shift smiled, 'the enemy's down at least thirty-six odd minions. That's something.'

'Unless the Maestro has a million at his command.'

Shift playfully punched his shoulder. He must've been weak because it hurt like crazy. 'Don't be so bloody pessimistic.'

'But—'

'Ah,' Auron shouted as he came through the wall, holding up a scolding finger. 'None of that. We defeated some bad guys. And if I've learnt one thing in all my years, it's to take the victory for what it is. Fo was powerful and had a jewel full of secrets the enemy will never get their hands on.'

'But—'

'Kid,' Auron said firmly. 'I'm not telling you a story right now because of your weakened state. But if you force my hand, I will tell it. I will also describe, in detail, the sexual conquest it led to afterwards. And it was with a Serian, so it'll get weird quickly.'

Nicolas made a big show of closing his mouth.

'My patient has awakened,' Garaz rumbled joyfully as he entered the room. The orc strode over to Nicolas and examined him. 'You had us very worried for a moment.' Garaz fussed with the dressings on Nicolas's wounds. 'When I applied my healing magic, you began to convulse. Your internal damage must have been more than I predicted.'

I convulsed? That's odd...

He was about to speak when Silva suddenly loomed over him. 'It is good to see you awake,' the warrior said flatly.

'Calm down with the gushing,' Shift said with a cheeky half-smile.

Nicolas looked past the warrior to the door. 'Are the others here?'

'No,' Garaz said as he inspected Nicolas's hip. 'They have dispersed.'

'Rex said, *You guys are crazy and dangerous, and I would happily not cross your paths again. But call me if you need me.*" Shift chuckled.

They don't seem sad to see him go.

He wasn't really sure why that idea made him happy.

'Alexi and Emelina left too,' Silva confirmed. 'Emelina told me to blow you a kiss, which I shall not do. Alexi said to tell you that he will kill you if he sees you again. I told him that if he did, I would decorate the nearest tree with his intestines.'

'Thank you.' He wasn't sure if it was the most appropriate response, but it was a response.

He can try again if he likes, and he can fail again. I'm not sure the guy is worth the coin.

'She cares in her way,' Shift smirked.

The warrior raised an eyebrow at the shapeshifter. 'And yet I was not the one constantly shooing Emelina from his bedside.'

Shift glowered at Silva, but no retort came.

'Gornak's going about his travels,' Auron said, his face betraying his longing for the life he'd lost. 'Apparently, there are many whoresons to slay. He's still also hoping to explain what happened to the guild before things escalate. Though I wouldn't bet anything on Gornak's powers of persuasion. Amazing warrior, poor debater.'

Just us then. I like that.

'Gornak did ask me to convey a message,' Garaz said, finally looking him in the eye. *"You are a worthy ally, Nicolas Percival Carnegie, not a whoreson at all.'* And he looks forward to the day your enemies tremble at the sound of your name.'

'How sweet,' Nicolas chuckled.

'He also got a chance to say goodbye to me properly,' Auron added. 'He got the *'murdering bitch,'* as he put it, to say the words to me. He didn't quite grasp the concept that I could hear him. But still, it was nice.'

That's good. But what happens now? After I—

Nicolas was suddenly aware of the others' eyes on him. 'What?'

'You didn't fail,' Shift said firmly.

'I never—'

'We all know how you think, kid,' Auron continued. 'You'll be kicking yourself for days because both Tavish and Fo died.'

Yes, but he wasn't about to admit to that.

'Despite what you may think,' Garaz smiled, 'you have honoured your parents' memories.'

'You have removed some terrible people from the world. Take comfort in that,' Silva added.

They were right. About all of it. Okay, so they hadn't achieved what they'd set out to achieve, but they had stopped some very bad people. That was something to be proud of, and he was. He let his disappointment wash away. They would have another chance. He was sure of that.

'There is one thing you need to do before we continue though,' Shift began. 'You need to say the name.'

Oh.

'Say it,' Silva commanded.

But...

'You should say it, it will do you good,' Garaz said softly.

Well...

'Kid, say the damn name.'

Letting out a single breath, Nicolas steeled himself. 'Koth.' Nothing happened. No demon appeared, and his life didn't suddenly get worse. 'Koth. Koth. Kothkothkoth.' He took in a deep breath. *'Kooooooooooth.'* Nicolas threw all of his frustration into the scream, venting every ounce of rage, distrust and paranoia so it would never bother him again. In theory.

'Excellent,' Auron smiled when he'd finished and slumped back, panting. 'Now you've earnt this.'

Garaz removed something from his cloak and threw it to Nicolas. He snatched it from the air. It was a small silver globe that fit in the palm of his hand.

'I was intrigued how Fo had managed to keep in contact with Tavish, so I searched his other boot and found this. It is a speaking globe,' Garaz explained.

Raising the object, he turned it around in his hands. It was smooth and cool to the touch, and something about it absorbed the eye. He almost dropped it as it began to glow green. Instead, he leaned in closer, understanding what this was.

'Hello?'

There was silence, but he could feel a presence.

'Is this the Maestro?'

Again, there was no answer, but he could sense that he was right. Part of him wanted to crush the globe in the hope it strangled this Maestro, but he guessed it wouldn't work like that. There was no way it would be that easy.

Instead, he spoke. 'Listen carefully,' he said firmly. 'I hope by now you know what happened to Fo, Tavish, and his men. How many of your servants have I killed now? How many of your schemes have I stopped? Yarringsburg, Sarus, Merida, the guilds. I don't know what you're planning, but I won't stop until your designs are burnt to ash. Just like my home. You hear me? I'm coming for you.'

There was a loaded silence.

'We shall see, child,' a distorted voice whispered back.

A moment passed, then Nicolas started as the globe cracked in his hand before crumbling to dust, which fell from between his fingers. He turned his palm to empty it before wiping his hand on what was left of his jacket.

'Hopefully, he's shaking in his boots.' Shift smiled.

Nicolas doubted it, but he liked the idea.

'We will get him.' Garaz nodded. 'No matter how long it takes.'

'It's a shame we killed all our leads.' Nicolas laughed.

Auron sighed. 'I do have an idea about that,' the spirit said hesitantly. 'But I don't really like it.'

Oh Deities...what now?

'How do you all feel about witches?' the spirit asked tentatively.

'Disgusted,' Garaz rumbled with a deep frown. 'They are base, craven creatures who have no business using magic.'

'You aren't going to have much fun at our next stop then,' Auron said, sucking his ethereal teeth.

'You know what,' Nicolas sighed. 'I'm fine with that. After all the trouble a bunch of humans caused us, I think it'd be easier to face a witch on our next outing. Or maybe a dragon.'

'Sorry kid. They're all gone.'

'Fine, just no more fauns then.'

A memory came to Nicolas. Something Fo had said. The faun had told Nicolas he had a large family.

I don't think we've seen the last of them. Dammit. I hate recurring villains. I had enough of that with the necromancer.

'We can worry about our next opponents later.' Shift gestured at the others to grab chairs and sit down, which they did – save Auron, of course. Shift sat back themselves and smiled at him warmly. 'So then, Nick. Tell us all about your parents.'

Instantly, the loss struck him like a war hammer to the chest. They were gone. His mother. His father. Dead. For a moment, the grief threatened to overwhelm him. But he had been overwhelmed by so much already recently, that his self control was starting to become honed. Nicolas wouldn't allow it to consume him. He knew he had to talk about it, about them. And here he was surrounded by friends ready to listen.

Family, even.

Taking a moment to gaze at the sun filled horizon beyond the window of his room, Nicolas summoned his fondest memories of his mother and father. His eyes closed as he played out some of the best times he'd had with them; like when he had snuck into the bakery early one morning and was caught eating a cake that had been just too tempting to ignore. His mother, who had frantically run from the house shouting his name when she'd realised that Nicolas wasn't in bed, had scolded him for sneaking out of the house in the dark. But his father had taken the blame, saying he had summoned Nicolas, thinking it was about time he started learning the family business. He still clearly remembered the knowing wink as his father leant in close and whispered *'besides, you have a cake to replace'*. His mother had done a poor job of pretending not to hear him.

Right then, he wasn't grieving. Instead, he felt blessed to have so many treasured memories to call on. When he turned back to his companions, each was waiting attentively for him to begin.

With a half smile toward Auron, he started to tell those tales. 'So, this one time...'

EPILOGUE

The banging on his door was urgent and insistent.

Who in the Underworld wants me at this hour?

'Who in the Underworld wants you at this hour?' Beba echoed his own thoughts as she stirred in the bed next to him. That was why he'd married her; they were so alike in some respects but so different in others.

'A Lord Commander's work is never done.' He smiled thinly as he rose from the bed.

The huff from Beba was gratifying.

Always nice to know I'll be missed in the marital bed.

Below, he heard the shuffling of his servant walking to the door. Good, that gave him time to look the part at least. Walking downstairs in his nightshirt wasn't the impression a good Lord Commander of the City Watch conveyed. That said, he needed to look the part quickly.

Trying to dress at speed whilst not waking your wife more than she already was required care and precision. Luckily, he had plenty of practise.

Maybe not luckily actually.

Suitably attired but wishing he was still in his nightshirt, Lord Commander Greer stepped from his chamber, taking one last forlorn look at his bed and the woman who occupied it. Just before the door closed, he heard a murmured voice. 'Stay safe. I love you.'

'I love you,' he whispered back.

And, Deities, was that not the truth.

When he reached the top of the stairs, Sergeant Tallith was shifting nervously in the entrance hall, along with two other men of the watch.

Bollocks.

Mind you, Greer had known what to expect. One didn't wake the Lord Commander in the middle of the night to tell him everything was all fine and dandy.

'Thank you, Hellig,' he said to his servant as he reached the bottom of the stairs.

The old retainer gave him a polite bow before retiring to his chambers.

Greer looked at his sergeant. He was young, and a little idealistic for Greer's tastes. But he had skill, which was why he'd made sergeant. Some might've put it down to nepotism but never in earshot of Greer. 'Out with it then, lad.'

Tallith looked reluctant to answer. It was too late at night, or early in the morning, to leave him waiting, and he widened his eyes slightly in impatience.

'There's been another one,' the sergeant said finally.

Bollocks.

Greer massaged the bridge of his nose. 'Where?'

'An alley by Coombes Street.'

Bollocks.

How delightful of the killer to pick the worst place to leave a body.

Greer didn't say a word. Instead, he struggled into the armoured chest plate that was a snugger fit since he'd been promoted—more desk time and more fine dining to blame for that—then placed his helm on his head and took his baton of office. Turning back to the sergeant, he gestured for him to lead the way.

This was going to be a long night.

****

By the time Greer arrived at the scene, there was already a crowd. What were so many people doing up so late? Good, respectable citizens needed their sleep. At least his boys had cordoned the alley off and were engaging in some enthusiastic crowd control.

Good. This could turn into a dung sandwich at any moment.

Could?

Would.

Tallith and his boys shouldered him a path through the mob. People passed dark, veiled murmurs between them as they parted. That wasn't good. In his experience, that meant a pot was simmering.

Passing the cordon to the salutes of those on guard, Greer proceeded into the alley.

It was dark and littered with bins and boxes. An ideal place to commit murder. And it was beside a tavern, so the ideal place to have that murder discovered quickly by some drunk wandering down the alley to decorate the wall with his urine.

Two of his boys were guarding the body, and Linnerman, the healer – who's main talent was now useless here – crouched over it.

'Young woman. Human,' Linnerman said without looking up.

As well as a macabre fascination with death a necromancer would've been envious of, Linnerman also had an amazing sixth sense for who was around him.

'Same as the rest?' Greer knew the answer as he asked it.

'Yup.'

Chatty bloke, Linnerman.

Greer risked a peek over the healer's shoulder. He wished he hadn't. There was something about someone dying so young that made the murder seem all the more brutal. All those potential years of life...gone. He loathed murderers. A good trait in a Lord Commander of the City Watch.

The young woman's face was frozen in horror. Trails of blood ran from her eyes, nose, ears, and lips. Like the others, there were tell-tale burn marks on the parts of her bare skin that showed. Sadistic bastard, this one.

'Still no idea how he's doing it?'

Greer felt the waves of frustration emanating from the healer. 'No,' he answered finally.

The thin, elderly man rose and turned to face him. Long ago the healer had learned to keep his beard neatly trimmed, lest it end up inadvertently dipping into something gross. The lads at the Watch House still laughed about how he'd learnt that lesson.

'There is no sign of physical wounds beyond the burns,' Linnerman informed him. 'I suspect the heart is in the same condition as the others, but beyond that, there is no outward sign.'

'That'll mean magic then.' Greer sighed. He hated dealing with magic. It was always easier with a good old-fashioned knife. Or strangulation. They were certainly easier to prove in court than *Yes, Your Honour, the victim was killed by a lightning strike unleashed by the accused from two streets away.'*

Bloody wizards. Robe-wearing bastards, to a man.

'All right. lads,' Greer said, turning to his men. 'You know the drill. Comb the scene and question anyone who was about. What about the person who found the body?'

'Not in a fit state to talk yet,' one of the men answered, indicating it was because of ale and not shock. An unreliable witness. Greer's night was getting better and better.

Sergeant Tallith gave an awkward cough before he spoke. 'Maybe if we reached out to the Hall of Guardians—'

Greer rounded on his sergeant, who shrank under the Lord Commander's shadow. 'I will not have some up-his-own-ass hero sniffing around my crime scene and running around my city lopping people's heads off so some bard can write a sonnet for him to listen to whilst he fiddles with himself. Is that clear, *Sergeant?*'

'Yes...yes, sir.'

Bloody heroes. Bunch of drunks and miscreants to a man. They were hardly reliable anymore. More likely to start a bar fight than be of practical use. And who would have to clean that up? Oh yes...him.

Greer raised his voice to ensure all his men could hear. 'We are the men of the City Watch. We do not shirk in our duty, and we do not outsource it to mercenaries. Now step to it and do what you're paid to do.'

Cheeky little shit, suggesting that they call in—

Oh no. The natives are getting restless.

From beyond the cordon, Greer heard raised voices.

Here we go.

'What was a human woman doing in *your* quarter?' someone shouted.

'What do you mean *your?*' another challenged.

Dammit. If only she'd been killed two streets over. Approaching the barricade, Greer gave his men the nod to unsling their batons.

'I think it's pretty clear what he means!' another voice helpfully chimed in.

'Typical *human* talk,' came a retort.

'You gotta problem with humans?'

'Who hasn't, nowadays?'

They were all inebriated and angry. Greer doubted the finest orator in all Etherius would find the words to calm this lot down. Still, he had to try.

Let's see if appealing to their community spirit helps.

'All right, folks,' he said, holding his hands high. 'We are investigating this matter, which is not helped by insults being thrown around. This is a time for us to come together, rather than look at what divides us. So behave.'

The crowd stopped throwing insults. Instead, they started throwing punches. Within moments, the crowd had become a scrum, people piling on each other to express their opinions with physical violence. Thankfully, the level of drink they'd all consumed ensured that most of the blows struck air and more often than not caused the one throwing the punch to stumble over. Still, the lack of ability didn't dull their enthusiasm.

That escalated quickly.

Greer sighed and massaged the bridge of his nose again. 'All right, lads, get stuck in.'

At his command, the watchmen used their shields to drive the crowd back, giving anyone who wouldn't comply a wallop with their baton. Greer wasn't going to have this developing into a riot. The city had been built as a symbol of peace. Greer was sure the designers of the place would raise an eyebrow at the state of it now. But at least it wasn't cold. It ought to have been at this ridiculous hour, but the professor's new system ensured the city stayed warm. Quite the marvel, really.

The crowd may have been drunk and all worked up, but they dispersed quickly enough. This time. Great, now he could get on with some actual police work.

'Lord Commander...Lord Commander...' The boy ran up to him. As he came to a stop, he doubled over, puffing and panting as he fought to catch his breath.

Greer indulged him. No point trying to get a message from a messenger who couldn't breathe.

The lad finally stood upright and looked at him sheepishly. 'The governor's already heard about this and wants to see you. Now.'

Bollocks.

Acknowledgements

Gosh darn (for want of stronger language), I felt like I was walking the trail of death myself with this one.

There are two things I have found really difficult about being a writer. The first, is assuming that just because I am writing it, it is therefore good. Secondly, is overthinking my writing to the point I make changes that make it worse. These should be two polar opposites, but in this work they came together in perfect harmony, and I didn't even know it.

I'll explain...

When I first started writing the series, I had an image of a single scene in my head. That scene became chapter one of this book. From that grew the idea of having the group travel a road and get jumped on in every tavern they visited. Which I found amusing to write, but I forgot to include much of an actual plot. In my obliviousness to this issue, I instead obsessed over the character arcs, thinking I'd made them too subtle and ending up dialling them up to a point where the book became a bit of a depressing slog.

Naturally, I was oblivious to all of this.

Thank the Deities for Dani, my ever amazing editor, who reality checked me. She pointed out these mistakes and I worked (very) hard to correct them and create the book you have just read.

The first four books, for me, were really the beginning of Nicolas learning what he needed to in order to quest. To get over his reluctance to get out in the world, to face his fear, not let the excitement of adventuring carry him away and then to accept that sometimes, the bad guys need to die. After the Underworld and all that business I thought a nice, all action adventure would be a good change of pace for you, the reader. I hope you found it refreshing.

Because my readers deserve nothing less than the fun fantasy adventures they've come to expect from this series. I am forever thankful for you following Nicolas and his companions on his adventures, and I want to make sure this series continues to be the very best fantasy nonsense you can read.

Of course, Dani has a big hand in that too, a thousand thank yous to that very talented lady. I also need to thank my mum and proof reader, Christine. Without her effort, all sort of tpyo would peper this book and make it les fun too read! And of course, I give the usual shout out to my awesome Kickstarter backers, who help get this book from a Word document on my computer, to an actual, honest to goodness, novel!

I really hope you've enjoyed this book, and have learned to stay the heck away from taverns!

Until book 6,
Keep adventuring,

Andrew

KICKSTARTER CREW

As I said before, I couldn't have made this book without those awesome folks who backed my Kickstarter campaign to get Trail of Death edited.
  I name you here so that all generations will know what part you played in making this happen, you awesome people!

Leigh Walker,
Joe Rixman,
Alexandra Corrsin,
Heiko Koenig,
John Idlor,
Andrew Wainwright,
Terry S,
J Mills,
Lisa Heiser,
Katherine Shipman,
Sharon Howes,
Andy Meredith,
Mark PJ Nadon,
Jill Vance,
G Clatworthy,
Brendan Noble,
Franchesca Caram,
Caitlin Attard,
Hannah Wilkinson,
Jason and Nisa Martinko,
Michael Yeh,
Simon Mark De Wolfe,
Malfor,

Becky James,
Samantha Landstrom,
H. M. Clarke   ,
Corrine Brucks,
Emma Hainer,
David Holzborn,
Vancil C Thomas,
Jean Pace,
PJK,
Rik Geuze,
Gerald P. McDaniel,
Justise Briones,
Jenna Levitski,
Cline,
Greg Levick,
Hugo Essink,
Travis Glenister,
M T McGuire,
Karen Wrobel,
Chris,
phoenix17,
Mistrill Merendras,
Sydnie Harman,

Rod Steinberger,
B. Plaga,
Kirsty Grandfield,
E.M. Middel,
Agnes Metanomski,
Adam Nemo,
Duncan Wilcox,
Abdul Hadi Sid Ahmed,
John Gilligan,
M. Mazzone,
Russel,
Jason Joyner,
Kelly Stirling,
Lorenza,
Ellen Pilcher,
Alex van Renesse,
C. Niehot,
Elena,
Geoff Parkinson,
Rob Davis,
Nikki Thompson,
Andy99000,
Tonel,

About the Author

Andrew Claydon has an imagination, one full of variety.
Sometimes it's funny, sometimes it's adventurous, sometimes it's shocking, and occasionally it's outright strange...but it's never boring!
Andrew is a UK author who grew up loving fantasy movies such as Conan, Krull, Beastmaster and Willow. The epic worlds and battles of swords and sorcery therein inspired him to create his own fantasy worlds, adding to them his own brand of irreverent humour; because sometimes it's good to chuckle in between sword fights!
He wants to inspire the imagination of others, just as he's been inspired; with dashing heroes, epic quests and vile villains.
So reader beware, you aren't just opening a book, but a doorway into Andrew's imagination. It'll be a strange journey, but an entertaining one!
When he isn't writing, he loves to read sci/fi and fantasy novels. It's one of the things that inspires him to write himself. He also enjoys playing Warhammer 40,000 and is a keen wrestling fan.
He has degrees in both history and psychology, as well as black belts in several martial arts.
When he isn't creating vast fantasy worlds and populating them with good guys and bad guys to run around fighting each other, he works as a supported employment coordinator, helping others to try and achieve their aspirations.
Subscribe to my newsletter for the latest publishing news (and a FREE prequel novella) at: www.andrewclaydonauthor.com
Or follow me on social media:
Facebook: Andrewclaydonauthor
Instagram: @authorandyc
Tiktok: @authorandyc
If you enjoyed the book, then please leave a review with your preferred retailer.
Reviews are really important to indie authors to help them get their work out there.
If you do take the time to leave a review, thank you.

ALSO BY

Chronicles of the Dawnblade Series
The Simple Delivery
Strange Companions
The Odd Sea
Wrath and Wraiths
Trail of Death
Demons and Disorder

Novellas and short stories
A Grudge is Born
The Gathering
Don't you know who I am?